FIVE WEEKS

A SEVEN SERIES NOVEL

DANNIKA DARK

Also By Dannika Dark:

THE MAGERI SERIES
Sterling
Twist
Impulse
Gravity
Shine

NOVELLAS
Closer

THE SEVEN SERIES
Seven Years
Six Months
Five Weeks

ACKNOWLEDGMENTS:

I want to give a huge thanks to my team of betas: Amber, Teresa, Erin, Kelly, and Mikaela. Some of you were thrown into the mix mid-series and somehow managed to hang on for the ride. Everyone in life has a story to tell, and sometimes there are things in our past we spend our lives running from. This book is dedicated to those who have retired their running shoes and found a piece of happiness they can call home.

I spent a lifetime running away from my problems…

Until I had a five-week collision course with fate.

PROLOGUE

J ERICHO STRETCHED OUT HIS LONG legs and noticed his arms were pinned to the mattress. He dipped his chin against his chest and saw a luscious blonde on his left with a dragon tattoo inked across her shoulder, and a brunette on the right. The blonde had her nude body flush against his chest and hip. The brunette, on the other hand, was drooling on his right bicep and twitching in her sleep.

He glanced around and didn't recognize his surroundings. After jamming all night onstage with his band and having a few shots with the groupies, things had gotten crazy. Nothing he wasn't used to, being a Shifter. The Cole brothers all had a touch of inherent wild in their blood.

The Shifter community was comprised of a wide variety of animals; Jericho was a wolf. The last thing he remembered was briefly shifting in hopes of getting the girls to follow suit so he could find out what their animals were. Like most Shifters, they were evasive at first. One of the girls had brought Sensor pops—a candy spiked with emotions by a Sensor— and everything became fuzzy after that. More drinks, a lot of kissing, and no recollection of whether or not they had sex. He was certain he didn't with the brunette, because he remembered her animal was a deer. Jericho preferred women with bite.

Shifters were prohibited from changing into their animal in a Breed bar, but he'd been known to do it at the end of his act. It had gotten him kicked out of a few clubs, but nothing beat the reaction from the women when he revealed his animal onstage. Not to mention he had a pretty wolf—a warm shade of brown mixed with cream and orange.

Then he'd shift back and show them what *else* he had to offer when his clothes wound up in a heaping pile at his feet.

After living in Austin for a year, Jericho didn't perform that act anymore because the groupies had come to expect it. The women were too easy to get, and he liked the thrill of the chase.

Groupies were one of two kinds: either the office girls who wore slingback pumps and cherry-red lipstick, trying to find a piece of wild before returning to their mundane lives, or they were batshit crazy. Unfortunately, groupies were the only women who would give him the time of day. He'd never met a good woman who could handle a man like him; they were put off by his tattoo, long hair, and rocker lifestyle. Then again, why should he care? It's not as if he was looking for a mate. Jericho didn't want someone who would tie him down and make him turn in his Les Paul for a BlackBerry. He'd been living this lifestyle for decades, and it was the only life he knew.

Two of his brothers, one of whom was his Packmaster, had settled down with mates. Their large house was becoming a solid pack, but it was beginning to make him feel like the odd man out. Even his younger brother, Denver, had settled down just a little bit after taking over the role as Maizy's watchdog. Maizy was the human child who lived with them, and woe to the man who made that little girl cry. Denver fiercely protected her and would pound anyone's ass into the ground who hurt that child. Just ask the smart-ass at the gas station who, after looking at her tiara and wand, made the mistake of asking her if she rode the short bus to school. Reno had taken Maizy's hand and walked her out to the car while Denver shined the floor with that man's ass, and deservedly so.

Nobody messes with the Weston pack.

Most Shifters lived with their own kind. But Austin, the Packmaster, had fallen in love with Lexi. She'd grown up thinking she was human until she had recently gone through the change—a Shifter's transition to adulthood when they shift into their animal for the first time. Lexi had been stolen from her Shifter family by a human when she was just a baby. That explained her resilience in all she'd been through, because that was the Shifter way. After coming to grips with the truth, she'd moved in with the Weston pack, mated with Austin, and that was that. The brothers accepted her mom and little sister as family, even though they were human.

They weren't the only humans in the house. Reno had recently hooked up with one of Lexi's coworkers, and they were as good as mated, except that mating wasn't legal between humans and Breed. April had moved in several months ago, and they had a chemistry that couldn't be matched. But it was less "in your face" sexual than the Austin and Lexi phenomenon. Those two were like watching the mating rituals of wild animals. April was a great girl, but more of a bookworm. At first the pack had tried to steer Reno away from her. The brothers insisted it wasn't a wise decision for Reno to pursue a human. But after saving Reno's wolf, April had earned their respect. When Reno asked her to be his life mate, the pack let go of their grudges and accepted her into the family. That's what brothers do.

Jericho didn't have a mate, despite the two bombshells curled up next to him. He loved the ladies and loved them good… in bed. But outside the sheets, no woman had ever made his wolf pace restlessly. No woman had ever made him feel an inexplicable desire to behave irrationally, all for the sake of making her smile. No woman had ever made him want to be a better man, one who would spill blood to protect what he loved. No woman had ever incited the hunter in him. No woman had ever denied him.

Except one.

CHAPTER 1

THE ONLY THING IN THIS world I loved more than a frozen chocolate shake on a hot spring day was combustible sex on a kitchen table.

"Hell's bells," I groaned, rubbing my forehead when a brain freeze struck me.

"You drank it too fast, Izzy. How many times have I told you to suck on it slower?"

I smirked and glanced up at Hawk, who seemed oblivious to his own innuendo.

I was born Isabelle Marie Monroe, which didn't fit my spirited personality in the least, so everyone called me Izzy. I came from an interbred family of Shifters—something frowned upon by most Breeds. My dad was a wolf and my mother a cougar. *Talk about cats and dogs.* All my siblings were cougars, so growing up the lone wolf in the family was no cakewalk. Shifters don't go through the change until their late teens or early twenties, but kids often show telltale characteristics of their animal early on. When they began to sense I wasn't one of them, my sisters and older brother turned on me. After I went through the change, it confirmed their suspicions.

So I learned how to fight.

It took me three long years to build up enough courage to go out on my own, and when I did, I couldn't escape that house fast enough. A charismatic young Shifter named Jericho took me under his wing. We met about twenty years ago when he worked as a roadie for a popular band touring around the country. We were two Shifters from different worlds who found each other in a rainstorm. It was a lifetime ago, but Shifters live for centuries. I still looked a graceful twenty-five.

I lived and traveled with Jericho for five years. We had a magnetic chemistry, as if we'd known each other in another lifetime. But Jericho would often ditch me in a bar and run off with some floozy who caught his eye. It couldn't be helped; the man was gorgeous and women threw themselves at him. Except for me, because all we ever were was best friends. Then things got twisted between us, and I bailed.

Recently I'd found out my parents had divorced. A loner by nature, my mother had finally given up fighting my father's desire to join a pack. As for him, he ended up joining a group up in Colorado. By that time, my siblings had scattered across the country, and we didn't keep in touch.

Avoiding pack life wasn't advisable for single women because rogue wolves were a constant threat, though a pack led by a good Packmaster offered protection. But I'd never known that life, and it frightened me. After all, my own family hadn't looked out for me. How could I expect strangers to? Because of that distrust, I never revealed my animal to anyone except close friends or lovers. I'd never experienced what it meant to be in a pack, but the instinct called to me in quiet moments.

I bounced around the lower states for years and then moved to Texas with a friend who wanted to join a pack. She'd heard Austin was thick with Shifters, and you can bet your red panties she found a Packmaster within the second week, which left me without a job or a home.

And that's when I bumped into Hawk. We met at a Laundromat of all places, and I sensed his Breed energy when I sat next to him. After letting his jockeys tumble with my G-strings, we decided to take it to the next level and have been living together for the past month. I didn't know what he did for a living and didn't care, so long as he treated me right. He'd just gotten me a job at a Shifter bar called Howlers, which is where we were headed.

When I noticed only a few slurps of milkshake remained, I hurled the cup out the window.

"What the fuck!" Hawk rolled up my window from his panel and sighed. "Why don't you act like a lady?"

"Why don't you treat me like one?" I quirked a brow and smiled.

He touched his mustache, and I could feel him glaring at me from behind his black sunglasses. I wasn't really into the whole 'stache look, but it suited him in a yuppie-biker kind of way. Hawk didn't own a motorcycle, just a red sports car. Two doors, meaning whenever one of his buddies came along, I had to squeeze into the back seat, which felt like a suitcase.

"You're in one of your moods today, Iz. Sure you aren't a cat? I think you might be since you're partial to those damn hissy fits," he said with a dark chuckle.

I hated it when he pulled out the cougar card. He knew how I felt about growing up the lone wolf, but Hawk didn't seem to mind digging in his talons with a joke here and there.

I crossed my legs seductively and stroked my hand down to my knee, seizing his attention as the car slowed at a red light. "I do have a kitty," I said with a provocative purr. "Want to pet her?"

Hawk lifted his glasses over his head and didn't look as amused as I thought he would. "Don't pull that shit tonight, got it? You're sexy as sin, Izzy, but I'm getting real tired of the way you shake your ass at other wolves to make me jealous."

I folded my arms. "Maybe if you gave me some attention, I wouldn't have to."

He slid his glasses back on when the light turned green. "I give you *plenty* of attention when it counts."

It only *counted* five seconds before he had an orgasm, or if I was on my way home and he wanted me to stop off at the taco stand. Hawk took care of me and we got along, but the chemistry was nonexistent, as it was with almost all the guys I'd dated. I'd concluded that mated Shifters were all extraordinary liars. Hawk didn't make my toes curl or my insides tingle. He didn't make me slide down in my seat and fantasize about what I wanted him to do to me. Hawk took me to Chili's every Friday, paid the bills, tuned up my car, and let me sleep with the remote control. I guess that's love.

"I'm not sure that I like your work attire," he grumbled, staring down at my long legs.

I tilted the vent away and twisted around to face him. "This isn't my uniform, so just drop me off and keep all the snide remarks to yourself. I don't want you coming in and picking on my customers. You *know* how Shifter bars operate, and I've done the waitress gig before. At the end of the day, I'm there for the tips, not the compliments. I may shake my ass and throw them a few winks, but I'm monogamous, and you *know* that."

He eased up to the front of the building and pinched my chin. "Better be. If I hear you're messing around, it won't be pretty."

"You're right, Hawk. Nothing makes me wetter than serving a bunch of jackasses beer and nachos. Give me a kiss."

A smile curved up his cheek, and he pulled a lock of my red hair. "Your fiery temper is going to land you in trouble one of these days."

"It already has. I'm with *you*."

And wasn't that the truth? Hawk was a nice guy, but whatever he did was illegal. He'd come home on more than one occasion with bruised knuckles and a look of satisfaction. It seemed out of character because I'd never seen him lose his cool, no matter how much smack he talked. Hawk wasn't the perfect boyfriend, but then again, what sense of normalcy had I ever had? The only stability I'd ever known was with Jericho, and God knows where he was. The last time I saw him, he was lying in our hotel room in *my* bed with a girl straddling him and rocking her hips mercilessly.

Wearing *my* Pink Floyd shirt.

Jericho knew how much I loved that shirt, and he gave it to some whore who probably cut it up and made it into a hideous beach-bikini top. He'd crossed a line, which led me to believe he didn't value our friendship as much as I did.

I'd never had sex with Jericho because that wasn't what our relationship had been about. What had once existed between us was a close bond that I'd never experienced with anyone before or since.

"Look, it's the only Breed job I could find you on short notice," Hawk said. "You're the one who insisted on finding work, but I'm fine with you staying home. Actually, I like this idea less the more I think about it. Nervous?"

"First-day jitters. You know how it is." I stared out the window. "I need to stay busy and work or else I go nuts."

"Well, this'll be a trial period. I make good money, so I don't know what you're trying to prove."

I chuckled softly. "You'd be surprised what a girl can make in a place like this."

Howlers was a low-key bar that catered to Shifters, and that was my kind of place. I felt more comfortable around my kind; Vampires and Chitahs made me nervous as heck. Some Breeds lacked distinct characteristics and could pass as human, so they weren't as easy to identify. A Mage looked no different than anyone else, but as a creature of energy, their presence could be felt by a sweep of chills across your body that could easily be mistaken for the shivers. All the Chitahs I'd met were tall, had predatory body language, and eyes the color of amber or firelight.

"Last chance," he offered.

"It's gravy." I opened the door and got out. "I'll be fine driving myself to work from here on out."

"Izzy, we talked about this. I don't want you driving out here alone."

"I know, but it doesn't look so bad," I said, glancing around the parking lot. The bar was sandwiched between a pawnshop and an open field. "It's not like we're in the hood."

"Iz…"

I slammed the door and bent forward, staring through the window as he rolled it down. "Hawk, I know you're trying to look out for me by driving your girl to work, but if you show up late, then I'm stuck here. If something happens and you can't make it, I end up taking a cab home, or the bus. Do you want me walking the streets or hanging out with some of these clowns in the bar?"

"No can do. I won't be late."

"Kisses, honey. But I'm driving to work from here on out. Pick me up tonight at twelve and wait outside. If you come in and get me fired, then we're done."

I strutted across the parking lot and jumped when he beeped his horn. Hawk laughed and sped off.

Jerk.

He always had to have the last word. Sometimes I wondered

why I hadn't already left him. Maybe I liked the idea of having a companion, but the truth of the matter was I had no good reason to leave him. He treated me decently, offered protection, and gave me a place to stay.

"Ho-ly shit," someone yelled out. "Redhead alert, boys."

Nothing I hadn't heard before. Shifters had a soft spot for redheads because there were so few of us. I had wavy, wild hair that favored a lighter shade of red—like copper and honey fused together. Sometimes men complimented my green eyes, but they were always about the hair. I stood at around five-nine and loved wearing heels to boost that up. A few small freckles marked my nose and cheeks. I'd discovered a long time ago that if I freckled or sunburned, it could be erased by shifting. My inherent healing ability took care of it, but I was stuck with the ones I'd gotten as a child. Jericho hated when I did that—he once said I reminded him of a constellation of distant stars. Then again, he was stoned. Funny how Jericho had been on my mind lately.

"Does anyone know where I can find the boss man?" I asked, walking toward the bar.

A few fingers pointed down a narrow hall to my left. I gripped my purse strap and headed down the hall until I came to a door on the right with gold lettering that read *Jake*.

After three knocks, a voice grumbled for me to come in. We'd only done a phone interview, which was unusual. Most managers of Shifter bars wanted to see a potential waitress before hiring her. But when I'd mentioned my red hair, I guess that sealed the deal. Some bars prohibited redheads from being on their payroll, so it was something I needed to disclose up front.

"I'm Izzy, reporting for duty."

Jake was a round man with thinning hair. He looked nice in a white dress shirt, but the room was hot, and the fan on his desk didn't seem to be doing much good, judging by his ruddy complexion. Jake set down his pen and looked me up and down, but not in a creepy way.

"So you're Izzy Monroe?" he said with a private chuckle. Jake pointed a finger toward the door. "The girls change in the room across the hall. I have a few rules, so pay attention. No sex on the premises. I don't care if it's with your mate; that's the golden rule. No riling up the men without settling them back down. Nothing worse than having to break up bar fights, and it puts a bad reputation on my establishment. And finally, no dipping in the tip jar. I'm pretty fair about letting each worker pocket what they're tipped instead of splitting an even cut of the gross. But there are two locations in this establishment where customers can tip the bar itself. It's a way to support the kind of place I run, and every dime of that money goes into fixing things around here. The jars are blue and you can't miss 'em. You steal from there and you're stealing a repaired toilet, new shirt, and clean glasses. Make sense?"

"I gotcha. It's all gravy. My last boss had the same system going, and he made a killing. Except Tony used that money to take us all to the races as part of a work vacation."

His lips twitched. "Is that so? You're real good about working your stories into suggestions, Red."

"Izzy."

"Sounds like a real hoity-toity bar you worked at. Around here, we serve a bunch of roughnecks. They get wild, they break chairs, and damn if they don't bust out a toilet at least once a month. I keep the place running smooth, clean, and tip-top. I fired the last girl because she decided to show her tits for a big tipper who was waving a Benjamin at her. If you pull something like that, you'll be right on the street with her. I take care of my girls," he said, leaning back in his chair. "You'll get good tips if you know how to handle the customers and work the tables. If someone's pushing you to do something or holding out, I wanna know about it. I don't like cheapskates coming into my bar who won't pay my girls for the hard work they put in."

I rocked on my heels. "What about the uniform?"

He dabbed his forehead with a handkerchief. "Your shirts are tight, but they'll cover you up. The shorts are short because it gets hot around here, and there's nothing wrong with a pair of lovely legs. But don't even think about taking scissors to the shirts I provide you. Same rule as any respectable bar: watch how you bend over tables. If you know anything about wolves, then you know that's a green light for them to come on to you. I'm a fan of dipping, and the girls here will show you their moves if you aren't familiar."

"I know the drill," I assured him, not revealing I was a wolf. Jake was a chatty fellow, but I liked him right away. "I'll get changed and have one of the girls show me around before it gets busy. When do we peak?"

Jake chuckled and leaned forward on his elbows. "Ten to three. You up for that, honey? It gets slammed here on Friday nights; you picked a helluva night to start your shift. You sure you don't want to start out with the morning crowd?"

"No offense, Jake, but I work tables better than most. I'm a fast learner, hard worker, and I thrive in chaos. Do you have live bands?"

"Yep. Usually two nights a week."

"Super. My kind of place." I loved a busy bar with music, and I especially loved getting to know the regulars because that made it a friendly place to work. "Anyone you want to warn me about?"

His eyebrows sloped down. "How's that?"

"You know," I said with a shrug. "Sometimes there's that girl who likes to steal customers or the bouncer who gets a little frisky."

Jake pointed a finger. "If any of that goes on, then I want to know about it. I have a good staff, and if you have personal problems with them, that ain't my business. The bartenders look out for my girls, and no one is stealing tables without answering to me. Get with Rosie and have her show you the ropes. She's the best one to train you—been here the longest. I have to finish up some work and go home for the night, so if you have any questions, see Rosie."

I spun on my heel and smiled. Jake was an all-right guy.

The uniforms for Howlers were sleeveless black shirts with the bar logo on the left breast, and black shorts. The bartenders had similar shirts to show off their biceps, but they wore jeans instead of shorts. I made my way across the bar, smiling at some of the patrons who whistled at me. I had a non-sluttish way of beguiling men that occasionally made them blush and feel guilty for catcalling me. Hawk called it the *girl next door* hex.

I approached a woman in uniform leaning against the bar. "Are you Rosie? Jake said you would show me the ropes."

Rosie was a curvy woman with caramel skin, thick legs, and a generous cup size that no T-shirt could disguise. She exuded confidence in every subtle gesture. Her false eyelashes slowly fanned as she looked me over and smiled.

"The boys are going to love you," she said. "I don't deal with catty, so if you're one of those backstabbers, then I'll find out and cut you up."

Gulp. *Was she serious?*

Rosie laughed and touched my shoulder, as if emphasizing she was only kidding.

"You're a dainty little flower. What's your name, hon?"

"I'm Izzy. Izzy Monroe."

Her red lips turned down. "What kind of a name is Izzy for a girl? Don't you want to come up with something a little sexier for work? You don't want these boys treating you like a pal; you'll never make tips that way."

I gave her a broad smile and jutted my hip out. "Don't worry, Rosie. When I'm on the floor, I work my assets. I may look like a dainty flower, but I'm really a wild weed."

For emphasis, I spun around and gave her my best walk.

She giggled and leaned against the bar on one elbow. "That all?"

"Watch my dip."

I simulated setting drinks on a table and sashayed to the other side after doing a swivel. I gave men just enough that if there were any wolves in the group, they would order more drinks to see it again. If a girl gave them too much of a show, they'd lose interest.

Rosie applauded quietly. "You need to teach me that little move. I'll show you something that'll get you a few tips if there are any leopards in the house. We don't get them often, but they don't play around when they tip." She curled her finger for me to come closer, and I did. "I'm sure you know the game, but don't tell anyone your animal. They want the illusion that we could be one of them and it drives them crazy when they aren't sure. Bear, wolf, deer, leopard, mountain lion, eagle… whatever. I have a hunch what some of the girls in here are, but we don't even tell one another. Just watch and learn the best moves and work what you can in your section. No table-hopping; Jake doesn't like that."

"We talked. He told me. I think I'm going to like it around here. But do me a favor and don't give me any nicknames because of my hair. That gets old really fast, and it sticks with some of the regulars. Just call me Izzy."

"You got it, hon. You have a boyfriend?"

"I sure do. Why?"

"Keep him out."

I laughed and sat on the barstool next to her. "I know. We already had *the talk*."

"I'm just saying. Nothing will kill your action in here faster than a regular knowing you're hitched up with someone. We get a few men who drop serious cash; the regulars are our bread and butter."

The Breed had money to burn and some tipped over a hundred percent. Howlers was a Shifter club, but since it wasn't marked exclusive, other Breeds were allowed. Immortals had fat pockets, and plenty of Packmasters lived high on the hog. They liked to flaunt that money and believed in paying for services rendered. Chitahs were also big tippers, but I was uncomfortable around them. Maybe it was the way they looked at me with those predatory eyes, but I preferred being around my own kind. I knew what Shifters wanted and fell into conversation more easily with them. While waiting tables brought in good money, I'd never been able to put away much of it with all my traveling. Not to mention I'd found out a few lovers in my past had been dipping into my stash.

"How are the bartenders?" I asked, knowing I'd have a close working relationship with them.

"Fabulous," Rosie said, sipping her cola through a tiny red straw. "They're flirtatious as sin, so don't fool around with them outside work. Jake doesn't like the drama."

"I said I had a boyfriend."

Rosie set down her short glass and giggled with closed lips. "I don't judge."

———◦◦◦———

Six hours into my shift, my heels were attempting first-degree murder on my feet. I had made the fatal mistake of not breaking them in, and every trip to the bar made me want to drop to my knees and crawl.

"It looks as though you have your hands full," a formidable man sitting in my section remarked.

I sensed a strong alpha vibe, and he looked like one of the ancient ones. What stood out were his multicolored eyes—brown and sapphire. His dark hair was neatly pulled back in a ponytail, drawing all the attention to his chiseled face. He possessed a powerful inflection in his voice that signaled he was an alpha. They often came from strong genetic lines and lived more than a few hundred years.

"I'm Izzy," I said, placing a paper napkin on the table for his draft. "Can I bring you something to eat? I've tasted the burgers, and the cook is on fire tonight."

A smile tugged at the corner of his mouth. "You must be new," he said in a silken voice, glancing at his watch. "No one ever recommends the chef on this shift."

Shit. Fatal error. The guy who made my burger had left an hour ago.

When he saw my cheeks flush, he sipped his beer and then folded his arms on the table. "Why don't you bring me one of those hamburgers, and I'll let you know."

Not wanting to ruin my tip, I cocked my hip in a way that caught his eye and gripped the chair, allowing my hair to cascade over my shoulder. "How about I order you a supreme pizza from the Italian shop up the road? On me. You look like a man with an appetite, and one of these burgers probably won't tide you over. I'll arrange it real nice on the house tray so no one will know I ordered it special."

He laughed handsomely, and I shivered when I felt another wave of energy. "I'm Prince."

"Charmed," I said with a sly wink, making my way back to the bar.

Close save. I had a feeling this guy was a regular, and I wanted to stay on his good side. Men like him were generous with gratuity.

I was pretty sure alphas had psychic powers and knew who the wolves were. Female wolves go into heat once a year, and I'd once met an alpha who could sense it coming before anyone else.

Talk about embarrassing. I'd never known a man powerful enough to scent it more than a week in advance, but it still unnerved me. Alphas were too serious for my taste, and I was a girl who liked a man with a sense of humor.

Not that Hawk was a barrel of laughs, but he had his moments.

After ordering the pizza, I wiped down a few tables and took a break. The bartender was about to end his shift, and so was I. Jake had allowed me to work six hours and said he'd talk with Rosie before giving me his decision on which shifts I'd be able to work. If he felt I could handle the crowd, then I was going to dip into some of that peak money. Only the queen bees got the full shift through peak hours, so I was fortunate that Jake wanted to give me a shot. Managers usually selected the girls who brought in the most money.

"How are you holding out, hon?" Rosie blotted her face with a paper napkin. She had the most perfectly lined lips I'd ever seen. Black hair fell in large curls, all loose and pretty around her face.

"Peachy," I lied, wanting to throw my shoes into the eternal fire of damnation. "Where are all the women? I thought there'd be more."

"Oh, they like to make a late appearance," she said, rolling her eyes. "They want to have the men good and riled up before they make their entrance at the door."

"Oh, brother."

"You got that right. If you think that's bad, you should see the turnout on ladies' night. They show up as early as possible to start getting free drinks, and by midnight, it's the hottest mess you've ever seen. Don't get me wrong, some of the girls are classy and looking for an honest Shifter, but we have a few doozies."

"Don't you mean floozies?"

"That too," she said with a flurry of laughter. "It keeps things interesting. Never a dull moment. You're doing an outstanding job,

Izzy. I'm impressed. I've seen a few girls make rookie mistakes or run out screaming on their first day. If Jake asks, I'm going to recommend you for a few peak hours. But take the early evening, hon. You don't want the after-midnight crowd. It takes thick skin, and I'd rather see you ease into the place before we scare you off."

"Trust me, I've seen it all," I assured her.

That was no lie. I used to work in a bar that serviced bikers. Those guys loved to shift in the parking lot and have an all-out fight, taking bets on which animal would win. I once called animal control and a couple of them were picked up. My boss fired me after that, but I had a good laugh knowing they had spent the night in the kennel until one of their buddies released them by filling out adoption papers.

"Why don't you take off and soak your feet in hot water," Rosie suggested, picking at her fingernail. "I've been watching you hobble around in those heels all night and it was funny at first, but now it's not so much. I see you wincing every time you reach the bar. Jake doesn't care if you wear sneakers in here, just so long as you look polished and are wearing the uniform."

"I'm not really a sneaker girl at work, but thanks for the tip. Let whoever takes over my tables know that the alpha over there—"

"The one staring at your ass as if he were decoding hieroglyphics?"

"Yeah, that's probably the one. I ordered a pizza for him."

She knitted her brows. "What's wrong with our food?"

"Well, he challenged the cook's skills."

Rosie looked at her gold watch and frowned. "I *knew* he was killing our business. I'm going to bring that up with Jake again."

"Anyhow, I want his pizza on one of our serving dishes, and fix him up real nice. I won't get the tip, but I don't leave my guys hanging."

She nudged me with her shoulder. "Neither do I, hon. I leave 'em stiff so they're left wanting more."

I laughed and a few heads turned. "Thanks, Rosie. I'll look forward to hearing from either you or Jake. He has my number; just let me know what time my shift begins."

"Nighty-night," she sang, sipping her cola.

After changing into my jean shorts and turquoise blouse, I kicked off my shoes and held them between my fingers, walking out barefoot.

I turned the corner to the right and strolled out the front door, taking in a breath of fresh air.

"And what of my pizza?" a deep voice inquired. I glanced down at Prince, who was sitting on a bench to my right with his long legs stretched out and crossed at the ankle.

"Sorry, I had to end my shift. Your new server is going to take good care of you. I told her to set you up."

He cocked his head to the side. "Maybe she's not the one I wanted to tip."

I rocked on my heels, looking into the parking lot for Hawk's car. "Well, you obviously want to tip the person who takes care of you, and I didn't do a good job of that tonight."

After a slight pause, he stood up and approached me, reaching for the door. Then he suddenly leaned close and drew in a deep breath. "Five weeks, Freckles."

"What do you mean?" I was a little insulted if he was insinuating that's how long I'd last working there.

A carnivorous grin spread across his face, and he gave me a lascivious wink. "Five weeks until you go into heat."

My eyes widened as he turned and went back inside.

A pair of headlights from a red sports car temporarily blinded me until I covered my face. I grumbled when Hawk beeped his horn. He knew how much I hated being honked at.

A good-looking man wearing a sleeveless black shirt jogged in my direction—presumably the bartender who worked the late shift. I could see why Jake would want him during peak; he had a mess of sexy blond hair and an athletic build. I guessed him to stand just shy of six feet tall.

"How's it going, honeypie?" he said, jogging up the steps and giving me a friendly wink.

I slid a last glance at the entrance to Howlers before getting in the car and ending the first night of my new life.

CHAPTER 2

M Y EYES SNAPPED OPEN WHEN someone slapped my ass and jolted me awake.

"Get up, sexy."

I flew at Hawk, clocking him in the jaw with my fist.

"Holy fuck, girl! What the hell is your problem?"

"You *know* what!" I caught my breath and sat up against the headboard, knees to my chest. My heart pounded out of control as I remembered when my sister used to shift into her cougar and prowl on my bed in the morning. "I told you I don't like being woken up like that."

I preferred soft kisses to the back of my neck by a lover, or even a plate of food beneath my nose. I often had violent outbursts when I was startled awake—sometimes shifting into my wolf.

And nobody wanted to tangle with my wolf from what I'd heard. She had a nasty temper and represented my alter ego with a proud wag of her tail.

"I'm not in the mood to fry bacon just to wake your ass up. Deal with it. I'm heading out to take care of business. It's already two in the afternoon, so I think you need to get moving and shower for work."

"Maybe my customers like me stinky." I snatched up an automotive magazine from the end table in our garish bedroom.

Whatever he did, Hawk made money. Good money. He also liked to flaunt it, and a man with money and no taste was not an agreeable mix. Seashells and birds decorated our mauve bedspread, the oval tables were made of etched glass, the brass lamps were shaped like a woman's nude body, and don't even get me started on the hideous drapes. It wasn't the style so much as the money he coughed up to make it so atrocious.

"I'm letting you drive to work tonight, but if you come home late, the deal is off."

I swung my legs over the bed and stood up. "Letting me?"

He spanked my ass again, and I scowled at him. "Yeah, *letting* you. Just remember who pays the bills around here."

"Not for long!" I snarled, slamming the bathroom door.

That just rubbed me the wrong way. Hawk could be a real jerk when he wanted, bragging about how he brought in the cash and how grateful I should be. He didn't think I could pull in much money as a waitress, but little did he know. I had this niggling feeling that our relationship was doomed. Eventually Hawk was going to become insecure about his woman making money and would give me an ultimatum. I'd never allowed anyone to dictate how I live my life. Maybe I didn't look like much of a tough girl with my slender frame and innocent face, but a female wolf either learns to be assertive or becomes nothing more than a submissive bitch.

And I was nobody's bitch.

I'd seen the influence some corrupt packs had on their women. I felt sorry for those girls. Not the ones with a sharp tongue, but the girls who'd lost their identities after being swallowed up by the dominance of an unworthy mate. It wasn't the Shifter way, because most of the men revered their mates, protected them, and supported their desires to work or raise a family. Shifter women were outspoken and headstrong, but it frightened me to think I might end up in the wrong pack.

At least with rogues, I didn't have a sense of being trapped. Lone wolves were sometimes involved in criminal activities in order to pay the bills. They saw themselves as badasses who didn't need to follow orders, but most were just men who had issues. Only a rare few were alphas. Alphas instinctively formed packs, but once or twice I'd run into a lone alpha. Those were the dudes I stayed far away from.

Scary dudes.

After my shower, I shaved my legs and gave them the full shea-butter treatment. I used to wear pants, but now I dressed the way

I wanted, and if I ended up with a scratch or mark, I'd shift long enough to heal it. I just had to deal with my wolf getting pissed at me for not letting her stay out. Hell, maybe some of her attitude helped me get through a rough night. Eventually I'd succumb to the call—like all Shifters do—and allow her two nights a week to run loose.

Not on the streets, of course. I didn't know my way around Austin well enough, so I'd been confined to the backyard after I'd torn up Hawk's drapes. I guess my wolf didn't like his taste either.

I threw on a pair of frayed jean shorts and a sleeveless white shirt. There were a few things I needed, so I headed to the drugstore. By then, Hawk had already left the house.

While driving, my cell phone rang, and I quickly answered. "This is the party to whom you are speaking."

A laugh bubbled on the other end. "Izzy, this is Rosie. I talked to Jake and put in a good word. I think you work harder than some of the other girls, but don't tell them that. And a few regulars were asking about you after you left. Jake's offering you full peak hours if you want them. Can you handle that?"

I found a parking spot outside the store and shut off the engine. "Of course! That's great news. Thanks so much, Rosie. I won't let you down. I'll keep the drinks and food moving, and let me know if you need any help with promotions. I used to hand out flyers on the weekdays to promote special events. I don't know the laws around here for posting them on poles, but I can do that too."

"Thanks, hon. I'll tell Jake, but we got a guy who does that already."

"A guy?" My flats crunched on the asphalt when I stepped out of the car. "Nothing sells a gig like a girl. Most of our customers are men and they need a little motivation. Their girls get sexed up by the band, they flirt with the waitresses, and everyone goes home and gets a little nookie."

"I knew it!" she exclaimed. "I said to Jake a long time ago I thought I could walk the streets for money, and he didn't think it was a good idea."

I belted out a laugh and strolled into Walgreens. "If you said it like that, Rosie, then I'd have to agree with him. Do you want me to be there at eight?"

"If you want to come in early and prep or have dinner, that's okay. Staff eats for free, just so you know."

A young man in flip-flops and long shorts gave me a cheesy grin. I didn't return the smile. Handsome or not, I never cared to see a man's hairy toes wiggling in a pair of sandals.

"Sounds gravy. Look, I need to let you go. I'll see you tonight?"

"I'm there every night, hon."

Rosie hung up, and I perused the nail-polish aisle. My hair swung from a loose ponytail, and the only makeup I had on was tinted lip balm and a little blush. Occasionally I'd apply eyeliner for work, but over the years, I'd learned to accept my flaws as part of what made me Isabelle Monroe. I realized that beauty had more to do with confidence. I'd seen plenty of knockouts who walked with their head down, and men didn't give them the time of day.

The trick was to walk with your chin up and center your eyes on a man, as if you had a sexy secret. Then, just as you pass him, look down and nibble on your lip. But always look back over your shoulder at him. Men are perceptive about body language—something I'd learned working in bars.

I lifted the orange nail polish and examined it under the fluorescent light.

"Try the matte green," a young woman on my right suggested.

I glanced over at a girl with striking beauty. I admired the trendy cut of her blond hair—short with long bangs sheared at an angle. She looked at me with charcoal-lined eyes and lifted a curvy bottle from the rack.

"Normally I hate the stereotypes about redheads wearing green, but this color would look great on you because of your fair complexion."

"Thanks," I said. "Looks like it's on sale."

"The top shelf is half off, so check out some of the shimmery colors with a touch of pink. Sorry, don't mean to be nosy."

"Not at all. You seem to know your stuff, and I never turn down free advice," I said, noticing the bright purple polish on her nails. "I'm Izzy. I just moved here a few weeks ago."

She dropped a bottle of electric blue into her basket, and it rolled over a paperback novel. "I'm April Frost. Where are you originally from? I don't hear much of an accent."

"All over," I replied with a soft laugh. "We'll see how this goes."

"It's not a bad place to live as long as you don't mind hot weather. I work a few blocks down at Sweet Treats."

"What's that?"

She shrugged and examined an eyeliner pencil. "It's a candy shop, but it's not just for kids. I guarantee you'll find something in there you like. Stop by and I'll give you the first item for free."

"Very savvy," I said, noticing her eyes flash up to mine. "A local business, right? No need to work your charm, you have a new customer. I know how important it is to reel 'em in."

She laughed and passed the basket over to her other hand. "I'd recommend going there even if I wasn't the manager. We have the best chocolates you've ever tasted."

"Yum. So, I see you like reading?"

She blushed and twisted the basket away, trying to hide her romance novel. "My best friend is going to kill me for getting this. I try to buy everything on the e-reader he gave me, but I can't seem to walk into a store that sells books without putting one in my basket. It's like crack."

A man walked by with a bottle of shampoo, rushing toward the register. April accidentally backed into him, and one of her jeweled sandals slipped off. She blushed and smiled apologetically before he kept going.

"I'll swing by this week, April. Nice meeting you, and thanks for the polish tip."

"You too, Izzy. I like that name."

She disappeared toward the shampoo aisle, and I wandered up front and placed a box of protein bars in my basket.

"Will this be all for you, ma'am?" the cashier asked.

"Yes, please."

I hated being called ma'am. I knew I still looked in my mid-twenties, but I hated being addressed so formally, even if I understood the reason behind it. Personally, I never called my customers *sir*. I learned their names and established a relationship with them. But humans had their customs.

An insistent ring chimed from my purse, and I pulled out my phone. "This is the party to whom you are—"

"Izzy, goddammit."

I paid the cashier. "Hi, Hawk. Did you forget something?"

Like telling me how much he loved me. Which he never did; we didn't have that kind of relationship. He loved my ass, loved my meatloaf, and he even loved my red hair. But he didn't love *me*.

"Where are you?"

"Shopping for the necessities."

"I need you to necessitate your ass home. I ran into some trouble, and I want you to get off the streets."

Get off the streets? Who says that?

"Hawk, I'm fine. Nobody in this city knows who I am, let alone where I am," I said, walking toward my cute little blue car.

"Izzy," he warned.

"I have to pick up some groceries on the way home and buy a new bra."

"Izzy…"

"I'm hanging up now…"

Hawk was mad. I could hear it in the inflection of his profanities. "Get your fucking ass home right fucking now. I will *find* you, come get you, and drag you home if I have to."

"Fine," I growled in the phone, stuffing it into my purse.

I slumped in my car and shut the door, wondering why it was so hard to find a good Shifter. Either they were bossy or they would treat me like one of the guys. Maybe I wanted to be spoiled once in a while. But Shifters could be abrasive, belligerent men. Except with their life mate. I'd convinced myself those women possessed a secret love potion they weren't sharing with the general public—one that tamed the primitive ways of a Shifter and made them do romantic things like buy flowers and rub their woman's feet with scented oils.

Deciding not to argue, I turned the key and rolled down the windows, ready to head home.

Until a long arm reached through my window and yanked my keys out of the ignition.

"Hey!" I squinted and glanced up, wondering if someone was playing a prank.

"You sure that's her?"

A man with a black mustache shaped like an upside-down horseshoe bent over and looked at me with droopy eyes. It looked like a biker mustache, although I didn't know all the different names for facial hair. It resembled a long set of handlebars to me.

"Yeah, that's her," he replied.

As soon as I reached for the passenger door, he caught my left arm in a tight grip.

"Haul her in," the other voice said. "Let Delgado decide what he wants to do with her."

"Let me go!"

Handlebars tugged my arm and glanced up at my hair. "You a real redhead?"

I bit my lip. Redheads learned not to answer that question; it always led to another question we had heard a million times before, one about the carpet matching the drapes.

"Come on, sweetie." The door clicked open and he jerked me to my feet. "We're not going to hurt you."

"What's this about?" I wrenched away and held on to the door.

"It's about your boyfriend, Hawk. He's been overcharging and taking a cut. Our boss doesn't like people stealing from him."

I furrowed my brow. "Is this about drugs?"

Handlebars stirred with laughter and shifted his eyes at the guy behind me. He was a scrawny little bug-eyed man, missing a front tooth. I didn't sense this guy was Breed. I felt confident dealing with humans, but the last thing I needed was for my wolf to get cocky and shift in broad daylight. That kind of stunt could land me in trouble with the authorities.

"Ain't she adorable?" Handlebars chuckled and leveled out his tone. "I say we keep her. Yeah, sweetie, it's about drugs. Your boyfriend was set up this morning by Delgado and busted in the act. Before our guy could take him out, Hawk fired a few rounds and took off. We're looking for him, and we know he'll be looking for you."

I stilled in shock. *Drugs? Exchanging gunfire?*

"How do you know I'm Hawk's girlfriend?"

"Sweetie, Delgado makes it his business to know everything."

He jerked my arm forward and I dug in my heels. "I'm not going anywhere with you."

Handlebars suddenly bent over, hooked his arms around my waist, and threw me over his shoulder. I pounded my fists against his back and cursed. Then I ran my hand over his back pocket, hoping he'd have a switchblade in there.

"Why don't you put the girl down, and I won't slam your face into the asphalt. How 'bout that?" a voice threatened, making all the tiny hairs on the back of my neck stand up. This guy was *definitely* Breed.

I peered around and saw a fierce man sitting on a Triumph motorcycle. I caught a glimpse of a gun strapped beneath his arm. *Was he a bounty hunter?* He got off his motorcycle and stalked toward the little guy, throwing a hard fist and knocking him out cold before the poor human could give him his best "go to hell" speech.

Then it was between him and Handlebars.

"This is none of your business. Walk away," my kidnapper said in a cool voice.

I couldn't see any of the action because I was ass-out, waiting for the stranger to either save my life or get himself killed.

Then I heard the click of a gun and froze. *Oh my God! He's going to shoot me in the ass!*

"Let me go!" I screamed, wiggling and flailing like a dolphin caught in a fisherman's net.

"Shut the hell up!" He smacked me so hard on the back of my leg I cried out in pain.

A gunshot went off, Handlebars bent forward, and vertigo took over as I was about to meet the concrete.

"Gotcha," the motorcycle man said. Strong arms caught me from behind, and he tossed me into my car.

I didn't care for being manhandled, but I didn't hesitate to leap into action when my keys landed in my lap. I shoved the key in the ignition with a shaky hand, barely closed my door, and threw the car into reverse.

The last thing I saw was Motorcycle Man kicking the shit out of Handlebars, who was clutching his bleeding leg. When April came jogging out of the store, I almost slammed on the brakes. The thought was extinguished when she grabbed Motorcycle Man by the collar and dragged him away with a scowl on her face.

Texas was going to be an interesting place to live. Who knew such a quiet girl hung out with one serious badass who carried a gun?

A man I didn't know, but I owed him.

CHAPTER 3

"HONEY, YOU DON'T LOOK SO good tonight," Rosie said in a glum voice. She set down her glass of Dr Pepper and began filing her nails.

"I think I'm just having one of those days." I tried to brush off the fact that a man with tacky facial hair had been trying to kidnap me until a biker shot him in the leg. "How do you like my new nail polish?"

"It's green." She turned up her nose and showed me her nails. Rosie had broken one and was filing it down, but the rest of them had been given the full treatment at the salon. Rosie was the kind of woman who believed a good manicure was a religious experience. "Is that all you're going to eat? You need energy if you want to keep up with this crowd." She stared at my salad and wiped a smudge of ink off her hand.

"I'm not especially hungry," I said truthfully. I hadn't heard from Hawk and wasn't sure if those thugs knew where I worked. It wasn't likely or they would have already shown up, but that didn't stop me from taking the long, long way to work.

"A big act is coming in tonight, hon. You should fuel up on a hearty dinner, because the ladies will wear you out with their orders."

"What act?"

Rosie set down her nail file and sipped her drink from a narrow straw. "They're a hot local band. Jake had them in here once before and the show tripled his income, so he's been trying to work out a deal to make them regulars. Be real nice to them because Jake wants to seal the deal; they're a little skittish about signing an exclusive contract. Just keep the drinks moving. Once the girls bust through that door, it's chaos."

"Ah, one of *those* bands. Girls flinging their panties at the stage?"

She smothered a laugh. "Right before hurling their drinks in the bathroom. Try to push the expensive appetizers and weak drinks to start so they'll spend more. If you serve the hard liquor first, they'll be gone by the second song."

"You bet. Do you guys sell anything on the side?"

She reapplied her lipstick and snapped the mirror shut. "Like what?"

"Sensor pops?"

Rosie narrowed her eyes. "I know that it's become commonplace to pass out candy spiked by Sensors, but Jake doesn't like that mess in his place. I personally don't touch that stuff. It gives me the willies to think about feeling someone else's emotions."

Sensors were paranormals who, like Shifters, lived an extended lifespan. While some did investigative work, most earned their money by harvesting emotions and selling them to buyers looking for a thrill. Sometimes they drew in business by imprinting emotions on candy so people could sample their wares. Their customers would experience arousal, elation, anger, an adrenaline rush, and other emotions—except in a subtle and controlled way. Just enough of a taste to decide if they wanted to call the number on the wrapper and schedule a transfer.

I poked my fork in my salad bowl and took another bite. "It doesn't cost the bar anything since it's promotional advertising for the Sensor, and Jake can charge a small fee for each piece of candy. There's nothing illegal about it."

Rosie waved at a gentleman leaving the bar and sighed. "We had an incident two years ago where the distributor didn't give us what we requested. He wasn't a professional and put too much into the candy. People went crazy and we had to shut down for two days."

"Wow," I said, chomping on another cucumber. "You don't have to explain further."

"Well, you just don't hand out *anything* to a bar full of drunken Shifters. That's all I'm saying. We had a fight break out, and one guy almost died from a bite to the jugular when he fell unconscious and couldn't shift."

I'd never dealt with a Sensor because I'd heard stories about it leading to sensory addiction. Those with less-than-exciting lives would spend all their money reliving an emotional experience in their life, or one that they purchased. I had good vibes about working in a bar that took pride in their establishment, so I dropped the subject.

"Where's your family?" she asked. "Did they move here with you?"

My stomach knotted and I sipped on my ice water. "We're estranged. Sibling rivalry and all that. It's a long and uninteresting story."

"Sorry to hear," she said, her attention already elsewhere. Rosie was a woman who had undoubtedly heard it all. She looked older— maybe in her early forties. In Shifter years, there was no way to tell how old she *really* was. Everyone aged differently, and sometimes it depended on their animal.

Suddenly, two hands covered her eyes and a handsome man kissed her on the head. "How's my Rosie?"

She giggled like a smitten teenager and reached up to fix her hair. "Denver, stop. I want you to meet the new girl."

He stole the chair on my right and gave me a dazzling smile. "This is Izzy Monroe."

Then his smile waned. "Izzy Monroe?"

"That's what they call me," I said, taking a monster bite of salad.

He studied my hair and then narrowed his eyes.

"Izzy, this is Denver. He's pretty to look at, but don't let those baby blues fool you. Denver's all talk."

I set down my fork and leaned back, crossing my legs. I caught him looking down at them before he erased his interest.

"Your name is Izzy." It wasn't a question.

"And you're Denver. The bartender, right? I saw you come in last night at the end of my shift."

"That's it? That's *all* you have to say to me?"

I stood up and patted his back. "And you're smokin' hot, Denver. Can't wait to start having babies with you."

As I walked off, I heard Rosie giggling hysterically. "You really need to work on your game, Denver."

———⊶◦⫘◦⊶———

Just after midnight, the band arrived at Howlers. They swaggered through the front door and heads turned, but I kept my attention on the customers. Rosie wasn't kidding. The scantily clad women showed up in droves, wearing tight-fitting skirts and do-me pumps. Some had hiked their G-strings above their low-cut jeans. I vehemently hated that look. Those were always the girls who swung an attitude my way, made me work extra hard on their table, complained about my service, and never left a tip.

Someone did a sound check on the mic and tapped it a few times.

"Denver, two daiquiris and three margaritas," I called out.

"Doesn't anyone just want a man's drink? A beer? Anything?" he shouted, holding his hands up and staring at the ceiling.

I laughed and stood on my tiptoes. "In a bar full of women? They want fruity drinks. Suck it up and keep your blender on standby. While I'm waiting, I need another pitcher for table nine, handsome."

When I turned around, a napkin floated to the floor. I dipped down to pick it up and after placing it on the bar, came face-to-face with Handlebars.

Super.

"That's quite a move," he said in a leathery voice. "You're a real pro. I can tell you've been working tables a long time… or maybe a pole."

I glanced down at his black jeans where he had been shot.

"Got a guy who patched me up and prescribed some good painkillers. Turns out your knight in shining armor had bad aim and only grazed my leg. Hurts like a bitch, let me tell you," he snarled.

"Don't start anything in here; you're in the wrong place for that," I said sharply. "This is *my* turf, so you play by my rules. Got it?"

This guy had no idea what a bar full of Shifters would do to him if he put his hands on me and I screamed. Guys were touchy-feely all the time, but when a girl said no, and *especially* if she did it while screaming, knuckles flew from all directions.

"Where's your boyfriend?" Handlebars pressed.

I tugged at the ends of my black shorts and gave him a nasty glare. "I have no idea."

And if I did, I'd probably turn Hawk over to my new stalker out of spite. I'd tried calling him all day, but it kept going to voice mail.

Denver handed me a tray and gave Handlebars a good once-over before retreating to a group of rowdy girls trying to snag his attention by polishing the bar with their breasts.

Jake's voice sounded over the speakers while I delivered the drinks, and I struggled to hear a woman placing her order.

"Ladies, gents, it's my pleasure to present one of the biggest acts in Austin. You're in for a real treat to see them up close and personal. Put your hands together for…"

"Rosie!" I shouted, weaving my way toward her. "The woman in blue wants a Zipper. What the hell is that?"

"…the baddest Breed group in town. Welcome to the stage, Izzy Monroe!"

I whirled around and my jaw dropped.

The main lights went out and cheap lighting illuminated the stage. A guy tapped his drumsticks and started the beat.

"Izzy, did they just say your name?" Rosie yelled over the music.

I gave her a quizzical look. "What the hell is going on?"

"I don't know. Same guys, but a different name. Do you know them?"

Ho-ly shitola.

Walking onstage with swagger and truckloads of sex appeal was a man who could bring a woman to orgasm by merely brushing his lips against the nape of her neck.

After all, I should know.

His hair was shorter than I remembered, now cut to the shoulders, and he had dyed it different shades of brown. It obscured his face, and I desperately moved around people to get a better view. All I could see was his tattered shirt, torn jeans, and his signature move of swinging a guitar over his shoulder as he approached the mic.

"I'm Jericho," he growled.

Grown women screamed and rushed the stage.

My heart hammered in my chest, my mouth as dry as the Sahara, and a roar of tingles moved through my body. At first, they were the good kind that made me feel warm and aroused. Then they spiraled into the kind that made me feel woozy—like I might faint from shock.

Jericho Sexton Cole.

Twenty years ago I was destitute, and Jericho had taken me under his wing. He worked as a roadie until I'd convinced him he could sing the hell out of those bands. He took me up on a dare one night and went onstage as Sexton Cole. The name stuck, and was one he lived up to. Those were the best five years of my life, but gradually, Jericho had succumbed to the addictive lifestyle of hard drugs and cold women. It shattered me to remember the last time I'd seen him perform, because he had crawled onto the stage and passed out.

Damn, he looked as stunning as ever. Even more so now, because I could tell by the way he moved and sang that he was sober.

Jericho's raspy bedroom voice filled the room with a seismic tempo that had the hips of every woman in that bar gyrating. He made love to his microphone—body and soul.

My name. Why did he name his band after me? I couldn't breathe.

"I have to get out of here."

"Honey, you can't leave now!" Rosie shrieked, eyes wide with horror. "We're swamped! Now you shake your little ass and keep the drinks flowing. This is Jake's big night, and we need to pull in some serious cash. Push the specialties. And just tell Denver you want a Zipper. He knows what it is."

Rosie spun around with a tray over her head and vanished into the crowd. I could feel the heat on my back from the burning sensuousness in his hypnotic voice—his words caressing my soul like a distant dream. A man I'd thought was dead after all these years.

The first man I'd ever shown my wolf to. At the darkest time in my life, Jericho had been there like a beacon of light. He'd once taken me to the beach in California at midnight and we'd run into the ocean with our clothes on, because that's how he seized the moment.

Too much history was rushing back at once. People were shouting orders, and I nodded, moving like a zombie toward the bar.

Denver leaned forward on his elbows and gave a tight-lipped smile. "Enjoying the band?"

I ignored him, lost in a nebulous of memories. "I need a Zipper."

Denver turned around and began mixing the order. "They change names when their act gets stale and people want a fresh sound," he yelled over his shoulder. "I know *all* about you, Izzy Monroe." He slammed the glass in front of me and pointed his finger. "You're the bitch who almost killed my brother."

When he turned away, I lurched across the bar and grabbed a fistful of his shirt, yanking him back. "What did you just say?"

"First, I called you a bitch, and I think we both know where I'm coming from."

Yeah, I did. Not in the derogatory sense, the way humans used it, but Denver knew I was a wolf.

"Second, you left my brother to rot in a hotel room from a drug overdose. I was the one who had to pick him up at a *human* hospital," he emphasized. "Jericho almost died because of your apathy."

"Overdose? What?"

"I'm a nice guy, Izzy. I get along with everyone. But I don't forgive anyone who leaves my brother dying on the floor of a run-down, sleazy hotel."

I gasped, furious and horrified all at once. *What had Jericho told them?*

Before I could speak, someone jerked me around, slapped his hands over my thighs, and threw me over his shoulder. After a few pats to my behind, I heard him say, "Taking my old lady home."

I recognized that flat ass. *Handlebars.*

"Put me down, you jackass!"

The music roared and nobody heard me; they were engrossed with the sexual sound of Jericho singing about pain to the wailing cry of a guitar. Darkness blanketed the room. The only exception was the bar area. I looked up and saw Denver leap over the bar, his legs sliding across the surface as he moved out of sight. Jericho's voice tumbled in my head, which was quickly filling with blood from being upside down.

I reached beneath my attacker's shirt and pinched his skin as hard as I could. He shouted in pain and I straightened my back, trying to grab his hair. Handlebars swung me around, using me to block Denver's punches. When he lost his grip, the singing abruptly stopped. I didn't know which way was up and I fell backward, striking my head against the edge of the bar. The shouts faded to murmurs, and my eyes closed as tiny pinpricks of light lured me into unconsciousness.

"*Izzy?*"

———————⧖———————

Jericho didn't feel a shred of guilt when he showed up late for their gig at Howlers, because it drew out the suspense. The owner, Jake, didn't seem to mind and was pleased to have him; most places were. They pulled in serious cash, even with the frequent name changes.

He walked onstage with a black guitar pick clenched between his teeth. This particular song began with a slow beat, but then midway through, they'd hit the gas and bring down the house with their adrenaline-pumping performance.

Jericho's eyes settled on a blonde in the front row working her fingertips around her nipples, twisting them until they poked through her white shirt like bullets. Unable to concentrate on the lyrics, he steered his attention toward the back of the room. He saw nothing but a sea of faces in the dark, except by the bar.

Some action was going on, and Jericho continued strumming his guitar as the song built momentum. A large man with a long mustache had thrown one of the waitresses over his shoulder, and it looked like things were getting rowdy. Nothing he hadn't seen before, but the red hair snagged his attention as it swung around.

Denver slid over the bar and hit the guy in the face. That's when the girl straightened up and smacked her assailant in the head. Pack instinct kicked in when he saw his brother throwing punches, and Jericho buried the primitive urge to fight by Denver's side.

He kept playing, singing into the mic, but suddenly not feeling in the moment. His heart raced unexpectedly, and he didn't know why.

Then Jericho saw her face.

Isabelle Marie Monroe.

"Fuck," he said into the mic.

"Yeah!" a woman shouted. "Fuck *me!*"

He lifted the strap off his shoulder and threw the guitar down. Feedback from the amplifier screeched, and those standing near the speakers winced. His band stopped playing for a few beats before picking back up without him.

Christ. It couldn't be.

He leapt off the stage and pushed his way through the crowd—*fought* his way through.

Women desperately clung to his shirt, and the men were giving him shoulder bumps.

By the time he reached the bar, the young woman was sprawled out on her back with one leg bent at the knee. A blanket of wavy red hair surrounded her head like a fiery halo.

Jericho stood catatonic. It *was* her.

"Izzy?" Rosie said, smacking her cheek. "Izzy, wake up."

Jericho threw a glance at Denver, who was still fighting the asshat who'd tossed Isabelle around. "You got this?" The two men swung at each other and a Shifter from the sidelines jumped in for the hell of it.

"In the bag," Denver shouted between swings.

Jericho's eyes were wide with disbelief as he stared at a woman he thought he'd never see again.

"Izzy, wake up. It's Rosie," the waitress continued.

The band kept playing after Jake made a speech to hold the crowd over.

"She needs to go home," Rosie insisted. "Even if she shifts, she hit her head pretty hard, and I wouldn't feel right about making her wait tables."

The man with the long mustache stumbled off, quickly leaving the building. Denver leaned over the bar and grabbed a stack of paper napkins, wiping the blood from his nose. "Jackass."

"Who was that?" Jericho asked, still looking down at Isabelle.

Denver knelt down in front of the redhead and wiped his nose again. "A human who walked into the wrong bar to start shit. What's her address, Rosie? We'll call a cab."

"I don't know, honey. Jake pays us in cash; you know that. He doesn't like to be in everyone's business, and it's not as if he has to file taxes," Rosie said with a shake of her head. "He just needs your name and number, and that's all she wrote. And you can't put her in a cab while she's still unconscious!"

Denver laughed. "Why not? I see people leaving here like that all the time."

"Move out of the way," Jericho said gruffly, kneeling down and cradling the back of her neck. "I said *move*!"

Rosie stood up and ushered a few waitresses back to their tables. His bass player took over singing, and it made Jericho cringe to hear him off-key.

"Why don't you just leave her unconscious on the floor?" Denver suggested. "Like she did you."

Jericho snapped his head around. "Shut the hell up. You don't know what you're talking about."

"You're a bag of nuts. Don't forget who showed up to save your sorry ass."

With careful ease, Jericho lifted Isabelle into his arms.

"Mmm… no," she mumbled as her eyelids fluttered. "I don't know what a Zipper is."

Man, did she look *stunning*. She always did, but time and experience had worked a beautiful magic on this girl. Isabelle had amazing lips—the kind that made a guy lose his train of thought. His train jumped the track and derailed when she licked them.

"That how you like 'em, Mr. Rockstar? Comatose?" a man heckled.

In a smooth voice, Jericho walked by him and said, "That's how I got your old lady."

The guy's face tightened, but no way would a Shifter take a swing while Jericho was holding an injured girl in his arms.

As soon as he found a private spot in the field next to the parking lot, he gently laid her down in the soft grass. Isabelle needed to shift in order to heal that nasty bump on her head.

Jericho softly stroked the nape of her neck and whispered, "Shift."

Hopefully her wolf was inside and paying attention. He remembered the old tricks—Isabelle always had a fondness for having the back of her neck touched. It was a technique her wolf also responded to, so he continued stroking and calling to her.

Her eyes began to open, but before she looked up, Isabelle shifted in a fluid motion. He fell back when her wolf bared her teeth at him. She'd always been a badass bitch, but never to him.

"Easy, Isabelle," he soothed, scooting away and creating distance between them. "You hit your head and you're confused." Some Shifters remembered the first few seconds or even minutes into their shift, but she might have blacked out and let her animal spirit take over.

Her wolf was smaller than most. Fur just as white as snow, and her feet were black, as if she'd run through a tar pit.

"Come on, Isabelle. We're in the middle of the goddamn city. Shift back."

He glanced over his shoulder when a horn blared. Headlights briefly shone on them before the sedan drove through the parking lot. When Jericho looked back, Isabelle was gone. Only a pile of clothes and her heels remained.

"Isabelle!" he shouted, standing up and scanning the property. The city was no place for a wolf to be wandering. It was too easy to get hit by a car, shot, or taken in by animal control.

"*Fffuck.*"

He jumped when Denver slapped his arm around his shoulders and gave him a tight squeeze.

"She ditched you again, huh?"

He shrugged Denver off and faced him, stepping close and curling his lips. "What's your deal with Isabelle?"

"You mean Izzy, right? The name of your band. The name of the girl who left you overdosing in a hotel. You almost *died*," Denver yelled, shoving Jericho in the chest. "You were lucky I only lived an hour away and they called me on time. It took me for-fucking-*ever* to get you to shift. You said some shit—"

"What shit?" Jericho demanded, shoving at Denver's chest. "I don't remember saying a damn thing."

"No, because you're Mr. Fucking Rockstar who can shoot up heroin and doesn't need anyone. You were *crying*, Jericho. I went back to the hotel to find out what had happened. A maid said she went in to do housecleaning and found you facedown in your own vomit. That little redhead was digging in your back pocket and stealing money out of your wallet. She didn't care if the maid saw her. She cleaned you out, stole your guitar, and left you there to *die*."

Jericho shook his head. "You're full of it. That's not what happened."

"You don't even remember what happened. You've been living a lie. That girl is toxic, and I don't want that poison seeping back into your life. Let her go. You'll be lucky if Jake still wants you to come back after what you pulled tonight, but he's not firing Izzy just because you two had a thing. So get your act together. I don't like being the serious one around here. Life shouldn't be that damn complicated," he muttered, kicking up a clump of dirt and heading back to the bar.

Denver was about as laid-back as they came. Jericho loved a good party, but Denver was the *life* of the party. It's why he excelled at bartending; he was a born people person and knew how to make anyone smile. So Jericho didn't like the serious turn this topic had taken. He respected his pack and didn't want to break that bond. Family wasn't about blood but who had your back. His brothers always had his back and vice versa. So they had learned to get over the petty shit and stay tight. He decided this wasn't worth fighting over.

Jericho lit up a cigarette and pinched it between his thumb and index finger, watching the smoke haze across his view of the quarter moon. He decided to shake it off and get his ass back onstage. Jericho had never been a quitter.

But for the first time in his life, he felt like quitting something. Isabelle.

No woman had ever made him feel so alive and capable of doing anything. She had seen the potential in him and pushed him into singing. Then one night she disappeared without a trace. All these years later, he thought some terrible fate had befallen Isabelle. Had he known she'd picked his pockets, stolen his guitar, and left him overdosing, he would have buried those sentimental feelings about her years ago.

It was time to get out the proverbial shovel and bury those feelings once and for all.

CHAPTER 4

WAKING UP IN A STRANGE bed is disorienting enough, but nothing quite tops waking up naked in a vegetable garden.

I bolted upright and wiped the dirt from my face, alert and soaking in my surroundings. I was lying in a tomato patch on the side of a house near an open gate. My wolf had dug up the dirt so that it made a soft bed to sleep on. Even worse was that I'd been snuggling with a rubber snake, no doubt placed there to scare away the birds.

"Oh hell's bells, Izzy," I muttered under my breath, staring at the tall wooden fence beside me.

The last thing I remembered was playing carnival ride on Handlebars. Now I had dirt in places that would require a carwash to get clean. My wolf was a dirt roller and would take a patch of Texas clay over a roll in the grass anytime. I hated her for it, and after this fiasco, we weren't going to be on good terms.

It was predawn and I needed to get my rear in gear before the lawn-mowing husbands came out in their black socks and sandals. I scurried to a small shed and peered inside. Unfortunately I didn't find a full wardrobe, or at the very least, gardening attire.

I used my long hair to cover my breasts, flattening it out strategically. Beside the shed door sat a large paper sack overflowing with empty plant containers. I turned it upside down, tore a hole in the bottom, stepped inside, and slowly shimmied the bag up my legs.

"Please God, I'll never eat another donut again," I whispered, praying it would fit. Once I had the bag in place, I ran.

Ran like a bride to the altar.

"Oh my God, oh my God," I sang, hurrying up the sidewalk. My hair blew away from my shoulders and I stopped, concealing my breasts again. It was the only time I'd ever been thankful for a modest cup size. I glanced at a familiar street sign and headed north. The bag made ripping noises that scared me enough to shorten my steps. Sunrise continued to push its way to the horizon, ready to give birth to a new day.

With Howlers to my right, I crossed the street and kept jogging. There was no way in Hades I was going to show up at work half-naked and covered in dirt just to get my work clothes out of the locker. Those girls would never let me live this down.

I heard another tear and slowed down again, trying to hold my hair in place. Maybe I could pull this off and just casually walk up the street with a grocery bag around my Bermuda Triangle. I'd seen women wearing less.

"Chilly morning for a stroll."

I cringed at the familiar voice.

After patting down my hair, I prepared to face the worst person I could have possibly run into while naked.

"Hello, Jericho."

Sweet Jesus, did he look good. He leaned across the middle of a blue truck with the most indifferent look on his face. Maybe he seemed so attractive because of how coherent he was—not at all the man I remembered from years ago. Or maybe it was the way he styled his long hair so that it looked tangled, as if he'd just rolled out of bed. Could have been the silver rings and leather bracelet with the small spikes.

Might have been the tattoo.

It was most *definitely* his sea-green eyes. The ones that slid down the length of my filthy body until they settled on the paper bag that barely covered my coochie.

"Thought you'd run off for good, Isabelle. You seem to have a knack for that," he added.

"Sorry, Jericho. I almost didn't recognize you with your dick in your pants. If you'll excuse me, I have to get home."

I tried to flounce off, but walking in short steps with a paper sack around my hips wasn't a graceful way to make an exit.

He rolled the truck beside me and the engine rumbled, but he didn't say a word.

So I walked a little faster.

He drove a little faster.

Finally, I broke into a run. Jericho hit the gas and kept up with me.

"Get in the goddamn truck, Isabelle."

"No."

"You're a female wolf running naked in the street. Get in."

"I'm not naked," I panted. "I'm wearing recyclables."

Which suddenly ripped. I stopped and waved my hand behind me, feeling a cool breeze against my cheeks. I twisted the bag where it had torn and held it tightly to my hip.

"Why bother? It's not like I haven't seen a naked woman before," he said. "In fact, I've seen a *whole lot* of women."

"Jericho, you smug, arrogant—"

"Horny," he added with a bored wink.

"I hate you."

"You still want to fuck me."

Exclamation points were appearing over my head. "Don't flatter yourself. I may wear recyclables, but I don't want to have sex with any."

He flinched. "Maybe no one will care if you're half-naked since we're on the Breed side of town, but I'm guessing it's a long walk home."

I stared at my bare legs. Yep, this would certainly get me arrested by the human police. Shifters didn't care about nudity so much. It was a little silly to be rehashing past drama like a couple of children on a street corner when I only had a veil of paper covering my feminine mystique.

"Fine," I conceded in a miserable voice, walking toward the door. "But you're not allowed to say a word to me. All I want is a lift."

"Is that so?" he said in an annoyed voice, his left wrist draped over the steering wheel. He licked his lips and I tried not to notice, but the way his tongue swiped across them should have been against the law. "And why not?"

"Because…"

Because *oh my God*, after all these years, I still felt something for him. My traitorous heart leapt against my chest, despite the fact it still carried a scar. All those old feelings rushed back and there we were again, except there we weren't. We were two different people, and I didn't know who had changed for the better and who for the worse.

"Finish what you were going to say."

I leaned in the window. "Because you were an insensitive friend," I said in a somber tone.

The doors locked and Jericho sat back in his seat, revving the engine.

"Wait a minute, are you going to leave me here?" I exclaimed.

"You got it, Sexybelle."

When he sped off, I chased after him. "You can't leave me here!" He left me there.

On the side of the road at dawn, wearing dirt and a torn paper sack. I finally felt like the trash Jericho had thrown away all those years ago.

"Hey, sweetie! Want me to help carry your groceries?" a man razzed from his truck window.

I gave him the finger and stormed across the street as he laughed and turned the corner.

———⋅◦⋙◦⋅———

I gasped for air and sprang to my knees. "Don't do that!" I shouted, feeling the residual sting on my rear from being slapped. My fingers gripped the sheets on our bed, and I blew out a hard breath.

"Miss me, Iz?"

I tore the covers away, a sheen of sweat covering my chest and the room feeling uncomfortably stuffy from the afternoon sunshine pouring through the windows. "Hawk? Where have you been? I tried calling you."

"Pack your bags."

"Huh?"

He yanked a suitcase out of the closet and stuffed it with his boxer shorts and dress shirts. "We're moving."

"Moving where? Wait a second. What's going on? Some psycho has been following me around looking for you."

"Yeah, that's why we're moving. What's with all the dirt on the kitchen floor and ripped-up paper?"

I swung my legs over the bed and slipped on a T-shirt. "I'm not going anywhere with you. Not unless you tell me you've fixed whatever you messed up. I've always accepted you for who you are and haven't interfered in your business affairs, but I'm not about to get mixed up with someone who has lunatic humans chasing after him. This isn't the life I want."

"I don't give a shit what kind of life you want, Izzy. This is the life you *get*. So quit looking a gift horse in the mouth," he said, backing me up to the wall. "You need to get it in that thick head of yours that life isn't about good times and getting what you want."

"Oh?" I said, doing one of those neck swivels that I'd only seen women on TV do. "And what is all this?" I waved my arms around the room. "A two-thousand-dollar sofa, Hawk. That's insane! And what about the boat you never take to the lake, or the trips to the casino where you come back with a hangover and empty pockets? What about your fancy suits—"

"Really, Izzy? You want to bring up my suits when you dress like a hooker?"

I slapped him. I'd never slapped a man before, but Hawk brought out something venomous in me I didn't like.

Neither did he.

Hawk wrapped his fingers around my wrist and gripped my neck with his right hand, squeezing hard. "Don't *ever* do that again. I take good care of you, Izzy. I'm only saying you need to appreciate it, but it always feels like you're holding out for something better.

There *is* no better. I'm the best you've got and the best you'll ever get. Maybe it's time you show me some due respect."

I fought hard to keep my snarling wolf at bay. The only way I could protect her from getting hurt by a pissed-off Shifter was to stay calm. "Let go of me."

He laughed and released his hold.

"Take it back, Hawk. You know I'm a good girl. Maybe I work as a waitress, and maybe I like wearing shorts instead of gowns, but that doesn't make me a whore. And the last thing I want is to sleep with a man who sees me as nothing more than a streetwalker. So take it back."

He shook his head. "Fine. I take it back. Now pack your shit."

"No, thanks." I marched toward the bathroom with attitude in my swing.

"Excuse me?"

"I'm not about to become an outlaw. I have nothing to do with whatever you're involved in, but if I start running with you, then that makes me look just as guilty. I'll pack my things and leave, but I'm not leaving with *you*."

"And where are you going to go?" He followed behind and joined me in the bathroom.

I squeezed a dollop of toothpaste on my red toothbrush and began giving my molars a vigorous scrub. "You're talking to a girl who has traveled through thirty-four states, hitchhiked with the best of them, and has always found a way to make it on my own. Do you think sleeping under a bridge scares me? Think again. I'll do whatever it takes to survive in this world because I'm a fighter."

He swept my hair away from my neck and rested his chin on my shoulder. "You're too damn foxy to be living in a city full of Shifters without a pack. I can offer you the protection you crave and all the freedom you want. If someone gets wind that you're a wolf…"

"They won't." I shuddered, because his words seemed like more of a threat than a statement.

"But if they do, then you'll become nothing more than a pack bitch. When was the last time you were in heat?"

I shrugged him away and spit in the sink. "Don't ask me

something that personal, Hawk. We haven't been dating *that* long, and I have no intention of mating with you."

Going into heat meant hiding out for a few days, if not longer. Being aroused for that length of time was exhausting. Heat was the female's body screaming to reproduce, and males responded. They could scent a bitch in heat, and male instinct kicked in to sate her animalistic needs. It helped having a boyfriend who could detect it a couple of days before I could. Then I'd make reservations at a motel to ride it out. I'd never been with another man during my cycle because it almost guaranteed pregnancy. I'd heard rumors about how exquisite sex was during heat, and some women said it shortened the time they had to endure it. Good for them, but I didn't want babies with a man I didn't intend to mate with.

"You might change your mind," he murmured softly. Sweetly. "I've got a lot to offer a woman, Iz, and you're not getting any younger."

I wiped my mouth and snatched my hairbrush. "Straighten out your life, Hawk. Then we'll talk. Maybe."

"As long as I've got someone after me, they're after you. I can't afford to have something happen to you."

"Then *fix* your problems."

I squeezed around him and grabbed my duffel bag from beneath the bed. I bent over and he gently held my hips, rubbing them methodically. "How about a going-away present?"

"Not in the mood." I found my favorite pair of sandals and stuffed them in the bag, shaking my ass to loosen his grip.

Never shake your ass at a wolf.

He pulled up my T-shirt in the back and cupped his hand over my sex, insisting I stay for a few extra minutes. Admittedly, it felt good. Hawk never lasted long in the sack, but he knew how to get things heated up. Every lover I'd known had flaws—none had ever kept my engine roaring from beginning to end. Some finished the race early, some never finished, and others wanted me to spend too much time shifting his stick. Maybe perfect sex was only a fantasy— embellished stories conjured up by mated women who had exceeded their limit on tequila.

Hawk kept working his hands. "Come on, Iz. I've got something that'll make you change your mind."

"I'm not in the mood," I reiterated, turning around to face him. My fingers splayed across his chest, and I locked eyes with him. "I can't do this."

"You weren't too good for it before."

"That's before I knew this was about drugs. I had a feeling you were doing illegal stuff, but honestly I thought you were a loan shark or organizing poker games in a basement somewhere. Drugs change the game. I've seen what it does to people firsthand, and I can't sit back watching you deal it to them."

"They want it. It's not as if I'm forcing it on anyone," he retorted, swiping a finger across his mustache. I found it ironic how much Hawk looked like a cop and yet he was the one selling narcotics.

"This is scary stuff. It's not my scene. Don't justify what you're doing because you have paying customers, which, by the way, you're ripping off. I heard about your scheme of overcharging to fill your pockets. You didn't think you'd get caught?"

Hawk stared at me long and hard. I got the shivers because he could be an intimidating guy. Hawk wasn't his real name, but he'd earned it because he had a way of watching you and reading your every thought.

"Coming or not?"

I shook my head. "I'm giving you a second chance to make things right because I care about you. Everyone deserves a second chance. Call me when you've made up your mind on what's more important in your life: drugs or me."

CHAPTER 5

"**I** NEED A JELLY DONUT," I declared, wiping down a table and taking my break.

Rosie pulled up a chair in what had become our regular gab session. "Girl, you need more than a donut if you want something for a man to grab on to."

Donuts were my favorite thing. I also avoided them like the plague because I had no self-control and would stuff myself into a sugar coma. They were my weakness. Especially the chocolate-glazed ones. And *most of all* the chocolate-glazed ones with a cup of hot chocolate I could dunk them in. Throw in a few marshmallows, and I'd be your girl for life.

Rosie fanned herself. "That was some show you put on last night. Who *was* that creep with the long mustache?"

"I don't know, but he sure enjoys picking me up every time we run into each other. Maybe he doesn't work out at the gym enough. Thanks for talking to Jake and smoothing things over. I don't want to lose my job, and I promise that idiot won't be a problem again."

"You bet your sweet bottom he won't. If you bring human trouble in this bar again, Jake won't be so nice. He's taken a shine to you, so don't mess it up."

"I can't imagine why he's been so generous," I said, biting into my tuna sandwich.

"That little sneak thinks you're secretly screwing the singer. He admitted that after hiring Jericho's group, he noticed your unusual name on the job application your boyfriend submitted to him. Jake thinks keeping *you* around will keep the *singer* around. Nobody names their band after a girl who doesn't mean something."

I snorted and took another bite. "I don't think my name is a term of endearment for Jericho."

She grimaced and took a sip of her Dr Pepper. "Don't tell Jake that, hon. If he thinks you'll drive them away, he'll fire you in a heartbeat. If you're smart, you'll stay away from those boys. Don't rock the boat that keeps you afloat."

"Wise words."

She reached out and swept a lock of hair away from my face. "How's your head? Did you shift?"

"I've been told I'm hardheaded."

I licked my finger and watched one of the servers bend over for a napkin. Some girls were inexperienced servers, while others were masterful at earning tips outside the club with unmated males. They would target the wealthy alphas because they had a healthy sexual appetite and didn't mind the attention lavished on them. As long as it didn't drive the customer away, most managers turned a blind eye.

"I don't want to get off on the wrong foot, Rosie. I have a past with Jericho, and I don't want to talk about it." I took a sip of my lemon-water, the condensation from the glass dripping onto the table. "*Denver*. I should have *known* they were related."

"Brothers," she said, turning a ruby stone on her finger. "That's the only reason the band is giving Jake a chance. A dive like this compared to what they could be earning in the upscale bars and other events?"

I had to laugh. Jericho wasn't about fancy bars. He used to love outdoor events and small clubs, but I kept that to myself.

"I'd forgotten his brothers were all named after different cities. I don't want there to be any weirdness with Denver. He seems to like you, so do you mind helping me get on his good side? I don't need to be best friends with him, but it's going to be tough if he's slinging low blows and riling me up while I'm working."

"I'll talk to him, but I can't promise anything." Rosie shined up her lips with gloss. She often wore a lighter shade of lipstick or tinted gloss than her lip liner.

I parted my wavy hair to the right side and brushed my fingers through it, thinking quietly. Of all the places to settle down, why did it have to be the city Jericho lived in? And on top of that, the same bar!

"You look like a girl who just lost her man."

When my eyes flashed up, she smiled knowingly.

"I've seen that look before," she said with a shrug. "A girl like you will find another Shifter in no time. A girl like me? Not so much."

"Don't be ridiculous. You're a knockout."

"I'm also mated."

A laugh burst out, and she giggled along with me. "Very funny, Rosie."

"Well, when you've found *the one*, there's no need for another man to come along."

"He's that good, huh?"

She nodded before answering. "The best. He treats me like a queen, stays out of my business, knows how to be a man and not let me run over him, and he sure knows how to smooth out all the rough edges," she said with a purr. "He has a bubble bath and a glass of red wine waiting for me every morning when I get home."

"Sounds like heaven."

It was getting busier, so I quickly finished my sandwich and stood up. "I need to get back on the floor."

I did a little hip shake on the way to the bar when I saw a new group of men walk through the main door. Regulars chose their section based on their favorite server. I didn't care if they had a regular waitress; my plan was to lure them over to the Izzy side. The girls who took it personally were usually the catty ones I stayed away from anyway. Unseated men were fair game, and all the girls knew it. Once they sat down, the rules changed and everyone respected each other's stations.

Denver's shift hadn't started yet, so I chatted with the bartender about house specials until he got busy with customers. A burst of noise came from the front of the bar, and I smiled at a familiar face.

"Hey, April!"

She had on a cute pair of black Capri pants and a blue top that slid off one shoulder. Her nail polish matched her blouse perfectly. I couldn't help but admire how stylish she was in an offbeat way.

"Hi," she said shyly. "You recognized me."

"And you recognized me."

She hopped onto the barstool and faced the open room. "How can anyone *not* recognize hair like yours?"

"What are you doing here? This doesn't seem like your scene."

"It's not," she admitted, looking at me over her left shoulder. "But I try to get out once in a while and put on my social-butterfly wings. My guy likes having a few beers and showing me off. He's always bragging to people about how I'm a store manager. Plus my best friend, Trevor, is always dragging me up here. I think he gets discounts on the drinks, but don't tell Jake."

I smiled and leaned in. "How does he get discounts?"

"Denver is in our pack and doesn't charge him full price."

Crap. My small world was getting infinitely smaller.

"Has Denver mentioned me?"

April tilted her head and tucked a strand of her straight blond hair behind her ear, showing off the graceful curve of her neck. "Why would he? Are you two seeing each other?"

I touched her shoulder. "No, you don't have to worry about that." I slid off the stool and sighed. "I need to take some orders. Those guys look thirsty," I said, pointing to a table nearby. "Your boyfriend is the one with the bike, right?"

"Yes. What was all that about the other day at Walgreens? *Holy smokes!* I saw your car speed off and Reno had shot the guy, but he didn't tell me what happened."

I sighed and straightened out my shirt. "Just some idiot messing with me. I'd like to talk to Reno and thank him if you don't mind. Please don't leave without letting me do that. If it gets busy in here, just grab me off the floor before you head out. It gets crazy in here this time of night, and I might lose track of you."

"Will do."

"And April?"

"Yes?"

"I want you guys to pick out whatever you want on the menu. I'm buying. It's the least I can do to show Reno my gratitude for helping me out the other day. You're a lucky woman."

Her smile gradually spread, and it became apparent she didn't need to be told by someone else how lucky she was. I'd seen that look on a woman in love.

Sigh. I had no idea how it felt, but I sure loved admiring it. I don't know what had compelled me to show my face in Jake's bar after what happened with Handlebars, but I realized it wasn't just about the paycheck. I refused to let Jericho run me off again. I was tired of running.

Except in that very moment, I wanted to run.

Jericho swaggered through the door as a song by Audioslave cranked on the speakers. My heart galloped against my chest and I swallowed thickly, deciding I had no choice but to avoid him if I wanted to keep my job. I approached my table with a gracious smile. My shaky hand pressed the tip of my ink pen against the notepad.

"What can I get for you men?"

I hated calling the opposite sex "boys." Shifters didn't care much for that kind of talk, and yet I'd heard it too often in human bars.

The older one with the scruffy beard and black bandana wrapped over his head leaned forward and licked his lower lip. "How much for a shake?" he said with a dark chuckle.

"That comes free when I go to the bar and collect your drinks. So what'll it be?"

A man with hairy arms chortled. "She's a firecracker."

The guy with the bandana leaned back in his chair, hooking one arm over the back. "It's them green eyes. Those green-eyed girls are dragons."

I smiled and cocked my hip. "I only breathe fire when I serve men who don't know how to tip a lady. But I'm sure that won't be a problem with any of you."

Effortlessly, I laid down the challenge. The other three men looked amongst one another, as if silently agreeing they had no plan to look like cheapskates.

"How about I start you off with a round of beers? Then you can decide what you're up for. I'm also going to bring out a plate of hot onion rings, because if you don't get them now while they're fresh and delicious, you'll regret it later. Be right back," I said with a coy smile, batting my eyelashes.

As I turned away, I rolled my eyes. I had a feeling they were going to be my difficult table for the evening.

My shoulders were killing me, and I knew it was because of nerves. I had a bad habit of hunching them when feeling tense. I sent the order for onion rings to the back.

"A round of beers," I shouted at Denver.

He ignored me while salting the rim of a large glass. I rubbed my bare shoulder and worked my arm around in a circle. The sleeveless shirts were actually nice. At the last place I'd worked, the owner made us wear cutoff shirts that revealed our midriffs. I felt a little classier in my new work attire, albeit the shorts were a little snug, but it made a difference not to have my breasts hanging out of a low-cut blouse. Especially since mine weren't as voluptuous as some. I had a soft, feminine curve that suited my slim physique.

"Denver, table twelve needs a round. Four beers, please."

A pretty brunette was occupying his time, but she seemed disinterested in his advances. Denver was a handsome man who could easily be a male model. But some women preferred the rough-looking Shifters who gave off an air of authority. They equated that with men who had protective animals.

I tipped an empty glass over and spilled backwash onto the bar. It caught his attention and he cannibalized me with a hostile glare. He held up a finger at the brunette and breezed over with a clean rag.

"Do that again and I'll—"

"Tattle? Don't be one of *those* guys. Look, we have no choice about working together, so can we be civil? What happened between Jericho and me is not only personal, but it happened *decades* ago. It's our personal business to resolve, but I'm still going to be here every night waiting tables. I need to know you'll have my back if I'm in trouble. And each time drinks move out slowly because you're in one of your moods, it not only affects my tips, but it hurts *Jake*. Truce?"

He polished the bar with his rag, causing the muscle in his bicep to flex. Denver wasn't ripped, but just nicely defined. I could see a little of Jericho in him, but they were definitely two different personalities.

He bent forward on his elbows. "If you promise to stay away from Jericho and not mess with his head, I'll cut you some slack."

"No problem."

His eyes flashed up. "I smell bullshit."

I wasn't a drama queen, and his implication that I had plans to become a train wreck in his brother's life made me bristle. "Four drafts, please."

Denver smoothed out all the rough edges in his expression and patted the bar with the palm of his hand before he turned to the object of his affection.

That's all I needed. We were good.

"You two old lovers?" a woman sitting on the barstool to my right inquired. She had blond tresses dolled up in an old-fashioned style, like Marilyn Monroe. "I'm a Sensor. I don't always have to touch things to pick up on emotions."

"No, he's just a brother of someone I used to know."

"Ah," she said in a husky voice. "One of *those*. For five hundred bucks, I can make your job a lot easier." The woman absently ran her finger around the rim of her glass.

I leaned in closer. "What do you mean? You can't remove emotions without someone knowing." She'd have to place her hands on Denver's chest in order to complete an emotional transaction—whether it was giving or taking.

"Just between you and me, he won't know a thing. He looks like the kind of man who might pay for a little action, if you know what I mean. I've got a whole drawer full of erotica," she said, tapping a finger on her temple. "People pay good money, but maybe I'll offer him a free session. During the transaction, I'll bring you up conversationally and remove all that hostility without him even realizing it. If he starts to guess I'm pulling the emotion, I'll slip him some kinky sex that'll make him soon forget."

Sensors were sneaky beings. They worked hard for their money and established reputations in many clubs.

"No, thanks. I'd rather him hate me to my face."

She took a slow drink. "Your call. But it's a harmless exchange and everybody walks away happy. I'll be here if you change your mind, dearie."

Encounters like that made me skittish about non-Shifters. I didn't know who I could trust.

Hours passed, and a steady flow of customers kept me busy. I spotted April at a table on the far end of the room and decided to say hello.

"Mind if I join you for a minute?" I asked, holding the empty chair on the left next to Reno, my motorcycle hero. April touched his right arm and smiled proudly.

"You look beat," she said. "I don't know how you do it. I'm scrambling with a bunch of kids in my store, but this is *chaos*."

I smiled and an awkward moment passed as I waited to be introduced to her pack—Jericho's pack.

"Everyone, this is Izzy. We ran into each other shopping. Izzy, that's Wheeler, Trevor, and *this* is my Reno," she said, leaning against his shoulder. He quickly wrapped his arm around her and gave me a brisk nod.

Wheeler was the kind of guy I'd be wary to have in my section. His arms were covered with tattoos, and he wore a sleeveless shirt to show them off. All Breeds had healing abilities to some degree, so the body absorbed the ink, and the tattoo would disappear. The only way to seal the design was to use a salve called liquid fire—a painful process that made any tattoo or scar permanent. Laser removal didn't apply. No smile touched his face behind the facial hair that surrounded his mouth but didn't extend up to his ears in a full beard. His scruffy brown hair was styled shorter on the sides and fell all over the place on top. He had a morose expression as he leaned on the table and sipped his whiskey, sliding his bright eyes up to mine without saying a word.

Trevor seemed like a laid-back young man. I loved the way he styled his hair over his forehead. Not many men his age wore button-up shirts and nice watches. He had the kind of celebrity charisma that made girls bashful.

"Nice meeting you," Trevor said with a friendly wink.

I got butterflies when Reno turned to face me. He had a compelling appearance—handsome, but in a rough and dangerous "don't fuck with me" kind of way. Maybe it was the canvas of muscle that pressed against his tight-fitted shirt, or the sharp cut of his jaw, or the concealed weapon beneath his shirt. But it was definitely the stony expression on his face.

His musky cologne filled my nose, and I waited impatiently for him to speak. I wasn't sure what Denver had told them or what they knew about Jericho and me. "I just wanted to thank you for saving my butt yesterday. My boyfriend is mixed up in some trouble I didn't know about. I'm really glad you showed up when you did; I don't want to imagine what could have happened if my animal had come out in broad daylight and killed a human. You only grazed his leg, by the way."

"I never miss my intended target," Reno replied. "He's human, and I couldn't take the risk. Your boyfriend needs to sort his shit out."

"Yeah, he does," I agreed in a disgusted tone. "Anyhow, I hope you guys ordered something good to eat because it's on me, so don't be cheap. It's the least I can do. I really appreciate that you stepped forward for a stranger. You didn't have to do that and—"

"And yeah, I did. I don't turn a blind eye to a man handling a woman that way. There's a line you don't cross with me, and it wouldn't have mattered if you were a human or another Breed. You treat a woman right," he said, kissing April's forehead in a possessive way that clearly showed his devotion to that human.

I smiled at both of them and touched his broad shoulder. "We need more good men like you. Anyhow, hope you guys enjoy your evening. April, I'd love to swing by your store this week. Hopefully you have some of the old-fashioned candy I love so much."

"We sure do. I usually work the afternoon and evening shift," she said. "I'll make you up a special bag for your first visit."

As I left the table, contentment filled me up. I'd always thought it was important to show respect when someone stretched out their neck for you. It's what Jericho had taught me during our years on the road.

Ugh. And there were those thoughts of Jericho surfacing again.

As I approached the bar, a tall man sitting on the stool pivoted around with a cigarette tucked behind his ear. He had brooding, wanton eyes, and despite my irritation with him, they still made me flush all over. Jericho wasn't built like Reno, or even Denver. He was over six feet tall with slender muscles, but not skinny. I didn't have x-ray vision, but back in the day, he used to have a six-pack that made the girls salivate. Jericho knew damn well how to wield the sex appeal that God blessed him with. He'd pulled back his hair into a loose ponytail, several strands falling around his face. His black jeans and concert shirt fit him snugly, and I got a better look at the tattoo on his left arm. It was a guitar half-filled with ink, like a yin-yang design with sexy curves.

He watched me with jade eyes rimmed in black—a creamier shade than mine. They stood out because he was wearing smudged eyeliner, and I found myself noticing little things about his appearance. Like the rings on his fingers, and the long chain that hung from his back pocket and attached to one of his belt loops.

Ignoring him was an exercise in futility. So rather than pretend what we both knew I *couldn't* ignore, I casually approached him and leaned on my left elbow.

"How was your walk home?" he asked, his lips twitching.

I munched on a salty pretzel from a bowl on the bar. "I've always enjoyed an early morning stroll. The fresh air does amazing things for my skin. I should do it more often."

Tension crackled between us—the urge to slip into our old banter battled it out with the animosity I felt.

I dusted the salt from my fingers, and a few rowdy men shouted from a nearby table. I glanced their way when Jericho suddenly hopped off his stool and roughly pinched my chin. He was a good seven inches taller than I was, so he bent down to examine me closer. He brushed back my hair and tilted my head.

"What is wrong with you?" I finally said, knocking away his arm. As I leapt off the stool, he corralled me against the bar and pulled my hair back, gripping it with a tight fist. I couldn't move and was three seconds away from calling for help, although I had doubts Denver would gallantly leap over the bar to break this one up.

Jericho brushed his fingers across my jaw. "Who put that mark on your neck?"

Warmth touched my cheeks. I had no idea what he was talking about. "Huh?"

"Your neck, Isabelle. There are fingerprint bruises in the places that someone would grab you if they were pinning you to a wall."

I wriggled free. "And how would you know something like *that*, Jericho?"

Wrong. Jericho would never lay a hand on a woman, but I was piping mad.

His jaw set. "I may not like you, Isabelle." He captured my wrist and tugged me a little closer with each statement. "I may be mad as hell for what you did to me all those years ago—making me think something bad had happened to you. I may want to have Jake fire your ass and toss you on the streets. I also may want to stop coming in here so I won't have to run into you at every turn. But *nobody* puts his hands on you."

And there it was. An indirect declaration that Jericho still cared about me, if even a smidge. It could have been sheer principle that I was a woman who had been manhandled—although I hadn't noticed any bruising when I'd left the house. But the intensity that burned in his eyes left me with a question mark about his feelings for me.

"My life isn't your business anymore," I said ruefully.

He let go and turned away, drinking his beer as if I'd never been there.

A knot formed in my stomach as I stared at his back. I wanted to know why he was so upset with me when *he* was the one who'd destroyed our friendship.

"Izzy, hon, your table is about to have a conniption if you don't take their order." Rosie pointed at a group of men who had reached their limit.

"I cut them off. They've had too much to drink and I'm not going to be responsible for them driving home drunk and killing someone."

"Then bring them an order of hamburgers, but if you don't shake your ass over there, they're going to cause trouble."

Jericho slid a half-interested glance over his shoulder.

I pressed my lips together and approached my table. "Now, how about I bring out some cheeseburgers?"

A hand slapped my ass. "How about I have a taste of *this* juicy burger?"

"Don't put your hand on me again," I said in a tight voice.

"Whoa. Those redheads like to give orders," a guy in a leather jacket said with a deep chuckle. "A fiery temper in the sack warms the cockles of my heart every time."

"She can warm *my* cockles," the man to my left said, cupping his leathery hand around the back of my thigh. "I love a girl who looks sweet in the face. I bet you'd look real sweet down on your knees."

"I think you've had too much to drink. Why don't you—"

I gasped when someone snatched the back of my shirt and hauled me aside. I gripped a chair to keep from falling and looked up at Jericho, who lit up a cigarette with a flick of his silver lighter.

"Who invited you?" one of the guys spat.

I shouted for Denver when the men rose from the table. Jericho kept his cool, taking a long drag of his cigarette before blowing smoke in their faces.

My heart raced. *What do I do?* We didn't have bouncers in this bar; that job had been left to the bartender and a few guys in the kitchen.

Reno, Wheeler, and Trevor materialized behind Jericho without a word. My table seemed more concerned with the likes of Wheeler, who folded his arms and incinerated them with his molten gaze. Jericho's brothers took a stance that left no question they were a pack—and a pack lived, ate, and fought together. I didn't know what kind of animals the idiots at my table were, but they looked intimidated.

Jericho pulled another drag from his cigarette and smashed the butt in the ashtray. "Why don't you walk outta here before we take matters into our own hands? I don't like seeing greedy men putting their hands on a woman disrespectfully, and neither do my brothers. Don't fuck with the Weston pack."

To my surprise, the men spat a few obscenities and cowardly walked away.

"They must have been deer," Trevor said with a cocky laugh.

"More like chickens," Wheeler suggested, his arms still crossed.

Trevor looked disappointed as he turned away. "Well, I got my wolf all amped up for nothing. How about next time we don't deliver a threat and just beat their sorry asses?"

Reno chuckled and messed up Trevor's hair. "Some battles aren't worth fighting."

As the men dispersed, a warm feeling slid over my body when I looked up at Jericho. His eyes were hooded and low, but when he melted me with a possessive gaze, my feet cemented to the floor.

He moved toward me with the grace of a panther—slow and predatory. The external noise from the bar faded away, and all I heard were his silken words as he caressed the ends of my hair, looking at it between his fingers.

"You haven't changed," he said in quiet words.

"What do you mean by that?"

Jericho bent down and his mouth brushed against my ear. "Still sexy as sin and making me protect you."

Goose bumps erupted over my arms. "No one said you had to protect me. I'm not the shy girl you once knew." My heart raced. The inflection in my tone wasn't as harsh as I'd planned it to be, my words breathy and unsure.

His warm body pressed against mine and when I stepped back, I bumped into a wooden post that pinned me to him. Tingles raced through my body uncontrollably, and I lost the ability to think rationally when I smelled his cologne. Men *never* had this kind of effect on me. His power slid down my body like hands against my naked flesh.

Jericho had a smile that aroused, and combined with his voice, it became an aphrodisiac.

Or maybe it was the way his callused fingers lightly stroked the back of my neck, as if I were an instrument. As he played me, memories flooded my mind, and I shoved him away, panting and trembling.

Jericho worked his jaw in a frustrated manner, his brows slanting down with a look of disbelief. He shook his head and then backed up.

A brunette appeared out of nowhere in a revealing top that displayed her breasts like cookies in a bakery: warm, tempting, and something you'd regret later.

"How's my sexy man?" she asked, tucking her fingers possessively in his jeans and nipping on his arm. "You want to go have some fun?"

His eyes stayed locked on mine as he circled his arm around her waist and pulled her against him. She moaned playfully as he squeezed her hip, testing if I had my temper under control.

So I played his game.

"Can I get you a drink, honey?" I asked her. "Maybe some milk in a dish?"

Sometimes I could spot the cats. It was all in the purr and the way they slinked their bodies.

"No, thanks," she replied. "I have something else in mind I want to put in my mouth."

When she stroked his crotch, I blinked in surprise. Not just because she had the audacity to do that in front of me, but the fact that Jericho tilted his head and gave me a "so what?" look.

So what?

Maybe he was right. All that connected us were five amazing years, and that was a lifetime ago. Seeing him made me raw again. Those feelings caught up with me like a shadow that had never let go. Part of me wanted to squeeze him tight and tell him how much I'd missed him—because I had. Jericho had shown me the private side of himself he never gave to others, and I'd done the same for him. Another part of me wanted to hate him for the anguish he'd put me through. And yet, I couldn't help but feel elated knowing that despite his insolence, Jericho wasn't lying in a grave as I'd imagined. He'd somehow assembled his life into something meaningful and gotten a grip on his demons.

Meanwhile, my demons were currently on the rampage and waving pitchforks.

So I said cutting words that hurt because I meant them, and yet I didn't.

"I wish I'd never met you."

CHAPTER 6

A T FOUR IN THE MORNING, I swapped out my work clothes for loose jeans, flip-flops, and a thin sweatshirt. My feet had survived another brutal night in my new shoes. I stuffed the black heels in my locker along with my work attire. Lockers were assigned to all the employees to store our personal belongings. Without a home to go to, I had no access to a washer and dryer. What I really wanted was a shower to erase the smell of cigarettes and spilled beer, but I didn't have that luxury either.

I'd temporarily split with Hawk, and I'd have to stand by that choice, even if it meant smelling like a barnyard animal.

I also had a psychopath human shadowing me, and I didn't feel safe sleeping in my car. This put me in a predicament. I'd slept on the streets in my younger years, but I'd long since left that vagabond lifestyle behind. Hawk had pocketed my first night's worth of tips, saying I owed him. Reno's tab maxed me out for the night. We still had a week before payday, and I didn't have a place to stay.

"Bye, Rosie. See you later tonight."

"Drive safe," she said, yawning and sleepily looking at her watch.

I headed out the main door and strolled across the dark parking lot. When I reached my car, I leaned against the door and wondered where to go. The girl I came to Texas with had joined a pack, but you didn't just roll up to a Packmaster's door and invite yourself in to crash with them for a little while. That was a big no-no as you could only stay by invitation. We hadn't spoken in a month, and frankly, I didn't know her all that well.

"If you stand out here much longer, you might grow roots."

I glanced over my shoulder and turned around. A lovely woman with a long braid strolled in my direction. As she neared the lamppost, I could make out her warm complexion and earthy eyes. She looked Native American from her strong bone structure and elegant demeanor. The wind kicked up her long skirt and she reached down and gripped it with her fist.

"Are you having car trouble?"

"No. I'm just… tired from a long night at work. I waitress here." I pointed at the building and she smiled.

A strand of hair blew free and tangled in front of her face. "I'm Ivy. A brother of mine locked his keys in his truck again, so I came by to drop off a spare set."

"Maybe he should keep his spare set in his back pocket," I suggested.

She laughed, and the apples of her cheeks glowed. "He would probably lose those too. I'm not one to be nosy, but I don't like seeing someone in need. I'm not sure exactly what you're in need of, but you have that look about you."

Ivy seemed like an expressive soul, and I got good vibes from her right away. "I've temporarily split with my boyfriend until he can get his act together. I don't think it hit me until I got off work that I don't have a home to go to."

"Then you'll stay with me. What's your name?"

"My name's Izzy, but I can't impose like that."

She shook her head in disbelief. "And why not? You need a place to stay, and I live in a large house with plenty of rooms. We should help others so one day they can return the gesture to someone else. I'm not asking just to be nice, Izzy. I truly want to help so I can put my good intentions into the universe. Maybe one day some of that goodness will come back to me. Don't deny me this because you think it's imposing. Truly, it's not."

Wow. This girl could sell. She had a way with words that made you feel as if you were in the wrong and she was imparting her wisdom upon you. What could it hurt?

"Ivy, I'd love that. Just one day is all I need to get myself together. I promise I won't be in your hair; my body is in dire need of rest, so I'll probably sleep until midafternoon."

"Have you eaten?"

"Yes." The pretzels on the bar counted a little bit, so not a total lie. Usually I ate breakfast at dawn and went right to sleep, but I didn't want to be a bother.

She eyed me skeptically. "I'll call my Packmaster and let him know about our arrangement. Follow me."

I blinked. "You're in a pack? Oh, in that case…"

"Don't worry." She lifted her hand and smiled. "He's a compassionate man who will not turn away a woman in need. Shifters should stick together. Regardless of what your animal is, you're welcome in our home. I'll drive slowly," she said, walking toward a hatchback.

I followed her taillights and switched on the radio, singing along to an oldie by U2. A fragile smile touched my face as the song reminded me of a time in my life when strangers had given me a meal or a ride to a new destination. It would have been a dangerous proposition for a single girl, but I'd had Jericho at my side to protect me.

I had been adrift for so long that coming back into the Shifter community felt like home. While I'd worked Breed bars in recent years, they were in small towns, and their clubs served other Breeds, including humans. The calling to be near my people had become stronger in the last year or two. I'm sure it had to do with my ovaries putting pressure on me to mate. Those two bitches needed to mind their own business.

When Ivy turned up a private road, it led to a magnificent house with a large stretch of land around it.

"Wowzer," I muttered, gaping at what looked like an old-fashioned mansion. It was lit by a pale moon, and I could make out white flowers around the property and upper balcony. One of the trees in front had an old-fashioned rope swing tethered to a lower branch, and several cars were parked on the left side of the house. Ivy waited for me by the steps of the wooden porch while I parked my car.

"Everyone's asleep," she whispered as I walked up the steps. "Sometimes they get up in the middle of the night and raid the kitchen, so if you're hungry—"

"I'm fine," I promised her. "I just need some shut-eye and I'll stay out of everyone's way. I don't want to be a nuisance."

We approached the door, and she held out her key. I noticed a sign nailed to the siding that said *Weston*. Something about that name sounded familiar.

"You're no trouble compared to some of these boys," she said in a low voice. "I'll take you up to your room. Do you have any bags?"

I shrugged. "Most of my stuff is still at the house. I did pack a few things, but I'll grab them when I wake up. Is it okay if I take a shower before I leave for work?"

She nodded and opened the door. "Our house is yours, Izzy. Please, come in."

The floor creaked when I stepped inside. She hung her keys on a nail over the letter *T*. "You can put your keys on my nail," she said in a soft voice. "I don't have a car, but they wanted to include me in the lineup."

On the right was a row of keys hanging on the wall. I found the letter *I* and looped my keychain over the rusty nail that was above it.

Ivy kicked off her shoes in the corner, and I followed her lead, putting my flip-flops beside her flats to the right of the door. We entered an open living room with another adjacent room on the right. Straight ahead was a fireplace, and to the right of it, a hall that led to the back of the house.

Ivy tiptoed toward the stairs on our left and turned around, lowering her voice to a whisper. "We have a little girl in the house, so please don't shift. She's human and doesn't know you."

I nodded with a bemused look as we reached the top of the stairs. It wasn't common for humans to live in the same house as Shifters, but Austin seemed like a progressive city. On the second floor, I stared at two separate hallways shaped like an L. One led to the back and had doors on either side, while the other ran along the front of the house. Ivy led me toward the back until we approached a room on the left. She switched on a small lamp beside the bed and turned around.

It was a quaint little room with a bed on the right, a window straight ahead, and no other furniture. I'd heard most bedrooms in

Shifter homes were small to accommodate more people in a growing pack. This room didn't appear to be inhabited by anyone.

She turned down the bed and closed the drapes.

"If you need anything, let me know. My Packmaster is already aware you're here, but he hasn't told everyone else yet since they're either asleep or not home."

"Thanks again, Ivy. I'll find a way to return the favor," I said in a quiet voice.

She touched the end of her lovely braid and her dark lashes fanned across her cheeks. "Good night."

After she closed the door, I collapsed on the bed and got a whiff of the clean sheets. "Oh my God," I groaned, feeling a dull ache in my bones. I barely pulled my legs beneath the covers before my eyes slammed shut. After wiggling out of my jeans and sweatshirt, I tossed them on the floor. It felt wonderful to know I wouldn't be sleeping in my car, but I needed to think about my plans for tomorrow. That meant getting up early and finding a place before my shift started.

Random thoughts tumbled in my head as I switched off the lamp and scooted to the left side of the bed. Hopefully I'd be able to figure everything out in the morning. I nestled my face against the cool pillow, grateful for Ivy showing up when she did and for her generosity.

<hr/>

The bed lightly shook, and I covered my head with the pillow. Hawk loved startling me awake, and the curtains did little to block out the morning light. I felt a tug at my hair, and my wolf began to stir.

"You got pretty hair," I heard an angelic voice say.

Something in my brain switched on, and I remembered I wasn't at home. My wolf instantly submitted to the sound of a child's voice. This was Ivy's house. I peered out from the pillow and glanced over my left shoulder. A young girl with sparkling blue eyes sat behind me, her tousled blond hair tumbling past her shoulders. She had on a bright pink shirt with a wide collar that had slipped off her shoulder, and her fingernails glittered with purple nail polish.

"I wish I had hair like this," she said, holding up a strand.

I smiled and rolled over, the covers tucked beneath my arms. "And I wish I had dimples like yours. I'm Izzy. And who is this pretty little face brightening my morning?"

She giggled, and I noticed a missing bottom tooth. "I'm Maizy. We both got *Z*s in our name."

"We sure do. I think your hair is much prettier than mine. Want to trade?"

Maizy smiled and touched my wild hair again. It had picked up a wave from all the tossing and turning. Against the white sheets, it looked like a blaze of fire.

"My mom wants to know if you're hungry."

"Did she send you in here?"

"No. She asked Miss Ivy, so I decided to come ask you myself. They're in the kitchen making lunch."

I leaned around and looked for a clock. "What time is it, honey?"

"Noon o'clock," she said with a smile.

I sat up and rubbed my face. "I need to go. Tell your mommy not to worry about fixing me anything to eat. I'm going to take a shower and then I have to leave. It was nice meeting you, Maizy."

She leapt off the bed and her wide collar pulled down in the back, revealing some of her shoulder blade. I caught a glimpse of a birthmark and watched as she scrambled to fix her shirt. "Oops. You weren't supposed to see that," she said, her cheeks flushed.

"I promise I won't tell anyone," I said with a curious smile. Human children were so endearing.

Her worry evaporated, and she swung open the door. "Nice to meet you, Miss Izzy."

After the door closed, I snatched my clothes off the floor and wrapped a throw around me so I could hunt for the bathroom.

I checked two rooms in the hall before I found it. I slammed the door and took a quick pee while waiting for the shower to get hot. Then I began rifling through the cabinets in search of towels. I needed to get moving and find a motel—hopefully one that would accept a late payment.

After I rushed through a hot shower and shut the water off, I remained in the tub and dried my legs with a hand towel because it was all I could find. They must have had a linen closet in the hall where they stored the big towels, unless they just walked around naked.

When I heard the door open and close, I stood paralyzed with fear. Through the frosted shower curtain, I watched a shadow move to the left and lift up the toilet seat.

Oh. My. God.

I wasn't used to locking bathroom doors and must have forgotten. This was embarrassing. It was past the point I could say anything since they were already unzipping. I touched the towel to my hair so the water droplets wouldn't tap against the tub.

I covered my eyes until he finished, and when the toilet flushed, I blew out a quiet breath of relief. Then I heard the sound of pants dropping on the floor and someone getting naked.

Very naked.

The kind of naked you get before taking a shower.

Eek!

My eyes went wide, and the little hand towel would only cover one private area of my body, so I chose the southern hemisphere. Before he could tear open the curtain, I grabbed the end and blurted out, "Occupied!"

Silence followed for what seemed like eons.

"Occupied? What the fuck?"

The curtain tugged, and I gripped tighter. "Don't you dare come in here!"

"Who the hell is in there?"

When the curtain moved to the left, I screamed. It was a shrill scream—the kind heard in horror movies. While I had no problem with nudity, I had a real problem being naked with a stranger in a confined space.

The door kicked in and someone entered the room.

"What's going on?" another man said in a deep voice. I got butterflies in my stomach and knew it was the Packmaster.

"Don't look at me. I sing tenor, not soprano. I thought the last person finished up in here. Who the fuck *is* that?"

I peered around the edge of the curtain, my wet hair dripping as the cold began to make me shiver. To the right stood a fierce man with dark tattoos inked on his shoulders and upper arms. Like me, he didn't have a shirt on, and a medallion glimmered against his chest. He had dark hair and the bluest eyes I'd ever seen.

As soon as he saw me, his eyes narrowed at the man to my left, who wore nothing but a pair of silk boxers. "Did you touch her?"

The guy in boxers looked just like Wheeler—the Shifter with the tattoos April had introduced me to last night. They shared the same eyes, mouth, face, and dirty-brown hair. The striking difference was that he had no facial hair or tattoos. He seemed a little softer than what I imagined Wheeler must look like beneath his clothes, but they were unmistakably twins.

"Ben, get out," the Packmaster ordered.

"What's going on in here, Aus?" another voice said. I cringed when Denver moved into sight. His eyes widened when he saw me peering out from the corner of the shower. "What the hell is *she* doing here?"

Hell's bells, this was *Jericho's* pack!

I looked at his threadbare T-shirt with Popeye on the front. "Nice shirt."

He ignored me and tipped his head at the Packmaster. "Do you know who that is, Austin?"

"Our guest."

"*That* is Izzy Monroe. Ring a bell?"

Austin's jaw set, and another person squeezed into the room.

"Is this a party?" Jericho blanched when he saw me.

"I really don't want to be rude, because I appreciate that you let me stay the night and use your shower, but could you all leave the room? I'm naked."

"I'm Austin," the Packmaster said, stumbling over his words and looking at Jericho. "That's Izzy? *Your* Izzy?"

"I'm nobody's Izzy. I'm *naked*," I reminded him. "Could you all leave before I completely lose my mind and start screaming? No offense or anything, I'm just naked in a room full of strangers!"

They hustled out of the room and slammed the door. I listened to them argue in the hall while I slipped into my baggy jeans and thin sweatshirt without drying off. I needed to make a quick exit. My shirt soaked up the water from my hair, but at that point, all I wanted to do was finish brushing my teeth with my finger and get the heck out before an explosive fight erupted.

I swung the door open and noticed everyone had left.

Except Jericho.

He had his arms folded and was leaning against the wall across from me with his leg bent at the knee. Reno and Austin were solid in height and stature, but Jericho snuck in just an inch taller. "Can't seem to stay away from me, can you?"

"I didn't know you lived here or I would have passed on the offer," I said, closing the door behind me. I leaned against it as we stared at each other, just a couple of feet apart.

He stepped forward and dropped his arms. "What kind of trouble are you in?"

"My boyfriend is sorting out some personal stuff, and we're temporarily separated until he figures it out."

Jericho moved a little closer and tingles prickled at my neck. "Broken up or did you bail on him too?"

I sighed hard and pulled my hair back. "Look, Ivy was kind enough to offer me a place to stay, and you know I'm not a drama queen. I don't want to do this with you right now—not with your pack around. I have a lot on my mind."

My heart quickened when he closed the distance between us. His eyes lowered, and when I glanced down, I realized why. My wet hair had soaked the front of my shirt, and my nipples were pressing against the fabric. Jericho tilted his head to the side and engaged in a conversation with my chest.

"Where are you going to stay tonight?"

"That's where I'm heading now. I'm going to check out some of the motels near the bar."

His eyes—I swear I could feel him touching me. Jericho had only looked at me like that once before. I remembered it so vividly in my mind…

It was the night before he screwed that girl in our hotel room. We were lying in bed, watching a comedy show like we'd done a million times before.

Jericho spilled his Coke on me when he reached over to set it on the nightstand to my right. I called him a few names and laughed, taking off my shirt and tossing it across the room. That was the first time he had ever looked at me like that.

Wild and ravenous.

His eyes roamed over my chest like a force of nature, studying the white fabric of my bra and the shape of my breasts. He licked his lips, and his mouth looked like he wanted to taste.

I didn't want to become another notch on his bedpost. Especially not with Jericho, because he slept with women left and right.

Before his lips met mine, I turned over and showed him my back.

"No, Jericho," I said. "Let's not go there. We're not going to have sex because you're having a moment of weakness. You can watch a movie if you want, just turn the volume down. I'm beat, so why don't you go back to your bed."

Jericho didn't leave.

He pressed against my back so I could feel him in an intimate way that I never had before. The full length of his body, the warmth, and the desire.

He spoke sweetly against my ear. "Are you sure you want me to go?"

"Yeah." That was the last thing I wanted. Being near him felt safe and good—too good. He brushed my hair out of the way and began caressing my arm with a silky touch of his callused fingers.

"Can I just kiss your neck? Nothing else, Isabelle. I promise." Restrained desire clung to his words and melted my resistance.

I didn't respond. Part of me wanted to see if he'd get up and go back to his bed. His soft mouth touched the back of my neck and ignited my body all the way to my core. No man had ever turned me on so quickly.

"Does this feel good?" he whispered, slowly kissing and stroking my neck with his warm tongue.

Oh God, did it.

I clutched my pillow and pulses of pleasure touched my sex like a heartbeat. Erotic thoughts went through my mind of him sliding my panties down and taking me roughly. Jericho was gentle with his women—I knew this from conversations we'd had. But the wolf inside me wanted more. Instincts I'd never felt for another Shifter erupted, warming my blood with ancient heat. I wanted to hear his textured voice whisper my name against my skin over and over, but I was terrified to say anything.

Terrified that it meant more to me than it did him.

But I thought about it.

His mouth journeyed around the nape of my neck, and I clenched when his tongue ran straight up. When he licked a sensitive spot, I shuddered, becoming wet. Every press of his lips sent another wave of need through me, and my body began to tighten, curl, and stretch. When his teeth scraped my skin with a greedy bite, I moaned.

"Want me to stop?" he asked, nipping on the lobe of my ear. "Say no, Isabelle."

I said nothing.

He bit my neck with more force and I clutched my pillow, trying to figure out what I was allowing to happen. I wanted him to stop, and I didn't want him to stop. I wanted our friendship to stay the same, but I wanted a claim on him that no other woman had. It was an unattainable wish, and Jericho wasn't at a place in his life where he desired a mate.

"Can I touch you, Isabelle? I need to touch you," he said, his voice breaking apart.

His kisses worked up into a frenzy, mixed with light sucking, and when he curved around to the left side of my neck, an intense tightening began to release.

Jericho's hand searched for the one place that needed to feel him. His hand memorized the shape of my body as it leisurely made its way toward my thighs. When he suddenly cupped his fingers over my sex, I came to a full orgasm with one deep stroke of his finger. The intensity *shattered me, and I made a soundless gasp, gripping the pillow tightly. Jericho nestled against me and nipped my left shoulder while I rode it out.*

All from a kiss to my neck.

No man, before or since, has had the power Jericho held over me, unleashing a frenzy of desire from within that made my wolf pace and howl. And I wasn't even in heat.

Afterward, I was so embarrassed and confused by what had happened that I leapt out of bed and bailed on him. I'd spent the next day confronting my feelings for Jericho and realized that I must have meant more to him than the other women, and maybe we could build a relationship from the strong foundation of our friendship. It might pull him out of the chaos he'd gotten himself into with the partying and drugs.

Maybe loving him out loud would make a difference.

The next evening, I returned to our room and decided to apologize for running out on him. I went with my heart on my sleeve, and that's when I walked in on Jericho having sex with another woman.

In my bed. The very bed he had pleasured me in not twenty-four hours prior.

Standing so close to him in Austin's hallway conjured up all those buried memories—good *and* bad.

I pushed at his chest and felt him resist. "I have to go."

"Go where?"

"I don't know. Away."

He slipped his hand behind my neck. When I felt his fingers against my bare skin, I pulled his arm until he let go.

"Why do you keep touching me, Jericho? One minute you hate me and the next you can't seem to stop groping me."

He jerked his neck back. "Groping?"

"Yes, groping. I'm sure your girlfriend wouldn't appreciate you hitting on other women."

"That woman you met at the bar is *not* my girlfriend," he said, a smile tugging the corners of his mouth as his jade eyes centered on mine. Why did he have to have such provocative eyes?

"What happened to the Jericho I remember? Is he still in there? Or has he been replaced by Sexton Cole?"

He blinked and stepped back, brushing his hand across the thin fabric of his black shirt.

"Was that sealed with liquid fire?" I asked softly, admiring the ink on his arm.

Jericho touched the image of the guitar on his left arm. "I had it done a year after you split."

"It's beautiful," I said truthfully. "It suits you. I'm just glad you didn't get something silly, like a cartoon duck."

I stared at his lips and noticed how perfect they were. I secretly used to call them sugar stamps because every woman coveted his sweet kisses, but I'd never seen him stamp anyone.

Jericho had the most sensual mouth—the kind that when his tongue swept over it, you wondered what he tasted like. And that man knew how to work his tongue. He could stare at you from the opposite end of the table, slightly drawing in his bottom lip and licking it with a slow and deliberate stroke, only showing you the tip of his tongue. I used to think of it as his opening act, and it's how he got the girls to stay for the big show.

He pulled a cigarette from behind his ear and popped it in his mouth, letting it flick up and down between his lips. Jericho eyed me, from my damp shirt all the way down to my bare feet.

"Never thought I'd see you again, Isabelle."

"How come you've never called me Izzy?"

He bit the cigarette between his teeth and rocked on his heels. I snatched the stick from his mouth and threw it down the hall.

"Quit trying to be the badass rock star in front of me. I know the real you. Not the one you pretend to be because maybe that's who you think you are now. This is an image—a projection of what you thought a rock star was supposed to be to women, the public, and maybe yourself. I remember the guy who used to laugh so hard that he'd cry. I remember the guy who laid out a blanket in the back of a pickup truck in a motel parking lot so we'd have a place to sleep and watch the stars. I remember a guy who beat up four Shifters in the biggest fight I'd ever seen, all because one of them called me a whore. I remember a guy who canceled a big show so he could buy me donuts at the coffee shop on my birthday." Tears wet my lashes, and I wiped them away. "What happened to that guy? Is he gone for good? Because if he is, I don't want to keep having these run-ins. What existed between us was years ago; we're in different places now. If we can't settle what's between us because of the shadows from our past, then I may need to move on. I'm not the quiet girl you met at a bus stop on a rainy Saturday—I'm tougher. But that's kind of how life molded me."

With a stoic expression, Jericho backed up against the wall and slid to the floor, draping his arms over his bent knees.

I knelt in front of him and searched his eyes. "I've missed you."

When his eyes lifted, they were remorseful. I felt the pain of decades within them—years of being lost.

"Are you mated?" he asked.

I sat back on my legs. "We just met. I'm not mated, but I'm in a relationship. We've been living together for a month. You know me—I'm as monogamous as they come. So the touching thing isn't working for me. I don't know how serious it is with Hawk after the stunt he pulled, but until we're officially broken up, I'm off-limits. Thanks for taking care of those guys at the bar. Sometimes customers get touchy-feely, and I always put them in their place, but it doesn't erase the humiliation I feel when I'm seeing a man."

"You didn't initiate it," he said in my defense.

"You're right. I also didn't initiate it in this hall when you touched me a minute ago, and you *know* that was more than a friendly gesture." I gave him a look of reproach and sighed.

"I won't put my hands on you again," he promised, his voice edged with anger. "Do you want to tell me why you let your boyfriend wrap his fingers around your throat?"

"We had a fight, but it's not what you think."

"What he did was unconscionable. A real man *never* puts his mark on a woman." He paused for a beat and sharpened his gaze. "Has he ever handled you like that before?"

I averted my eyes. Hawk wasn't an abusive man, but he could be a little rough. He knew I didn't like to have my ass slapped in the morning but did it anyway because he thought it was funny. Sometimes he jerked me around by the arm, but there was never any hitting or violent behavior between us, not like there was in the house I grew up in. That was the level of violence I compared everything against, so anything less was manageable.

Jericho nodded with an intolerant glare, as if I'd given him the answer he wanted. "Did the fight with your boyfriend have to do with the jerk-off who threw you against the bar and knocked you out?" He leaned forward.

"Someone's after Hawk, and they think they can find him through me. Hawk's lying low until the dust settles. I have no idea where he is, but it doesn't seem to matter to these guys."

Jericho rose to his feet and walked around me. "So you have someone after you and no place to stay."

I got up and squeezed the ends of my wet hair. "You summed it up very nicely, Jericho."

"This isn't funny, Isabelle. You're staying here."

"No," I said, moving past him. "That would be a disaster waiting to happen." I jogged down the stairs with him close behind.

"You can't wander around in a city full of Shifters."

"Sure I can!"

"Isabelle…"

I grabbed my flip-flops and keys before flying out the front door. Jericho tried to grab my shirt, but I picked up speed and jogged across the yard. Oh God, I needed to get away from all this drama.

"You don't really want me here," I yelled out. "And we might end up killing each other. I told Hawk if he doesn't pay this guy back, then it's over between us. I've given him an ultimatum, and I'm not really a fan of those."

When I unlocked the car door, he pressed his arm against the frame and squinted in the bright afternoon sun.

A butterfly briefly landed on his shoulder before fluttering off. I put my hands on my hips and softened my voice. "Why are you trying to stop me?"

"I can't help it, Isabelle. I have a strong instinct to protect you, and damn if I can't suppress it. You've always deserved a good man. I just don't think I can stand aside while you settle for some sonofabitch who thinks he can put bruises on you. Let's get one thing straight: if any man ever puts his hands on you again, I'll end his life. I don't care if you're mated to him."

I smiled and touched his cheek, feeling his smooth shave and searching his haunted eyes. "Maybe the old Jericho's still in there after all—the one who cares about people and doesn't shut them out of his life. I'm not expecting us to be friends again. But there are no other waitress jobs on the Breed side of town, and I *need* a paycheck. I'm tired of drifting. I've been moving around for years, and I want to get rooted somewhere and…"

"Find a pack?"

I blinked and tugged at the door.

"You're a wolf, Isabelle. It's natural to feel the need to join up with a pack. Stop living in denial… Stop fighting what comes natural."

"I know what I am."

He nodded and looked at me slyly. "You sure do. But when are you going to accept it?"

He knew me too well. I'd always struggled with my upbringing in a house full of cougars and had never known what it felt like to be bonded with anyone.

Except Jericho. In a strange way, I used to think of him as my pack. Maybe that's why I still felt a strong connection with him. He was the only one who knew my fear of joining a family. It's an instinct all Shifter wolves had, including myself, and even Jericho once admitted he'd one day settle down in a pack. I'd always told him it didn't matter to me.

I'd lied.

CHAPTER 7

USTIN WAS A BIG ENOUGH city that I knew the odds of running into Handlebars again were slim to none—as long as I stayed out of Hawk's territory.

I checked out a few motels, but the prices were outside my budget. With my hair pulled back in a messy knot, I parked my car in front of McDonald's and called Hawk.

"Better pick up," I murmured.

"Yeah," he answered.

"Hawk! I've been trying to get a hold of you."

"Miss me already?"

"Are you sitting around waiting for this to go away or doing something about it?"

"Working on it," he replied.

"Does that mean you're paying him back what you owe? I have a man after me. He's big and he's scary, but he's still a human and my wolf can kick his ass."

"You aren't supposed to shift in front of humans."

"And you aren't supposed to work for drug lords. Hawk, please. Let me know how this is all going to work out so I can make plans."

"Where are you staying?" he asked.

I shifted in my seat and watched a kid inside the restaurant smearing ketchup on the window. "You know where to find me if you want to talk, but don't start any trouble and get me fired."

"I can protect you, Izzy. Say the word and I'll come pick you up."

No way. I kept wondering why I was giving Hawk a second chance, but I saw the good side in him and believed in redemption. What if my staying made all the difference in turning his life around?

"Say yes. I want you back."

Was I overreacting? No one said relationships were easy. "Where are you hiding out?"

"Can't tell you, but I can show you. Come on, Iz. I don't like the idea of you sleeping God knows where or with who. Help me sort this shit out and we'll go back to the way it was."

I tapped my finger on the steering wheel, feeling the angel on one shoulder and the devil on the other, each trying to give me sage advice.

"Who's watching out for you? Huh? Come back to me and I'll make it right. You can't keep running when things don't go your way."

Hypocrite. Although, he had a point. I could have bailed on him, but I was tired of being the girl who always ran out on people. If I left him, he wouldn't pay off this Delgado guy, and I'd still have that crazy human tackling me every chance he got. Going back to Hawk seemed like the obvious choice to me. I'd be able to talk some sense into him and find out what was really going on. If it didn't work out, I'd make him call this big-shot dealer and let him know we weren't an item anymore and to stop chasing me down. I also didn't have a dime in my pocket.

And my gas was running low.

"Do you promise you'll sit down and tell me everything? Be honest with me from here on out?"

He chuckled. "A promise is a promise. Where are you?"

"Pick me up after work. I get off at four."

<hr />

After Isabelle stormed out of the house, Jericho had let his wolf run loose on the property to release the tension that had built up. Isabelle had a way of working him over like no other woman could. She'd wind him up until he felt constricted by his emotions.

Jericho didn't like feeling emotions. It's why he'd turned to drugs all those years ago. Things got worse when Izzy had walked out and Denver forced him into a human rehab center. Those kinds of places didn't exist in the Breed world, so he didn't have a choice. In confinement, he couldn't let his wolf out, so he was forced to confront the emotions he'd repressed for years. Feelings of inadequacy among his brothers, feelings of solitude when fame hit that had made him feel like nothing more than a used napkin that women wanted to blot their lipstick on.

Years had passed since then, and every now and again, he still enjoyed a little weed. But never the hard-core stuff. The best numbing agent? Avoiding the things that caused him pain.

Relationships.

Love.

Success.

And recently, traveling. He'd seen many cities, but the emptiness consumed him, despite the fact he always had someone to warm his bed. So when his younger brother, Austin, called everyone up and said he wanted to form a pack, Jericho had thought, *"Why the hell not?"*

By then, he'd already formed a new band, and they'd made a name for themselves at local clubs who were eager to book them. The success wasn't on the same level as he'd experienced years ago, but he liked the pace.

The Cole brothers had recently moved to a new house and were a tighter family than ever before. Austin might have been the youngest brother, but an alpha was born to lead and maturity came naturally to them. He made an exceptional Packmaster, and Jericho respected his ability to not only make sound decisions, but to be humble enough to take advice from his brothers. Austin believed in tough love, but sometimes that's what it took to set someone straight. He looked after his pack above all else.

So things had been good. Real good.

But all Jericho could think about lately was Isabelle. She'd always had amazing legs, but it was that sexy hair he loved the most. Her faded freckles reminded him of long summers in California. Man, he loved the way they mirrored her innocent heart. Most girls who were born with those wholesome looks skanked it up, but Isabelle kept it classy. More than that, she'd grown to become a tempting balance of two halves. Confident and timid; angelic with the tongue of the devil; fierce and fragile—a woman who made him feel unworthy of her affection.

She was his past and present—his heaven and hell.

After letting his wolf out for a long afternoon run in the woods, Jericho put on his work clothes: jeans shredded above the knee, a studded belt, dark lace-up boots, and a black jacket. No shirt meant a kick-ass, unforgettable show. He slipped on a few thick rings and grabbed his necklace with a pendant in the shape of a razorblade. Jericho put his guitar in its case and swiped the keys from the nail in the wall above the letter *J*. He stuffed his gear in the back seat of the blue pickup truck. He didn't have his own car, so he'd claimed the family truck that had once belonged to Austin.

It was after midnight, and Howlers was packed. He smirked when he saw that Jake had used two orange cones to reserve a spot for him up front.

Jericho ran over the cones and parked.

"Hey, man. Where ya been?"

He glanced at his bass player—a scrawny guy named Chaz with a black goatee and a bad reputation.

"Had to go for a run. You know how it is."

"I hear that. You wanna do a few lines before the show?"

Jericho lifted his guitar and slammed the door. "You know I don't touch that stuff."

"Don't act like a virgin to the white lady. I heard about your past."

Jericho turned his sharp eyes to Chaz. "Who the hell told you that?"

Chaz sneered and picked up a small pebble, rolling it around in his hand. "Denver talks a lot when he's drunk. Come on, I won't tell anyone. It'll take the edge off."

Words Jericho had heard more times in his life than he cared to remember. Words that tantalized him in a way he hadn't expected. He thought about how good it would feel to dull the pain and enjoy the show without having to watch Isabelle move around the bar while men leered at her.

God, how close he'd come earlier to kissing her at the house. Just being in close proximity and smelling her sweet skin, touching the smooth nape of her neck and watching her pupils dilate roused something primal in him. A feeling that had been dead since he'd last seen her.

Two men stumbled out the front door of Howlers, laughing and singing as they made their way across the parking lot.

"No thanks, man. Not my scene anymore. Take that shit somewhere else."

Chaz leaned against the truck and stroked his goatee. "I forgot— you only do the pussy shit. You think you're a real rock star, don't you? Walkin' around with your little dime bag of weed."

Jericho tightened his fist, tempted to turn around and knock the shit out of him. Chaz always acted up before a show and then disappeared. The drugs tapered down his attitude and made it easier to work with him—that man had some serious issues he hadn't learned to cope with.

"How about you get your ass onstage in five minutes?" Jericho bit out as he stormed up the steps and yanked open the main door.

The rock music blared, and on his way to the back of the room, he pointed at Denver. "We're talking later," he yelled, watching Denver wipe down the bar with a bewildered expression.

One of his groupies sauntered up in a white, strapless dress. Most wore the skintight ones, but not Trix. She liked easy access when he'd take her in the back room, or even behind the building. Trix was the kind of girl who had her sights on Jericho because of the slice of fame it gave her. The problem with a girl like Trix was that she had a tendency to crowd his space.

"Hey, sugar," he said, giving her a squeeze. "How's the crowd tonight?"

She flipped back her blond curls and smiled up at him. "I'm keeping 'em warm for you."

He popped her on the ass lightly and winked. "Go on, we'll catch up later."

When he walked through the room, several beautiful women

swiveled on their barstools and followed his movement. His brother, Wheeler, looked like an ailing seal hunched over his drink at the bar.

Jericho sat on the stool to his left. "How's it going?"

"Going," Wheeler replied, looking in his direction but not at him.

"Where's Ben?"

His face tightened. "Do I look like his keeper? You're his brother too. Why don't *you* tell me where the fuck he is?"

"What happened between you two? You guys used to get along. Then you got all dark and diabolical."

Wheeler ran his hand over a tattoo that wrapped around his wrist. "People change."

"You got that right. Maybe I don't like seeing you two at each other's throats all the time. Dig? Look, I have to get ready for the show. Catch ya later," he said, slapping Wheeler on the back and heading backstage.

"Denver! Three pitchers," a familiar voice called out.

He turned his head and watched Isabelle serve a tray full of burgers to a table of young men. The women were drawing nearer to the stage, anticipating the show. They caught sight of him walking with his guitar slung over his shoulder and began all that lip-biting and whispering.

Jake had a private room set up in the back where the band could hang out and get ready. Most Breed clubs offered private rooms to unwind, although this one was pretty damn small. Jericho liked to kick back with a few beers, strum a few chords, and kiss a few girls. When he walked in, it looked like Joker, his drummer, had already started. A girl in the tightest leather pants he'd ever seen was straddling him and licking his nose.

It was enough to make Jericho shudder.

"Where's Chaz?"

Jericho unzipped his case and pulled out his guitar, handling her with experienced hands. "Helping a nun cross the road. But he'll be back as soon as he saves a drowning puppy."

They snorted a few laughs, and Ren tossed a wadded napkin at him.

Jericho sat down and began tuning his guitar as he listened to Jake on the mic, giving their introduction and warming up the crowd.

Joker patted his friend on the ass and she gave a wicked laugh and stood up, sauntering over to a tray of hors d'oeuvres.

"Where the hell did you get the name of our band?" Joker asked, tapping his drumstick on his boot. "Because wouldn't you know it—I ran into a waitress out there by the name of Izzy. Sweet little titties, but not big enough for my mouth. She had a hot ass; I wouldn't mind getting my hands on that. Do you two know each other or something?"

"Let's go," Jericho said, knowing one more word about Isabelle's hot ass and he was going to pound Joker in the face. "Saddle up, boys. Showtime." He took his black guitar pick out of his pocket and put it in his mouth as they made their way up the side steps to the stage.

The audience howled and cheered as the lights dimmed, leaving only the stage illuminated by a few spotlights. Jericho scanned the crowd and didn't see Chaz.

"Where the fuck is he?" he said in an angry breath.

The backup guitarist spat out a curse and plugged in his guitar.

Jericho played it cool and turned his back to the crowd. "I'll give him *one* song to get his ass onstage. If Chaz isn't here by the end of this song, he's fired and we're going to have to wing it. Let me have this one, guys."

His guitar was a curvy Les Paul with a mahogany body that faded to black around the edges. It had a sweet tune when played just right, and Jericho knew exactly how to stroke the lady to make her sing. He adjusted the pickups and tone until the sound was rich and full-bodied.

He approached the mic. "Something a little different to start off the show tonight."

Sweat formed on his brow and as the room buzzed with anticipation, he began to play "Yesterday" by the Beatles. Jericho dragged out the guitar melody, and the crowd soaked it in.

As soon as the lyrics rolled past his lips, he realized he'd never performed this song in public before. The only time he'd ever played it was in the late hours of the night in the hotel room he shared with Isabelle. He'd quietly sing as he watched her sleep, dreaming of a better life. Every word became an explanation to Isabelle. He glanced toward the back of the room and saw her suddenly freeze as she walked to the bar, pivoting around slowly to face the stage. She set the tray on the bar without taking her eyes off him and stepped forward. The light from the bar illuminated her hair, and *damn*, she looked angelic. Every word of the song replayed a regretful moment in their lives, and he wondered if he was half the man he used to be, before all the drugs.

When he sang the line about why she had to go away, Isabelle wiped her cheek and tilted her head.

No one else in that room existed—only her.

His yesterday.

The crowd swayed to the sound of his smoky voice that mimicked some of the greats. Soulful and broken.

Isabelle lowered her somber eyes and shook her head. He sang louder and tried to reach out to her with his words, but she turned around and headed toward the restroom.

Then he was alone.

Alone in a room full of people who clung to his every word, except for the one person who mattered. His heart splintered.

Chaz suddenly appeared and leapt onstage, hooking up his gear. "Fuck, man. Sorry 'bout that." He wiped his nose and widened his eyes at the crowd.

Jericho wrapped up the song and released a heavy breath. Time would never erase his mistakes, and he wished more than anything that he could go back and do it differently. All that regret—why did he have to be such a fuckup?

That girl still owned his heart. All the bullshit aside, he wanted Isabelle back in his life. But it was too late. She had a man, and all Jericho had was his guitar. That's all he'd ever wanted, and that's exactly what he ended up with.

He wondered what she had done with his first guitar—the one she'd swiped from their motel room. Isabelle knew how much that instrument had meant to him. He used to fool around with the guitars backstage when he worked as a roadie, setting up equipment for bands. Isabelle had said he had a God-given talent. Wouldn't you know it? That girl had taken every penny she'd saved waitressing and bought him a butt-ugly Fender Stratocaster with a powder-blue body from the local pawnshop. She'd told him he was destined for greatness. Despite its second-rate quality, he loved that damn thing.

In the end, Jericho had destroyed everything he valued in his life because of his addictions. She must have realized she was too good for him. And she was right. But how could she have just left him there to die? He wanted to follow Denver's advice and hate her with every fiber of his being.

But he didn't.

He *couldn't*.

CHAPTER 8

"**H**ON, WAKE UP."
I moaned and lifted my head from the wooden
table where I'd dozed off. Rosie peered down at me
with her purse slung over her shoulder.

"I'm about to head out. There's a bubble bath waiting for me
with my name on it. Don't you need to be going home? Rush hour
is over and the birds will be chirping soon."

I sat up and stretched out my arms. "I was just waiting around
until the donut shop opened."

She gave me that look. The one a person gives when you're
shoveling manure and they can smell it. The bracelets on her wrist
slid up her arm when she touched her hair. "Take care of yourself."

"See you tonight," I said with a pitiful smile.

"I have the day off." She jutted her curvaceous hip. "The mister
is taking me out to dinner and salsa dancing."

"Salsa?"

She winked and waved her fingers as she walked toward the
door. "Hold down the fort, honey."

I yawned and took a sip of warm water from my glass. Only a
few customers remained, mostly drifters. We stayed open twenty-
four hours since some immortals worked odd shifts and had no
qualms about having a few beers at six in the morning with their
breakfast plate of sausage and eggs. Because of the tumbleweeds that
blew through this time of day, only one girl worked the floor from
five to nine. From what I'd heard, moms brought their kids in for
breakfast, but they weren't big tippers, so most of the girls didn't
want to waste their time working the early shift.

Remembering how Jericho had sung that Beatles song gave

me the shivers. Hell's bells, he was phenomenal. I'd heard him sing plenty of rock songs, but the ballads had always been my favorites, especially that one. He used to play it in our hotel room late at night when he thought I was asleep. His voice had poured through the microphone like smooth bourbon, and I'd become drunk listening to him. But for a fleeting moment, I could have sworn he was looking *right at me*. I knew Jericho often looked toward the back when the women became a distraction in the front row, but it just felt like his eyes were on *me*.

It was a good thing they weren't, or he would have seen me running to the bathroom in tears. I'd stayed in there for another full song and finally found a way to pull it together and put the past behind me.

It wasn't just that he'd slept with that woman all those years ago, because we had never been exclusive or even in a relationship other than being friends. But walking in on him having sex had made me realize I didn't *matter* to him. I'd falsely believed I was special, and when things had heated up between us the night before, I'd thought it meant we might be moving in a serious direction. To be fair, I was young and too foolish to realize a man like Jericho could never settle for just one girl.

All that history shouldn't have mattered now, but it did. I couldn't endure losing him twice—once was hard enough. If I had to go through that again, it would break me. After the night I left him, I'd never once dated a musician. How could I expect a man who had the most beautiful and available women at his disposal to be monogamous?

Jericho had addiction problems: sex, drugs, and rock 'n' roll. A drug addict must abstain from all drugs to be clean and sober, but it was unrealistic to ask someone to become celibate. By no means did I think I was vastly superior to him—I had my own drawer full of dirty socks. I just didn't air my laundry out in the open the way he did.

A plate of scrambled eggs and bacon appeared in front of me. Jericho stood across the table and spun the chair around, straddling the seat and folding his arms over the back. He was wearing a black suit jacket with no shirt, and the hickey on his chest soured my stomach.

"What's this?" I asked.

"Just the way you like it. Bland as all fuck." He shoved a saltshaker toward me. "Go on and eat. You've been passed out for the last thirty minutes, and I don't remember seeing you eat dinner earlier."

"It's hard to serve on a full stomach." I lifted the fork and shoveled in a few bites. "Usually I just snack on protein bars and save the big meals for the afternoon. What are you still doing here? Your show ended hours ago."

He reached across the table and broke off a piece of my bacon. I noticed most of his eyeliner had smeared off. "Decided to hang out for a while and play a little pool with one of my brothers," he said, chewing on the bacon.

"Is he the one who sucked on your chest?" I asked, pointing at the purple bruise.

Jericho pulled open his jacket and glanced down at his left pec with drowsy eyes. Then his mouth widened in a fiendish smile. "We spilled popcorn. I had a mishap with the vacuum cleaner. Swear it."

"How come you never talked about your brothers? They seem decent, and I only remember you mentioning them once or twice."

He slowly licked his finger and then sucked off the remaining bacon crumbs. "I was in a different place back then. Austin was just a kid, and my parents didn't want me around; they thought I'd be a bad influence. They were right. By then we were all living on our own, but the other guys would return home for long intervals to bond with Austin. It was always weird when I showed up. I got a lot of shit from some of my brothers for not visiting as much, and I guess they could see what I'd gotten mixed up in. Reno was afraid I'd get too famous and people would eventually notice I wasn't aging. You know how the Breed feels about fame."

"I'm glad you've sorted it all out. I'm sure they've always loved you, but you were a handful back then."

He pulled a cigarette from behind his ear and gingerly tapped it on the table. "I wasn't that bad."

"You walked naked into a gas station and bought Twinkies on

a dare. You didn't run, Jericho. You walked in there just as cool as a breeze."

He leaned back with a nostalgic expression. "I forgot about that. Now tell me, Isabelle, whose idea was it? I can't seem to recall what kind of deviant person would have made such a dare."

I kicked him under the table, and it roused a smile. "I had no idea you'd go through with it."

"You wanted Twinkies."

"Actually, I wanted those little cupcakes, but I guess you'd forgotten by the time you walked across the street and went inside."

He shrugged. "It was chilly that night."

I took another bite of my eggs. "Thirty degrees with snow flurries, as I recall."

We both laughed, and a moment of silence fell between us, one thick with memories and tender feelings.

"I like your hair better now," he suddenly said. He frowned and quickly bent forward so a veil of hair obscured his face. "What I mean is it's not braided like you used to wear it."

"I've learned to accept the wild nature of my hair and just roll with it. Thanks, though."

"How's your family?" he asked in a stony voice. Jericho knew about my tumultuous upbringing.

"My parents divorced."

His brows rested at an indifferent slant. "And your siblings?"

"We don't keep in touch. We're related by blood, but I have no love for them. You have no idea what it's like growing up in a house where you're the odd animal out. After they went through the change, they used their animals to intimidate me, and because no one stopped them, it progressively got worse. My mother would defend them, saying they were just acting on instinct against another predator."

"Bitch."

"Yeah, calling her own child a predator when I was the one who was prey in that family. I'm not surprised about the divorce; they fought all the time. My dad isn't so bad, he's just… distant. Maybe it's because he's an older wolf."

Jericho popped the cigarette in his mouth and pulled out his lighter. Light gleamed off the silver shell, and he snapped it shut with a click.

"You didn't use to smoke," I pointed out.

After taking a short drag, he blew the smoke over his shoulder. "Started up after… Well, I just picked up new habits and got rid of old ones."

"Do you mind?" I asked, holding out two fingers.

"Yeah, the hell I mind," he said in a harsh tone. "You don't need to pick up any bad habits."

"How do you know I don't smoke?"

Jericho smiled cunningly and pulled another taste from his cigarette. "I've seen the way you wrinkle your nose in disgust when leaving a table full of smokers. Don't pretend to be someone you're not."

"Maybe I want to see what the fuss is all about. It's not like Shifters can die from cancer."

"No, but your breath won't be as pleasant as it is now."

I arched my brow. "And what about *your* breath? Do you think women enjoy kissing an ashtray?"

Jericho tapped the ashes into an empty glass. "It's not my lips they usually want their mouth on." He smiled invitingly and broke off another piece of bacon, watching me squirm in my seat as I tried to pretend his suggestive comment wasn't sexy.

"Do you ever miss traveling?"

"We do small tours around the state sometimes," he said. "I don't miss sleeping in trucks and doing shit jobs for a few extra dollars to buy dinner."

I sighed. "Me either. Although…" I glanced around and laughed softly.

Jericho leaned in tight. "Is Jake paying you good?"

"Fair. The tips are decent, but the guys are holding back because I'm new. That's why I haven't been able to put any to the side. I know the drill. They do that with fresh blood because they think they can make me work harder for them. The other girls don't like telling how much their regulars tip them, so it'll take me some time to figure it out."

His jaw set. "Let me know the next time that happens."

"Are you going to beat them up?" I wondered aloud, poking a fork at my eggs.

"No. But I'm going to have a talk with Denver. He knows what's up around here."

"Denver doesn't want to be bothered with that kind of thing. We're not on friendly terms."

He quieted, as if he knew I was right. Denver held a grudge against me, and although we maintained a working relationship, he wasn't about to bend over backwards to do me any favors.

Jericho watched me stabbing my eggs. "Eat, Isabelle. Or else I'll pin you to the table and shovel it in."

I set my fork down. "Always such sweet words rolling off your tongue, Mr. Cole."

He snorted. "Ladies seem to have no complaints about my tongue."

Which killed my appetite.

"I need to get going," I said, rising from my chair and stretching. "I'm beginning to wonder if I can work these late hours every night."

He sat up. A thin necklace with a razor on the end slid across his chest from behind the lapel of his jacket. "What did I say?"

"Maybe I don't want to constantly hear about how much other women want you. Maybe that's not the kind of thing that turns me on."

I spun around and walked toward the locker room to get my purse. My face heated with embarrassment. *Did I just say that out loud?*

As I opened my locker, the door closed on my right. Jericho leaned against it with hooded eyes.

"What do you want?" I asked. "I have to leave."

He kept his intent guarded as he walked behind me, lightly brushing my hair away from my shoulders. His hands never touched my body, but I shivered when he blew a soft breath against the back of my neck. I felt a flurry of tingles between my legs and stepped forward against the lockers.

"Jericho, don't touch me."

I felt the heat of his body behind me, then the caress of his words moving across my neck like silk. "I'm not touching you, Isabelle." He blew on my neck again, concentrating the intensity of his breath so that heat snaked across my skin.

I reached in the locker and gripped my purse, making a soft and almost complaining moan. He placed his hands on the lockers, and I felt the faintest movement of my hair, as if he might be moving his nose through it and smelling me.

A lick of pleasure raced down my body, quickly extinguished by an intrusive thought that crossed my mind. *This* was how Jericho seduced all his conquests, and I would be no different from them if I let him continue.

I turned around. He tilted his head—eyes alight and buzzing with arousal. I focused on the only thing that would turn me off, and that was the hickey on his chest. "How come you haven't settled down with a mate? You're not getting any younger."

"Never found anyone worth settling for."

"Maybe you're attracting the wrong women."

"I could say the same about you. Only men, not women."

I touched his nose and smiled. "You haven't met the men in my life."

"Nor have you met the women in mine," he countered.

My fingers traced the outer edges of his hickey. "This tells me all I need to know."

Jericho's rings suddenly bounced across the floor, and he rubbed his chest as if he were trying to erase the mark. "If it bothers you that much…"

Faster than a blink, Jericho shifted into his animal in a fluid motion. The beautiful wolf I remembered stood before me, proud and tall with his head held high. He licked my hand and sat back on his hind legs. I squatted down and ran my hands alongside his face, burying my fingertips in the angel-soft hairs behind his ears. Jericho's wolf was a spectacular creature—earthy brown with shades of cream and orange. In certain spots, the tips of his hairs were black, especially around the tail. Most Shifter wolves were easily identifiable because of unique markings, unless they were a solid color. But sometimes you could simply tell by looking in their eyes.

He lapped me up with those jade eyes rimmed in black, and I laughed. I never had to worry about his wolf putting on a façade. Like all wolves, his loyalty ran deep for those he loved. Because of our travels, we'd learned to trust and protect each other. There were nights when Jericho's wolf had kept me warm and guarded me with his life. We didn't always have a bed to sleep in, but I'd never had any fear as long as he was by my side.

His eyes bubbled with familiarity as he excitedly licked my face and greeted me after years of separation. Wolves are pure and not polluted with all the hang-ups humans carry around like spare change.

"I missed you," I said, trying to keep my mouth closed as he continued licking.

His tail wagged and he whined, but I could still see in his eyes a flicker of Jericho, who hadn't let his animal take complete control.

A knock sounded at the door and I gasped when Jericho unexpectedly shifted into human form. My hands were wrapped around his naked thighs and my face was right in his crotch, just as Hawk strode in the room with a look of disgust on his face.

"You did that on purpose," I snarled, glaring up at Jericho.

He winked.

"What the fuck is this?" Hawk exclaimed.

"It's Jericho being funny," I said, rising to my feet. "Hawk, I'd like you to meet an old friend. This is Jericho Cole."

"Yeah, so I see," he went on, anger stamped on his features. "You have a funny way of saying hello to an old friend, Izzy."

Hawk was wearing his button-up blue shirt. I hated that look because he always undid the first four buttons and subjected the world to his chest hair. Not that it was venturing into grizzly-bear territory, but enough of it poked out that gave everyone a peep show.

"Hawk, don't be ridiculous. He shifted to play a joke on me."

Hawk stepped forward aggressively and sliced the rock star from head to toe with his sharp eyes. "I don't find my girl's face in your balls very funny."

Jericho hiked up his jeans and buttoned them. "Neither do I, but that's another story," he said as smooth as molasses. "So you're the big bird? Hawk? Is that your animal too? My wolf likes to eat them for a light snack."

Hawk stepped around me and folded his arms. "Why don't you keep on talking? I'll show you what the fuck my animal is."

To be honest, I'd never seen Hawk shift. He alluded that he was a wolf, but we always shifted separately. The way he laid down the threat put me on edge.

"Hawk, let's go." I touched his arm, but he shook me off.

Jericho bent down and fished through his blazer until he found his pack of cigarettes. He put one between his lips and began sliding his rings back on. The anger on his face was palpable. He left his jacket and broken necklace on the floor and faced Hawk wearing nothing but jeans, the rings on his fingers, and holding a leather belt in his hand. "Go ahead, Tweety Bird. Scare me with your badass talons and beak. I haven't eaten breakfast and could use a little… chicken."

I dove between them and shoved at Hawk's chest. "If you start a fight and get me fired, I'm not going home with you," I whispered. "Let's go."

Hawk pointed his finger at Jericho. "You lucked out this time. Next time you won't be so fortunate."

We turned toward the door and Jericho made clucking sounds. Hawk froze.

"Jericho," I said, my voice lowering an octave. "Let it go."

He lit up his smoke and tucked the lighter in his back pocket. "Sorry, Isabelle. Just thought he might try hitting something else for a change besides you."

Hawk pushed me to the side and his voice became chillingly calm. "Say again?"

"You heard me, *compadre*. I noticed you like putting your hands on women. Did you see the marks you left on her neck, or is that *your* version of a love bite?"

The tension became electric, and my breath caught since I'd seen firsthand the damage Jericho could do in a fight.

"You think you're going to whoop me with that belt, boy?"

Jericho shot me a glare. "All these years, Isabelle, I thought you had higher standards than a man who uses 'whoop' and 'boy' in the same sentence. I know we're in Texas, but I think we can be a little more sophisticated than that."

Hawk stepped in front of me and obscured my vision with his wide frame. "I think you need to quit running your mouth at *my* woman and talk to the man in this room."

"That's fine by me, Tweety. Be sure to point out who the other man is whenever he comes in the room. Let me tell you a little something about me. I fight dirty—no holds barred. I'll use my belt, my lighter, the pen in Izzy's purse, and whatever the hell else I feel like using that's going to cause more damage. I've been in enough fights that *nobody* talks a good enough game to make me tremble in my boots. All it does is amp me up. Cross me the wrong way and I'm your worst nightmare. And putting your hands on Isabelle stepped right over the fucking line and pissed on it."

I jumped when I heard the sharp crack of a belt.

"So do me a favor and quit running your mouth, Tweety."

Jericho didn't give warnings—he stated the facts. He was a lover, a singer, a man with an easygoing personality and a cool demeanor. But anyone who had ever made the mistake of crossing Jericho ended up on the receiving end of an unforgettable beating. He was tall, toned, and terrifying. His lips would curl in and those rings would be the first and last thing most men saw, if they were lucky. The rest had to endure Jericho unleashed. I'd only seen it happen a couple of times, and each fight was justified. I wasn't so sure what was going on here because I'd rarely seen Jericho provoke a fight.

"You two have fun in the sandbox," I said. "I'm going home."

I stormed toward the locker, nudged Jericho to the side, snatched my purse, and flew out the door.

"Ridiculous!" I shouted at nobody. I still had my heels on and jogged down the steps to the parking lot.

Unbelievable. There was nothing sexier than having a man fight for you, but only for the *right* reason. All that chest-beating in there was about male ego, not me. How did I get mixed up in such a blender full of drama?

Then an unexpected wave of tingles spread between my legs, reminding me just how provocative it was to have Jericho so close without touching me. Had one finger grazed my skin, I would have known he wasn't a man of his word. But his restraint impressed me, as did the fact he had kept his promise.

But I knew what he was really trying to accomplish. It became a game to get me so worked up that I'd be the one to initiate touch. He wanted to break my willpower and prove how irresistible he was.

"Izzy!" Hawk shouted. "Stay where you are."

I heard a car door slam, but I'd already made it across the street. When I stepped up on the curb, my heel caught between the jagged cracks of the sidewalk. The force of motion caused me to lose my balance and fall forward, landing on both knees. I broke the fall with the palms of my hands but hissed when I pulled my foot out of my shoe and saw blood on my knee.

Hawk's red sports car screeched up to the curb on my left. He got out, hooked his arms around me, and hauled me into the car. A shoe flew through the open door as he slammed it.

Yeesh.

Once Hawk buckled up and merged into traffic, he glanced at my knee and said, "Don't bleed on my seat."

"My things are in the trunk of my car. Go back."

"You didn't seem too interested in retrieving them five seconds ago," he said, gunning around a corner and staring in the rearview mirror. "We'll buy you some new shit."

I glanced over my shoulder. "Is someone following us?"

My body hit the door when he made a sharp left turn.

"Hawk, slow down! I need to go back and get my car."

"Your car will stay right where it is."

"How do you expect me to go back to work?"

He reached in the glove compartment and flipped it open. A few maps fell out, and he tossed a package of napkins on my lap. "You're not going back to work. I don't like the idea of my woman slinging beer and onion rings all night to a bunch of horny men. Is that what you want to be for the rest of your life, Izzy? Some bar slut?"

"Well done. You've managed to belittle my worth in a matter of a few sentences. Pull the car over; this was a mistake."

Hawk ignored my complaints and made a hard right turn. His erratic behavior began to rattle me.

"Pull the car over! What's gotten into you lately? I'm not up for this kind of craziness!"

"Crazy? Just *how high* do you think your expectations deserve to go?" he asked in a cool voice. "Izzy, Izzy. No man seems to be worthy of you."

"What are you talking about? If you had just paid this guy his money, we wouldn't be driving around the city like Bonnie and Clyde. You're acting like a maniac!"

"And you're acting like a ball-sucking whore. Do you know what I risked to drive all the way out here and pick you up, knowing Delgado could have one of his men casing the bar? I walk in and you have your face cozied up in another man's crotch. Classy, Iz. Real classy."

My head felt ready to explode. I didn't even want to argue with him. He should have trusted me, and while I knew it wasn't an ideal situation to walk in on, the fact he was berating me began to rile me up. It made my wolf want to bite him in the ass.

"Stop the car and drop me off. I made a mistake. Izzy Monroe made a big, fat, *whopping* mistake. There. I said it. I'm not saying you're evil and I'm good and that's what this is all about. We're just not compatible. We're not even combustible in the sack together. I'm not even sure why you're hanging on to a girl like me if you clearly don't respect what I do for a living. And by the way, I love my job. Maybe I have to deal with a few jerks, but that goes with the territory, and I don't think any job is jerk-free. I serve. Why do you have such a problem with the fact I serve others? Maybe if you tried it once in your life, you'd have a little humility. Not everyone is meant to be a doctor or banker. And who are you to talk, Mr. Drug Pusher?"

Oh hell's bells. Evil Izzy just walked in the door, put her boots on the table, and ordered a drink of devil's tongue.

"I own a house and pay for your fucking clothes. *That's* who I am to talk."

Did he just say that to me?

I turned to my left and wagged my finger at him. "First of all, the money you used to purchase that house came from drug addicts. Men and women who have an addiction and need help. All you do is feed them pain and misery and take away their hope. You don't seem to care that you might have been responsible for some of them overdosing or committing crimes!"

"Like you're Miss Goody Two-Shoes."

"Yes, I smoked a little grass when I was young, but I've left my wild ways behind. At some point, you have to grow up and do the right thing. You're not doing drugs, Hawk, you're distributing them. And on top of all that, you're stealing. Not stealing from a collection plate in church. *Nooo.* You're stealing from a drug lord."

"Delgado is not a drug lord. He's a businessman who owns a few strip joints in the area. He's also a human who doesn't have a clue of the street value of his drugs and what people will pay for them. His stupidity is my gain."

"Let me out."

Fear swam through me with every sharp turn and throttle of the engine. I'd been trying to change my ways about giving people second chances because I wanted to believe others would do the same for me. But his aggressive and unpredictable behavior put a knot in my stomach, and I didn't have a family or pack to protect me.

I slowly wrapped my fingers around the door handle, my heart racing. When he stopped at a light, I opened the door and leaned to get out. Hawk seized my left arm.

Pulling it free was as impossible as his grip, and when I turned to fight him off, he punched me hard in the face.

"Lights out, Izzy."

CHAPTER 9

A RINGING SOUND DREW ME OUT of a torturous slumber. I moaned, struggling to open my eyes. I began to feel pain in various places, from the throb in my head to a dull ache on my cheek. I'd never had anyone punch me in the face before. Ever. Not even in the house I grew up in. My conniving siblings had devised subtle methods of abuse, but they'd never struck a blow with a closed fist.

"Hello?"

It was still dark, and I thought the lights might be out until I felt something tight against my face. Not only that, but my wrists were bound. When I moved my legs and fabric brushed against my knees, I felt a stinging pain where I had skinned them. I could sense I was lying on a bed, but the house didn't smell familiar.

"Hawk?" I croaked. I attempted to clear my throat and turn my stiff neck. I heard the sound of a television in the distance.

"Hawk," I called out in a loud voice.

Footsteps approached, and a door opened. "I see someone's awake."

"Take this off me."

"No can do."

"I hate to break the news on your kidnapping attempt, but I might as well let the cat out of the bag. I already know what you look like."

"Yeah, yeah."

"Did you drug me?" I still felt groggy and didn't think he could have knocked me out that long with a punch.

"Brought something for you," he said.

"Ah!" I cried out when something icy touched my cheek.

"Hold still. It's just an ice pack."

I turned my head away. "Why don't you let me shift and heal?"

"Because, Izzy," he began with an intolerant sigh, "that would mean letting you free, and I don't feel like chasing your crazy ass down."

"Who says I'll run?"

He chuckled. "You'll run. That's the thing you do best in this world."

That hurt worse than a punch to the face.

"What is this about? You don't love me enough to tie me up to a bed." My fingers stretched out and I realized those weren't ropes around my wrist. It felt smoother, like a cord.

The bed depressed as he sat to my left. "And how do you know what I feel?"

I frowned. "Don't pretend you love me when all you feel is a sense of possession. You buy things for the sake of having them, not because you need or want them. You've done a great job at keeping me in a gilded cage, but I'm not a bird. I'm a wolf, and you can't cage a wolf."

His fingers combed through my hair. "I only want to keep what's mine."

I bit my tongue, deciding it was not in my best interest to argue.

"Can you at least remove the blindfold?" I asked in a calm voice. "It makes my head hurt worse when I can't see. Please, Hawk. Just the blindfold."

"I like the submissive side of you," he said approvingly.

My hair tugged in the back, and I winced as he untied the heavy cloth and pulled it away. I blinked through blurry vision and widened my eyes in an attempt to see more clearly. Hawk's shaggy hair covered the tops of his ears, and his jaw was peppered with black whiskers.

"You want a bottle of water?" he asked.

The civility of his question contradicted with the thin cords that painfully bound my wrists to the bedposts.

"Whose house is this?"

"Ours."

I let that word hang in the air for a minute. Ours. That meant this wasn't temporary, and he planned to keep me here. Bile rose in my throat when I glanced down at my body. I was no longer wearing my work clothes, but a white satin nightgown that stretched all the way to my ankles. And it wasn't mine. Did he buy this while I was unconscious? Or did it belong to someone else?

"What do you mean by *ours*?"

"Maybe it's about time we get to know each other a little better," he suggested, getting off the bed and tossing the blindfold on a dresser. "You said you didn't want any secrets, and I need to see if what we've got between us is going to work out. I own three houses. This one is smaller than the others, but it's a good place to lay low."

I glanced around the windowless room. The walls were the color of cement, and while I couldn't see the floor, I thought it was wood from the sound his shoes made walking across it. The only light in the room came from a brass lamp on the nightstand next to Hawk. The wall in front of me had an open door on the left and a closed door on the right that looked like a closet. Unlike the other house, there wasn't a single shade of pastel blemishing the room. This was cold and depressing, perhaps reflecting a darker side of Hawk I'd never seen.

Until now.

While he rummaged through the dresser, fear gripped me stronger than ever before. I wasn't sure how to play Hawk's game so he'd let me go. He wouldn't respond to arguing, so I needed to earn his trust. No one at work would care if I didn't show up. Rosie was the only one I'd bonded with, and she had the night off.

I crossed my ankles and decided to keep them locked. A flush of heat overtook my body from the stuffy air in the room, but all I wanted to do was cover my body with the blanket.

"Last chance for a drink."

"Yes. Water would be great," I said.

I just wanted him to leave. Once Hawk changed into a white T-shirt and boxers, he left the room. I leaned forward and glanced at my wrists. The cords were thin, and I couldn't tell if the material was plastic or metal, but he must have bought it at a hardware store because it didn't look familiar to me. The cords were secured to the bedposts and wrapped around several times. I tugged, but they only tightened around my wrists and bit into my flesh. I didn't want to lose circulation, but my shoulders were beginning to cramp. I twisted to the left and then to the right, turning my arms and trying to stretch out some of the soreness.

Hawk returned and unscrewed the cap from a plastic bottle. He moved around to my right side and lifted my head, holding the rim to my mouth. I took a few deep swallows and water dribbled down my cheek. He wiped it with his hand and placed the bottle on a stereo shelf to the right. It was one of those old systems with the turntable on top and massive speakers on either side.

"See, I'm not such a bad guy," he said in a velvety voice. But I could see right through him. He *enjoyed* having me bound and at his mercy—it empowered him.

"Can you untie me?"

"No can do. Stretching the arms and binding them will keep your animal from shifting."

"Hawk, you can tie my wrists together, but this position really hurts. I'm losing circulation in my arms. I don't know what your endgame is here, but I don't think you want to injure me to the point where you've done irreparable damage."

He rubbed his jaw and gave it consideration. "No, you're still too pissed off. I can see it in your eyes."

"My black eye?"

His expression darkened with annoyance. "We'll talk in the morning, Izzy. It's late."

I stretched my right shoulder and lifted my head to look at him. "Hawk, can you cover me up?"

He flipped the thin blanket over my legs and switched out the light. To my relief, he left the room and closed the door behind him. I released a breath, thankful my situation wasn't going to get more desperate than it already was. Any feelings I once had for him were now dead, so nothing he initiated sexually would be consensual. That left me with the primal fear of being violated by a man who felt like he owned me and had rights to my body like I was property.

Men who treated women as livestock and abused them received no mercy when caught. Shifters had zero tolerance for abuse against women, and I'd heard stories about what had happened to some of them who were turned over to the packs. I hoped that Hawk wasn't that kind of man, but as the cord pinched my skin, I had my doubts.

After Isabelle dashed out of Howlers, Jericho had been left with adrenaline pumping in his veins. He wanted to finish off Hawk and give him a nasty dose of his own medicine, but Hawk predictably ran out after her. Jericho knew about men like him. They liked to push women around to feel superior in their inferior lives.

Afterward, he got in his truck and drove aimlessly. The sun winked at him from the treetops in the distance as he coasted down a busy street. Dawn swallowed up the dark night and replaced the stars with splashes of apricot, yellow, and a pale azure.

Jericho swung by a diner and ordered a plate of Belgian waffles. He mostly stared out the window, smoking his cigarette, wondering why he couldn't just walk away from Isabelle. Why did she have to pick a loser like Hawk to settle down with? Just imagining that guy pushing her around made his wolf thirst for blood. She might have been tall and sassy, but Isabelle wouldn't be able to fight off someone his size. No pack would allow one of their women to be treated with such disrespect. He knew how rough she'd had it growing up, and that's why he'd promised years ago to look out for her.

Maybe that's what made it harder for him to turn a blind eye.

After finishing his coffee, Jericho headed home. He wished he had been the one to run out after her, but now the two of them were probably curled up in bed together, so he put it out of his mind.

When he pulled up the driveway, Lexi stalked toward his truck with her hands on her hips. She had on a pair of cutoff jeans and a brown T-shirt with a logo on the front promoting barbecue.

"Austin's going to kill you," she announced, tucking her straight brown hair behind her ears. "You were supposed to be home with the truck two hours ago. He needed it to haul dirt for Mom's garden so she could do some work before it got too hot."

Jericho rolled up the window and popped open the door. She continued to lecture him as he pulled his guitar out from behind the seat. A sick feeling gnawed at his stomach that he couldn't shake, as if he were in the middle of a waking nightmare. It's something that had begun not long after Isabelle ran out of Howlers, and it had progressively gotten worse.

He ignored Lexi and headed toward the house. All the roses were in bloom—huge bushes filled with exquisite red blossoms. Lexi's mom, Lynn, crouched in front of one, pruning a thorny branch with her shears. Austin had built her a little wooden stool for gardening, and Maizy had painted it bright yellow.

Jericho swatted at a mosquito on his neck and realized he had left his jacket at the bar. It wouldn't be the first time he'd come home from a show shirtless. The waitress at the diner hadn't raised any complaints; she'd refilled his coffee cup at least six times.

He tromped up the porch steps and went inside, hanging his keys on the nail above the letter *J*. He didn't bother taking off his shoes but created a calamity of noise as he stormed up the stairs.

"What's up with you?" Austin asked, pulling a white tank top over his head as he walked down the hall.

Jericho ignored him and went straight for the game room. He took a seat at the bar and poured himself a shot of whiskey. After he knocked it back and grimaced, he poured another.

"You wanna tell me what's bothering you that you're drinking this early in the morning?" Austin put his left forearm on the doorjamb and leaned against it.

"Ghosts," Jericho murmured.

"Is one of them named Izzy?"

He polished off the rest of his glass, and when he pushed it away, it tipped over and rolled around. "Have you ever met a girl who was so wrong for you she was right?"

Austin laughed richly and entered the room, swaggering up to a barstool and easing onto it. "I'm living with one. I've always thought

Lexi was too damn good for me. I wanted her for a long time; I just never thought I deserved a woman like her."

"Yeah," Jericho agreed. "That about sums it up."

"Denver told me what happened back in California. Are you sure you aren't putting a girl on a pedestal who doesn't belong there?"

"She's different."

How could he explain it? Isabelle still retained that purity that had drawn him to her all those years ago. He resented the fact that she'd stolen from him, but he could hardly blame her for leaving his ass. Jericho had done plenty of unforgivable shit back then. He'd once gotten so fucked up on coke that he had left her alone at the beach with a group of strangers they'd just met. He simply forgot her, thanks to the drugs. She'd worshipped him, as if he could do no wrong, and he'd never taken a moment to appreciate what they had together. He'd abused her trust and friendship, and in the end, he'd gotten exactly what he deserved.

He couldn't help but look back with remorse. There were ugly parts of their friendship he'd just as soon forget. Sure, it was nice to remember the night she slept against him, snuggled close to keep warm. But the reason they slept in the alley that night was because Jericho had blown all his money partying. Isabelle knew why, but she always stayed by his side, and a man rarely found that kind of unrelenting devotion.

In the beginning, Jericho had drifted through different towns, struggling to find his place in the world. It's something many wolves did before joining a pack. Then he met Isabelle and discovered they shared a common spirit. He showed her how to live, and she showed him how much potential he had. It wasn't until after he formed his band that the lifestyle had swallowed him up.

"Where are you, Jericho?" Austin snapped him back into the present.

"Do you believe in second chances?"

Austin rubbed the cleft in his chin and stared into the mirror behind the liquor bottles. "I'd be a fool to say I didn't. The thing about second chances is there's more to prove the second time around, and more to lose. You fuck it up, and it can never be fixed."

"I can't stop thinking about her, even when she's not around." Jericho began combing his fingers through stringy hair in need of a wash. "On top of that, she's playing house with a complete asshole," he added.

"So you think she'll be better off with a partial asshole?" Austin chuckled and leaned on his left arm to face him. "Come on, Jericho. You're not a wolf who's ready to settle. Why are you so hung up on this woman?"

Jericho tapped a pack of cigarettes against the palm of his hand and pulled out a slender stick, admiring the neatly trimmed paper. "Because we never really ended it. I never got the final word. We never had the fight where she would have told me what a failure I was at being her friend. I just woke up and she wasn't there anymore."

He lit the end of his cigarette and blew a donut ring in the air. It floated toward the ceiling, and damn if that didn't remind him of her too.

"It sounds like she's got something else going on in her life now, brother. If you care about her, you'll leave her alone. If you don't give a damn about her, you'll mess with her head and ruin her life. I don't know who Izzy is, but if she's poison, then I don't want my brother mixed up in that. You're not adrift anymore. You're part of a pack, and I have a responsibility as Packmaster to look out for my family." Austin rapped his knuckles on the bar and looked around. "Just keep in mind that those years you two spent together were the years you were lost to us. Lost to everyone. If she had anything to do with that—"

"She didn't. That was all me. Fame tasted pretty damn good back then." Jericho set his smoke on the ashtray and ran his finger across his bottom lip, pinching it out a little. "How's Lexi getting on with the business?" he asked, changing topics.

Austin smirked and turned around so his elbows were on the bar. "That woman is something else. She's still scoping out buildings on the Breed side of town, and I think we've got a contender for the next Sweet Treats location."

"Is she still doing the pastry thing?"

Austin nodded. "She's got the cookies and cakes down pat, but she's trying her hand at donuts and breakfast foods. I told her she's getting in over her head—maybe she should just keep the shop open in the afternoon and see how business goes. *Hell no.* Lexi wants her store open morning and night. Her goal is twenty-four hours, but I'm not having that. We're not a fucking 7-Eleven."

Jericho snorted. "That would cut short your time in the sack."

"Nooo doubt," Austin agreed. "If she can hire staff to accommodate the hours, then I'll agree to it. But money will be tight in the beginning, so I don't see that happening."

"You sure it's a good idea? The old shop is running just fine."

Austin slid off the stool and stretched back. "I give my woman whatever she wants, including her dreams. We need to move the business to the Breed district so we can get out of all that mess with taxes. I liked the last place we looked at; Wheeler's negotiating a price to see if we can get him to come down."

"So you'll need staff?"

Austin patted Jericho's arm. "Yeah. You feel like dropping the microphone and serving cookies?"

"That would be a negative. I might have someone in mind if she needs help."

Jericho wondered if Isabelle would like that kind of job. She wouldn't have to put up with drunken men, and the girl loved her donuts.

"What if you sang in the store now and again? It's going to be a pastry shop that also serves coffee. Lexi wants a place where people like to hang out, and a singer would really draw in customers. We could set it up so you'd have a little area in the corner to play your acoustic. No mic, just a stool. Real casual." Austin tucked his hands in his pockets. "You won't have women throwing lingerie at you, but you might like the change of pace. It'll put a little extra money in your pocket if you also put out a tip jar. I think it's safe to say the ladies will pay well to hear you sing."

Jericho swiveled around and stretched out his left leg, staring at the pool table. "I might do it for some free donuts."

Austin strolled toward the door. "I think that can be arranged."

"Unlimited supply," Jericho added.

"Don't push it."

A knock sounded at the door downstairs.

"Are you expecting someone?" Jericho hopped off the stool and followed Austin.

"Lexi's going to a movie with Naya. She doesn't like coming over here because—"

"She's a diva?"

"I don't think she gets along with Wheeler, so she stays away to avoid the drama. Don't mention anything about it," Austin murmured as they hurried down the stairs.

"Naya, come in!" Lexi said excitedly.

"Is that what you're wearing, chickypoo?"

They made it to the bottom just in time to see Lexi staring down at her cutoff shorts. "What's wrong with what I'm wearing?"

Compared to what Naya was wearing? *A whole damn lot.* That woman was sexilicious, even by Jericho's standards, and he wasn't into brunettes. Naya had on a white slim-fitted jumpsuit. The shorts were short, and the top was a sleeveless V-neck that buttoned up. You could see her black bra beneath the light fabric, and Jericho wondered what the view was from the back. His eyes traveled down her suntanned legs to the silver anklet above her right foot. Naya had luscious brown curls and burgundy lips that were full and seductive. She couldn't be more different than Lexi, but they used to be neighbors and had forged a strong friendship. Jericho wondered why he'd never been lucky enough to live next door to an exotic dancer.

"Why don't you change into something a little feminine?" Naya suggested, tapping her hoop earring. "You look like you're going to a baseball game. All you need is a footlong and a baseball cap."

Lexi curled her fingers around Austin's arm. "Well, I might have to go upstairs for the baseball cap, but I have the footlong right here."

Jericho burst out laughing and coughed in his hand to cover it up. Austin popped her playfully on the rear, and she jumped forward and squeaked.

"Now *that's* what I like to see," Naya purred. "Nothing sexier than a—"

"Footlong?" Jericho finished.

Naya cut him a steely glare. "I don't believe we've met?"

"We met once, but you were on your knees," he said with a chuckle.

Last year, Austin's wolf had killed Lexi's ex-boyfriend to save her life. Afterward, Jericho had swung by the apartment and found Naya on her hands and knees, cleaning blood and roses off the floor. She'd also called someone to dispose of the body.

"The name's Jericho."

Her eyes sparkled, and she brushed her hair away from her shoulder. "I know you. I've seen you gyrate those hips onstage before; you could give me a run for my money."

Jericho took a seat on the stairs and twisted one of his rings around his finger.

"Do you think I look okay?" Lexi whispered to Austin.

He slipped his hands around her ass and crushed his lips against hers. "Good enough that I might call off your movie," he murmured against her mouth, nibbling on her bottom lip.

Jericho saw a little tongue action and looked away.

"No, no!" Naya folded her arms and tapped her foot impatiently. "This is a planned event, and I won't let my girl be distracted by—"

"A footlong?" Jericho suggested.

Naya picked at her fingernail. "You're getting less funny."

"That's okay, honey. You're getting less sexy."

She feigned indifference and sighed. "Lexi, are we ready?"

"Yeah. Just about. My purse is upstairs. I'll be right back."

As she jogged past Jericho, Lexi did her hip shake thing, and Austin's pupils dilated. He swiped his tongue across his bottom lip and growled, "Be right back." Austin hiked up the stairs like a man on a mission, two steps at a time.

"I swear, if he makes us late again…" Naya sang to herself as she strolled toward one of the windows on the right. She held the lacy curtain between her fingers. "This is pretty."

"Lynn decorated the house."

Lexi's mom suffered frequent episodes of what Jericho liked to call *storegasms*. She had multiples too. Every time she walked into the home section of a store, she would load up her cart. When they bought the house last year, it came unfurnished, so there were a lot of rooms to fill. Lynn was the only one around there who had a professional touch.

The front door swung open, and Wheeler ambled in, kicking off his shoes and slamming the door behind him. He was shirtless and red in the face. The tattoos on his arms were a collage of images he wore like sleeves. Wheeler didn't believe in putting animals on his body; he'd once said it was bad luck for a Shifter to do that unless the image was of his own animal, so the only one he had was a wolf. His chest was free of tats, but he had one on his back.

Wheeler wiped his sweaty face and unbuckled his belt, throwing the leather strap on top of the pile of shoes.

"Where the hell have you been?" Jericho asked.

"Lynn wanted that space on the right side of the yard dug up for a garden. I got a real problem with the fact everyone took off and left me to hoe up that dirt by myself and lay down topsoil." A drop of sweat fell from his head onto the floor, and he slicked back his brown hair. "Manual labor is not my thing."

"I had my doubts you were capable of doing anything laborious with your hands," Naya said. She was leaning against the wall on her right shoulder, studying her nails. Jericho could feel the tension snapping between them like live wires.

Wheeler hadn't realized she was in the room, and he swiftly headed toward the staircase.

"And I thought *I* was the only pussy in the room," Naya murmured, shifting her gaze out the window.

Wheeler had one foot on the first step and froze. "Say that again?"

"Which part? Pussy? By your reaction, you must not hear that word too often."

Wow. Jericho felt like he had just walked into the Twilight Zone. The animosity between these two was out of control. He stood up and tried to block Wheeler's view.

"Go upstairs and shower, man. No need to stir up any trouble with one of Lexi's friends. Dig?"

Wheeler's jaw clenched, and his amber eyes looked like hard candy as they narrowed at Naya's indifferent expression. She had turned to face him and tucked her hands in the little pockets of her shorts.

Wheeler watched her as she brushed one leg against the other, her skin making a soft hiss where it rubbed together.

Naya smiled knowingly. "That was the only one you'll ever have," she said in a way that implied there was an inside story behind the remark. She strolled toward the front door and ran her slender fingers over the right side of her ass as she turned around. "Tell Lexi I'll be waiting in the car." She ended the last part with a little purr and slinked out the door.

Jericho faced his brother. "What's the deal with you two?"

Wheeler blinked and turned around, tromping his way up the stairs. Lexi passed by him on her way down, and her eyes widened when she caught sight of his expression.

"What's wrong with Wheeler?"

Jericho shrugged. "He had to dig a trench."

She laughed her silly laugh and slipped on her shoes. "Poor guy. My mom would be out there digging it if it weren't for him, and she's in no condition to do that kind of work. See you later!"

"Stay out of trouble," Jericho said, following her outside. He leaned on the railing and watched her jog to Naya's car. The sun sizzled against his skin, and Jericho couldn't shake that bad vibe he'd been feeling all day.

Something felt wrong, and all he could think about was Isabelle.

CHAPTER 10

A HARD SLAP TO MY ASS startled me awake, and I lunged forward, grunting out an unintelligible word. Hawk laughed, and I realized I'd somehow turned my body over on its side.

"Take these off, Hawk. I can't feel my arms," I begged. I dug my heels into the mattress, trying to push myself into a sitting position, but my valiant efforts were in vain. The cords had pulled against my wrists in my sleep, causing the skin to swell and bruise.

My vision was a little blurry, and while I was unable to rub my eyes, I could see Hawk swinging a pair of handcuffs in a circle around his index finger.

"We're going to do this nice and easy, Iz."

"Can I at least stretch out my muscles before you put them on?"

He tucked the cuffs in his back pocket. "Fine. But if you try to bolt on me, then I'm not going to play nice. I'm going to hog-tie you. If you shift, then I'll pen your wolf in a crate so you can't shift back."

A flutter of anger pricked at my skin as my wolf began to prowl. Hawk loosened the cord on my right hand, and my arm immediately dropped. I shouted out and moaned at every rotation of my shoulder. Dull tingles made me nauseous, and instead of lying there and waiting for a slow return of blood to my limb, I began squeezing my fist and bending my arm. Hawk crossed to the left side of the bed and did the same with the other cord.

"Can we talk like civilized adults now?" I hissed through my teeth as I sat up.

"Civilized?" Hawk grunted as he sat on the bed.

He'd shaved and had on a pair of ironed jeans and a fresh blue

Polo shirt. Meanwhile, I was tied to his bed and looked like I'd crawled out of a dungeon. It made me want to shave that mustache right off his face and rip every chest hair out, one by one.

"You can't keep me here like this."

"Yes I can, Izzy. You've been living in the human world too long."

"What does that have to do with anything? Shifters don't hold hostages!" I rubbed my shoulder and grimaced when I bent my legs and felt a twinge of pain. On top of that, my right cheek was swelling my eye shut.

"Really?" he said. "Some Shifters hold to the old ways."

"You mean slaves? Come on, Hawk. That's not the kind of thing you want to get mixed up in. People who do that only prove how weak they are."

"Do you think you're the first bitch I've tied up?" he said coolly.

Chills swept over my arms.

A lecherous smile tugged at his lips. "Yeah, that's right. If a bitch isn't behaving, then I *make* her behave. If she still wants to be disobedient, then there are consequences. I've given you plenty of chances to show me you're a good girl. It's not too late to tame that wolf of yours. All you have to do is show me a little respect and do as you're told."

My voice softened. "Where are the other girls?"

He watched me for a beat and then asked, "Do you want breakfast?"

I was gobsmacked. "What happened to the other girls, Hawk? Did you hurt them?"

He scratched the back of his head and lowered his eyes. "I only killed the first one. I didn't care for cleaning up that mess and won't do it again. The other two I sold off when they didn't want to behave. I didn't realize how much you could get on the black market for a good bitch."

But our relationship had seemed so normal! Maybe he was only trying to frighten me as some sort of payback. I couldn't imagine Hawk doing something like that. Not the man who would sit next to me cracking pistachio shells while watching golf on Sunday afternoons. This couldn't be happening.

He clapped his hands together so loud I jumped. "So! Cereal or waffles?"

"I need to use the bathroom."

Hawk grabbed one of the cords and looped it around my neck. My fingers gripped the end, and he tugged. "Come on, sweetie. I'll walk you."

Jerk!

I scooted off the bed, feeling the itch to verbally thrash him as he led me to the bathroom like a dog on a leash.

"Can I take a shower?"

"That's fine. But you come out when I say."

The bathroom was right outside the bedroom door to the left. The shower curtain had seashells and starfish. After he shut the door, I quietly opened the cabinets and discovered he'd emptied everything except two towels. Even the towel rack had been removed from the wall, leaving unpainted holes were the screws had once been. I examined the plastic curtain rod but didn't stand a chance against him wielding a flimsy pole. Breaking the mirror would defeat the purpose of a surprise attack and injure me in the process.

And no windows.

I stripped out of the nightgown and stepped into a stream of warm water. Tiny grains of dirt were embedded in one of my knees. As my skin soaked up the water, my joints began to throb all over again.

Why had I given him a second chance? Never for one second could I have imagined that Hawk possessed the black heart of a psychopath. Nothing I'd known about him would have ever led me to believe he was capable something so abominable. Then again, what did I really know about him? We'd only been living together for a month. I'd trusted my instincts, deciding the things I didn't like about him were tolerable. Like his tendency to call me his bitch. The way he used it was possessive, and we weren't in a pack.

I quelled the anger rising within and stepped out of the shower to dry off. I needed to keep a cool head. I had nowhere to run this time, and even worse, I couldn't fight. Shifting would only exacerbate the situation, and my wolf could end up crated.

The reflection staring back at me was that of a stranger. Isabelle Monroe looked weary and beaten. The skin beneath my eye had bruised, and as much as I wanted to shift to heal, I couldn't be sure my wolf would change back. Once in animal form, I had no control over my animal. I could feel her tempestuous pacing, so I fought against the urge. My palms were scraped from the sidewalk incident, but nothing looked as shocking as my wrists. They were horribly discolored and raw—some of the skin surrounding the deep cuts had swollen. I rinsed my hands in warm water and patted them with a dry towel. Was this what it felt like to be human? I swept my wet hair away from my face and wondered if I should trim it someday soon.

Someday.

Please let there be a someday. Hawk couldn't have selected a better girlfriend to kidnap, because I wouldn't be missed. I'm sure Howlers had waitresses walk out on them all the time. Hawk was a wealthy man. What was he doing at a Laundromat when we met? Why hadn't I ever found that suspicious? Maybe that's where he'd found all his previous victims, because women with money and family didn't go to places like that.

Then I remembered the stories I'd heard about girls who went missing. Their captors had held them for decades. Men were kept for different purposes, like cage fights. It was illegal among Shifters, but everyone knew it still went on in the dark corners of the underworld. Packs that followed barbaric customs, and some Shifters were collectors. I'd once heard a story about a leopard who had his own zoo of women. He kept them locked in cages he'd built on his property—each of them a different animal. One woman had been with him for over two hundred years.

"Stop scaring yourself," I whispered, turning off the water.

A fist pounded on the door. "Time's up, Izzy."

"Did you bring my jeans?" I yelled out in a normal voice. Maybe if I played this out like I didn't mind being here, he wouldn't go to the extreme measures of roping me up.

He pounded harder, and I slipped into the nightgown and swung open the door.

"No, I didn't pick up your fucking jeans. That would mean going back to the house and Delgado's men finding my ass."

"Why are you afraid of a bunch of humans?" I kept my voice calm, but stepped back when his face tightened. "You're not a wolf… are you?"

If his animal was something meek like a deer, then he'd have no choice but to fight my wolf in human form, because my wolf would kill his animal. Maybe Hawk had been bluffing about being a wolf and wanted to find a submissive bitch for his own perverse need to dominate an animal more powerful than himself. I suddenly felt a surge of superiority, one that told me my wolf might be able to take him down.

Until he grabbed my arm and spun me around, cuffing my wrists behind my back.

"Think I don't know what's going through your mind? You're transparent."

"You can't stay in hiding forever," I said. "What happens when you want to go gambling or out to grab some tacos?"

He tried to wrap the cord around my neck, and I ducked to the right.

"Come on, girl. Let's go for a walk."

Hell's bells, Evil Izzy was about to show her face and this was *not* the time. I bit down on my contempt for him and kept a level head. "I'll walk on my own."

"Then walk."

I compliantly moved past him into the bedroom and had difficulty getting on the bed. When I crawled on my knees, it tugged my nightgown and I fell on my right side.

"Maybe you can just cuff one arm to the bed. That way I can at least move around," I suggested. "Maybe if you show me you can be nice, I'll be nice back."

Without a word, he unlocked the cuffs and pulled my left wrist to the post. The rails on either side were wrought iron, and he cuffed me below the horizontal bar so I couldn't escape.

"Where are your parents?" I asked. "Do you have any family? I don't remember you talking about them."

"*Now* you're interested?"

I shrugged. "I have no secrets to hide. You're the one who's been evasive about his past. I've told you all about my family."

"Oh yeah. The family you bailed on. You seem to like running out on your problems. You've spent years running from city to city, constantly searching for something better."

"Movement is life. You should be flexible to the ebb and flow of change."

Hawk chuckled. "Izzy Monroe, always the philosophical one."

"It's what attracted you to me, remember? I gave you a little food for thought, comparing laundry with life."

"Your ass and red hair attracted me to you. I don't remember what the hell you said to me in the Laundromat. I just noticed your basket of sexy panties and knew you'd be hot in the sack. I was right," he said, inching closer to the bed. Then he got that lustful look in his eyes.

"I think I want waffles," I quickly said. "Do you have any of those frozen ones? Also, a glass of milk with a little chocolate sauce would be great. Low-fat milk. But if you don't have any of that, then maybe some grapefruit juice. But only the kind in those little cans; you know I don't like the cocktail juice. What kind of cereal do you have?"

He waved his hand and left the room. I always knew the one way to turn that man off was to start running my mouth. Hawk wasn't a big talker. Even in the bedroom, the only sounds he made were a few grunts. He'd never been an aggressive lover, but now that I was tied up, I began to notice a change in his personality. He leered more, seemingly aroused by his new dominant role.

I squeezed my fingers together and tried twisting my hand in different ways to pull it through the cuff. He had tightened the link, and with my swollen wrists, it was a waste of time. I sat on the edge of the bed and quietly opened the drawer on the bedside table.

He hadn't cleared everything out of the bedroom. I noticed a ballpoint pen and a few notepads. I tried squatting on the floor to look beneath the bed, but I couldn't. So I extended my left leg underneath and slowly ran it to the right, trying to feel around. My toe touched a cord, but I couldn't get a grip with the nightstand in my way. I also felt a lightweight box, but my mind focused on the cord. He might have a phone hidden under there, which would have made him a certifiable idiot, but that's what I was counting on.

I stood up and rubbed my good eye, looking around. A picture hung on the wall above the bed, secured by a nail. *Could I use a nail as a weapon?*

So I had a nail, a pen, a lamp, and notepads to take down a man who weighed twice as much as me. I also possibly had a phone, or at the very least, a cord.

"Hell's bells, Izzy. What have you gotten yourself into now?" I whispered.

Discouraged, I sat on the edge of the bed and thought about Jericho. After all these years, he could still merely breathe on my skin and make me squirm like a virgin. Sometimes a woman has experienced too much life to have any blush left in her cheeks, but the man who puts it there is someone not easily forgotten.

Second chances. There was that phrase again. I'd been so eager to give that opportunity to Hawk, but unwilling to give it to the one person who really meant something to me. I knew why. Hawk was safe and easy. If it didn't work out, no tears on my pillow. But Jericho still held a piece of my heart. The last piece. The one that wasn't broken. If I took the chance of letting him back in, only to be cast aside again, I'd have no heart left to give.

I also didn't know what a second chance even meant with Jericho. Friendship? Forgiveness? Or maybe just a romp in the sack and I'd be over all that sex appeal? Though I highly doubted it. Jericho had a reputation for being a greedy lover, and his women became as addicted to him as he had once been to drugs.

Then I laughed. Was I actually sitting handcuffed to my ex-lover's bed, contemplating sex with Jericho? What made me think he'd even care? That's when it dawned on me that I still loved him. Jericho was my best friend and the man who made me believe I could be more than just an ornament in life. He'd taught me how to be spontaneous and experience the world with passion. Because of him, I'd traveled and met so many fascinating people. Goals, money, or even finding a mate didn't matter. He'd taught me the most valuable lesson in life: how to live in the moment.

A tear trailed down my cheek and lingered on my chin. I still loved him. The man I knew before he slipped over to the dark side was everything I could have wanted in a friend, a lover, and maybe a mate. I'd suppressed those feelings because neither of us had wanted that kind of commitment; we'd been too young, and I had valued our friendship too much to risk losing it to something that could never be.

Those tender feelings began to shift to resentment. I couldn't let it go. I couldn't get the pain out of my head of seeing him with another woman. Decades later, it burned my heart like a raw wound. You're never more exposed than when your heart is in your hand. I'd returned to our hotel room to have a serious talk with Jericho. I wanted to help him get clean, and I wanted us to do it together. I naively thought I would be enough for him to turn his life around, but I never got that chance.

Our relationship had become self-destructive, and if I'd stayed with him, I would have eventually been lost to myself. I needed to break free and figure out who I was. I needed to be able to love someone and have that love returned to only me.

As the pain in my body became a tolerable ache, I began to question myself. Was it wrong to bail when things got tough? It had saved me from the dysfunctional home I grew up in—raised by apathetic parents and treated as an outcast by my siblings. My father had been a lone wolf for too many years before marriage and had hardened as a man. Maybe that would slowly happen to me, and God, what a frightening thought.

"I hate you, Hawk," I whispered. I felt more than cuffed to a bed; I felt bound to the miseries of my past and forced to confront them in the silence of the room.

My survival instincts were beginning to kick in. I wasn't a frail girl who shut down when things got tough. The bed didn't seem too heavy. If I moved it a little to the left, I just might be able to reach what was on the other end of that cord.

Evening rolled around and Jericho hadn't slept in more than twenty-four hours. He'd tried to crash that afternoon but couldn't shake the ominous feeling that kept him pacing most of the day. Lexi told him it was probably the change in weather, but Jericho didn't even want to smoke. He tucked a cigarette behind his ear and occasionally would bite on the filter, but the urge to light up had completely left him.

He snatched the keys to the blue truck and headed over to Howlers with Wheeler. He needed to swallow his pride and apologize to Isabelle for the night before. Denver had the night off and had gone to play laser tag with Reno and Austin. Ben, Wheeler's twin, hadn't been around much lately. He'd been away for sometimes up to a week, playing card tournaments to earn money.

Wheeler crossed his left leg over his knee and wiped at a scuff on his black boot with his thumb. "You wanna spit it out? You've had a bug up your ass all day."

Jericho pulled the truck into a parking space and it jumped the curb. He threw it in reverse, and they bounced in the cab as he backed out. "I don't know. I've never had this feeling this strong before. Bad vibes—like a premonition or something. You believe in that stuff?"

"Maybe all that shit you did in your past is finally catching up with you."

Jericho shut off the engine and twisted the giant ring on his left index finger. "I can't stop thinking about Isabelle."

"Sounds like an addiction."

"We've got this… connection."

"Maybe you need to sever that cord," Wheeler suggested, popping open his door.

As they walked toward the building, Jericho glanced at Isabelle's blue car and wondered if she knew her taillight was busted.

The jukebox played an old Nirvana tune on low volume, and most of the customers were eating. Jericho and Wheeler slid up to the bar and greeted Frank, an older bartender who usually worked the afternoon shift.

"Slow night?" Jericho asked conversationally.

Frank fixed their usual drinks and set a beer in front of Jericho. "We don't have any specials running tonight."

Wheeler sipped on his hard liquor and watched a blonde at the end of the bar who had her blue eyes all over him.

Jericho glanced around the room. "Where's Rosie?"

Frank wiped down the bar and threw the rag over his shoulder. He was an older Shifter with a strip of silver hair on each side of his head. "She took the night off. We've only got two girls on the floor tonight."

That seemed unusual. "Why only two?"

"That redhead didn't show up. I guess she doesn't want this job if she's willing to flake out so soon. Jake isn't going to go easy on her; he expects his girls to call in when they're going to take the night off."

"She didn't call?" Jericho thought about her car out front, and alarm raced up his spine. "Do you have her number?"

"Nope." Frank walked over to the blonde and handed her a laminated menu.

This was all wrong.

"Looks like your girl split again," Wheeler murmured. "Drink your beer. You don't even know her anymore."

The room began to spin, and Jericho's heart pounded against his chest. He stood up and stared vacantly at the door. Moments after she stormed off the night before, that douche bag had turned chicken and refused to fight Jericho. He must have given her a lift, because when Isabelle got mad, she walked. Maybe they just went home and were busy having makeup sex, but Jericho knew Isabelle. She loved working and would never disrespect her boss.

"Frank!" Jericho leaned over the bar as Frank ambled over. "Do you know a guy named Hawk? Has a thick mustache, kind of big, Isabelle's boyfriend?"

"No. The girls don't bring in their men; it disappoints the customers."

Jericho stalked toward the back hall where Jake's office was. He knocked on the door and then opened it. Jake wasn't in the room, so Jericho knelt down in front of a filing cabinet and began to sift through the papers.

"What the hell are you doing?" Wheeler chided from the open door. "This isn't just going to get you fired; it's going to get you in legal trouble."

Jericho found her file and folded the papers, stuffing them into his pants beneath his shirt. "Are you in my pack?" He slammed the file drawer and confronted Wheeler. "If you're my brother, then you have my back. Isabelle's in trouble, and either you can help me find her, or you can nurse that addiction waiting for you on a paper napkin. We all have to fight addiction, but she's more than a craving. I don't care what Denver told you, I'm not turning my back on this girl when I feel in my gut something's wrong." He held a fist against his stomach. "My wolf knows it and I know it. Even if we didn't have all that history, it still isn't right to turn my back on a woman in trouble."

"Maybe you need to call in Reno and have someone a little more badass than you take over."

Jericho stared Wheeler down with cutthroat eyes. "If that asshole laid one finger on Isabelle, you're going to see an *epic* display of badassery."

He shouldered past Wheeler and shoved his hand against the front door, flinging it open. A guy stepped out of Jericho's path when he saw the vicious look in his eyes. Jericho hopped in the truck and slammed the door. He pulled the folder out and flipped on the interior light, heart racing like a bullet train.

The passenger door opened and the truck bounced as Wheeler got in. "Where are we going?"

CHAPTER 11

AFTER WATCHING ME EAT A bowl of cereal, Hawk left me alone in the bedroom for hours. He said if I behaved, he'd bring in a television. The last thing I wanted to do while handcuffed to a bed was watch *Wheel of Fortune*. I couldn't be sure if he'd left the house, so I'd spent hours strategizing an escape and decided that shoving a nail into his eye socket would only piss him off and get both of my arms tied up again. Hawk had the key to my handcuffs, and even if I tried to fight him, I needed the key to escape. Did he carry it in his pocket? I had to be smart about this.

Later, he reappeared with an overcooked pork chop and soggy green beans from a can. I drank the soda but left the food alone. I thought about what that alpha had said to me at Howlers about going into heat. The precursory tingles were already happening sporadically. Soon it would turn into waves of heat, filling me with an uncontrollable desire to mate.

That was unacceptable in my current situation.

I had to get out.

Without a clock or window in the room, I had no concept of time, and the hours melted away.

Hawk appeared and leaned against the doorjamb. "I'm going back to the house to pick up a few things. Delgado's men don't seem to watch the house at this time of night. Is there anything special you want me to grab while I'm there?"

A gun?

"My underwear, some clothes, my toothbrush, my soap because I don't like using your bar of soap, and can you bring the snacks we keep in the pantry on the third shelf? I have some special protein bars in there. And while I'm thinking about it, I need you to grab the pink box of tampons below the sink and a few razors, unless you want me looking like Sasquatch. There's an electric razor in the bottom right drawer if you don't trust me with sharp objects," I said sarcastically.

Irritation bled on his face.

I spoke in a dispassionate voice, as if we were having an ordinary conversation and I wasn't shackled to a bed. That was my plan. If I acted like a victim, he would feel empowered and begin to treat me like one. I also wanted Hawk to take longer so I could escape.

I crossed my ankles and readjusted the pillow behind my back. Hawk ran his finger across his dark mustache and lowered his voice. "Don't make any noise. If I come back and one thing in this room is out of place, I'm going to punish you."

He shut the door and I almost wanted to laugh. Half my brain was thinking this was still a joke. The other half I blocked out because I couldn't deal with it. After he left, I waited several minutes before I mustered the courage to stand up.

With my left hand cuffed against the post, it meant I had to move the heavy bed with my back to it. At first, the bed wouldn't move. But I began bumping my butt against the mattress and eventually it budged. I kept going until I'd moved it about a foot from the nightstand. I fell to my knees and swept my left leg beneath the bed again.

When my big toe touched the cord, I quickly pulled it with my heel. It didn't come all the way out, but when I stretched my arm beneath the bed, my fingertips recognized the feel of an old phone. I peered behind the bed, but didn't see a jack.

"Where are you?" I whispered. "Please don't be behind the dresser."

I wiped the dust off the phone and wondered if Hawk knew it was under there. When I pulled the nightstand away from the wall, I found the jack.

"Bingo!" I said excitedly.

I reached over and plugged it in, praying for a dial tone.

It was an old phone without a display panel. It came with a cradle, so I held down the hook and let go. My heart soared when

I heard a dial tone. My fingers trembled; I had to think about this carefully. The Breed highly discouraged calling human law enforcement because of the records they kept. Despite my current situation, I could wind up in more trouble if they filed a report. Unfortunately, Shifters didn't have a 911 equivalent.

After deliberating, I called Howlers.

"You've reached Howlers. This is Frank. How can I help you?"

"Frank! It's Izzy."

"You're calling in *now*? Jake's going to fire your—"

"Frank, I'm in trouble. Is anyone there?"

"No, Rosie's off and we're down to two girls. Jake's on vacation for the week."

Hell's bells. My rescue was unraveling into an epic fail. "What time is it?"

"You're kidding, right?"

"Please, Frank."

"Just past eight."

"Is Jericho there?"

There was a slight pause. "He was here earlier but took off with his brother."

"Do you have his number? Or Denver's number?" I faced the wall with the phone against my right ear.

"Why don't you leave me your digits and if he shows up, I'll have him call you? Look, it's picking up in here and—"

"Don't hang up! Just give me his number; this is an emergency."

"All right."

After he recited the number, I burned it into my brain and dialed with a shaky hand. "Please pick up."

"Denver. Who's this?"

"It's Izzy. Please don't hang up. I'm in trouble, and I need help."

He chuckled. "That sounds about right. What the train wreck is going on?"

"My ex knocked me out and kidnapped me. I'm handcuffed to a bed."

The line fell silent and his voice lowered an octave. "Say again?"

"Should I call the police? I don't even know where I am. What do I do?" I said frantically.

"Is this a joke?"

My heart beat at a hummingbird's pace. Hawk could come bursting through the door at any moment. "Denver, I know you hate me, and that's fine. But I don't deserve to be raped and killed over a grudge. Where's Jericho? He knows what Hawk looks like. I can tell you where he lives." I rattled off the address to his other house and described his car.

"You're saying that he cuffed you to a bed?"

I began shaking the more I said it out loud—the reality was sinking in like a waking nightmare. "Yes, that's exactly what I'm saying. He knocked me out and when I woke up, my hands were tied up with cords. He must have injected me with something to keep me knocked out for so long. Now I'm just cuffed, and I found a phone under the bed. He said if he comes back and anything's moved, he'll punish me. Look, I don't know if he's serious, or if he's just trying to get back at me for leaving him. This isn't the man I've been living with. I don't know who this guy is, but I'm freaking out. I don't know what to do."

"Calm down, calm down. Let me think. No, Austin, it's Izzy."

"Where are you?"

"Laser tag."

I blinked. "Oh. I heard that's fun."

"True that. Hold on."

He muttered something to Austin while I pulled the bed back in place. The phone fell from my ear and swung from the cord over the edge of the bed. I grabbed it and put it back to my ear.

"Izzy? Izzy?"

"I'm here."

"Describe your surroundings."

I glanced around. "I'm in a room with no windows, and I'm not familiar with the house. We could be anywhere. He told me not to scream, so maybe we're still in the city."

It sounded like he was relaying everything I said to Austin and whoever else was with him. I sneezed from the dust and tried to calm myself with a few deep breaths.

"If we give you a number, can you call it in about an hour?"

"What? He might be back by then!"

"Calm down, Izzy. We'll keep the number open so when you call, we'll be able to trace where you are. If he comes back, then wait until it's safe. You don't even have to talk to us; just hide the phone, turn off the ringer, and let us handle the rest. Don't put yourself in any danger. Is the phone hidden?"

"I was going to put it back under the bed."

"Good. Pull the cord out of the phone so it doesn't ring. Keep it close. Do you want to stay on the line for a while?"

"And talk about what? You hate me."

"I don't hate you, Izzy. I think you're a coldhearted bitch, but hate is a strong word. I used to hate you, but I'm over that. Did you shift at all?"

"No. He threatened to lock me in a crate. It's not worth the risk. If I shift, my wolf isn't going to let me shift back. I can feel her in there, and she's pissed."

He hissed through his teeth. "Bastard."

"I want to talk to Jericho."

"I don't know where he is. Austin's trying to call him but not getting an answer…. Wheeler's not answering either?" he asked someone in the background.

"Denver, I'm going to hang up. I need to put the room back together. Do you promise to keep the line open? I may only get one shot at calling."

"Cross my heart."

I snorted. "Good to know you have one."

"Shut it. Do you think you can remember this number?"

What choice did I have? If I could remember a table of orders, I was confident memorizing a phone number would be a piece of cake. Especially if I made up a song about it.

Denver recited the number five times until I felt like I had it down. We talked for another minute, and he asked a few questions about what Hawk did for a living and where he hung out. Then he quizzed me on the phone number and when I got it right, we ended the call.

I carefully pulled the bed to its original position and hid the phone underneath. After crawling between the sheets, a drop of sweat slid across my forehead. Making that call was the first time I'd allowed myself to think about what might happen if no one came for me.

The satin nightgown didn't help my situation. Hawk had closed the vents in the room and it left the air stale and warm. Despite my discomfort, I wanted to stay covered up when Hawk returned. The probability of going into heat soon left me in a quandary. Without knowing Hawk's animal, I had no idea if he'd react to it at all, but *I* sure would. I just hoped this emotional situation didn't trigger it to start early. If that alpha wolf was right in his prediction, I had just over four weeks left.

Once I glanced around for the millionth time to be sure everything was back in place, I began singing the phone number in my head to the tune of "Another Brick in the Wall." It made me smile when I remembered how Jericho had worked on one of their tours. We'd had some amazing nights under the stars, sharing deep thoughts about life after the show ended. I bought the concert shirt on the first leg of the tour and slept in it every night until Jericho complained he was tired of seeing me in it.

I missed that shirt. I'd seen it for sale online a few times, but it wasn't *my* shirt. Not the one with all the memories and music soaked into the fibers of summer nights with Jericho's arm around me.

Here I was in a crisis, and I couldn't stop thinking of Jericho. I groaned against the pillow.

I told myself I'd just close my eyes for a minute, but within moments, I'd fallen asleep humming the song.

⁂

Jericho burned the tires on his truck as he sped to the address listed on Isabelle's application. The prestigious neighborhood made him leery of what line of business her boyfriend was involved in. Jericho didn't think it was legit if he'd gone out of his way to buy a house outside the Breed community, as if he were hiding from someone.

"Park up the street," Wheeler said. "He knows what you look like. We need to take a stroll up the back way and look inconspicuous."

"Yeah, we blend."

"Let's just be chill and scope it out."

Jericho cut off the lights and parked behind an RV. "Maybe you should wait in the truck as the lookout."

"A lookout?" Wheeler angrily popped his door open. "That all you think I can do is sit around and play peepers? I'm your brother. Where you go, I go. So you can drop the solo shit, because we're doing this together. 'Preciate ya." He slammed the door and headed between two houses.

"Goddammit," Jericho murmured, jogging behind him.

"Look how these fuckers live," Wheeler said quietly as they passed a house with a four-car garage. "We have a big house for a growing pack. These assholes have twenty rooms for two idiots and a poodle."

"I used to break into homes like these with Izzy. We'd target a house when the owners were out of town and lounge in their pool during the summer."

"No shit?"

The neighborhood didn't have alleys, so they walked up the street behind Hawk's. A dog barked from one of the backyards, and Jericho slowed his pace. Luckily the fences weren't connected between houses and there was enough space between each home to see the street on the other side. "I think we're close. Let's cut through."

They scoped their surroundings to make sure no humans were watching and jogged between two houses. A motion-sensor light switched on, and they hauled ass. As they reached the homes on Hawk's street, they slowed down and skulked in the shadows.

"His address is fourteen twenty-four," Jericho murmured.

"This is it then." Wheeler tapped his finger against the brick house to his right. "The one across the street is the next odd number.

You want a boost into the backyard, or should we break out a window?"

Jericho locked his fingers behind his head, deep in thought. "The neighbors will call the cops if they see us climbing through a window. The fence around back will give us privacy. My goal is to get in that house and make sure Isabelle's okay. If he has alarms, then so-fucking-what."

"That's doubtful," Wheeler said with a grumble. "He might be hiding his ass in the human district, but I doubt he wants a security system to have a bunch of human police showing up at his house."

Jericho's eyes scanned all around. "I just hope he has cheap windows. I didn't bring my sledgehammer," he said, tapping his shoe against the fence.

"What if he's in there? He's going to hear you knock out the window."

"Then go up front and ring the doorbell. Create a diversion before I knock him senseless."

Wheeler stroked the hair on his chin. "Sounds like a plan."

When Wheeler hoisted him over the fence, Jericho sailed like a bird and then slammed down on a hard slab of concrete.

"Fuckwad!" Jericho gritted through his teeth. He was expecting grass, or at the very least, a bush. Hawk had poured cement in his entire backyard with only a covered hot tub and a few tables near the back door.

Jericho rubbed his shoulder and scoped out the property. There weren't any signs of security cameras or sensor lights, and Tweety didn't have drapes on his back windows. Jericho could see all the way inside the house, so he stood against the wall and peered in. The doorbell chimed, but no sign of movement.

Jericho took one of the thin cushions off the chair and held it against the glass door below the knob. He kicked it once as hard as he could—shattering the glass—but the sound was muffled by the cushion. After pulling a loose shard away to prevent it from falling, he reached in to unlock the door.

Glass sliced into his arm. His fingers found the lock, and he twisted it to the left, slowly opening the door. Jericho kept his eyes alert and his fists clenched. His restless wolf paced, snarling and thirsty for a hunt.

Hawk lived in a one-story house with a grand-fucking-piano and a fireplace. Tweety's fingers were too fat for playing the piano, and Isabelle didn't have a musical bone in her body. As he looked around at the expensive paintings and sculptures, Jericho came to the conclusion that Hawk was a collector.

He wrinkled his nose at the décor. It looked like a box of SweeTarts had exploded in there.

Jericho whirled around when glass crunched and the door shut behind him.

"Am I late to the party?" Wheeler twirled a small flashlight in his hand.

"Get your ass over here and watch my back."

Wheeler shone the light in Jericho's face. "It's not your best side, but I'll give it a whirl."

Wheeler stalked forward like a dark avenger, and they headed down one of the hallways to the right. Two doors were open and three were closed. All the rooms they looked in were empty, including a bathroom and closet. One door was locked and they passed it by. At the end of the hall, Jericho wandered into a bedroom with the same ugly décor. He lifted a delicate bottle of perfume from the dresser and held the sweet floral fragrance to his nose.

Isabelle.

The metallic taste of blood settled on his tongue from biting his lip.

"The other side of the house is clear," Wheeler said from the doorway. "When you're done sniffing her panties, why don't you come watch me kick down the locked door in the hall."

Jericho snorted and followed behind him. "This I need to see."

Wheeler stood with his back against the wall. In one swift motion, he kicked the door, which resulted in a shattering sound.

The second time, Jericho stood beside him. "On three we'll both go. One, two…"

Before he hit three, they kicked in the door and busted the frame. It swung open and hit the wall before closing again. Jericho pushed it open and they looked inside, Wheeler shining the flashlight around the room.

"What the hell is *this*?" Wheeler said, stepping in the center of the room, his voice reverberating off the walls. His shoes scratched on the gritty concrete as he turned in a slow circle, shining his flashlight across the floor.

On the cement floor were two metal pins with chains attached. It looked like something you might see in a zoo. Wheeler kicked the animal crate on the right, and Jericho shuddered when he saw a broken fingernail by the door.

Isabelle had never seen this room. She couldn't have known the vile acts Hawk had committed. Jericho became nauseous when he bent over to get a closer look at the fingernail. Isabelle's were painted green the last he remembered, and this one was red.

Wheeler squatted down and held the chain between his fingers. "What do you think he was doing?"

The room closed in and Jericho found it difficult to breathe. "Maybe just keeping them for his twisted perversions."

The chain clattered on the floor as Wheeler stood up. "Maybe he was selling them on the black market. That would explain why he's hiding on the human side of town."

"Fuck you," Jericho whispered at the insinuation that she could be gone for good.

Wheeler folded his arms and lowered his chin. "Everyone knows it still goes on, although they prefer selling young girls and not someone as seasoned as her. Packs living outside the Council's reach are always looking for submissive bitches. They can't find any locally without getting caught, so they fork over a big wad of money and—"

"So help me, if you don't shut up, I'm going to staple your lips together and chain you to the floor."

Wheeler scratched his chin and turned around. "Nothing I haven't heard before."

They were all aware of rogue packs run by the same men who had lived during the time when no Breed laws existed. They claimed land outside civilized society and made up their own pack rules, sometimes attacking organized packs and claiming their land. They were men who believed beating a woman into submission was the Shifter way. Barbaric men who did the unthinkable to women in order to establish rank among their pack.

Terror consumed Jericho as he looked at the ugly secret within the exterior shell of an extravagant home, knowing someone could be holding Isabelle captive in this dark underworld.

Wheeler stroked the hair on his chin. "We need to report this. Not just to Austin; this is bigger and the local Councilmen need to know what's going on and put a stop to it."

A door slammed in the other room and a light flipped on, illuminating the hall. Jericho spun on his heel and faced the door with all senses alert.

"Whoever the fuck is in my house is going to get a bullet in the head," Hawk shouted in a gravelly voice.

Wheeler appeared on Jericho's right and tossed the flashlight noisily on the concrete floor. "And boom goes the dynamite."

CHAPTER 12

I AWOKE TO THE USUAL SLAP on my ass. I thrust out my legs and viciously kicked as Hawk laughed haughtily.

How long had I been I asleep?

"Brought you a little present, honeybunch."

My curiosity was piqued when I heard unfamiliar noises coming from the front of the room. I peered over my shoulder and noticed Hawk had placed a table at the foot of the bed and was hooking up a television.

"I don't want to watch TV," I said, scooting up and rubbing my face.

"Oh, you'll want to see this," he said, connecting the cables in the back. Cables that ran out the door instead of plugging into the wall. "I have a special show I want you to watch."

"What time is it?"

He stood up and pressed a button on the remote. "Showtime."

The screen switched on, and a black-and-white image appeared.

"What is that?" I asked, staring at an empty room.

Hawk set the remote on the table and tucked the cables out of sight. "When I stopped by the house to pick up a few things, I ran into your boyfriend. You know—the guy with his dick swinging in your face."

My heart plummeted and my veins filled with ice. I looked closer at the screen and only saw a crate.

Oh God.

"Hawk, what did you do?"

"That asshole broke into my house. I put a cap in the guy who was with him, and your boyfriend shifted. Good thing I know a thing or two about how to get a wolf in a crate. I had plenty of practice with you."

"You what?" I gasped, my eyes widening. All this time I thought he'd kept my wolf in the backyard. Oh God, Hawk might have shot one of Jericho's brothers. Every thought revolted at the idea I'd been intimate with a man capable of such horrific crimes as these.

"That's right, Izzy. Your wolf is a mean little bitch, but once you learn how to handle a rope, it's easy to get them under control."

"Why? Why would you do that?"

"I had to make sure I could transport you if things didn't work out between us. You were easier to handle than the other girls who tried to leave. You're too forgiving, Izzy. That's your weakness."

I held my forehead in disbelief. "What are you going to do with Jericho?"

"I'm going to have fun, and you're going to watch. I can't believe you still hold a candle for a worthless bag of shit like him. Do you think you matter to a guy like that?" Hawk laughed sadistically and leaned on the television. "I can spot a user a mile away."

A wolf emerged from the crate, staggering about the room and groggily shaking his head. It was Jericho's wolf. I recognized his markings. *Oh my God, this wasn't happening.*

"Hawk, what are you going to do?"

"Nothing. The question is: what's he going to do to himself? There are enough drugs in that room to kill a whale. I want to see how long it takes before he buckles and gives in to his weakness. Sitting alone in a room for a long time makes a man reflect on his life. It's what happens when you're incarcerated. I was locked up in a human jail once. I had someone tracking me down, and it was the safest place I could lay low. Wouldn't do it again; it almost killed me."

"Please, Hawk," I begged. "Please let him go. Jericho won't be trouble, and he has nothing to do with us."

"Sorry, Iz. A man swings a dick in my bitch's face and he pays the penalty."

My cheeks grew wet with tears, and I looked away. "Turn it off."

"It's late and I'm tired. Let me know if you want me to heat up any popcorn," he said with a dark chuckle, closing the door behind him.

When I braved looking at the screen, the wolf was no longer there. Jericho paced naked around the room with his mouth moving, but I heard no sound. The door looked impenetrable, and on the floor beside the wall was a towel with some objects neatly laid out on top. Jericho knelt down with his back to the camera, looking at the items. Then he whirled around with feral eyes, shouting silent profanities at the camera.

I turned away from witnessing the cruelest torture imaginable. I'd heard stories about former addicts who overdosed because the first time they went back, they used the same amount of drugs they'd used at their peak. They forgot their body didn't have a tolerance to that level anymore. Shifters healed, but we weren't immortal.

Bile rose in my throat, and I swung my legs off the bed and stared at the lamp. I tried to remember the number Denver had given me, but I couldn't think straight. I kept wondering if the cables coming out of the TV led to Jericho's room or a computer. Was he in this house or another one? I strained to listen but heard nothing. Maybe Jericho's screams were behind soundproof walls or in a basement. Hawk seemed concerned that mine could be heard. Did I dare risk it?

I quietly stood up and concentrated on remembering the phone number.

The door suddenly swung open. "Here, I brought your clothes." Something hit the bed as I stood with my back to him. "What are you doing, Izzy?"

I stared at the solid base on the lamp.

"Izzy?" he said cautiously, his voice drawing closer from behind.

I gripped the base of the lamp and swung it around with my right arm. The cord caused it to jerk, but it smashed against Hawk's right temple.

Evil Izzy came out—enraged and eager to fight. I struck him several times with the lamp, getting him good on the forearm before he slapped me hard. Pain didn't exist. That word had been erased from my dictionary when I glanced at the television and saw Jericho pacing like a caged animal.

Hawk punched me in the gut, and I crumpled to the floor. The force of the fall caused the handcuff to bite into my already mangled wrist. Hawk shoved the table next to the dresser and out of reach.

"No more weapons for you, Miss… What the fuck is *this*?" he exclaimed, lifting the telephone cord.

He ripped it out from beneath the bed and then from the wall. "You little cunt!"

Then he beat me on my back with the cradle.

⸻

Days had elapsed, maybe a week. Time had eloped with the outside world and abandoned me to solitude. Hawk had reduced my meals to once a day after I kicked him in the groin.

Twice.

He didn't restrict me from bathroom visits, but showers were out of the question. My knees finally scabbed over, my wrists were a gruesome sight, and I no longer looked like Isabelle Monroe. Hawk had made me into an undesirable woman. My hair was unwashed and tangled, my face pale and bruised, my stomach flattening more than I would have liked. But what I looked like on the outside was not a reflection of the strength that burned within—a fire I kept tempered until the time was right. Shifters found courage to be more admirable than physical beauty, and that's one trait I had in the bag.

My back was still sore from when he'd hit me with the phone. Hawk hadn't raged since that night and remained his usual, poised self. Maybe the most disturbing aspect about it was how detached he'd become.

I had no choice but to cage my wolf. A skilled Shifter could switch to their animal form and slip out of things like jewelry and clothes, but it wasn't uncommon to get tangled up in them. Shackles, chains, ropes, and handcuffs—these were uncertainties for me, and because they restricted my movement, I didn't want to take the chance. If I didn't do it right, I could end up breaking her legs, and I was not a woman easily broken.

I wanted to be that sassy little redhead at the bar who made the toughest of men bashful when I handed them a beer with a beguiling wink. I wanted to sit on a beach at night and bury my feet in the cool sand, listening to angry waves crashing against the shore. I wanted to travel to South America and taste the flavorful dishes I'd heard about from acquaintances. I wanted to find a mate someday who would be able to love me, even after all this.

Maybe he'd be the kind of man who'd never give up on me. I'd never been more certain of wanting children as I was during my captivity. The mess of my own childhood became irrelevant; I just wanted to hold a baby in my arms so I could always protect and love him.

I wanted to live.

So my behavior became robotic, and it kept Hawk manageable. He subjected me to Jericho's video, leaving it on day and night. On one occasion, Hawk had snuck into the room and left behind a pail of water and a clean towel. Jericho was slow on his reflexes and didn't have time to react before the door swung shut. He might have seemed laid-back to most people, but Jericho possessed an intelligent, cunning mind. He had survival skills. He didn't waste the water, but dipped half the towel in there and used it to wash off while saving the rest for drinking.

I looked up at the television and watched him wrapping the towel around his waist. He didn't know I was on the other end watching him, because every so often, he'd hold his middle finger up to the lens.

It made me laugh every time.

I even talked to him. Whenever he'd settle down, I'd pretend we were sitting next to each other, bantering about old times. I began forming a relationship with a ghost on the screen.

Hawk opened the door and surprised me with a steak. "Last meal," he said. "Looks like I found a buyer. Sorry things didn't work out between us, Iz. But you can't say I didn't give you a chance. I'm making a run to the store for some protein shakes, and you're going to shift and heal up some of those marks. I don't think the buyer will care much, but I'd rather not hand over a mess or else he might change his mind on the price. I want to fatten you up, so eat every bite before you shift."

The door slammed, and my mouth watered looking at the steak. But what really caught my attention was his stupidity gleaming back at me.

Hawk had finally slipped up and made a fatal mistake: he left me a weapon.

I ate every bite of that overcooked steak and baked potato to stave off my hunger and give me strength. Then I covered the plate and fork with the napkin and concealed my steak knife under the pillow.

"Hawk?" I yelled his name a little louder a second time. He liked to play mind games, so I couldn't be sure if he'd really gone to the store.

I screamed his name at the top of my lungs and gasped when I saw Jericho stand up. He cautiously approached the door and pressed his ear against it.

"Did you just hear me?" I whispered.

My heart beat wildly against my chest with a fever of hope. I screamed so loud that my voice cut off and I began coughing. This time he pounded on the door with his fists. I leapt to my feet and strained to listen, but only heard the TV in the next room.

Jericho fell to his knees, covering his head with his arms, his fingers splayed. It was the look of despair, and it broke my heart.

"No, no," I whispered. "Please, no. I have the knife, Jericho. You have to wait for me. I'm going to come get you—I promise."

I pulled the knife from beneath my pillow and cut a hole in my nightgown, ripping away the bottom so it hung above my knees. I didn't want anything interfering with crawling, running, or kicking.

Next, I removed the picture from the wall and pulled the hard wire away from the back, stuffing it beneath my pillow. The stubborn nail was stuck in a plank of wood behind the wall, so I tossed the picture on the far side of the bed and examined the room. Hawk had moved the end table so the lamp and pen were no longer within reach.

I gripped the iron bars on the bed and pulled, hoping to break something.

At that point, I'd done everything I could do. I vowed I'd never complain again about breaking in new shoes. I was also going to let my wolf roll in the dirt all she wanted, and maybe treat myself to a few dozen donuts when I got out of here.

Hell's bells, I was going to dunk those bad boys in hot cocoa to my heart's content. Calories shmalories.

I didn't know how long Jericho could hang on, but I had to get him out of that room. He was the one who needed saving. Jericho had found his salvation through family and music. He'd finally given up the demons he'd battled, and sure, maybe he still slept around, but he was miles more of a man than he'd been before. I wished I'd told him that. I was proud of the Shifter he had become.

Except now, everything he'd worked hard for was threatened by a blanket of drugs inside a pressure cooker. Hawk wouldn't be gone for long, so I prepared to fight. I couldn't allow him to move me out of the house, or I wouldn't be able to free Jericho. This was my last chance.

Nothing could have prepared me for what I saw next.

When I glanced up at the screen, Jericho was lying on his back with something tied around his arm and a needle in his hand.

Convulsing.

I screamed for him. Screamed his name so loud that it ruptured time and space. I somehow managed to stand on my feet and pull the bed a few inches away from the wall.

No, no, no were the only words pouring out of my mouth.

When Hawk burst into the room with a plastic bag in his hand, my eyes went wild with rage.

He moved toward me like a cyclone. I pulled out the knife and stabbed him in the chest. He stumbled backward, clutching the black handle, eyes wide with surprise. I grabbed the wire and thrashed him with it.

"You killed him! How could you kill that beautiful man!"

Red slashes appeared on his skin from where I mercilessly struck him. He gripped his hand around the handle of the knife and pulled it from his chest, holding his hand to the wound. Hawk stepped back and glanced at the television. A sadistic smile stretched across his face as he savored his victory and my anguish.

"Now you see, Izzy. Our weaknesses define who we are. That's what makes selling drugs to these addicts so damn easy. Did you really think he'd be able to abstain from the only thing that matters to him? Eventually they all give in, and they'll pay whatever it takes for just one more trip. I'm glad you enjoyed your meal. I put something extra in there to make you go nighty-night."

I screamed like a feral animal, still clawing the air, blinded by my hot tears. I finally collapsed on the floor, pulling at the cuffs so forcefully that blood trickled from my wrist.

"I'll be back, Iz. Once I shift and you're knocked out, we're going to have a real good time before I hand you over to my buyer," he promised, shutting the door behind him.

CHAPTER 13

J ERICHO STARED VACANTLY AT THE ceiling, saliva running down his cheek. Isabelle infiltrated his thoughts. He turned his head to the side, heart racing, the band still tied around his bicep and pinching his skin. The concrete floor felt like a sheet of ice against his back in the stuffy room.

Jericho could survive without food longer than most people. He had rationed the water and drank as much as he could to stay hydrated and alert.

He thought about the shrill scream that had almost stopped his heart. The second time, he knew without a doubt it was Isabelle. She was somewhere in this house, and he didn't want to imagine the kind of torture that animal was inflicting upon her.

Jericho wanted to crush Hawk's bones and incinerate his remains. He thought about the drugs in the corner and how that was his ticket out of here. If that sicko wanted to watch Jericho self-destruct on camera, then it was time to put an end to his twisted game.

So he faked his overdose.

If Hawk was watching, he'd eventually come into the room to dispose of Jericho's body. That was the plan, so Jericho stayed absolutely still.

Not an easy feat when he heard another scream in the distance that sounded animalistic and nothing like the last. His heart pounded so fiercely he could scarcely think.

Slow breaths.

Nice and easy.

Relax.

The door unlocked, and a sheet of plastic dragged across the floor.

"Knew it wouldn't take long for you to drop like a fly," Hawk murmured. "Damn shame I missed watching it live, but I'll catch the rerun." He chuckled darkly and let out a grunt.

Jericho waited patiently like a skilled predator waiting for his prey to move within striking distance. Hawk approached from behind and hooked his arms beneath Jericho's, dragging him in front of the door. It was easy for Jericho to fake an overdose, because he'd experienced the real thing.

Hawk crawled on his right, swinging a large bag around. When the timing was right, Jericho raised a needle he'd been concealing in his right hand and drove it into Hawk's jugular, pushing the plunger all the way in. Jericho gripped him by the hair and threw him off-balance.

"How's that feel, *boy*?" He kicked the sonofabitch in the gut and noticed blood oozing out of a partially healed wound on his chest. As much as he wanted to go animal on him, Jericho needed to find Isabelle.

He shut Hawk in the room and locked the door. Maybe punishment would be served if he was left there to rot—to decide if he wanted to go crazy from starvation or end it all with another fix.

The towel around his waist dropped to the floor as he walked down the hall with a purposeful stride. The bleak hallway looked like a prison, as if Hawk had customized the basement and built rooms. When he reached a set of wooden stairs, he made his ascent. Jericho opened the door, and the sweet bliss of central air cooled his skin. The shutters on the kitchen windows were thick slats of wood that blocked out the light.

Except it wasn't light outside.

"Isabelle?"

Plush brown carpet whispered beneath his feet as he walked through the living room. He paused behind a striped couch that faced a large television. An old war movie played, and the sounds of explosions filled the room. An object tickled the bottom of his foot, and when he stepped back, he saw a large feather. Just as he'd thought.

As he approached a dark hallway, light shone from beneath a closed door at the end of the hall. He turned the knob and swung open the door, shocked at the horrific scene before him.

Jericho crossed the wooden floor and stepped in a puddle of blood. Next to his bare foot was a steak knife stained crimson and a piece of wire. The sheets on the bed were tangled. Isabelle sat on the floor, facing the bed with her left hand extended and cuffed to the rail. Blood trailed down her arm from where she had tried to escape. What a brave little wolf. Her white gown had been ripped in half, and sweet Jesus, a TV sat at the foot of the bed. Hawk had forced her to watch him—she must have seen him overdose.

"Isabelle!"

He rushed forward and carefully looked her over. He didn't see any stab wounds, thank Christ. She must have attacked Hawk and put up a hell of a fight.

"Oh, baby." He brushed her lovely red hair away from her face, revealing a bruise on her cheek.

Rage consumed him, and he shut his eyes.

"How come every time I see you, you're naked?" she mumbled groggily.

His eyes flew open, and he tilted her chin up. She blinked, tears still on her lashes.

"Come on, beautiful. Let's get you in the bed."

"I bet you say that to all the girls," she said, her smile sedate.

Jericho lifted her onto the bed so he could get a closer look at her injuries. Isabelle had always had the best set of legs of any woman he'd ever met. It looked like she had just skinned her knees, so he was certain they'd heal up in no time. It was the ligature marks on her wrists that made his blood boil.

She began singing a Pink Floyd song, except with numbers.

"Isabelle?" Something wasn't right. Hawk must have drugged her, but he didn't see any track marks on her arms.

"One hour, Reno said. Denver made me sing it," she said incoherently.

When she sang another verse, he realized it was a phone number. Reno knew how to run a trace, and that's what he must have been setting up.

Jericho covered her legs with a sheet and leaned close to her ear. "Stay here, Isabelle. I'm going to call for help."

That was a promise.

But first, he had to leave her alone for ten minutes. He had something more important to take care of, and that something was time alone with Hawk—no holds barred. Carnal thirst consumed his wolf, one that wouldn't be sated if Hawk were given the option of life, even if it were for a few more days in a basement. That animal didn't deserve an easy death.

As Jericho arrowed down the hall, he shifted into his wolf and then back into human form. This happened twice as man and animal became one in thought. He dialed the number Isabelle had been singing, and when Reno answered, Jericho dropped the phone and made his way down to the basement.

Shifters played by a different set of rules than humans did. Wolves avenged those who were abused in their pack, and with the full support of the law. Although Isabelle wasn't legally part of his family, she was in his heart, and that's all that counted. Justice would be served, no matter the consequences.

Jericho entered the basement and moved like a predator into the room, closing the door behind him.

Hawk's eyes widened with terror when Jericho's savage wolf emerged, pink tongue passing over his sharp fangs, promising a brutal death.

<hr />

When I woke up, it wasn't to a hard slap on the ass and ridicule followed by laughter. It was to the smell of maple bacon and fresh coffee beneath my nose. It soothed me and I stretched, slowly blinking my eyes open.

The first thing I did was chuckle when I saw a Led Zeppelin poster on the wall. A plate of food on a bedside table tempted me, but I glanced around at my surroundings. There was a door on my left, and as I sat up and pulled the sheet away from my legs, I noticed someone had dressed me in a clean T-shirt.

"I told them you liked sleeping in big shirts," Jericho said softly.

He sat in a beanbag chair to the right of the door, arms draped over his knees. A lava lamp bubbled on a small table to his left. Clean hair fell to his shoulders, and I smirked at the sleeveless shirt he had on—someone had done a terrible job of cutting the sleeves off it. He must have shifted and fed, because he looked fit and healthy again.

I tucked a pillow against the headboard and moved my sore body to sit up, looking at the marks on my wrists.

"Austin forced you to shift. Do you remember?"

I shook my head. "Just bits and pieces. Where am I?"

"My room." His voice was flat and deadly as he stared at me with jade eyes. "Isabelle, I'm going to ask you a question, and I want you to answer honestly."

"Okay."

The way he looked at me, with his hands resting on his knees, made me shudder. When he spoke, his lips peeled back, and he quickly relaxed his face. "Did he rape you?"

I closed my eyes and sighed. "No." When I opened my eyes, I tried to show him a smile. "But I kicked his ass, and if he had tried, I would have made him regret he had ever met me. Nobody messes with Izzy Monroe."

He threw his head back, staring at the ceiling with relief in his voice. "You always were a tough girl."

"Are you okay?" I asked. "You look okay, but…"

"What you saw on that television was a lie. It was a trap to lure him into the room."

He always was a smart wolf, I thought to myself.

The shifting hadn't happened soon enough. The marks on my wrists would either fade or scar.

"Lexi's mom dressed you, by the way. The girls took care of you. Lynn washed you up a little, but she's going to run you a hot shower when you're ready. I'll help you to the bathroom. Eat."

I pulled the plate onto my lap and chewed on the crispy bacon.

My eyes floated around the room in wonderment. He lived a simple life. A dresser sat at the foot of the bed, and the walls were covered with various rock posters. It felt like home.

"I can't believe you still have that," I said, pointing to a poster of the Stones on my left.

Below it were two guitars—one an acoustic and the other a Les Paul. He had amplifiers, cords, straps, and a few shirts sitting in piles around the room. Several guitar picks were scattered on the small table to my left. Still as messy as ever.

"Why don't you sit up here with me?" I offered, tired of staring down at him on the floor.

"Because I don't want to frighten you."

I set down my plate. "You don't frighten me."

"After what you've been through, you just might be a little scared of a man sitting next to you."

"You're no man, you're Sexton Cole." I cracked a pained smile.

One appeared on his face as well. He leaned forward and stood up, cautiously walking toward the bed. When he reached the edge, he leaned against it a little but kept his distance.

"You saved my brother," he said.

Then I remembered a little of what Hawk had said. "Was he the one who was shot?"

"We showed up at Hawk's house looking for you."

"How did you know where he lived?"

Jericho shrugged. "Stole your file at the bar. We rushed him in the hall and he shot Wheeler, then he shot me in the knee."

I gasped, and Jericho set the plate on the table and sat down.

"I was hurt bad so I shifted. Before I could shift back, he put me in a crate. Wheeler was left to die."

My hands were shaking and I wrung them together. "What makes you think I saved him? How did he survive?"

"You called Denver. You called my brothers and gave them the address. Because of your actions, they were able to get there in time, and Wheeler didn't die. Good thing he's a stubborn sonofabitch."

"Why didn't he shift?"

Jericho sighed. "He was shot in the head. It wasn't a fatal wound, but he might have eventually bled out since the bullet went clean through. I got him to shift once before he fell unconscious, so that helped him hold out a little longer. Austin hauled ass and got there in time to make him shift as many times as he could. Alpha wolves have the power to do that, and thank the fuck it worked."

"Is he okay? Any permanent damage?"

Jericho smiled. "Only to his ego. It's too early to know if he'll have any memory loss, but I think getting him to shift right after it happened healed up the tissue. He seems okay."

"I'm sorry I dragged your family into this. I had no idea what Hawk was doing—you have to believe me. Some guy started chasing me, and that's when I found out that Hawk was dealing drugs. I left him because of that, but you can bet I had no idea about all the other stuff he was doing. I feel sick to my stomach just thinking about it."

A strand of hair fell in front of my face. Jericho leaned forward and carefully tucked it behind my ear. "You don't have to explain."

"But I do. I gave him a second chance because that's what I believe we all deserve. I didn't love him, but I *still* gave him a shot to prove himself to me. I asked the wrong person."

"What do you mean?"

I took Jericho's hand and thought I saw a blush rise in his cheeks.

"All this time I thought a second chance was something I'd have to give you, Jericho. But I was wrong. I'm asking you to give *me* one. I'm sorry for running out on you all those years ago."

"I don't blame you; I was messed up back then. What's done is done. But I do have one question. What did you do with my guitar?"

Still holding his hand, I tilted my head to the side. "Huh?"

"That powder-blue guitar you gave me."

"I don't know what you're talking about."

His eyes narrowed. "Yes, you know. You stole it."

I pulled back my hands. "What? I didn't steal your guitar."

"It's okay, Isabelle. I'm over it. We were different people back then. I'm just curious."

I shook my head and gripped the covers. "I know we were different people, but I'm not a thief. I never stole your guitar."

Jericho angrily got off the bed. "Denver said the maid saw you swipe my guitar and empty my wallet. I would have wanted you to have the money because you went out on your own, but my guitar—"

I gasped and ripped the covers back, standing despite my weak legs. "I don't know what Denver was smoking with the maid, but I never stole anything from you, Jericho. I came back the next night to apologize and walked in on you and that redhead having sex. She was wearing *my* Pink Floyd shirt."

"Redhead?" Jericho turned around and locked his fingers behind his neck, something he did when he was thinking. "Redhead," he repeated twice more, searching his memories.

Then he collapsed on the beanbag, covering his face. "Oh shit. Oh shit."

"What?"

"I'm remembering. I thought she was you."

I clutched my chest.

Jericho lifted his stricken eyes to mine. "I hope you didn't pick up my bad habit of not locking doors, but you remember how I was. Some woman had followed the band back to the hotel and must have found out which room I was staying in. I don't know," he said, pinching the bridge of his nose as he remembered. "I just woke up in the dim room with someone kissing my chest… and all this red hair. I thought it was you. I called your name, but you never looked up. So we uh… well, we had sex. But then I wanted to see your face. All I could see was all that red hair and your favorite shirt. Then I lifted your chin, but it wasn't you. *Fuck.*" He threw back his head and covered his face with one hand. "It wasn't you. I threw her off and went to ask my mates if they'd seen you. Jimmy said you took off."

"I talked to him going down the stairs," I remembered.

"That's when I knew I'd lost you for good. I went on a binge to numb away the pain, and I don't remember anything after that."

"Oh my God." I sat on the floor, my eyes downcast.

Jericho wasn't the kind of man who would allow a woman to take advantage of him. He'd always chosen his women, not the other way around. Jericho had always been open about his sex life with me and said he'd never let a woman get on top, so I should have realized something was off with that scene. Even worse was knowing the reason he overdosed was because he found out that girl *wasn't* me.

I grimaced and tears slipped down my face. "I'm so sorry, Jericho. I didn't know I was the reason you almost died."

"No!" he shouted, crawling across the floor in front of me. He held my face in his hands and used his thumbs to wipe my tears. His eyes blazed with anger. "I should have gotten my ass up and gone to look for you. I took the easy way out, baby. I won't make that mistake again." His eyes fell to my lips and lingered. "By the way, you and that asshole are officially broken up."

I nodded and knew what he wanted—something I'd been fantasizing about for decades.

Jericho curved his right hand around my neck and softly petted my skin with his fingers. I leaned forward and pressed my tear-stained lips to his mouth. That first contact was electric, awakening nerves in my body and sending a rush of blood all over. When our lips parted in the slowest kiss ever recorded, we tasted each other with a soft and sensual stroke of our tongues.

I held my breath, and when I pulled back, I was panting. Jericho closed his eyes and pulled his lips in, licking them as if he'd eaten something delicious. "You taste like peaches."

"Will you give me a second chance? I won't run out on you again. I'm not expecting us to be an item, but I want to reconcile and become friends again."

He pulled my T-shirt forward and kissed the edge of my mouth, whispering against my lips. "Oh, we're a thing all right. The friendship is a given, but this is going exclusive."

"You don't do exclusive."

"Something you don't know about me, Isabelle, is that I've never wanted anything more permanent than a roll in the sack. Not with anyone… except you. I slept with all those women, but you were the one who cared for me in the morning. You were the one I drank orange juice with at the table while you'd read me the newspaper in that terrible British accent. You were the one who gave me a kick in the ass when I needed it and always forgave me. I'm twisted around your heart like a vine, and I won't let you go. And by the way, that whore wasn't wearing your shirt. That was hers."

Jericho stood up and rummaged through his dresser drawer. He turned around and tossed a T-shirt in my lap. "That's the vintage Izzy Monroe shirt. You left it in the bathroom on top of the sink. I've never let another woman put it on. It's sacred. Even though you weren't here, wearing it made it seem like you'd never left. That's some crazy shit, huh?"

I stared at the shirt in disbelief, pulling it to my nose and smelling it. He'd kept it all this time.

"First thing I'm going to do is go downstairs and kick Denver's ass for making me think you'd cleaned me out. If you're pissed at me for having sex with that woman, I get it. Looking back, I can imagine what that looked like; I had no idea you walked in on us."

He turned around and cursed hard. "Fuck!"

"It's in the past." I climbed to my feet and wobbled a little before regaining my balance.

"Second," he continued, "I'm going back to that house and picking up all your things. You're staying here until we figure out what's next."

He took two steps forward and cupped his hand around my neck, claiming me. "Baby, I'm not going to leave you. And you're not going to leave me, because we're going to work it out. I don't want you worried about me going off with another woman because that shit won't happen. I've spent years choosing women who didn't remind me of you. They embodied every quality you didn't have. It was just sex."

"But you've never been faithful to anyone."

"I've never had a good reason to be."

"And you do now?"

"Yeah, I do. I got my best girl back. Did I turn to drugs in Hawk's basement? No. Lock me in a room with a naked woman and it's the same deal. All I see is my weakness when I look at other women, but when I look at you, all I see is my strength."

A smile touched my lips. "Maybe you should put that in a song."

Jericho held my gaze with his pensive eyes. "Hawk's dead. Just so you know."

I nodded. "I had a feeling."

"You're a tough girl, Isabelle. Don't let what happened harden you, but don't let it weaken you either."

"How do I do that?"

He turned his left shoulder toward me and pointed at his tattoo. "Balance. I didn't fill in the guitar because I needed something to remind me. Not all black. Not all white. Not all full and not all empty. I'm not perfect, and I'll always be without something. But that's okay, as long as I don't let one or the other consume me."

I smoothed my fingers over the tattoo and looked up at him. "I thought maybe you just ran out of ink."

He burst out laughing and wow, what a smile. Jericho didn't just have nice lips, but his whole mouth worked in the most mysterious way. A sweep of his tongue, a casual smile, and the words he spoke. Not just in song, but in private.

"How come you only got one tattoo? I bet people gave you heat for that. No skulls, no daggers, no badass dragon?"

A current of possession rose in his tone. "Sometimes one good thing is all you need."

"I'm sorry that bitch stole your guitar. If it makes you feel any better, she's probably working on her fifth husband."

"The only thing she stole was my future," he said, pulling me against him and wrapping his arms around the small of my back. "But I got it back, and I'm not letting go."

A knock sounded at the door as it creaked open. An older woman peered in and glanced at my plate. "I've put some things in the bathroom for you to clean up with. Do you want something else to eat? I have a fruit salad in the fridge, and lunch will be ready in about an hour."

"No, I don't want to be any trouble. Thanks for what you've done for me."

"Lynn, I'm setting up a room for Isabelle down the hall. Tell Austin I'm heading out in a few minutes to pick up her things. I also need to grab some cheese popcorn."

I concealed my smile when he winked at me.

She peered suspiciously between us and closed the door.

"Lynn's having issues coping with some of the Shifter drama that goes on. We can't change who we are because a human lives in the house, but they're family and we protect them just the same. Austin thinks she's going to send Maizy away soon. His hands are tied since he's not the father. Lexi's trying to talk her into staying, but after this incident, I don't know. She's been pretty quiet this morning."

"Can you blame her? She's human and has a little girl to look after. Parents want the best for their kids."

"How many do you want?"

"What?"

Jericho chuckled. "How. Many. Do. You. Want?"

Okay, I started to blush. Especially when he tightened his grip and planted a soft peck on my forehead. Everything about the way he touched me was restrained and polite—Jericho handled me like a cornered animal who might run.

"Six."

His eyes widened and he leaned back. "Six? What the shit?"

"Don't you want a band?"

He gripped both sides of my head and kissed my forehead. "Still the same old Isabelle. Why don't you shift again? I'll leave you alone and you can let your wolf out for as long as she wants."

"I'll tear up your room."

Jericho leaned against the door and began fooling with a ring on his finger. "It's just stuff. I want those marks off your wrists."

I traced a finger over them. "I don't think they're going to heal all the way."

"*And* your back," he said in a controlled breath.

"Those marks don't hurt and they'll fade. Hawk put me through a lot, but you know I grew up in a fighting household. I'm not going to allow him to ruin my life. I'm going back to work this week and—"

"You are asshat crazy if you think you're going to work."

"Oh?" I put my hands on my hips and stared him down.

"Yeah. *Oh*. You can't go on pretending nothing happened."

"I can still work," I argued. "It shouldn't affect my ability to serve food and beer on a tray. Maybe at night I'll do a little crying in my bed and have some nightmares, but my life has to go on. Shifters are born with thick skin because growing up in the Breed world is no cakewalk. I'm not a delicate flower that needs to be protected from the wind. I'm a wildflower—a sunflower. Punish me with drought and heat, and I'll grow stronger."

"A week is too soon, Isabelle."

"Do you think moping around the house will put me in better spirits? Do you know why I like a service job, Jericho? It's because I love people. I enjoy laughing and hearing their stories of family and travel. I like building friendships and thinking of them as…"

"Family. That's what you mean, isn't it? You like working there because it starts to feel like a home. Maybe a pack."

I quieted, stilled by the truth that flowed from his lips. I'd never known what it was to live in a pack, and it intimidated me like nothing else. Someone with my history wouldn't fit in or be accepted by others. I grew up outside a pack and came from a mixed home. My job had always given me the acceptance I needed, and if it didn't, I could pack up and leave.

"Go on, Isabelle. Jump in the shower, and after you feel rested, you can shift in my room. Take as long as you need. You don't have to make all these heavy decisions right now, dig? Just take care of yourself," he said, pressing a small kiss to my forehead. "I'll be right here."

CHAPTER 14

―⋅∘≪❦≫∘⋅―

"TWO NUMBER TWELVES AND THEY want them atomic!" I yelled into the kitchen, handing the cook my order slip.

Jericho couldn't prevent me from going back to work a few days later. He tried, but I knew if I sat around the house any longer, I'd be miserable. The marks on my wrists hadn't faded, so April took me shopping and bought me trendy wrist cuffs. They were lacy and ran halfway up my forearm, almost like a glove. I chose the black to go with my sleeveless work shirt and had already received a few compliments on them. The fading marks around my eye were easily concealed with makeup, but a few men looked a little closer and didn't care for what they saw.

Most male Shifters won't tolerate abuse against women. Table nine looked ready to corner me and demand to know who did it, so Rosie took over my section while I relaxed in the back.

I was beside myself when Denver handed me a cheeseburger on a plate and sat down across from me. He apologized for having mixed things up. I couldn't blame him; the way the maid had described it, I would have come to the same conclusion.

In any case, we were square. I liked Denver—he was easygoing with a nutty sense of humor. Denver didn't have an endgame of finding a mate from what I sensed, but he loved to flirt. It seemed like a few of the Cole brothers had commitment issues.

Rosie strutted toward us and delivered a skeptical look. "Are you sure you're okay, hon?"

"Let the girl eat her cow patty in peace," Denver said.

She put her hands on her hips. "Such a smart mouth on you. I'll be sure to tell the cook what you think of his hamburgers."

"I'm fine, Rosie. I'll be better when everyone stops asking."

"You let me know if you need anything," she said, wagging her finger as she went back to the bar.

The main door swung open, and a cacophony of shouts burst into the room. Three men ambled up to the bar to order drinks—men I didn't know—so I told my heart to slow down. Some childish part of me thought Hawk might rise from the dead and come after me. Maybe that's why people have funerals—the mind doesn't seem to accept death unless you see the body with your own eyes.

"How's the room at the house working out, honeypie?" Denver asked, twisting the wrapper off a white peppermint.

"You guys have been great. I really appreciate it."

Everyone had a chaotic schedule, so I stayed in my room and rarely saw most of the pack.

"Maybe you should come eat with us."

I shifted uncomfortably and touched the lace on my wrist. "That's a family thing. I'm just going to stay out of your hair until I find a place of my own. If only these guys would give me better tips."

His face darkened, and he flicked the wrapper on the floor. "Are some of the customers holding out on you?"

I waved him off. "You know how it goes, Denver. I'm the new girl and—"

"Bullshit." He kicked back his chair and towered over the table, gripping the edges. "If someone tips low, I want you to signal me at the bar and let me take care of it."

"I don't want to cause trouble because then they won't sit in my section."

"If they want to keep coming back here they'll sit in your section. I'm serious," he said as he walked off. "Signal me."

I took another bite of my cheeseburger and washed it down with a sip of tea. Just as I moved to get up, Wheeler eased into the chair across from me.

He always wore sleeveless shirts, so the first noticeable thing was his tatted arms—all kinds of designs that blended into a canvas of art. It didn't look like he'd brushed his hair or trimmed his beard. He looked like a pirate, but in a good way. Especially with his bright eyes that were a pale shade of brown, like a glass of sweet tea warming in the sun.

During my stay in the Weston pack household, Wheeler had been noticeably absent. I presumed he had issues with me staying there given I'd almost gotten them killed because of my crazy ex.

"So here's the deal," he began. "I owe you. Big. You made a call that saved my life, and you made a move that saved Jericho's life. Regardless of the fact you were the one who got us in that mess, that's where it stands. If you want money, I can arrange something."

"I don't want your money," I said, pushing my plate. "It's all gravy."

He clipped a smile and sat back in his chair, studying me intently. "That all you have to say?"

"I'm back in Jericho's life, so you'll have to get used to seeing me around. But I'm sorry about how everything turned out. I didn't know Hawk was that kind of man, and I should have. I still don't understand how I could have trusted someone like him and not have seen his dark side. That's what gives me waking nightmares. I should have seen the signs early on."

"Sometimes people cover up what they don't want others to see," he said, staring at my wrist cuffs. "Secrets are truths that show what we've been through—what we've survived. I don't hide who I am," he said, raising up both fists and showing me his tattoos. "Maybe you shouldn't either. I want everyone to know exactly who I am and where I'm coming from. But sometimes people bury that shit deep and put on a façade. Those around them can't see the dark part of their soul they hide because it's not something they wear on their skin. It's a fracture that's deep and invisible. Why don't you show me what you've got." He nodded at my arms.

I slowly pulled off one of the lacy coverings and turned my wrist over so he could see the marks on both sides.

"You should keep them off," he suggested. "What do you think it says about you?"

"That I'm a victim, and I'm weak."

Wheeler shook his head and gave me a crooked smile. "You're serving these assholes whiskey and hot dogs. You know what that says to me? That you're tough. It takes a strong woman to move on with her life after something like that—and to show it off proudly as if it doesn't faze her? One badass bitch. You can't sit around beating yourself up because you didn't see it coming. Even if you'd known what he was capable of, what could you have done?"

"Called someone."

"Who? Unless you can prove someone has committed a crime, your hands are tied. You know the Breed's stance on slander. Without hard evidence, all you could have done was look away or walk away."

"At least I would have had the choice," I said glumly.

"People give signs when they want to be caught. Did he give any signs?"

I shook my head.

"Then he didn't want to be caught. He was too far gone. They're only careless in the beginning because they still have that thing called guilt riding on their shoulders. After a while, they lose their conscience and don't make any more mistakes. They don't want to be caught because they love committing the crime. It becomes less of a thrill and more of an addiction."

"How do you know?"

He wiped his face slowly with his hand in a downward motion, speaking in a tired voice. "I've been around long enough. Look, that's not what I came here to talk about. We're not even until I pay back my dues. You hold a favor in your pocket with me. Whatever and whenever you want, just let me know."

He rapped his knuckles on the table and took off.

I looked down at my wrists and peeled off the lacy coverings, leaving them on the table. Wheeler was right.

I strolled to the kitchen and the cook handed me an order. I proudly held that tray over my shoulder and walked to the table, giving the men my best dip as I set their glasses down.

"Here you are. Southwest burgers with extra jalapeños. Hope these are spicy enough for you. The chef uses fresh peppers—none of that canned stuff."

I set the plate down in front of a burly man and caught his gaze. I swiveled around and set down the last plate, but the men weren't eating. As I turned to walk off, one of them caught my hand and stuffed something into it.

It was a rolled-up fifty.

"There's another fifty if you tell me who did that," he said, leaning in tight and touching my wrist.

Ned was one of my regulars who had been shortchanging me. I smiled graciously. "He's taken care of. My job is to make sure *you're* taken care of, so when you need a refill on those drinks, just holler."

I returned to the bar and leaned against it, facing the open room.

"Honey, *what happened?*" Rosie's eyes widened when she caught sight of my wrists.

I leaned on my right arm to face her and lifted my chin. "Someone messed with the wrong girl."

"Damn right," Denver said, slamming the drinks on my tray. "She's staying with the Weston pack, so feel free to spread the word."

Rosie blinked. "You're living with a bunch of wolves?"

I patted her shoulder. "Rosie, I *am* a wolf. Maybe that ruins it for some of the guys in here who want the fantasy of something else, but I don't care. I should be tipped for my hard work and friendliness, not because I might be a cougar and take them home after work. You *hear* that?" I shouted at everyone in the bar.

The chatter died down and all eyes were on me. Crazy Izzy was coming out to play for a little bit, but I didn't care. I was proud of being a wolf, and it was time that everyone knew it.

"Some of you have been holding back on me because I'm the new girl, and you want me to work a little harder for your attention. I get it; I've been around the block. Starting tonight, tip me fairly based on how I serve your table. And by the way, sorry if this ruins anyone's fantasy, but I'm a wolf. A *proud* wolf."

Three tables erupted with cheers, clapping their hands and stamping their feet.

Clearly wolves.

Denver laughed and wiped down the bar. "Now you've done it."

"Well, maybe they'll tip me better and it'll make up for some of the cheap-ass snakes."

"You have lost your mind," Rosie said with a roll of her eyes. "Jake is going to have a hissy fit."

An entire table of men by the jukebox collected their drinks and moved to my section.

"Look what you've done!" Rosie said, pointing at my new customers. "Now you're going to end up with all the alphas, and the girls are *not* going to like this. Some of their biggest tippers are the Packmasters."

"Rosie, it's a Shifter bar called Howlers. Maybe you should drop some of the deadweight on the floor and hire a few wolves. Sixty percent of our customers are wolves."

"Incoming," Denver blurted out.

I heard a few girls making sexual sounds, and I got an eyeful when I looked toward the front. Jericho Sexton Cole swaggered in wearing jeans, a leather belt with silver studs, no shirt, and a black blazer. He had on a pair of black sunglasses, even though it was after dark.

"He is *so* working it," I said with a laugh, watching a sliver of a smile touch his mouth.

Jericho and I hadn't kissed since that morning in his room. He wanted to give me space to get my head together. We'd slowly begun rebuilding our friendship, and I realized that without that solid bond we shared, we'd never be able to make anything serious work between us.

"Does he have a show tonight?" Rosie wondered aloud. "I don't have him on my calendar."

Denver handed me a tray of shots. "Here, Izzy. Your new friends ordered these."

A familiar blonde slinked up to Jericho's side, so I blew it off and carried drinks over to my table. I didn't own the man, and I wasn't about to start acting like an insecure lunatic. I set the glasses in front of the men and caught a few stares. They certainly didn't like the looks of my wrists.

"You got a pack?" the more distinguished one asked. He wore a flannel shirt, and I'd never been a fan of flannel. He was the spitting image of Sean Connery. Minus the sexy accent and the sparkle in his eye.

"I'm currently staying with one," I said.

"That doesn't answer my question."

"She has a pack." Jericho appeared on my right and stood close. "How's it going, Turner?"

"Not bad," the man replied. "Just got a few boys here who think Izzy is the kind of girl they'd like to know a little better. Respectfully, of course."

"Of course. If she's interested in them, she'll let you know. Until then, no recruiting. Comprende?"

"I got it," he said with a laugh that dissipated into a wheeze. "You're a funny one, Jericho. A little protective for someone who's had about every woman in this room." Turner sipped his drink slowly, his eyes still on Jericho.

"Will that complete your order?" I said in a clipped tone. "Because I don't serve anyone who insults my friends. You can stay in my section and play by my rules, or you can mosey on over to Trina's section and fantasize all you want that she's a wolf when everyone knows she has hooves."

Jericho rocked with laughter and wrapped his arm around me, guiding me away. "That's enough, Isabelle. You don't have to jump to my defense."

"You're my best friend, and nobody demeans my friends like that. Especially someone who's paying me."

We kept meandering toward the door, and then he leaned in close. "I'm used to it. Doesn't matter what they think anymore; I know what I'm all about."

A sharp whistle pierced the air, and we turned to see Denver leaning over the bar with two fingers in his mouth. "She's still on her shift! You can't just walk out," he said, holding out his arms.

"Tell Jake I'll do an extra show," Jericho yelled back, and that was that.

"Where are we going?" I asked.

"Someplace."

"That sounds interesting. Hmm. The North Pole?"

"Nah. My nipples would freeze."

I stumbled on my shoe and Jericho held me steady as we walked across the parking lot.

"Outer space? I've always wanted to go there," I said, completely deadpan.

"Nah. The spacesuit would kill my image."

"Disneyland!"

"Isabelle." He scolded me with a tight squeeze. "You know I have an issue with people who wear giant costumes of animals."

"They freak you out."

"They do not freak me out. It's just creepy as hell." He opened the door to the blue truck and helped me in.

"Admit it, Jericho. Mickey Mouse makes you wet your bed."

He snorted and slammed the door, walking around the front.

"You're going to like this," he promised, starting up the engine.

As we merged into traffic, I was underwhelmed by my attire. "I hope wherever we're going, they're not going to give me the stink eye because of my outfit. Do I need to change?"

In the dark cab, Jericho put his glasses on the dash and gave me a quiet look, softening his voice. "No, baby, you look good."

I hid my smile and looked away. Jericho didn't say it often, and I didn't know if it was intentional. It's when he called me *baby*. Not babe in that arrogant way some men do. The way he said baby felt intimate. The only words I'd ever heard Jericho call women were sugar and honey.

Never baby.

All those years apart allowed me to get to know him all over again. Jericho was still the badass rock star with the sexy moves, sultry voice, and sinful body. But last night he'd lifted me off the sofa and carried me to bed after I'd fallen asleep reading one of April's books. I'd pretended to be asleep because I didn't want him to put me down. It was such a silly thing for me to do, but Jericho gave me butterflies whenever he did the unexpected romantic stuff.

"How are you feeling tonight?" he asked.

I watched the taillights on the car in front of us brighten. "Fine."

Then I felt him staring at me. "Isabelle, you haven't talked to anyone about what happened to you. It's not going to just go away."

"It's done with. What do you want me to do?"

"Feel?"

The light turned green, and he slowly pushed on the gas pedal.

"Feel what?"

"Something. Maybe I need to see you cry, and I never thought I'd say something like that, but it makes me nervous that you're not making a big deal out of it."

I gazed somberly out the window and knew what he meant. Sometimes people bottled up their emotions and allowed the contents to change them. Maybe he was afraid I'd run out on him again.

"Isabelle, stop thinking and talk to me."

I sighed in frustration. "I don't want to feel it again. Once was enough."

He breathed in deeply and put his hand on top of mine. "I'll let it slide tonight, but we're going to talk about it someday. If I have to get you rip-roaring drunk, we're talking."

I snorted. "I don't get drunk."

"No, you get tipsy and dance."

"Now you're just making things up."

Jericho turned his head slowly and arched his eyebrow. "Oh? What exactly were you doing in that bistro? You remember the one. We swung by there after hitting four bars."

"For your information, it was three bars, and I was just along for the ride. The bistro served amazing sandwiches and I was merely showing a physical display of my gratitude."

"Dancing."

"I'm going to disagree for five hundred, Alex. I was… moving in an exuberant manner."

Jericho chuckled and turned the corner. "You were shaking your butt, snapping your fingers, and singing a song about what was in your sandwich."

"I don't recollect that part."

Jericho began singing in a raspy voice:

I got a ham and cheese,
and it's good to me.
Because it satisfies all my needs,
all my needs. It's pa-nini, pa-nini.

"Oh hell's bells," I said, bursting with laughter. "Please tell me you're kidding." I could hardly control my laugh, and I bent forward, holding on to the dash. Jericho kept singing and really belted out the last two words. "Stop it! You're making my stomach hurt," I begged, clutching my belly and leaning back in my seat. Once he quieted, I wiped the tears from the corner of my eyes and he patted my leg.

"It's good to hear you laugh," he said in a low voice, as if talking to himself.

When I stole a glance, he didn't look away. Jericho's eyes were luminous, even in the dark cab of the pickup truck. I wondered if we were going to a concert. He didn't have on his usual charcoal liner below his eyes, so I didn't think so.

"We're here," he said. The brakes squealed to a stop and I leaned forward.

A nostalgic smile touched my lips as he got out of the truck and slammed the door. Jericho had brought me to a donut shop. When my door opened, he offered me his hand.

"Come on, Isabelle. My treat."

I stumbled in my heels as we headed inside.

The store was pristine, and the first thing that caught my eye was the display counter. I threw myself against it and drooled over all the delicious varieties to choose from—so many pretty colors!

"I'd like the one with the chocolate glaze. Jericho, do you want to get something else to split between us?"

"Hell no," he said, leaning on the counter. "I want a dozen of those chocolate ones and another dozen assorted."

My back straightened like an arrow. "You didn't just order all that."

"I did."

"You can't."

"I can."

"It's too much!"

"Someday I'll buy you something expensive. Maybe it'll sparkle and look real good on your finger. But right now, I'm buying you a box of donuts just the way you like them. Two cups of cocoa," he told the guy.

I didn't hear anything he said after the part about the ring. All I felt was a migration of little butterflies flitting in my stomach and tickling my nerves.

"Grab a seat, baby. I'll bring them to you."

I cupped my elbows and walked around him, scoping out the tables and trying to temper the blush that warmed my skin. Each time I felt the heat on my cheeks, it roused a peculiar smile on his face. A smile I'd never seen on him that gave me tingles—the good kind.

The rectangular tables were made of polished wood, and I chose a booth with yellow vinyl seats by the window.

When he appeared with two boxes, I laughed quietly. "I can't believe we're eating donuts at night. I haven't done this in a million years."

He slid the boxes onto the table and handed me my drink. I took a sip from the steaming cup and watched him flip open the first box, spinning it around to face me.

"Scoot over," he said. "All the way."

I slid against the window, and Jericho sat beside me with the other box in front of him.

He eyed the selection in his box. "I haven't had a donut since I was with you."

"Are you kidding?"

He picked at a candy-coated one and licked his thumb. "It just brought back too many memories. Plus, midnight donut runs were a *me and you* thing."

Good memories, I thought wistfully.

Jericho reached over and removed the lid from my drink. "Dunk away."

He remembered. I broke off a piece of the chocolate-glazed donut and dipped it in my cocoa. "Did you just come from a show?"

"Nope," he said with a mouthful.

"Why the outfit?"

"We're going to one," he mumbled. I almost didn't understand him because he'd shoved an entire jelly donut into his mouth. The jelly dripped down his chin, and he tried to lick it up with his tongue but couldn't reach it. I really needed to stop staring.

"Maybe you shouldn't eat all these. You might pass out on the stage in a sugar-induced coma."

"They're not all for me." He lifted his right arm and waved at three guys who had just walked in. "I want you to meet some people, Isabelle. You've already met my family, but this is my second family—my band."

Jericho stood up and greeted his friends, clasping hands and bumping shoulders.

"Isabelle, this is my drummer, Joker. Once he opens his mouth and puts his foot in it, you'll know why."

Joker had a sweet face and a slight overbite. He reminded me a little of a young Robert Plant. He scooted in front of me while Jericho patted the shoulder of a man wearing a leather jacket and sunglasses. His inky hair was spiked, and he had three lip rings. You couldn't tell how old a Shifter was in years by their looks, but he seemed young—like one of those guys who was trying to be cool but wasn't quite there yet.

"This is Ren, my rhythm guitarist who makes me sound good. Ren, have a donut."

When Ren sat down, he leaned his head against the back of the booth and his jaw hung slack, as if he were half-asleep. "Not hungry."

"And I'm Chaz, honey. Bass player and the reason this band sells tickets," the last guy said. Chaz was a gaunt man with hollow cheeks and acne scars. He tried to hide it with a black goatee that was scruffy and too long.

Jericho sat beside me and whispered, "Soon-to-be-fired bass player."

Chaz dragged a chair from a nearby table and sat at the end of the booth. When he reached for my box, Jericho seized his wrist and knocked it away. "No one touches Isabelle's donuts."

"No problem, sweetie," Chaz said, giving me a wink. "Just let me know when you want me to finger your hole."

I dunked my donut in my cocoa and let it soak up a little of the drink. "Sure thing. Just let me know when you get your thumb out of your ass and have a free hand."

Joker howled and rapped his hands on the table in a rhythmic flow. "I love her already. So you're the infamous Izzy Monroe. I've been wanting to meet the girl our band was named after."

"How many times have you changed names?"

"More than we've changed underwear," he said.

Ren chortled. "Speak for yourself."

"You want one?" I slid my box in Joker's direction. Chaz shot me an irritated glare.

"Nah. I'm diabetic."

"Sorry. Didn't mean to wave it in front of your face."

"You're cool. I'm not big on all that anyway. My weakness is ice cream. I can eat tubs and tubs of that shit."

"And he has," Ren added without so much as lifting his head from his napping position.

I finished off my first donut and looked between them. "You guys have a show tonight?"

"Big one," Joker said. "Not just Shifters, but it's going to be a mixed bag. They're organizing an outdoor event on five hundred acres of territory some rich asshole owns. Campers are bringing their RVs and tents. It's supposed to go on for three days."

"Breedstock," Ren said with a snort.

"How come I haven't heard of this?"

Jericho sipped his cocoa and began working on his third donut. "They have to keep it hush because of the limited space on the grounds. I don't think anyone got a human permit for this, so it should be interesting."

Joker fiddled with the napkin dispenser. "I heard Vamps paid a visit to the folks who live near the lake and charmed them away on vacation. I don't see how there could be a problem."

Ren reached over and snatched a glazed donut, cramming the entire thing into his mouth.

"Dare you to eat the whole box," Joker said.

Jericho leaned in privately. "I packed you a bag. I thought it would be fun to stay for the night and get away from the house. If you want to stay longer, we can do that too."

"You do realize you just made me into a target for mosquitoes after eating all these donuts?"

"Did anyone find out if we can shift?" Chaz asked, shoving half a donut into his mouth before spitting it out on the table.

"It's restricted from what I heard," Jericho said. "I wouldn't risk it. We'll have Vampires, Chitahs, Sensors—you name it. Bound to piss someone off if one of us bites them in the ass."

"You bringing her?" Chaz asked.

"Her?" Jericho eyed him coldly. "You call *her* Izzy."

"Is that what you're calling your flavor of the week?" he replied, drumming his fingers.

Jericho suddenly snatched Chaz's beard and yanked his face down to the table. In a swift movement, he pulled out a switchblade and with one clean slice cut off Chaz's goatee, leaving a mark on the wood surface.

"What the fuck!" Chaz yelled, knocking back his chair and standing up.

Jericho slowly rose to his feet and towered over him by at least five inches. "Here's what the fuck, Chaz. If you disrespect my woman again, it won't be your hair I cut off next. Get your junkie ass outside and I'll be along shortly." He snapped the knife closed and slipped it into his back pocket.

My heart was pounding as I looked between them. Chaz gave everyone the finger and scowled. "Bad move. I'm walkin'. See how you guys do without a bassist."

"What the fuck," Joker hissed. "We need him."

Jericho sat down and wiped his face. "That's exactly what he wants us to think so he can keep getting away with shit. You guys know anyone we can call on short notice?"

"News alert. We have one hour," Ren said, glancing at his watch.

"What about Trevor?" I suggested.

Trevor lived with the Weston pack. He and April were best friends, and he seemed like a cool guy. I'd walked by his door a few times and caught him putting together model airplanes, but every so often, he would be strumming his guitar.

"I don't think he plays bass."

"Maybe you should ask," I said.

Jericho pulled out his phone and dialed a number, stepping away from the table with his finger in his other ear.

"We're really fucked now," Joker said with a sniff. "I may need one of those pink ones."

I slapped his hand and closed the box when he reached for a donut. "How is it that you have diabetes? I've never heard of that with a Shifter."

"I'm a human."

I blinked in surprise. "Really?"

Joker laughed and flipped his sandy-blond hair out of his face. It was wavy and past his ears. "Jericho's an equal-opportunity kind of guy. They kept it a secret from me for almost a year before filling me in. I'm tighter with these two guys than my human friends. I guess I'll stick with the band until I become an old dog or they get sick of me."

"We're the old dogs," Ren said. "You're the old human. Get it straight."

"Shut up, Lord of the Lip Rings."

Jericho filled the space beside me and spun his phone on the table. "Looks like we have someone to fill in."

"Trevor knows how to play bass?" I asked in surprise.

"No. They're swinging by a pawnshop on the way and he's going to practice in the car."

A slow laugh began to build in Joker and he wiped his eyes. "This should be fucking *magical*. Why don't you call him up and hum the bass line for *Another One Bites the Dust*? We'll open and close with that one."

CHAPTER 15

A FTER STUFFING MY FACE WITH five donuts, I napped in Jericho's truck while he drove us to the music event. It reminded me of old times, before he'd formed a band. Now he was a talented rocker who could take on the world if he chose to. I knew he could have rocketed to superstardom because he was smart, talented, and wrote his own music. But that kind of fame puts a target on the backs of men who don't age at the same speed as humans.

I moaned and stretched, nestling my head against something soft.

Then hard.

My eyes widened when I realized my head was in Jericho's lap. I bolted upright. "Very funny."

"You're the one who laid down, Isabelle. I tried to wake you up, but you bit my arm."

"I did not."

He held up his arm and showed me the teeth marks. "I know you don't like being forced awake, so I let you snooze."

"Thanks." I rubbed my eyes and saw people walking everywhere.

Jericho sighed. "Hope this goes well. If not, we can probably wing it without a bass player."

"So Chaz has been a problem?"

Jericho honked the horn, and a few people moved off the road and out of our way. "You could say that. He's a junkie. It's been getting worse, and the rest of the guys don't want that shit around. We party, smoke a little weed, girls—you know. But Chaz started in with some of that hard-core shit. I let it slide at first because who am

I to talk? But he's been rolling in late to shows and not pulling his weight. That's bringing us all down."

"He'll be back. He's just throwing a tantrum so you'll be stuck in a bind."

Jericho tucked a cigarette behind his ear. "He's the one who's going to be stuck in a bind, because we're replacing him. I have two good men I don't want influenced by his bad habits. Come on."

He reached behind the seat, unzipped a bag, and handed me a pair of comfortable shoes.

I walked a pace behind him as we worked our way through the crowd. I'd never seen so many Breeds in one place. Vampires watched me with their onyx eyes, and I saw a few Sensors transferring emotions with their hands to someone's chest. I could always tell by the red glow.

Jericho peered at me over his shoulder and gripped my hand.

Onstage, a singer was winding up a cover of an Elton John song. When the music stopped, laughter and loud talking erupted from all directions. A sea of different Breeds filled the grounds, and I couldn't begin to guess how many there were. Some wore glow sticks around their necks. Two blond Chitahs were racing each other by a thicket of trees. Chitahs were tall, fair-haired, and built for speed. They weren't a Breed you messed around with because of their deadly instincts. Shifters were easy to spot because they stood in large huddles, and Packmasters usually marked themselves with special tattoos. I recognized a few regulars from the bar and waved.

Jericho let go of my hand and approached a vendor. He returned with two packages and ripped them open with his teeth. "Here. She said there weren't very many in this color."

He slipped a pink glow necklace around my neck and twisted two around my wrists as bracelets.

"This way I can spot you easily in the crowd if we get separated."

"Does this normally go on in Austin?"

"Nope. First time. Hopefully nobody gets killed and we can do it again."

A new band came on, and as the rhythmic beat thumped, Jericho tugged my hand and led me to the edge of the woods.

The pink glow from my stick illuminated his face, and he closed in on me with a carnal look in his hypnotic eyes.

Slow.

Steady.

Watching my lips.

I couldn't breathe. I licked my lips nervously as the energy pulsed between us.

He curved his right hand around the back of my neck and grazed his callused fingers across my nape. I shivered, and a rush of desire moved through me like strong alcohol.

Jericho closed his eyes and drew in a deep breath through his nose. He licked his lips and leaned in close, whispering against my ear.

"You're going into heat soon, aren't you?"

I nodded and his fingers curled in, sending a thrill through my body.

"Maybe you shouldn't be here," he breathed.

The music swelled, and laser lights beamed through the crowd, briefly passing over us.

Jericho moved closer, and I placed my hands on his bare chest. My fingers explored his firm abs and dared to move lower until they slipped inside his jeans. He sucked in his stomach and hissed through his teeth.

"Is it that obvious?" I asked.

His mouth moved away and paused on my cheek. "My brothers can't tell—not even Austin, and he's an alpha. Otherwise they would have mentioned it. He must not have a strong nose like he claims."

"Then how is it *you* know?"

"You have that look. I've seen that look. I *remember* that look." His left hand traveled to my hip and tightened.

In the past whenever I'd gone into heat, Jericho would leave me locked in his motel room. He protected me from everyone, including himself. He also slept outside the door to keep me from leaving. Only once had I begged him to let me take a man into my bed for relief, but he didn't budge. It was common knowledge among Shifters that sex would lessen the length of time a woman was in heat versus taking matters into her own hands. Most of the time it lasted for three days, but once it went on for almost two weeks. It's an uncomfortable feeling, like hunger pangs. Except a different kind of hunger.

I wasn't feeling it now. All I felt was Jericho's mouth against my cheek, sliding closer to my lips.

When he reached my mouth, he hesitated. A soft glow illuminated our bodies from the pink necklace, and as I stared intensely into his eyes, the flame of arousal lit between us.

The harder and deeper I stared into Jericho's soulful eyes, the more I wanted him to take me. I imagined him unbuckling his pants and pulling down my shorts, pinning me against that tree. My breathing became erratic, and my eyes hooded as I allowed the fantasy to overcome me.

Jericho lightly bit my bottom lip and pulled back—a claiming gesture. He let go and stroked the back of my neck with experienced fingers.

"Turn around, Isabelle."

I didn't want to break eye contact; I didn't want to lose the sexual energy that was becoming a dull ache.

When he stepped back, I turned around and held my hands against the bark of the tree.

Without hesitation, Jericho swept my hair off my shoulder and put his mouth on the nape of my neck. I cried out at the rapturous feel of his tongue, the soft and hard sucking he alternated between, and the scrape of his teeth. He blew a warm breath on my sensitive skin and suddenly cupped his hand between my legs.

When I moaned, he covered my mouth with his left hand.

"Shhh, baby. Not so loud."

His fingers began moving and working me over until all I wanted was Jericho.

He drew his hand up and slipped it inside my shorts. I was so close, and having my back to him felt so right—it was the way among Shifter wolves.

His fingers sank into my panties, and he slipped one inside me.

"So wet," he whispered in a shaky breath.

My cheeks flushed with heat—I couldn't take it anymore. Pleasure intensified with every stroke, lick, and kiss against my neck. When he growled, low and provocative, I reached around and unzipped his pants.

"Isabelle," he said in a silken voice. "Don't."

"Yes," I whispered against his hand, which had loosened from my mouth.

It became a race. The more I tried to unlatch his button in the struggle to free him, the more his fingers worked inside me. I felt a tightening sensation and finally his button popped free.

Jericho moaned against my neck, moving his mouth to my shoulder. "Stop, Isabelle. Don't touch me. I want to make you come. No sex has ever compared to making you come with one touch. *Let me touch you, baby.*"

His fingers went deeper, and I moaned with so much need and lust that I pulled down his underwear and stroked him behind my back. I reached up to wiggled out of my shorts when something stilled the both of us.

"Izzy Monroe!"

The crowd roared.

Jericho backed up. "Shit. We're on."

I slowly turned around, leaning against the bark of the tree with my shorts pulled halfway down my hips.

Jericho bit his lip. "I don't know if I can go up onstage with you looking at me like that, Sexybelle."

I tugged my shorts up and smiled at him. "I told you all those donuts would be nothing but trouble. Get up onstage. I want to watch you perform."

He stalked forward and kissed me hard, his tongue crashing against mine and igniting those feelings once again. "The first song is for you," he said.

Jericho zipped up his pants and headed toward the stage, the edges of his blazer flapping with his rapid pace. I pulled myself together and laughed quietly. "Jericho Sexton Cole, you're going to get me into so much trouble," I whispered, watching him climb onto the stage and swing his guitar over his shoulder.

The stars were magnificent overhead, and I slowly made my way toward the stage, hypnotized by his voice that called out to me in a song. It wasn't a song I'd heard before. He began the show with a bluesy acoustic melody—a ballad.

The audience was captivated.

I battled the demons that darkened my soul,
I broke into pieces but you made me whole.
I promise to make you a home in my heart,
we'll rebuild our lives, and we'll make a new start.
Mmm. My Isabelle, I can tell… by the look in your eyes…

My breath caught. The crowd vanished, and I gravitated toward a man who sang into a microphone that connected to my soul. His eyes roamed through the crowd and then found me. I lifted my bracelets and smiled. Jericho winked and finished singing the song he'd written for me.

On the spot.

I kissed the palm of my hand and raised it up in the air. He reached out as if to grab something and then held his closed fist to his chest. All the girls around me screamed and someone threw her panties at his feet.

I laughed and wondered how I'd gotten myself into this. Was I really standing here falling in love with Jericho Sexton Cole beneath a starry night? I'd always loved him, but this was something entirely different.

Maybe it was just seeing his sexy eyes searching for me in the crowd. Could have been his bare chest beneath his jacket, or the way his mouth caressed each word he sang into the microphone. It might have been the roar of tingles I felt between my legs when I thought about the way he'd gently handled me not five minutes ago and how I needed him.

More of him.

When the song ended, the band huddled together.

"Hey, Izzy!"

I blinked into reality and turned my head.

April approached in a white cutoff shirt and had about seven blue glow sticks tied around her neck. "Isn't Trevor amazing?"

I laughed quietly. "He hasn't played yet."

She brushed her blond bangs to the side. "You just wait. Trevor can do anything he puts his mind to, and he's going to knock their socks off. Plus, look at him! He looks so charismatic up there."

"Trying to make me jealous?" Reno said in a gravelly voice, holding her from behind. She leaned her head back and kissed him feverishly.

"Is anyone else here?" I asked.

"Everyone! Somewhere," she said with a laugh. "Except for Denver, and he's pissed about it."

Joker began a beat on the drums, and Trevor stepped forward and ran a bass line. Women screamed in unison, and April was one of them. Jericho laughed and shook his head, watching Trevor with disbelief.

The cocoa began working its way through me. "You guys have fun! Maybe we'll bump into each other again," I yelled over the music.

Jericho owned the stage, hammering out a rock song that had everyone throwing their fists into the air. I couldn't hear my own thoughts as I made my way to the portable toilets. That was one memory I didn't miss from our heyday.

After executing what I liked to call the "hovercraft pee," I used the sanitizer on one of the tables to wash my hands and found myself bobbing my head along with Jericho's band. As much as I loved hearing his covers of popular songs, I melted to his original stuff.

I bristled when a set of arms wrapped around me from behind.

"I'm so glad you're okay," I heard Ivy say.

I blew out a sigh of relief and turned around. "You scared me."

She looked stunning in a turquoise dress with a matching necklace. "I hope you don't think I've been avoiding you, Izzy. I keep to myself a lot, and you've been through a difficult situation," she said, reaching for my hand. "I know you don't want to talk about it, so I've been giving you space."

"Thanks, Ivy. I really am fine."

Her mouth twisted. "I don't believe that's true and I certainly hope you don't either. But it's okay not to be fine." She smiled warmly and squeezed my hand. "Have you eaten?"

"Jericho bought me a dozen donuts."

Her mouth parted as if she might say something, but her eyes were drawn to a few people in the crowd dancing.

"I love it here," she said. "I've never been anywhere like Austin, and the Shifters here are so different. Look at this." She waved her arm toward the crowd. "Have you ever seen so many Breeds in one place? We're stars, you know. Different, distant, young and old, but we're all made of the same stuff. We all shine just as bright as the next."

"Hey there, lovely ladies." A man greeted us in a jovial voice. The first thing I noticed was he didn't have a shirt on, and the second thing was that the zipper on his knee-length shorts was wide open, unbeknownst to him. His eyes were glazed over, his speech slurred. "You need a drink?"

"We're good," I said with a short laugh. "Is there a food vendor around here? You should grab something to eat before you miss all the fun."

He lifted both hands and squeezed invisible balls in the air. "Oh, I'll grab something all right." Then he snorted and threw his head back, looking down his nose at us. "I'm—"

"Just leaving," another person cut in.

A handsome Native American man with chiseled bone structure and dark eyes approached from behind. He was tall, formidable, and dressed down in a black tank top and dark cargo pants.

I felt the familiar prickle on my skin that told me our new friend was an alpha. He folded his arms in a tough stance with his chin low, and I shivered from the power rolling off him.

"Just talking to these pretty ladies," the drunk said. "There ain't no law against it, and this is a party."

Jericho's song ended, and the crowd went nuts screaming.

"It's fine," I said. "He's just had too much to drink." Nothing I hadn't seen a million times at work.

The shirtless drunk wiped his chest. "I'm nowhere *near*

intoxicated. I could drink another six-pack and balance an egg on my nose."

"I take it back. He's a drunk asshole. But we're okay here," I said, trying to defuse the situation.

"Hear that? We're fine," the man parroted.

The Native American took a step forward, dropping his arms to his sides. "You're not a Shifter."

"Bravo!" he cheered, clapping his hands. "Fuckin' genius."

My shoulders sagged. It could have been a perfectly normal conversation, but there always had to be one alpha who wanted to bare his teeth. I much preferred the tail-waggers.

"Leave," the alpha insisted.

The drunk pulled in his lips in a cartoonish fashion. "Make me."

I stepped between the two men, lowering my voice. "Wait. If he's a Mage, this won't end well for you. Let it go."

He glanced over my shoulder, and his eyes went wild. I pivoted around and saw the drunk had crept up behind Ivy and gripped her shoulders, giving them a squeeze and taunting the alpha with mischievous eyes.

Ivy was no fighter. She glanced over her shoulder at the man. "Please let me go, or you will be hurt."

Too late. The alpha clamped his left hand around the man's throat and walked him backward.

The drunk wasn't a Mage, or he would have attacked. I'd be willing to bet he was a Relic or Sensor, because his eyes were wide with fear.

"Let him go," Ivy said in a commanding voice. "He's not thinking clearly with all the spirits in him, but you have no excuse. Consider what your violent reaction will instigate in this public place. Eyes are already on you. Will you choose to be a man of control or a man without?"

The alpha's long black hair swished around as he looked between the man he was close to choking and Ivy.

"What's your name?" she asked him.

The alpha blinked. "Church. Lorenzo Church."

"Mr. Church, will you let him go? A child may be bigger and

stronger than an ant, but he is weak when he presses his thumb on the little creature to show off his power."

Ivy had no plans to watch this altercation. She spun around so fast her long braid snapped behind her. She hurried past me and vanished in a crowd of spectators.

I smiled and looked up at Lorenzo, curious as to whether he would succumb to his alpha instincts and give the man a lashing or allow a woman's words to nestle in his head like a seed of conscience.

Lorenzo shoved the man backward until he stumbled and fell on his ass. "You're fortunate this evening. If I see you again, you won't be so lucky."

He turned around and bowed his head curtly to me before walking off. I was impressed with the level of control he showed, but it also told me how dangerous he was. Lorenzo Church wasn't a man who suffered fools, and I'd seen his kind before.

I strolled through the crowd and noticed a few verbal arguments as alcohol and testosterone began to affect some like a poison. Ivy was smart for breaking up the fight. Humans might have cheered them on, but in this environment, some spectators were eager to become participants. Breeds were divided because of a history that couldn't be erased as long as the ancients were still around to remember it. The younger generations merely sought opportunities to fight, perhaps trying to prove they were a superior Breed.

What surprised me was how a woman with such strong words could be so physically passive. She looked like a trembling flower, and I wondered if her wolf was the same. If so, it would be hard for her to find a mate.

Shifters revered strong women, not demure wallflowers.

CHAPTER 16

"Izzy! Izzy!"

I spun around and scanned the crowd. This place was bazonkers! It was nothing like the human concerts I'd been to. There were activities going on that were specific to Breed. Sensors were selling their wares, Vampires were showing off their strength, but sadly, Shifters weren't allowed to roam around in animal form.

"Izzy!"

"Who's calling me?" I yelled out with a laugh.

I kept looking around and suddenly got the chills. No one approached me, and the voice quit calling. It was a voice I didn't recognize—a man's voice. I swallowed hard and pushed my way forward as Jericho wrapped up a song by Pearl Jam. I cupped my elbows and made it to the end of the stage, scoping out every face around me.

Strangers.

It just felt off. Maybe there was another Izzy. Then I laughed and shook my head. *Of course.* They were yelling for Jericho's *band.*

He pressed his lips against the microphone and made every woman within proximity wish that his mic was her breast. At the end of the song, cheers erupted and Trevor strutted to the front of the stage and took a bow.

Jericho smiled against the mic. "Trevor, ladies and gentlemen. Give a hand for the newest member of Izzy Monroe."

Trevor looked stunned as Jericho patted him on the shoulder. "You did good," he said, away from the mic. "If you want in, you're in."

Jericho peeled off his blazer, and his chest glistened with sweat. Two girls pushed by me toward the side steps. They quickly glossed up their lips and pulled their skirts higher. One of them was a knockout with never-ending legs and blond tresses that cascaded down her back to her tailbone. I glanced down at my knees that still had faded marks and frowned.

Naturally, the one with the big breasts wanted Jericho to sign her chest. Jericho held the pen cap between his teeth and signed where she asked. The blonde turned around and bent over, pointing at her ass. I focused on his crotch, searching for an erection. Shifter men could hardly control their animal instincts when a woman turned her back like that. He scribbled his name, and to my relief—and confusion—he wasn't aroused. Then she stood on her tiptoes and whispered something in his ear, tucking a slip of paper in his hand.

As they walked away, the blonde pointed to the left, signaling where to go. He looked at the paper and wadded it up, flicking it onto the grass.

I wanted to do a victory dance.

"Get me in on some of that action," Ren said, hustling down the steps with his guitar in hand.

Jericho slicked his hair back. "They're waiting over by the parking lot in front of the pretzel stand. By the yellow car."

"You coming?"

I inched back a little, hiding behind a man who was texting on his phone.

"Hell no."

"Not your type? I know you dig the blondes."

Jericho scratched his ear and glanced around. "Not anymore. I'm all about red. Have you seen Isabelle?"

Wow. A thrill moved through me, and I could have hugged the stranger who was still between us, texting away.

Until I saw Jericho's entire body lean dramatically to the right, peering around at me. "You're glowing over there," he said with a restrained smile.

I stepped into his line of vision and touched one of the pink necklaces, which was beginning to fade. "You were really good out there," I said, a blush rising to my cheek.

The rest of the show didn't matter, only those first five minutes when he'd opened his heart and wrote me a song. He knew it, and I knew it.

Jericho swaggered forward in his sexy pants, wiping away loose strands of hair that were stuck to his face.

"It's hot out here," he said conversationally.

I wiped a finger across his slick chest. "It sure looks like it."

A bucket of ice water splashed over his head and doused the front of my clothes. A few people standing nearby laughed and clapped. Joker swung the bucket a few times before tossing it aside. "Thought you could use a little… cooling off."

"Sonofamother!" Jericho yelled, flipping back his wet hair and glaring at Joker. "You just wait. What goes around and all that."

"You suck at paybacks, just so you know." Joker rocked with laughter and walked off.

"I like him," I said.

Jericho smirked and snaked his arm around me as we took a stroll. "You would. He's a good guy, all jokes aside. After our last show, he put a skunk in the back seat of Ren's car."

"How did you know he was the one who did it?"

"The skunk sprayed him in the process. He's lucky he didn't get rabies," Jericho said with a straight face.

I laughed, reminded of how wonderful it felt to have that old connection back. Not only that, but it was stronger than ever before. I remembered the one-way conversations I'd held with Jericho on the television screen in Hawk's bedroom—words of comfort that had never reached his ears while he battled vicious demons in that room. Those words formed an invisible thread that stitched his heart to mine.

Jericho slowed his pace until we stopped amidst a crowd. His eyes were stuck on me like peanut butter, and I thought he might kiss me. My heart pounded in anticipation as he touched my locks of red hair and smiled.

"What?" I asked.

His eyes sparkled. "Nothing."

"Say it."

"Sexybelle, you don't have a clue what you do to men."

"I serve them beer and hamburgers."

He pinched my nose and I wiggled free as we kept walking. Several people we passed looked at him twice. Unlike humans, most Shifters weren't into autographs unless it was on their body, for obvious reasons. One girl wanted her lower back signed, and I stood aside with my arms folded. Male Shifters usually responded to a female who turned her back, and this one was ass-up in his face with her low-rise pants.

He gave her a quick scribble without touching her and I watched his face closely. Jericho wasn't into it.

"Mind if I smoke?" he asked.

We reached a set of lawn chairs, and I sat down with him facing me. "You know I don't care."

"Trying to quit," he admitted. "When you went missing, I couldn't light up."

He popped open his lighter and a flame touched the tip. Jericho narrowed his eyes and regarded me with a curious expression. I pulled my feet up into the chair and hugged my legs.

"Are you cold?" he asked, widening his legs.

"Not yet."

"I brought your sweats. Just say the word and I'll grab 'em."

"Don't leave me alone."

Jericho's eyes slimmed, and he flicked the ashes from his smoke. "Why did you say it like that?"

I turned my mouth down and shrugged, looking around at the crowd in the distance.

"Isabelle…"

"It's nothing."

"No, it's something."

I traced my finger over a mark on my knee. "Can you change the name of your band?"

He took another drag from his smoke and flicked it on the ground. "Why do you want me to do that?"

"Because earlier someone was yelling Izzy, and I thought they were calling for me, but then I remembered that's the name of your band. It's just unsettling to watch you perform and hear people yelling my name. I don't know—after what I just went through, I'm a little edgy."

"Done deal. What do you want to name us?"

I barked out a laugh and stretched my long legs. Jericho lifted my feet onto his lap. He slipped off my shoes and began massaging the soles of my feet with his skilled hands. If it's one thing a guitarist knows, it's how to use his fingers. I relaxed and something intense flared up between us as he hit all those pressure points that connected to other places in my body. I scooted down, gripping the arms of my chair and resting my left foot on his stomach.

"I can't name your band."

"Why not? I've run out of names. It doesn't matter what we're called; people will eventually figure out who we are and buy up tickets."

"How about the Douche Bags?"

"All right!" he shouted with an enthusiastic nod.

"No! You better not."

He laughed softly and stroked the top of my foot. Jericho had callused fingers on his left hand from playing the guitar, so when he touched me, he pressed harder than he did with his right hand because his sense of touch wasn't as acute. The rough stroke made me feel like his guitar, and I wanted him to tune me up. He sexily bit his lower lip and leaned forward, lifting his chair and dragging it closer. It caused me to bend my knees, turning my foot massage into a leg massage.

"Give us a name, Isabelle."

"I'm not good at names."

"You need practice. Someday you'll have to name your children, so go on and give us a name."

I drew in a sharp breath and held it, as if to speak.

"Say it," he said.

"No," I said in an uncertain tone.

His fingers moved up my leg, and all I could feel were his warm hands caressing my inner thigh. He inched his way toward the one place I needed him the most.

"Say it," he whispered, his knuckles brushing against my sex and making me shudder.

I watched him with heavy-lidded eyes. "Heat."

He leaned forward and kissed my knee, giving it some rock-star consideration. "I like it. Heat."

"Speaking of, Jericho. I can't stay at your house if I'm going into heat soon. I need to go to somewhere private."

Jericho leaned back in his chair with a pensive expression. His wet hair had begun to dry, slicked away from his face and revealing his intense features. He had heavy brows that drew attention to his milky-green eyes.

"It's not that I don't trust my pack, but you're unmated and that would create a stir. Austin wouldn't agree to it. I can put you up in a hotel," he offered. "Sound good?"

"I'll pay you—"

"Bullshit, Isabelle. We're friends, and there are no paybacks. You just named my band so now we're even. How long do you have?"

"About a week."

"Do you want me to stay with you in the hotel?"

I laughed. Hell's bells would *that* be a royally bad idea. When I went into heat, I usually slept in the nude. Alone. Even my past lovers knew the drill. The pregnancy risk was too high. Human contraception? Forget it. Those who tried it learned the hard way how useless it was among our kind. Maybe humans didn't care about pregnancy, but Shifters took children seriously, so it was uncommon to see babies born from unmated couples.

I thought about Jericho's suggestion to stay with me in the hotel. My body would be primed—my sexual appetite off the charts. Males can scent a woman during her cycle, and from what I'd been told, it was like aromatic crack. I guess that's just nature's way of speeding things along, and it happens among humans too. Only they slap scientific words on it, like ovulation and pheromones. It's almost laughable how they try so hard to deny that they also have instincts and sometimes succumb to them.

"No, I don't think it's a good idea if you're sleeping five feet from me while I'm naked and writhing in the bed."

His eyes darkened a little. "On the contrary, I think it's an excellent idea."

"I'm serious."

"This city is filled with Shifters, Isabelle. This isn't like those small towns we used to live in. They might scent you out in that room."

"Jericho," I said with a heat in my cheeks. "I don't want to put you in that position."

He stood up and kicked his chair back. I clutched my chest as he dropped to his knees, gripping the armrests of my chair.

"I think it's about time I clear the air and tell you that I *want* to be in that position. I want to be in a whole lot of positions with you. If you need to take it slow, we'll take it slow. I've given you space this week because of what that asshole did to you."

His face was so close to mine that I could see the intensity flaring in his eyes.

"I sang that song tonight because I want you to know how I feel—how I've always felt about you. I wasn't good enough for you back then and if you'd hooked up with a guy like me, it would have messed you up. We've had good times and bad, sickness and health—so I think we've covered all the vows humans share. I love you, baby." He lifted his hand and cupped my cheek, brushing his thumb across my lips. "You're my sexy redhead. I love that you walked off after the first song because you're not just another groupie trying to get in my pants."

I reached out and stroked his temple with the tips of my fingers. "That's because I know the real guy beneath it all who's terrible at miniature golf. I know the man who spent every dollar in his pocket to buy a pair of new shoes for the little boy in the motel room next to ours whose mother was so cracked out she didn't care what happened to him. I love your voice and your music, but I love when you're just yourself around me."

He smiled, and his jade eyes simmered. "Anything else you love?"

"Hey, you two," Lexi said, excitedly running in our direction. "Jericho, stand up."

He glanced up at Lexi and rose to his feet.

She wrapped her arms around him. "Thanks for giving Trevor a chance. He's over the moon about it."

Jericho chuckled and patted her back as Austin strolled up. "He's awesome. Didn't know he'd been holding back on me."

Lexi backed up and landed in Austin's arms. He lazily dipped her for a kiss.

Jericho held the arms of my chair and bent down. "I'm making a food run. What do you feel like eating?"

"Lobster would be fabulous."

He rubbed his nose playfully against mine. "Typical fair food."

"If you see hot dogs, grab me one of those. You know what I like."

His face soured. "Yeah, that kraut."

"So what's wrong with sauerkraut?"

"I can't kiss you if you've been eating that stuff."

I tried to suppress my smile, but he was right there in my face. "Who says you're going to kiss me?"

"Oh, I'm going to kiss you, baby. And I want you to sit here, thinking about the lipgasm I'm going to give to you. I don't kiss other women, Isabelle. I've been saving my lips for you, so hang tight, and I'll be back with those hot dogs."

When he swaggered off, I felt like I needed a cold shower and a beer. Jericho found the switch that turned me on, and he didn't even need to touch me.

"Wow," Lexi remarked, plopping down in the chair beside me. "I've never seen Jericho acting this way before. So you two go way back, huh?"

"Eons. We lived, breathed, and ate together for five years on the road. He changed my life."

"For the better, I hope. Austin, honey, can you get me a funnel cake?"

Austin was jingling change in his pocket, his eyes alert and watchful. "Not sure I want to leave you alone with this crowd."

"It's a party. We're staying here, and if anyone tries anything funny, *bad* Lexi comes out to play."

His brows arched. "Bad wolf Lexi, or *bad girl* Lexi? Let me know if I need to go home and get my gloves," he said suggestively.

She extended her leg and tried to kick him as he chuckled and disappeared into the crowd.

"You two are great together," I said.

"He's my first love." Lexi smiled and tied her straight hair into a ponytail. "I didn't think he liked me back then, but I found out he'd been in love with me since high school. Boys just have a stupid way of showing it. Then they grow up into men who have a *really* stupid way of showing it."

I laughed. "That sounds right. So you've been together that long?"

Her brown eyes locked on mine. "No. We were apart for seven years. Sometimes you need time away to realize how you really feel about someone, you know?"

I removed my plastic bracelets and necklace since the lights had died out. Lexi had a point. I thought I'd known how I'd felt about Jericho years ago, but I was uncertain. I'd convinced myself it was just one of those infatuations. I was wrong. Seeing Jericho again was like finding the other half of me that had been missing.

"Do you… have a pack?" Lexi asked.

"No. I've never had one. I'm just… somewhat…"

"You don't need to explain yourself to me, Izzy. I don't blame you for being standoffish. Some of the packs around here are intimidating. I grew up human, so you can imagine how scared I was when Austin asked me to live with a bunch of men. This is new to me, but I've never been happier. Well, except for the toilet-seat situation they can't seem to comprehend. We all have our different personalities, but we're a tight group. We look out for one another."

"Do you know a man named Lorenzo Church?"

She arched her brows dramatically. "Where did you hear that name?"

"I ran into him earlier. He was pissing territorial lines."

"Oh brother," she said with a sigh. "That sounds like Lorenzo all right. He's one of the local Packmasters… and my cousin."

"Your cousin?" I asked in disbelief.

She held up a hand. "Not by blood. He's called once or twice to invite me to meet my real family, but I'm not there yet. I've had enough drama in the past year. Anyhow, my family's right here. I don't need a DNA test to tell me who loves me. Stay away from Lorenzo."

"Bad news?"

She twisted her mouth. "Not a bad guy... I don't want to make it sound like that. He's..." Then she sat up and turned her chair toward me, leaning forward. "Okay, here's how it is. Lorenzo is rich. Filthy rich. He runs one of the largest packs in the territory, and he's a man to be feared. I say that because he'll take the law into his own hands. He has... issues with people saying no to him. He also doesn't give his pack a slap on the wrist for insubordination. The wrath of Church is something to be feared. Was he hitting on you? Please tell me he wasn't hitting on you. Lorenzo has a few bitches in his pack he brings to bed, so he's not a monogamous wolf looking to settle."

I covered my face and smothered a laugh. "I wasn't planning on going to bed with him, Lexi. I just ran into him when he was about to throttle some unfortunate drunk in front of an audience. Ivy stopped him."

"Ivy?"

"She has a subtle way with words that seems to put men in their place."

Lexi leaned back and crossed her bare legs. "That's for sure. Ivy's not his type—she's too sensitive and demure. Lorenzo likes his women fiery, just like you. Sassy is the word I'm looking for."

"Thanks," I said with a generous smile. "Better than some names I've been called."

She rolled her eyes. "From jackasses in the bar, I'm sure. I click with you, so I hope it works out between you and Jericho. April's a good friend, and we get along famously, but she has a different personality type than me. Austin calls me feisty."

"That's attractive to an alpha."

"Yes, which is why you need to stay away from Lorenzo."

I swatted at a mosquito. "No need to worry. I wasn't the one he was looking at."

She furrowed her brow, but before she could reply, my phone rang.

"This is the party to whom you are speaking."

Lexi quietly laughed and looked at the crowd behind her.

"Hello?" I glanced at an unknown number. "Jericho, is that you?" The line went dead, and I set my phone on my lap.

"Who was that?"

"Wrong number. What does Austin think of all this?"

She pursed her lips in thought. "He's on the fence, but that's his job as a Packmaster. At the end of the day, he can't tell his pack who to love. I'm not saying Jericho loves you; I don't really know what your relationship is behind closed doors." She fidgeted and then sat up straight. "Yeah, this just ventured into awkward territory."

"No problem," I said. "I like your honesty."

Jericho and Austin reappeared with several white boxes and a six-pack. Austin sat on the ground in front of Lexi, and she spread a paper napkin over her lap before he handed her a hot dog.

"This isn't what I ordered," she said.

Austin rubbed his jaw. "If I had stood in that line, you would have never seen me again."

"That line was ridiculous when we left," Jericho agreed. He walked behind me and leaned over, presenting me with a sauerkraut-covered hot dog. I put the box in my lap, and he put his hands on my shoulders. "So, Isabelle has given our band a new name. It's a good time to shake things up with a little change now that we have new blood. I think with Trevor's looks, the girls are going to dig the new name."

"What is it?" Lexi asked after taking a huge bite of her hot dog. Austin reached up and wiped a dollop of mustard off her lip, then licked it off his finger.

"Heat. I think it's pretty badass."

"That's perfect!" Lexi's chuckle graduated into a cartoonish laugh that made her snort and cover her mouth. "That's what the women go into watching you onstage."

Jericho's fingers began rubbing my shoulders while he listened. Suddenly he leaned down and whispered, "What's wrong?"

"Nothing. Why?"

"You hunch your shoulders when you're stressed."

I moved out of his grasp and picked at my hot dog. "I'm not stressed."

"Isabelle…"

"Was it the phone call?" Lexi asked.

When everyone went quiet, Jericho walked around and knelt before me. "What call?"

"Just a hang-up call."

"Why would that stress you out?"

"I don't know. It felt like someone was following me earlier. Not just someone yelling out my name. It's that instinct that my wolf keeps telling me something's off."

Austin sat back and cracked open a can. "It's the energy in the air that's making your wolf nervous. Everyone's edgy tonight because of the mixed crowd. Earlier we saw a Mage escorted off the grounds for throwing his energy into a Chitah."

Fireworks went off in the distance.

Lexi gasped. "I want to watch!"

Austin chuckled handsomely and stood up, holding out his hand. "Come on, Ladybug. Let's go get you some sparklers."

They finished their hot dogs and strolled off, holding hands.

"I really like those two," I said. "They're perfect together."

Jericho drank a few swallows of beer and set it on the grass. "It's more obvious to everyone else but them. That's how it goes sometimes. Can't see the forest for the trees. They bicker, and she has her tantrums, but that's the spark that puts the passion in their sex life."

I leaned back in the chair and let my thoughts drift away from me. Fighting sure didn't put the passion in *my* sex life. It had the opposite effect on me.

I must have tilted my chair back too far, because Jericho suddenly lunged forward to grab me as the seat folded. It happened so quickly that when my back hit the ground, I couldn't stop laughing. He stood over me with his hair hanging down and a cheesy grin on his face.

"Isabelle, you're a nut."

A shrill scream poured out of my mouth and I flipped over. He tried to grab me, but I slapped him away.

"What's wrong?"

"Something crawled in my shirt behind my hair!" I kept screaming. Then I went into that body convulsion you do when a critter is on the loose inside your garments.

Jericho pulled the ends of my shirt and peeled it off.

In public.

With everyone standing around watching.

"Don't move."

Those two words made my eyes widen, and I stood as still as a tree. His hand slowly smoothed across my back and then he flicked his wrist. That was my cue to run and do the arm flap.

Jericho stared at the ground and scuffed his shoe across the grass. "That was the biggest damn water bug I've ever seen."

"Hell's bells. I'm going to be sick."

Someone wolf whistled and I crossed my arms over my bra. "Thanks, Jericho. Now everyone got to see the second act."

"At least it was a comedy show." He held up my shirt between two fingers. "Do you want to put this back on?"

"What are my alternatives, Mr. Shirtless?"

He chuckled and patted my shirt to make certain nothing else had crawled inside. I snatched it from him and slipped it on.

"I don't think I'm a country girl."

A slow laugh began to roll out of him. "You should have seen your face. I wish I had recorded that on video."

All the humor ebbed away from my expression, and I reached out and put my arms around Jericho. "I'm sorry Hawk did that to you. I had to watch you suffer on that television and it almost killed me."

His hands flattened on my back reassuringly. "It's okay, baby. He didn't hurt me."

"I wish you could have heard me talking to you so you wouldn't have been so alone in there."

His mouth moved against my temple. "I wasn't alone, Isabelle. I got you under my skin."

"Sounds itchy."

"It can be uncomfortable at times. More like a rash."

"Does it burn?" I said with a soft chuckle.

"Sometimes. Other times it feels like a heat that's out of control." His hands softened around my body, and I pressed a kiss at the base of his throat. "Isabelle, I rented one of the trailers on the grounds for the band."

"Why are you telling me?"

His ragged breath heated my ear. "Because I'm going to make love to you."

CHAPTER 17

AFTER JERICHO HAD ANNOUNCED HIS intent to seduce me in a private trailer, he led me through the crowd by my hand and made love to me with his eyes each time he glanced over his shoulder.

I, Isabelle Monroe, became aroused as the thoughts of what we were about to do stimulated my senses.

It wasn't just my senses being stimulated.

His steps became rushed, and at one point, Joker appeared. "Hey, Jericho! They want us to play another song."

"Later."

"I told them yes."

"Later!" Jericho shouted, his urgent pace now a jog. I struggled to keep up, my shoes in my left hand, but I kept stepping on sticks and pebbles.

"Ouch," I hissed, hopping on my foot.

Jericho spun around and lifted me over his shoulder. It was so cavemannish that it made me want to laugh. But I didn't, because I was too distracted with running my hands down his strong back.

"Isabelle, you need to stop doing that," I heard him say.

His words filled my head like a fever. I slid my hands into his jeans and grabbed his ass. When I felt his fingers claw at the waistline of my shorts, I wanted to knock him down and mount him right there in front of the crowd.

A squeak sounded, and he set me on my feet. "Get in."

"Is this ours?"

Jericho was panting and held my face so close I thought he would kiss me. I readied myself for it while staring at his lips.

"Get in, baby. I can't hold out much longer."

This was happening. This was *finally* happening.

He closed the door and turned the lock. The dim lights outside illuminated the cozy trailer with a frosty glow. I faced the door, and on my left was a small seating area with a table, like something out of a diner. The air was stuffy, and I could see the edge of a bed in the room to my right.

Jericho lifted the ends of my shirt over my head and dropped it to the floor. He cupped my breasts, rolling his thumbs over the lacy fabric of my bra until my nipples grew hard beneath. I swayed and gripped the belt loops on his pants. His hands disappeared behind my back to unlatch my bra.

"I've been wanting this for decades," he said in a rough voice edged with desire.

"Well, you've had plenty of practice."

His jaw rubbed against my cheek as he unhooked the strap. "Don't do that. Don't bring those women in here with us. Not a damn one of them can hold a candle to you, Isabelle Monroe."

The moment I heard the muffled snap of my bra coming undone, I felt myself coming undone right along with it. I'd never felt more naked in front of a man than when Jericho carefully slid the straps down my shoulders and let it drop to the floor. My arms remained at my sides, waiting for him to make the next move. I had been told I was an assertive lover, and I was afraid it might scare him off.

My shaky breath was the only sound in the room. Then his warm hands curved around my breasts, stroking my nipples and making me sway. He dropped to one knee and drew one into his mouth, sucking eagerly as I moaned and grabbed a fistful of hair.

He lifted his eyes to mine and wrapped his fingers around my wrist. "Let's go lie down," he said, standing up and leading me to the bed.

Before I could sit, Jericho unfastened my shorts. I'd heard his sex stories before and they typically involved him banging a girl against a wall, so I braced myself for a quickie.

The shorts hit the floor and he tossed them to the side. Then his fingers wasted no time pulling down my panties. "Sexybelle," he whispered. "My sweet little redhead. Lie down on the bed for me."

As soon as my panties tangled around my feet, I sat down. He placed the flat of his hand on my chest and coaxed me onto my back.

Jericho kicked out of his shoes and unbuttoned his pants, but he didn't bother with the rest when he saw me scooting up the bed toward the pillows.

"Where you going?"

"Nowhere," I said with a coy smile, bending my knees and holding them together.

He crawled up the bed with a sex-laced grin, parting my legs and resting his body between them. "There's no escaping me this time."

Oh God. He felt deliciously warm. Jericho studied my navel and circled his finger around it before mimicking the same strokes with his tongue.

"Ohh," I moaned, watching his eyes glitter as they looked up at me.

"You said you weren't a Southern girl, Isabelle, but I think I can change your mind," he said, moving his mouth south of the border.

I drew in a breath and held it as his rapturous tongue learned every stroke and flick that made me moan and squirm. Once he'd worked me into a tightly wound coil of desire, he began kissing my inner thigh and inserted his fingers.

"Peaches," he whispered, increasing momentum and returning with his mouth.

I grabbed a fistful of his hair and lifted my hips off the bed.

"That's it, baby. Give me more," he said, building me closer and closer to climax with his skilled hands and mouth.

I gasped and leaned forward, my body humming with desire. Then he flipped me onto my stomach. I heard his zipper and then him shucking out of his jeans. I eagerly climbed up on all fours and readied myself.

Jericho pushed at my back until I fell on my stomach. "Not that way."

"Why not?" I asked, knowing how most Shifters preferred sex.

His hot, naked body covered my back, and he parted my legs. "All fours or standing up is the only way I've done it. I want something different with you, Isabelle."

He put the blunt head to my core and eased his shaft in just a fraction. The girth made me shudder, and my entire body ignited. Jericho pulled my hair away from my neck and began a deep kiss against my nape, using all the right techniques of sucking and nipping.

I was trying to reach between our legs to get things going when he seized my wrists and held them so I couldn't move. He was gentle, and my body rocked with need.

"Come on, baby," he whispered against my neck. "I can feel you coming."

Hell's bells, he was right. My entire body tensed, and as he blew on my neck and ran his ravenous tongue in a circle, I lifted my backside, making him groan.

Hearing Jericho release all that caged sex filled me with heat.

And then it happened, like a twig snapping or a firecracker going off.

I forced my body back so hard it drove his shaft all the way in. All the restraints of pent-up passion crumbled away as he slammed his hips against mine.

I cried into the sheets, overcome by the possession I felt for him. His hands slid between the mattress and me and cupped my breasts, pinching my nipples. The sweet sting made me raise my hips, and he pumped even harder. Wood creaked as whatever flimsy contraption we were on began to shake.

"Jericho… Jericho…" I panted against the pillow as he pulled my hair.

He abruptly flipped me onto my back. "Better," he said, looking into my eyes tenderly. "I've wanted to look at that pretty freckled face beneath me for the last twenty years. You haven't aged a day," He kissed my cheeks and brow between his words. "Still as young… and beautiful… as ever."

"No need for the compliments, sir. I'm already yours." I gracefully draped one leg across his back.

Jericho arched a single eyebrow. "This isn't about sex." His mouth hovered over mine, as if he were uncertain if he could kiss me. I leaned up, and the friction between our lips barely touching was indescribable as he slid back inside me. He whispered so quietly that I almost didn't hear him. "I want to make love to you."

He gently lifted my left leg and rocked into me, kissing my neck so sweetly I could have wept. My fingers traced up his arms to his long hair, which felt like silk in my hands. Jericho moved his mouth to the right side of my neck, and through heavy breaths, he managed to plant the most sensual and giving kisses across my skin. Our bodies sank into each other, and I'd never had a feeling until that moment that I belonged to someone.

I felt like *his*.

The slower he moved against me, the more I needed him. He was hitting the sweet spot and my nails bit into his skin as a swell of desire intensified between my legs, making my body tremble and my muscles clench. I didn't want to come alone, and I knew he was holding back on purpose.

"Together," I said.

Jericho lifted his head and a smile hooked one corner of his mouth. "Ladies first," he insisted.

"Don't be a hard-ass. I want to do this together."

He thrust deeper, and I moaned. "I want to pleasure you, baby. Just let it go."

Frustrated by his stubbornness, I cupped his cheeks and leaned up, giving him my tongue, and our kiss went deep. So deep it felt just as intimate as the sex. When it broke, my mouth slid to his ear and I spoke words that broke his willpower as his hips crashed into mine.

"Sweetheart. Oh God, please come with me…" My words broke off into a series of moans, and I gripped the roots of his hair.

"Say that again."

"Come with me," I said in shallow pants.

He hooked his arm beneath my leg and pulled it up, driving harder as I held onto his shoulders.

"Not that," he said.

What had I said? What was it he wanted me to repeat? My brain scrambled. "*Sweetheart.*"

His body stiffened and felt like granite beneath my fingertips.

Jericho shouted and dropped his head, a shower of long hair curtaining my face as I cried out, still rocking beneath him. He picked up the frantic pace again, and we found our release… together.

One word we were always meant to be.

———— ∞◦⌘◦∞ ————

Jericho and I held each other for what seemed like an eternity. We nestled our bodies close, our damp skin sticking together. I traced my finger over his left bicep and circled over his tattoo. Jericho tenderly drew my hand to his mouth and kissed the marks on my wrist. I smiled against his chest.

"What's so funny?" he asked, absently brushing his hand through my hair.

"The song playing outside. Reminds me of the night we went to that DJ's house and you sat on a soda can that some rock legend had autographed… I forget who."

"That wasn't my fault. If you're going to get an autograph from a legend, you don't put it on a can of root beer."

"Maybe it's all he had with him."

"If that's the case, then I'm glad I sat on it. If I am in the presence of a rock legend, holding a can of root beer and a permanent marker, then feel free to tie my testicles to the bumper of a big wheeler and hit the gas."

I kissed his chest. "You *are* the rock legend."

He sighed. "Maybe that's not a title I want anymore."

I turned over and rested my arms on his chest, looking up at him. "What do you mean?"

"Lexi's going to open a pastry shop pretty soon. Austin wanted me to play there once in a while with my acoustic. I dig that scene. Reminds me of some of the places we used to hang out in when coffee was cheap."

"Yeah," I said wistfully. "But you're so good at what you do. Plus, there's no money in that. Not to mention the customers would line up outside the door and go crazy to see you."

He laughed quietly. "Maybe that's what Austin's thinking. It would draw in a crowd, and after a while, I wouldn't be such a big deal like I am onstage. I can do low-key."

"Is that what *I* am? Low-key?"

His eyes dragged down, and he shifted so that we were facing each other. "My favorite keys on the piano are the lower keys. They have the most depth and soul. Same with the guitar; the high strings are sweet, but the low ones will break your heart. Maybe it's time I tone things down. But fair warning—I still like to party and have a good time."

"Me too."

"I like to hang out at the bar and get rowdy."

"So do I."

He licked his lips. "Sometimes I have a little weed. Not often, but I usually have a few hits when I'm partying with a crowd."

"Does it still feel good?"

"Not so much."

I circled my finger on his clavicle. "Then maybe it's not a big deal if you just stop. I don't want to see you go back to that life again."

"Done deal."

"No, I don't want you to hold that against me."

"Same old Isabelle," he said, kissing my forehead. "I can drop the weed without blinking, but I can't quit smoking."

"I don't care, sweetheart. I'm not trying to change you. But when I ask you to put a mint in your mouth, you're going to obey."

He rocked with laughter and grabbed my thigh, giving it a firm squeeze. "What if you took a job helping Lexi out in the new shop when they open it? She's going to need experienced staff because she'll be too busy working the register and making pastries. Austin talked about hiring a couple of girls."

"She should have table service. Why be like everyone else? People like to be seated and waited on. Sometimes they don't feel so important in their daily life, and having someone take care of them is a big deal."

"You always had a sweet heart," he murmured, kissing my forehead again.

"I can always spot the lonely ones. I spend more time talking to them so they feel like someone cares. It's not just about slinging beer."

"I know that, baby. You think I don't respect what you do? That's why I asked about the pastry shop. Nobody keeps a cool head in chaos better than you. It's not about all that hip-shaking you do in the bar for tips, but damn, Isabelle. You *shine,* and it's infectious. That's the effect you had on me when we first met. You made me feel like somebody."

"You *are* somebody. You always were; you just didn't see it."

He smoothed his hand down my arm. "That's what I mean. You have a gift. I've seen you work your magic, and it blows me away. You pick out the meanest bastard in the room and make him feel like he just might have a heart."

My lip quivered, and I turned away. "It's not true, Jericho," I sobbed. "You can't say that to me."

All the emotion I'd kept bottled about Hawk began to seep out.

"Hey, now. What's going on? Shhh… Baby, talk to me," he said, whispering against my shoulder.

With my back to him, I sniffled and tried to keep my voice level. "How could I have been with such a monster? What does that say about me? I can't bring out the best in anyone, Jericho. Maybe I bring out the worst."

He propped up on his arm and his voice darkened. "Why the hell would you say that?"

And then it came out. "Because look what I did to you!"

He turned me onto my back. "You think you're the one responsible for me shooting up? Do you?" He sighed hard and tenderly brushed my hair away from my face. "I never had a purpose in life like my brothers did. Reno was the bounty hunter, the twins were good with numbers, and then I came along. I carried that with me my whole damn life. When the fame hit, I wasn't ready for it. The drugs were recreational at first, but eventually I needed them."

"Why?"

"Because I felt like a dirtbag. I wanted to be numb. What good was I as a Shifter? I toured with humans, lived in the human world, and for what? To have women thrown in my face and drugs shoved up my nose. That downward spiral that you seem to think is *your* fault was me trying to forget what a loser I felt like. You were the best thing I had, Isabelle. You're the best thing I'll ever have."

Jericho wiped the tears off my cheeks and lashes.

"Don't ever talk that way again. It's not you," he said in a softened voice. "Hawk was a deceptive sonofabitch who got what he had coming. You're trusting, and you gravitate toward people who need help. Maybe he looked like he had all his shit together, but you must have sensed he needed someone. You look for the best in people. That's not a fault, Isabelle. It's not a weakness. It's what makes you the best damn woman I know. So go ahead and let it out."

"I don't want to cry anymore," I said decidedly, pulling the sheet to cover my waist as I sat up.

He smirked. "Your hair looks like a Pomeranian caught in a tornado."

I smiled sweetly at him. "But you still love me."

"Yeah, baby, I still love you," he said, kissing my lips.

"Even though I don't have a tattoo?" I said jokingly.

He snorted. "Seriously, Isabelle?"

When he pulled his head back to look at me, I shrugged. "It's no secret what kind of women you date. Blondes who are well-endowed and inked."

He threaded his fingers through my hair. "First of all, you're the only redhead I've ever knowingly been with for a reason. And on a side note, I think your tits are *spectacular*. Candy-red nipples," he whispered against my ear, "and more than a mouthful." His fingers grazed along the feminine curve of my chest. "As for the tattoos, I don't want you getting one because you think it's a requirement on my checklist. Some ink is invisible, and I know all the stories that mark you."

"Not all," I said.

"Yeah, we got some catching up to do. Look, I'm sorry, Isabelle."

"For what?"

"For being such a dick and leaving you on the street that morning wearing a paper bag."

"You were just being your usual cocky self."

He was quiet for a couple of beats and working something out in his head. "I want you to stay here; I'll be back in a little bit."

"Where are you going? Do you have to go onstage again?"

"I need to run a quick errand. There's a toilet in here, but the shower is questionable. You might have to take a bath in the sink."

"Super. Be sure to pick me up a rubber ducky before you come back," I said through our kisses.

"Maybe I'll just lick you clean, Sexybelle."

"Mmm, sounds good," I said, tasting his bottom lip.

"Hey, what are you doing?" He glanced down at my palm where I held one of his chunky rings, the one that depicted a vicious wolf's head.

"I want a piece of you with me while you're gone," I said, sliding it on my fattest finger. "Plus, I like this ring."

Jericho blew a burst of air against my neck, making a terrible sound. I lifted my shoulder and squirmed away from the ticklish effect. It was so easy to fall back into our friendship—the way we were before it all fell apart. After a minute, he hopped off the bed and pulled up his jeans. "Be back in two shakes of a stripper's ass. You have a change of clothes by the bed, and there's some junk in the bathroom to brush your teeth with."

"Super. I love brushing my teeth with junk."

"Stay sexilicious, and don't go anywhere. I'll keep my phone in my pocket if you need to call."

"Oh," I said, looking around. "My phone is by the lawn chairs. When I fell, it dropped in the grass."

"I'll grab it on my way back." He headed down the hall and turned on a low lamp. "I'm going to lock the door behind me. Don't let anyone in unless they're holding a six-pack."

"What if they're wearing one?"

"Then you'll know it's me and you can open the door."

CHAPTER 18

D AMN IF JERICHO DIDN'T WALK out of that trailer whistling.

Whistling!

After grabbing a plain black tee, he drove away from the campsite. As much as he wanted to stay behind and hold Isabelle, Jericho couldn't put off this deal any longer. Since he didn't have the right connections, he called Wheeler as soon as he sped onto the main road.

Wheeler had a contact, so with reluctance, he arranged for Jericho to meet with him. When Jericho pulled up to a large glass building, he parked the truck halfway on the sidewalk and got out.

A gentleman puffing on a cigar dropped his stogie to the ground and smashed it out with his brown cowboy boot. He was a robust man with a silver beard and blue dress shirt. "My name's Tony," the man said with a brisk nod. "Wheeler's a friend of mine from way back. He tells me I need to fix you up."

Jericho slammed the truck door and wiped his nose. "I don't have much time. Show me what you got."

"Come inside and we'll make a deal." Tony jangled his keys and unlocked the door. Jericho moved to the center of the room, hands shaking, feeling jittery.

Tony's gait was slow as he went to the left side of the dark room. "Looks like you got it bad. Come over here and I'll set you up."

Jericho moved toward the counter and watched anxiously as Tony flipped on a few lights.

"What's your poison?"

Jericho cleared his throat. "Engagement rings."

Rings weren't really the Shifter way because jewelry sometimes got lost during the shift unless you were careful to take it off first or remembered where you'd left it. But Jericho couldn't help himself— he wanted Isabelle to have the whole damn fairy tale.

Tony chuckled. "You had that look in your eye; I figured as much. Do you have something in mind? Platinum, white gold, marquise, princess cut?"

"I don't know." He leaned over the counter and eyed all the glittering jewels.

"Well, tell me about your woman. Is she one of those shy girls?"

Jericho snorted. "Hell no. She's confident, beautiful, and strong. But she has a kind heart. I don't deserve someone like her."

"May I recommend a solitaire? One stone for one girl—the *only* one. Speaks volumes. If you told me the first three, I'd say go for flashy, but if she's good-hearted, then she's the kind of woman who doesn't give a shit what her friends think."

"Yeah, that's Isabelle."

Tony led him to a display of rings and pulled them out. After a confusing glance around, one ring caught his eye.

"A beauty, isn't she?" Tony smiled and pulled the ring from the case, holding it between his fat fingers. "This one is special. She's a one-carat diamond that sparkles like no other because she has over one hundred and thirty facets. It's like wearing a star on your finger. Fourteen-karat white gold. Hold her in your hand."

Jericho slid the ring halfway up his finger and grinned. "This is it. She's the one."

"If you said that to your woman, then I do believe it is."

"How much?"

"Free."

Jericho flicked his eyes up. "Bullshit."

Tony shrugged and took the ring away, carefully pushing it in a black box. "Wheeler's picking up the tab. You guys can sort it all out."

Jericho leaned heavily on his arms. "Look, I'm not having my *brother* pay for my woman's engagement ring."

"And do you have five large on you?"

"Shit."

Tony sighed and strolled over to the left, sliding open a display. He slapped a white box on the counter. "Or, you can probably dig out what you have in your pocket for this cheap piece of shit. Each time she squints and tries to see the stone, she'll remember it's your love that's important and not the ring."

He wanted to reach across the counter and strangle Tony. What money Jericho didn't spend on partying, he gave over to Austin to help with bills. It would only take a few weeks for him to pay back Wheeler. The bastard. "I'll take *this* one," he said, tapping the black box in front of him.

"Excellent choice. You can bring her in later if we need to have it resized."

While Tony locked up the counter, Jericho made a quick call. "Wheeler, I'm going to kill you."

"You wanted the best, right?"

Jericho spun around and whispered harshly into the phone. "How do you think I feel, knowing my brother—"

"Save it," he replied. "You're paying me back; this is just an advance because of the short notice. I wouldn't buy your woman's ring—that's too fucking weird. Did you tell Austin?"

"Hell no. I think I should tell Isabelle first, don't you?"

Wheeler grumbled on the other end. "If you say so. Just remember, the Packmaster has the final say in who stays in the pack. It's common courtesy to tell him your intentions. After what went down with Hawk, he might not let her in."

"I doubt it. Keep your mouth shut until I ask her. Shit," he whispered. "I'm fucking nervous."

Wheeler chuckled darkly. "Where is she?"

"In the trailer I rented."

"That's sweet. So you left your girl to go shopping."

Jesus, Wheeler could be a pain in the ass. Jericho paced around the middle of the room and heard music coming through the phone, but it didn't sound like a live band. "Where the hell are you?"

"I split. Not my scene. I'm at a strip club, and don't go blabbing to Austin. He thinks I went to grab another beer. Do me a favor and keep him in the dark." Wheeler hung up.

Tony flipped off the light and handed Jericho a bag. "Here you go. Good luck, son."

That put one nervous butterfly in his stomach that was more like a winged demon breathing fire. All of a sudden, his impulsive idea was giving him cold feet. *What if she said no? What if this was too soon? What if she wanted a different ring? What if she didn't want a ring?* Well hell, he'd buy her whatever she wanted. Emeralds, rubies, donuts… any damn thing.

The thing is, her saying yes wasn't just about accepting Jericho, but it also meant joining the Weston pack. She'd never known stability. She'd never known a family who loved her unconditionally.

Isabelle had clung to him all those years ago because he had given her those things. If she wouldn't live with his pack, then Jericho would be faced with a choice: love or family.

That wasn't a choice he wanted to make.

—◦◦◦◦◦—

After Jericho left, I got dressed and snooped through the drawers in the trailer. Most were empty, but I found some food in the kitchen and made a peanut-butter sandwich. A blues band played outside, and I wondered if the music would go on night and day.

The trailer was beginning to get stuffy, and I had no idea how to turn on the air—if it even had air. What I really wanted to do was grab a lawn chair and sit by the door with a cold beer in my hand. Jericho had locked me in with the best of intentions, but this was a festival. I had never once been to a festival and spent it locked inside a vehicle! Then again, I'd never been to an all-Breed festival, so he was probably right.

Someone rapped their knuckles on the front door, and I froze mid-bite. The second series of knocks sounded more urgent.

"Izzy? It's April. Can I use your toilet?"

I laughed softly and put my sandwich down. "One second."

When I opened the door, April rushed by me. "Oh my God, I hope you're not naked," she said, running in short steps down the hall. As she used the toilet, she left the door open so she could talk to me. "I'm so sorry. I went to those portable outhouses and I can't. I just *can't!* There's no telling what kind of cooties are in there."

"That's okay, I understand completely."

After another minute, April emerged, her expression more relaxed. "I feel so much better," she confessed, taking a lazy stroll toward me.

"How did you know we weren't in here knocking boots?"

April raked her blond hair away from her face. It fell to her shoulders in an angular cut that was shorter in the back and longer on the sides. She took a seat at the tiny table. "I ran into Wheeler earlier and he told me you were by yourself."

"How did Wheeler know Jericho left?"

April pulled off her shoe and shook out a pebble. "Wheeler saw him get in the truck and drive off."

My stomach did a flip-flop. "Drive off? He left the festival?"

"You didn't know?"

I glanced at a clock and noticed over an hour had elapsed. "Was there an emergency with the pack?"

"Not that I'm aware of. Denver's still at the bar, and we think Ben took off an hour ago. I can't find Reno," she said irritably. "He's always forgetting his phone. The last time I saw him was by the fireworks. I went to get water, and when I got back, he was gone. He probably went looking for me when I told him to stay put. God knows where he is! I should have stayed where I was, but I had to go, and I knew Jericho's trailer was parked over here. Holy smokes, he's going to kill me."

"Doubtful. How did you know which trailer?"

"Trevor pointed it out when we were walking around. Joker told him the band always rents a trailer during these outdoor events in case one of them wants to take a nap or get away from the crowd."

"Well, maybe you should go back to where you were standing by the fireworks," I suggested. "I'm sure Reno will find you. If not, maybe you can talk one of the singers into paging him."

She laughed. "He'd really kill me if I embarrassed him like that." She pulled a tube of lip gloss out of her purse and ran it over her lips. "Wandering around is only going to keep us separated, so it's better if I stay in the spot he last saw me. Maybe I'll call Lexi and see if she and Austin can keep me company."

I stood up and pulled a can of soda from the fridge mounted in the wood paneling. "It's cold. I don't know how the power works out here."

She cracked open the can and gulped down several swallows. "Mmm. I love orange soda. Reno said the guy who runs the property got it all hooked up with power. I think he wants to do this every year because he's making good money. Tickets went on sale weeks ago for a limited time, and he tacked on a parking charge per night. I can only fathom what he's making off *these* things," she said, tapping her fingernail on the wall of the RV.

I settled in the seat across from her. "So… you're human? And you live with the Weston pack. How's that working out?" I didn't want to be rude about it because I'd heard of interbreeding between couples of different Breeds, but not humans.

"Love takes you strange places. I know it's not conventional, but his family accepted me like one of their own. That's not to say we didn't hit a few bumps in the beginning, but I think once they saw how much I love Reno, none of the other stuff mattered as much. The boys can be a pain in the rear, but I really like our life and wouldn't trade it for anything. He takes good care of me. The only thing I'll miss is working with Lexi every day. She's going to open up a new store pretty soon."

"I heard. Jericho asked if I might want to work there," I admitted with hesitation.

"You should!" she exclaimed. "I'll make the suggestion. It's not going to tip like the bar, but maybe you could just part-time it for a while."

"Maybe."

"I'm sorry about what happened," she said quietly. "With Hawk, I mean."

"Me too."

"It's a good thing you got out of there. I've heard horror stories about what they do to Shifters on the black market. No one would care about a human, but Reno still keeps a close eye on me. There are a few packs around here that give me the creeps."

April was right about that. You could always spot the ones running something illegal. A glint of sin reflected in their irises.

"Jericho didn't tell you where he was going?" she asked suspiciously, slurping on the rim of her can.

I touched the wolf ring I'd taken off his hand and placed on my finger. The festival had everything we needed from food to clothes because of the vendor stands. Why would he just take off?

An errand.

God, please don't let it be drugs. I knew addicts were compulsive liars and I wanted more than anything to believe Jericho was on the straight and narrow. But what if I had been duped once again? How could I *not* question my judgment after Hawk? I had no doubt Jericho cared for me deeply, but maybe he was ashamed to tell me he hadn't completely stopped. No, that couldn't be right. If that were true, he would have caved in Hawk's basement. No user could resist that kind of temptation, could they?

"Izzy?"

"I'm sorry, just thinking. He didn't tell me where he was going. Maybe he forgot a guitar he wanted to use in the show later on."

"I didn't think about that. You're probably right."

A hard knock sounded at the door.

"Reno," she said with a roll of her eyes.

"Wait," I whispered, stretching out my arm. I quietly moved toward the door and peered out the window. *Hell's bells.* It was Handlebars.

I looked at April with my index finger pressed to my lips for silence. He was only a human, but so was April, and she could easily get hurt.

"Go hide in the bathroom," I whispered. "Now!"

"I can't leave you," she whispered back.

"April, I'm a wolf. If I shift, I could accidentally hurt you, and Reno wouldn't be able to deal with that. I wouldn't be able to deal with that. Go!"

She made fists with her hands and her brows knitted. The

moment of uncertainty passed and April hurried into the bathroom, locking herself inside.

Handlebars beat on the door again. "Open the goddamn door. I know you're in there."

"What do you want? Hawk is dead."

"Yeah, so I heard," he said in a gruff voice. "But there's one small problem."

I paused. "What?"

"Delgado still wants his money and his drugs."

"Did you check his house?"

He hammered his fist on the door. "Yes, bitch. We checked his house. Now open up."

"There's no money or drugs in here."

"No, but your ass is in there, and your ass is going to show me where they are."

"I don't *know* where they are!" I screamed. "We split up and he tried to kidnap me. I had no clue he was selling drugs!"

He violently pulled on the door and it shook. These doors were not meant to keep strong men out. I turned around to find a weapon when the door wrenched open.

"There you are."

I widened my arms. "Here I am. Sure you want to tangle with me, Handlebars? I bite."

"That ain't my name."

I stood my ground as he entered the small room and ducked to avoid the low ceiling.

"How did you know I was here?" I asked.

He laughed once and it died just as fast as a mouse in a trap. "Coincidence. I just happened to be strolling by. Now tell me where the stash is, and I'll be on my merry fucking way."

The music blasted outside, and the crowd in the distance cheered. "I'm not playing stupid with you—I really don't know. Do you think I enjoy all our run-ins? I'm telling you I have no idea where that stuff is. If you'll get off my back, maybe I can help find what you're looking for. The only problem is Hawk told me he had other homes, and I have no idea where they are."

"Hawk wasn't stupid enough to keep valuables out of reach. He would have kept his money and stash close by. I had one shitbag who hid the drugs in the floorboard of his wife's car. You know why? Because if it's found by the law, it won't be in his possession. But I ain't the law."

"Then give me time to look."

"Time's up."

I stepped back as far as I could. "You can bark at me all you want, but nothing is going to make that money magically appear. Or the drugs. Which one does Delgado want?"

"Both. All."

I heard something clatter in the bathroom, and April quietly cursed.

"Who the hell's in there?" he said, already moving his way toward the back.

I stepped in front of him and pushed. "No one. Go outside and let's talk."

"Get the fuck out of my way," he said, shoving me.

"If you touch me again, I won't be so nice," I said through clenched teeth.

Handlebars smirked and cocked his head to the side. With one finger, he foolishly poked me in the chest.

CHAPTER 19

WHEN JERICHO PULLED INTO THE festival grounds and got the call from Austin, he broke into a hard run as soon as he parked the truck. A few drunks called him an asshole as he plowed through a group of spectators. The trailers were on the opposite end of the grounds, and the crowd was dense because people were dancing in large groups. He bumped into an immovable Vampire who eagerly showed him his fangs.

Jericho ran around him.

"What's going on? Where's Isabelle?" he shouted, slowing down.

Austin stood outside the trailer, his arms folded and his eyes alert. "We've got a human down," he confirmed in a low voice, eyes scanning the crowd in the distance. "This is bad news, Jericho. A dead body in *your* trailer. If a Chitah doesn't sniff us out first, a Vampire might have heard."

"Not many Vamps are here," Jericho said out of breath. "I've only seen a handful. They have to concentrate harder to block out the loud music, and do you mind telling me what the fuck they would have heard? Isabelle!"

Austin shoved him back and blocked the doorway. "Calm down. Her wolf is in there, and that'll get ugly quick."

Jericho paced in a nervous circle, forced to obey his Packmaster. "Don't call me with a level-fucking-red and stand there telling me to be calm."

"Be calm."

The sound of Reno's motorcycle rumbled and slowed down like a heartbeat as he pulled up. He cut off the engine, opened the kickstand, and swept his leg across the back to get off. "Move outta my way. I'm going in." He reached inside his button-up shirt for the gun strapped to his chest.

"The hell you are," Austin said, moving toward him.

"Let me at that bitch."

Jericho swung at Reno and almost knocked him off his feet. Reno was a big guy, so that was saying something, but Jericho was taller and not intimidated by anyone.

"That's Isabelle in there, not some bitch," Jericho bit out, pointing his finger at the trailer. "I'll take your ass down if you lay one finger on her."

"Take your best shot, Jerko."

"Pull it together," Austin said impatiently in his alpha voice. "Here's the situation: We have a dead human in Jericho's trailer we can't get to because Izzy's wolf won't let anyone inside. It's pretty clear what went down, but not why. April shut herself in the bathroom and would have called you on your phone, Reno, if you had it with you," he said with a scowl. "She can yell out information, but that just riles Izzy's wolf up."

"Where's her wolf?" Jericho asked.

"Lying on top of the dead body."

Shit. That sonofabitch must have pissed her off something fierce to make her wolf take claim of his body like that. "Her wolf knows me, Austin. She trusts me. I can get close to her and get her out."

"I don't *want* her out," Austin said calmly. "Out means trouble. She's covered in human blood, and we got Shifters out there looking for a reason to shift. There's already talk about how unfairly we're being treated, while the other Breeds get to practice their magic. If she runs into the crowd, that'll be like the gun they fire off at the races. It'll start a riot if everyone starts shifting. Lexi and Ivy went to find a crate. If you want me to lock your ass up in there, then I have no problem with that. But if she doesn't shift back, we crate her home, and you're going to be the one to put her in there."

"We need to get April out," Reno said, his voice caged with fury.

Austin tossed him his phone. "Call her up. She's fine."

Reno turned around with the phone pressed to his ear.

Jericho stepped forward, locking eyes with Austin. "Let me in."

"You sure? She could go wild on you. Izzy has blood in her mouth, and you know how hard it is to come down from that. I went in and tried to force her to shift, but I have little control over the human inside. She bit me," he said, holding up his left arm. Dried blood streaked down the back of his forearm from a set of puncture marks.

"Why don't you stay out here and shift to heal up. I'll go calm her down."

Austin stepped aside. "Be my guest. I may have control over my alpha enough to shift here, but I'm taking the stitches on this one. Don't shift, Jericho. I'm warning you. I want everyone to keep their animal in check. I have a big fucking mess to clean up here, and I'm only doing it because it took place in *your* trailer. Do you realize what kind of trouble she's caused by killing a human? This involves all of us now, and I don't need this kind of trouble surrounding my pack."

Jericho glanced back at Reno, sitting in the grass with his knees pulled up, talking on the phone and clearly stressed out. He was holding his palm out and moving it in a motion that looked as if he were calming someone down.

That someone was April.

Jericho opened the door, and a low growl rumbled from the left. "Easy, girl. It's just me," Jericho said, stepping into the trailer.

Her lips peeled back and she bared sharp canines. She had beautiful white fur that made her ebony nose stand out. The same nose that was sniffing the air as he slowly took a seat on a bench to the right.

The scene was gruesome. Jericho's eyes roved around the room at spatters of blood everywhere—visible even in a dim room lit by a small lamp with low bulb-wattage. She must have latched on to his jugular. What the hell did that bastard do that had made Isabelle's wolf lash out so ruthlessly?

It looked like he'd tried to run away. His arms were contorted in a peculiar manner, and Jericho couldn't see his face—only a pool of crimson surrounding his head like a halo. Isabelle's wolf had snuggled up beside his chest as if she were claiming her prey.

"Isabelle, you were always one badass wolf," he said coolly, half smiling. The ring she had taken off his finger was sitting on the counter, and her clothes were in a pile right below. "Why don't you shift back now? It's over."

She growled, telling him it damn well wasn't over.

"Jericho?" April said in a weak voice from the bathroom. Isabelle's wolf lunged at the door and made her scream. Her wolf had never met April, and that was a common reaction.

Jericho stood up and reached for the door, expecting Reno to come barging in. Instead, he heard his brothers arguing outside.

"Shut up!" Jericho yelled. "You're pissing her off."

Her wolf growled with each breath. Jericho knelt down and crawled toward her fearlessly—head first, neck extended.

He looked her square in the eyes. "You know deep down I'd never hurt you, baby."

Isabelle's wolf snorted and released a high-pitched whine. Her tongue swept out a few times, and she looked around, confused by her surroundings.

"That's just April in there, and you're scaring the piss out of her. Come over here, baby. I'm not going to make you do anything you don't want to do. If you want to stay in control and keep Isabelle sleeping, then fine by me. But we're going to put you in a crate and take you home where you can run around the property and roll in the dirt all you want. Yeah, that's right," he said, watching the light glimmer in her eyes. "I know you're a dirt roller. I still remember the time you went rolling in the mud back in Seattle. Poor Isabelle woke up covered from head to toe like some kind of swamp creature."

Her wolf staggered to her feet and paced forward with her head down. They'd bonded a long time ago, so he didn't have second thoughts when he reached out and ran his fingers through her coat. He knew exactly where she liked to be scratched, and it was on the back of her neck.

"Yeah, that's my girl." He smiled as she sat down and shook her head.

A light knock sounded at the door.

"Open the door slowly," Jericho said, keeping his eyes on Isabelle. "Don't come in; just stand at the door."

As the broken hinge creaked behind him, Jericho kept methodically stroking the sides of her face and rubbed her ears to keep her calm.

"Jesus. You're crazy, anyone ever tell you that?" Austin said. "Lexi brought the crate. Hurry up; we need to get rid of the body and get this trailer off the premises."

Austin slid the crate in and shut the door.

Jericho pulled the crate next to him and ignored her disobedient groans and growls. He opened the front and patted inside. "Come on, baby. Let's go home."

———— ⁙ ————

"Careful!" Jericho yelled, banging his fist against the back of the truck window.

Austin had hit a pothole in the private road that led up to their house—one Reno was supposed to fill in last week. Isabelle wasn't doing well in the crate. He had tried to steady it with his own body, but the bumps in the road and sharp turns had her biting the wire door.

When the truck stopped, Jericho stood up and looked down at Austin. "Unlock the front door and I'll get her inside."

"You can't bring her in the house. Lynn and Maizy are in there."

"I'll lock her up in my room."

Austin slammed his door. "Absolutely not. My priority is to protect my pack. I'm sorry, brother, but Isabelle is not my pack. Lynn and Maizy are. She was getting on my good side, but this just took her down a few notches. This could do more than damage our reputation; it could break apart our pack."

Jericho cursed and opened the bed of the truck. Isabelle's wolf was barking out of control, and he needed to calm her down. That meant stabilizing her crate and taking her somewhere safe. Reno had stayed behind with the girls to take care of the trailer—he knew a few cleaners who worked independently and, for a hefty fee, wouldn't report their findings to the Council.

Austin helped him with the crate and they set it down in the dirt. A few crickets were chirping in the darkness, and Jericho glanced at a silhouette standing in the window.

"So you want us to sit out here in the dark?"

Austin slammed the bed of the truck closed. "You got it. Don't go anywhere near the house. I called Lynn earlier and told her to keep the doors locked up tight so Maizy doesn't wander outside. She likes wolves but she's too young to realize she can't run up to a rogue. Find a soft patch of grass and camp out for the night." Austin returned to the front of the truck. "I need to head back. After we clean up the mess your girlfriend caused, we're going to stick around, have a few beers, and listen to some music. Then we're coming back to deal with this. You're lucky the music was loud enough to drown out the drama. Maybe the wind was in our favor. Who the hell knows."

"Pass the word to my band that the show is off." Jericho felt like crap about it, but what could he do?

"Doubt it," Austin replied, getting back in the truck. He slammed the door and rested his forearm on the edge of the open window. "Have you heard Trevor sing? He went up there for kicks and played a blues number. Girls went crazy. As did a few men," he said with a comical grin.

Jericho turned his back and lifted the heavy crate, causing every muscle he owned to flex and harden.

Austin's truck kicked up dirt as he headed down the road and back to the festival. Just another night for the Weston pack. They didn't bat an eyelash at this kind of drama, but the humans who lived in their house had a tougher time wrapping their heads around the perils of the Breed world.

He found a nice spot under a tree with a soft patch of grass. Jericho knelt down and opened the cage, speaking in a mellow voice. Isabelle's wolf sprang out and then circled around, sniffing her surroundings and nervously eyeing him. The blood had dried on her white fur, more noticeable around her muzzle.

"It's fine, baby. We're home." He fell on his back and stared up at the sky, kicking off his shoes. How could decades ago feel like yesterday and another lifetime all at once?

Isabelle nestled beside him, tucking her muzzle on his shoulder and licking his ear. They fell back into a familiar groove, and he hummed the song he'd sung to her earlier at the concert, hoping that would draw her out. Isabelle was in there somewhere, even though she wouldn't remember this. But there was a way you could talk a person out of their animal and coax them to shift.

What bothered him was her reluctance. An hour went by, and while her wolf trotted around and checked out the property, she didn't show any signs of tiring. Jericho could usually sit it out—the animal needed their time to run free, but Isabelle had shifted that morning and it wasn't like her wolf to take control.

Jericho pulled out his phone and punched Reno's number.

"Reno."

"Hey, you got a second?"

"What's up?"

Jericho paced in a circle. "I need to know what happened in that trailer between Isabelle and their attacker. What did April say?"

"She said he was looking for drugs and money. He worked for someone Hawk dealt with."

"Did he know about Hawk being dead?"

"Yeah, she overheard that part of the convo," Reno said, out of breath. The music in the phone began to fade, and it sounded as if he were distancing himself from the crowd. "April knows who the ringleader is."

"What do you mean?"

"The guy said a name—Delgado. That's the same sonofabitch who sent one of his lackeys after April. He's a loan shark, but it looks like he has his finger in all kinds of pies. Drugs, for one. I know for a fact he's been buying up strip clubs in town. *Breed* clubs."

"So he's human," Jericho said, wiping a few blades of grass off his arm.

"Yeah, that's problematic. He put his finger in the wrong fucking pie, but we can't do a damn thing because he's human, and he knows it. Delgado has other men do his dirty work and stays out of sight. That's how the big boys like to operate."

"Why does he think Isabelle has Hawk's stash?"

Reno's voice sounded tired. "Guess they did a search and couldn't find it. You better check your girl out; she might know where it is."

Jericho turned around and looked at her wolf pawing a hole in the dirt. "She doesn't know."

"Bullshit."

"Look, Reno, I know this girl like the back of my hand. She would have done the right thing if she knew because that's the kind of girl she is. But if we don't give that asshole what he's looking for, he's going to keep coming back for her until I kill him. You can tell Austin we'll sleep outside tonight, but if he tosses her on the street because of this shit, I'm going with her. That's a done deal."

"Hold up—"

Jericho hung up the phone and sat on his knees. "Come here, Isabelle."

She trotted over and nuzzled against his chin, licking his mouth.

"If you want to make out with me, you're going to have to shift." He stroked her face and looked deep into her green eyes. "Come on, baby. We'll figure this out together. I'm not going anywhere and neither are you. I know you're freaking out in there and that's why your she-devil wolf is on the prowl, but she's not going to fix your problems, and you can't hide from them forever. Maybe you're scared. After what just happened with Hawk, I don't blame you. But you need to trust me."

Her wolf sat down and cocked her head. *Yeah, something was wrong.* Isabelle had a badass wolf, but she'd never been stubborn with him. She also wasn't acting herself. Usually her wolf liked to dig in the dirt and roll around, but she stayed calm and almost protective of Jericho as she turned her back and kept her eyes sharp and alert.

Jericho glanced back at the house and saw Lynn had switched off the lights.

Maybe Isabelle was mad at him and not ready to come out. When he'd ditched her to make a run to town, he didn't have any concerns about leaving her alone. She wasn't a child. That human stood no chance against her wolf, but he wondered if Isabelle had fought him in human form. That seed planted in his head and made his wolf stir with anger. He surged to his feet, wiping the dirt off his pants. What he really wanted to do was take care of her problems by finding the piece of shit who went by the name Delgado.

Isabelle had been through enough, subjected to the worst kind of betrayal by an asshole boyfriend she'd thought she could trust.

Then again, who was Jericho to talk? He had turned his back on their friendship for drugs and women.

He clenched his fists and paced. They better have taken care of everything with the dead human, because killing a human was against the law. Self-defense had to be proven, and no one had found a weapon on the body. The higher authority could arrest Isabelle and charge her with murder.

The protective instinct was too powerful to resist, and Jericho's wolf emerged.

CHAPTER 20

MY BACK ITCHED. WHEN I rolled to my side, I could feel blades of grass stuck to my skin. I squinted as the morning light pierced my eyes like a reckoning, and I shielded my face with my arm.

There I was, lying naked in front of the Weston pack's house. Super.

When I sat up and twisted around, Denver waved from a chair on the front porch.

All I could think about was my uncontrollable craving for popcorn. Every wolf had a different craving after shifting back to human form, and nobody could explain why. I once knew a girl who had a thing for green olives, and a Shifter I'd met up in Topeka had an expensive craving for caviar. He told me he'd never eaten caviar, and it took eight years after he'd gone through the change before he finally figured out what his body desired. Someone offered him an appetizer at a fancy party and after one small bite, he recognized a flavor he'd never tasted before. Who knows? Maybe we've all led past lives.

My craving was popcorn, but specifically cheese popcorn. I licked my lips.

"Craving?" Denver said with a snicker. He popped a knuckle and then swatted at a gnat.

I dusted the grass from the back of my thigh and rubbed dirt off my face. "Can you get me something to put on? Where's Jericho? What happened?"

He stood up and took a few steps, tossing me a dress. It looked like something Ivy would wear—strapless cotton the color of chocolate. I slipped it on while Denver took a bottle of bubbles from the porch step and set them on a table by the door.

"It looks like Jericho took off. Austin called and said not to let you in the house. I came home as soon as I got off work. You've got a mean wolf, Izzy."

"I've heard." I tied the little strings around the waist and wiped more blades of grass, which had left imprints on my skin, off my arm. After I got myself together, I walked up the steps onto the porch.

The front door swung open and Maizy ran outside, as vibrant and full of spirit as any girl of six or seven. Her blond hair swung in two little ponytails, and she had on a pair of jean overalls and a pink shirt.

"Denny, can I come outside now? The lady isn't naked anymore."

I quietly laughed. Denver rubbed his chin and looked over at her from his chair, his dirty-blond hair disheveled. "Did you eat breakfast, Peanut?"

"Yep," she said, taking a seat beside him. I noticed how she imitated the way Denver was sitting—her right leg stretched out, leaning on her left arm.

"And what did you eat?"

"Um…"

"Get inside and eat some cereal. Then you can come out and play."

She stuck out her pink bottom lip. "But I want to be outside with you."

He relaxed his posture and smiled at her. "Don't make me the bad guy. You get inside and eat three pieces of bacon and toast."

"But I'm not hungry."

He looked thoughtfully at the clouds and leaned forward. "Looks like a good day for ice cream, but it's too damn hot."

She looked up at him hopefully. "No it's not."

"Maybe if you cool off with some orange juice and a few pieces of bacon, I might think about it."

She bolted out of the chair and beamed at him with the most endearing smile. "You mean it?"

He frowned. "You want a strawberry cone or not, little girl? Skedaddle!"

Maizy squealed and ran back inside.

"And don't forget the toast!" he yelled at the door.

"You're good with kids," I said, taking the empty spot to his right. "Even though you're kind of a dickhead with adults."

"Hey, I gave you a dress." He combed back his hair and settled his indigo eyes on me.

"Yeah, but how long did you sit on this porch staring at my ass?"

"I'm pleading the fifth." His eyes darted toward the road. "Here they come now. Have fun with that. I need to grab something to eat," Denver said, standing up.

At the end of the private road, a cloud of dust swirled behind a black Dodge Challenger and a vintage motorcycle. I swallowed hard and tried to remember the last thing that had happened. It was…

"Oh my God, is April okay?"

"She's fine. That's her on the back of the bike."

I buried my face in my hands. "Oh, hell's bells. I almost had a heart attack."

"I'm taking you to work in a little while, *after* Austin has the ugly talk with you."

"Work?"

"Yeah. Feel free to get fired if you want, but I happen to know your shift starts in a few hours. I talked to Rosie and she said there's an extra T-shirt and pair of shorts in the dressing room. I didn't explain why you needed them." The door slammed as Denver went inside.

That's how Shifters rolled. We dealt with drama and soldiered on. Even the trusted humans among our kind rarely related to our lifestyle, so I was surprised to see how well some of them were getting along within the Weston pack.

As soon as the black car prowled to the parking area on my right, Austin got out and stalked toward the house. He lifted his arm and pointed at me.

"You, away from the house. Now."

My stomach did a flip-flop.

"Austin, wait!" Lexi ran up beside him. Fury colored his face, and the power in his alpha voice compelled me to get off my rear and do as he said.

"Lexi, stay out of it. This is between the Packmaster and—"

"Austin," she hissed. "Don't you pull that alpha shit on me."

There was a little standoff between them, and my brows popped up, not having seen many women talk back to a Packmaster in front of the pack. Lexi was tough, definitely an alpha female. After she narrowed her eyes and he folded his arms, she conceded defeat and stormed past him.

He playfully popped her on the behind. "We'll kiss and make up later, Ladybug."

She slammed the door. Austin caught my arm, helping me down the steps and toward the tree with the wooden swing. When he motioned for me to sit in it, I obliged.

Behind him, April warily looked in our direction as she joined Lexi inside. Reno headed our way, and I began to feel outnumbered and a little confused.

"Did anyone tell you what happened?" Austin asked.

I shook my head, gripping the rope tightly.

"You killed a human in Jericho's trailer." He slid his jaw from side to side. "What happened before you shifted?"

I took a deep breath, and Reno tossed his helmet to the ground. He was wearing the same button-up blue shirt as the previous night, his short brown hair neatly combed. Austin, on the other hand, had messy hair and a wrinkled white tank top.

"April stopped by because she'd lost track of Reno, and we started talking. Then this guy shows up at the door, pounding on it to get in. I told April to hide in the bathroom, and he forced his way inside."

Austin folded his arms. "Who was he?"

"He works for Delgado—the guy Hawk was selling drugs for. I found out Hawk was taking an extra cut by jacking up the prices on the drugs he was selling. Now Delgado wants the money *and* the drugs."

"Then give it to him."

I laughed and threw my head back. "That would be so easy, if I actually knew where he stashed them. I'd happily give it over because I could care less about any of it. I just want this guy off my back."

"You sure about that?"

I stared at the cleft in his chin and realized what he was implying. "The money means nothing to me. You could shred it into ribbons and I wouldn't care. I'd never put Jericho or any of you in danger on purpose."

Austin and Reno looked at each other. "She's telling the truth," Austin murmured.

"This Delgado has been a problem," Reno stated matter-of-factly. "He's a human, but he's knee-deep in the Breed world. He got a taste of our money, and he's been buying up local Breed clubs."

"Shit," Austin breathed.

Reno pulled his sunglasses off and tucked them in the collar of his shirt. "He's trouble, and we can't do jack about it."

"Yeah, that's a problem if he's human. It makes him untouchable unless we can get human law enforcement involved."

"Which gets them involved in *our* business," Reno emphasized. "Then we'll have to deal with the higher authority."

No one wanted the higher authority meddling in Shifter business. They weren't a governing body of Breed law—more like judge, jury, and executioner.

Denver strolled barefoot across the lawn, wearing a baggy orange shirt and a pair of jeans. His hair was still messy, and he looked indifferent to the crisis unfolding as he munched on a bowl of cereal.

"'Sup?" he asked with a mouthful. "Is she still being a stubborn bitch?"

"What can I do to help?" I stood up from the swing, still holding on to the ropes. "I didn't mean to bring this to your doorstep, but tell me what to do and I'll make it right."

Austin stuffed his hands in his pockets and paced in a small circle, staring at his shoes. "If he thinks you have the drugs and money, then Hawk hid them somewhere. You need to find them. I don't have time to be chasing down a human."

I gazed up at the tree and watched the leaves shake in the light breeze. "I'll give the house another search, I guess. And the house you found me in," I said with a shiver, not wanting to go back and see that room again.

"Denver will take you to work. After your shift, Reno will—"

"Uh, hold up," Reno said in a private voice. "I got a thing planned with April tonight."

"Can't it wait?"

A smile appeared. "No."

Austin tipped his head to the side. "Whatever it is, this is more important."

Reno stood his ground and threw back his shoulders. "I ain't gonna church it up for you; I have a date with my woman, and she bought sex lingerie. Would you make Lexi wait? Yeah, didn't think so."

Denver snorted, and milk dribbled down his chin. "Don't you mean *sexy* lingerie?"

Reno snapped his head around and glared at Denver. "No, because as soon as she puts it on, we're gonna be having sex."

Denver wiped his chin. "Might be hard to have sex with all that fabric on."

"Look—" Reno began, pointing his finger.

"Cut it out," Austin said tersely. "I don't have time for this shit. Fine. You get a free pass, but the next time I need you for something, Reno, you'll do it. Get a hold of Wheeler. Tell him when Izzy gets off work. I want him to go with her to the locations." Then he turned his eyes toward me. "I cleaned up your mess last night, and in case you haven't figured it out, your wolf leveled that human with one bite. I figure my helping you out makes us square for the call you made that saved Wheeler's life. Wheeler won't be getting involved—he's just going to keep an eye on you."

I folded my arms. "In case I decide to get greedy and run with the money? I really wish I could understand why you think I'm that low of a Shifter."

Austin stepped forward and softened his voice. "I don't know you. All I know is that Jericho was doing just fine until you showed up. Now we're hiding bodies and cleaning up our tracks. This isn't just about you. The Council has the authority to dismantle my pack if they don't think I have it under—"

"Ho-ly shit," Denver exclaimed. "Check out Jericho."

We all looked toward the high grass on the right, and Jericho's wolf emerged. He was a magnificent shade of brown and powerful in size. Between his fierce jaws was a dead rabbit, and he walked aggressively toward us, making the other men tense.

Jericho's wolf dropped the rabbit at my feet as an offering. It was a gesture of loyalty and love. If I had been in wolf form, we would have shared the bounty together. It's something I'd heard of mated couples doing but had never seen. Problem being, I wasn't his mate, so the dead rabbit made all the men look between one another. What's more, a Shifter only did this when his mate was in wolf form. Here I was, in human form, and Jericho's wolf had hunted for me.

"He must be confused," Austin said quietly.

The wolf sat on his haunches, impervious to the men's reactions. He smacked his tongue around his mouth and looked up at me expectantly. I brushed my hand over his soft ear, my heart thumping wildly.

"You shouldn't confuse a wolf like that," Reno said quietly, staring down at Jericho.

"I didn't."

"Then why the hell is a dead rabbit lying at your feet?"

Denver snorted. "Maybe he thinks she needs the foot for her keychain."

CHAPTER 21

————⊶⊙⊄⊘⊃⊙⊷————

"**I**ZZY! I NEED YOU TO cover my tables."

I glanced over my shoulder across the bar. "What's wrong, Rosie?" She held up her left hand, and I stared blank-faced at a broken nail. "Really?"

Rosie smiled guiltily. "How am I supposed to give a good impression looking like a hobo who clawed her way to work? I'll be right back, honey."

I reached in my pocket for a black band. Instead of a full ponytail, I took the hair from both sides of my head and tied them back.

A familiar face strolled into the bar. The customers tapped their feet to a folksy song playing on the jukebox, not taking notice of the alpha. Lorenzo's black hair fell over his brown shoulders, just as smooth and straight as could be. He looked like the angel of death—dark hair and eyes, dark tank top and pants, and a look of menace. My eyes skated to the skull-and-crossbones tattoo on his left arm. Leather bracelets with tassels adorned his wrists, and a rope necklace looped around his neck.

Lorenzo caught sight of me at the bar and strolled up, easing into the seat to my left. Denver had taken the night off to go to the concert, so Frank was filling in. He handed Lorenzo a drink without asking for his order. "Here you are, Church."

Lorenzo's eyes flicked down to the ligature marks on my wrist, and he unexpectedly snatched my arm, holding it up for a better look.

"Did the Weston pack do this?"

I pulled back. "No."

His steely eyes narrowed. "If you lie to me, I'll find out. If I discover they aren't treating their women right, there'll be trouble."

"They treat their women like gold. We should all be so lucky to be in a pack like theirs."

He shifted in his seat and gave me a critical stare. "Then why aren't you with them? Word is you're a wolf. A good bitch shouldn't be alone without a strong pack to look out for her."

Lorenzo took a short sip of his drink and waited for an answer.

"Maybe some of you guys who live in a pack aren't so nice to your unmated girls," I implied, careful not to insult an alpha. "There's a difference between a sense of belonging and belonging to someone. I have a great job and—"

"Ligature marks on your wrist."

"That was an ex."

"Did Cole take care of that ex?"

I grabbed the tray of drinks Frank handed me. "Don't worry about the Cole brothers; they take care of things just fine. Let me know if you want something off the menu and I'll put a rush on it," I said in a friendly voice. Nosy or not, Lorenzo undoubtedly had tip money in his pocket waiting for a lucky girl, and I had no idea who his regular was.

After delivering drinks to my customers, I dipped down and lifted a black wallet off the floor. "Did you drop this?" I asked the dark man with the friendly smile.

"It's not often you find an honest person," he said in a baritone voice, taking the wallet from my hand.

"Well *that* was an experience," a brunette said, flouncing by and collapsing in the seat beside him. After kissing his cheek, she wrinkled her nose. "The bathrooms are nasty. Can we go somewhere else?"

He tucked the wallet in his back pocket and lifted his eyes to mine. "I think we'll stay a while and order something off the menu."

"The avocado burgers are amazing," I suggested. "I know the cook on this shift, and he's a genius."

"Bring one for each of us. Fries?"

"Coming up."

"Uh, I want a salad," the woman complained as she tried to cross her thick legs.

I lifted the tray. "I'll have them put the light salad dressing on the side. Would you like lemon-water?"

She smiled appreciatively. That was one thing I loved about my job: turning people's moods around. "Yes, please. Thank you. Oh, and got any pickles?"

"You bet. I'll have your order out as soon as possible. Be right back with your water, miss, and if you gentlemen need another round, just holler."

I subtly turned, not wanting to offend the woman with any ass-shaking, and went to retrieve her water.

After a few tables cleared and my avocado-burger table left me a hefty tip, I slid into a booth in the back and officially went off the clock.

"Honey, what's going on?" Rosie asked. "You seem like such a sweet girl, and I don't like the look in your eyes."

"What look?" I nibbled on a wedge of pickle and sipped root beer from a short glass.

"Every time someone comes flying through the front door, you freeze up and clutch your heart. I saw you drop a tray an hour ago when a couple of rowdy men slammed their fists on the table while playing cards."

I grimaced and hoped none of the patrons had caught me doing that.

"Sorry, Rosie. My ex has made my life a living hell, and I'm just trying to move on."

She laughed melodically and leaned back, the turquoise earrings swinging from her ears. "Oh, I know all about that. My first boyfriend came along when I was about twenty." Rosie shook with silent laughter and waved her hand. "I was a late bloomer. His name was George, and I thought he was the one and only. He was a handsome young man with curly hair and a sweet mouth who kissed me every chance he could."

My brows drew together. "What was wrong with him?"

"He was like Jekyll and Hyde. Just the sweetest boy, but behind closed doors…" Rosie shook her head. "An animal. Lucky for me, I have big knuckles," she said, making a fist.

I finished my pickle and licked the juice off my thumb. "I don't like fighting; maybe that's why I bailed all those years ago from my home life. Yours is the kind of story that scares me because… it happened to me. I feel so stupid, like I should have seen who he was."

Rosie leaned forward and patted my hand. "Honey, the devil paints the prettiest masks. Some of us learn that the hard way, but don't blame yourself. I did that for years, and no good ever comes of it. Someday you'll meet a man and you'll be awful to him. You'll say mean things and push him away, but he'll keep pulling because he'll see beyond your pain. Just don't keep pushing. At some point, you have to let him in or you'll lose him for good. Don't look at every mark on a man as a reason to leave him—we're all marked. Maybe it's the ones who seem too perfect that are anything but," she said contemplatively, tapping her chin. "The one thing I remember is how perfect George appeared. Everyone just loved him and said I was a lucky girl. I felt undeserving of that kind of man. Only later did he show his true colors, but maybe a man who hides his flaws is hiding something more wicked."

"So you're saying I need to find a flawed man with issues?" I sat back in my chair and thought about Jericho. With him, I knew all his imperfections, so there wouldn't be any surprises.

Hawk was another story. But in retrospect, I could see the warning signs. He'd known slapping me in the morning made me volatile and sometimes shift, so why did he provoke me that way? Maybe that was a subtle hint of a larger fissure on that man's soul. Jericho had never done anything so thoughtless. His flaw wasn't that he would hurt me physically, but I knew the risk that he could break my heart.

"Who's the guy who's been watching you all night?" Rosie asked, sipping her drink.

I snapped out of my fog. "What?"

She craned her neck and peered over the divider. "The man

who… well, he's gone now. I thought maybe you were dating him, or he was the ex."

"What did he look like?"

The ice in her glass clinked when she set it down. Rosie pulled out her makeup mirror and applied more lip liner. "I haven't seen him in here before. He ordered one beer and watched you for the last hour, but not the way a man looks at a woman when they want to sleep with them, you know? Kind of… mad."

Her eyes should have been on the mirror, but they were on me.

"He's not the ex. What did he look like?"

"Plaid shirt, tight jeans…"

"I don't mean what he was wearing."

She clipped the mirror shut and slipped it in her purse. "He's a little taller than you—not a big guy. Stern. He looked like anyone else wandering in. Either he was naturally bald or shaved his head—I couldn't tell which. He also had a tattoo on his hand, but I don't remember what it was."

That gave me the creeps. "Was he a Shifter?"

"I can't always tell unless I get up close. He sat in the corner by the door; we don't get many customers who fill that area."

Chills ran up my arms. I wondered if Delgado had sent someone else in to follow me. God, was I going to be paranoid for the rest of my life?

Heck no! my brain shouted. *Get out of Dodge before it's too late! Time to bail and get out of this city before you end up buried in it.*

"Is Jake going to fire me? I haven't been the best employee," I asked, ignoring that irritating voice in my head.

Rosie chuckled with her mouth closed. "Not as long as you're keeping Jericho around. Plus, I think he likes having a redhead on staff. You don't see many redhead Shifters, so it's a treat for the boys. Some of them stay a little longer and drink a little more, just so they can watch you work."

"Then maybe all the girls should dye their hair red."

She leaned in and her voice fell to a whisper. "One time, Trina did that. She colored her hair like a stoplight on her first day of employment. Now Jake and I knew she was a blonde, but she thought she was going to be slick and pull in all the tips," Rosie said with a giggle. "*Nooo*. You can't pull one over on these boys. I don't know if they can smell red hair or maybe something didn't match up, like her skin was a little flawless or she forgot to dye her brows, but they *knew*. In fact, they were so irritated by it that she didn't get any tips that night. Jake threatened to fire her if she didn't get herself together, so she came in the next day with black hair because the red wouldn't come out. Oh, honey, she looked frightful. Like a little Morticia Addams."

I laughed, feeling a bit sorry for Trina. I knew what that was like. I had once worked in a Shifter bar and dyed my hair brown, hoping to avoid the attention. Somehow, they knew. I'd catch them studying my hair, examining my eyebrows, as if looking for any small clue I wasn't what I portrayed myself to be. I'd even covered my faded freckles with makeup, but I don't know. Some things just can't be explained, and almost all Shifter men had an inherent attraction toward redheads. The other Breeds could care less.

I had an inkling why. I'd only met two redheaded Shifter wolves in my life, and they were both alpha Packmasters. *Strong* alphas. If red-haired males were more likely to be an alpha, then mating with a redhead might increase a man's chances at having an alpha child. Not all wolves will have an alpha child, so it's a great honor, and most of them are the firstborn. Cole's family was the rare exception. It explained why a few Packmasters had more than one mate. If the firstborn wasn't an alpha, they could always try their chances with another woman. I had mixed theories about all this.

I didn't see what the big deal was. I wasn't any different than the next girl.

"Ready to go?" a voice beside us asked.

Rosie and I looked up at Wheeler, who stood with his arms folded. Rosie didn't seem to care for all his tattoos, nor the scowl on his face, so she left the booth.

I left Wheeler while I changed clothes in the bathroom, slipping into a pair of flats and a short cotton dress the color of storm clouds. I decided if we got caught snooping around Hawk's place, I didn't want to look conspicuous by wearing dark clothes this time of year.

No one messed with Wheeler as we cut through the crowd. They stepped aside and let us pass. He possessed an ominous presence and was the only Cole brother that put me on edge. Despite the fact he said he owed me one, I felt terrible that he'd almost died. My phone call resulting in Austin getting there on time didn't erase the fact my psychotic ex had put a bullet in his head.

Halfway across the room, my purse got hung up on something. I spun around, and a man with a shaved head was tugging on the strap.

The next thing I knew, Wheeler's arm flew out and seized the guy by the throat. "Let it go or I'll shatter your nose," he said in slow, menacing words. His fingers gripped so tightly that the bones in his hand were visible.

The purse popped free, and I blinked, heading swiftly toward the door. Wheeler held my wrist and led me across the parking lot, walking two steps ahead. I finally twisted my arm free from his grasp and slowed my pace as we approached his car.

"Spiffy wheels," I said, admiring the gunmetal-grey exterior.

"It's a 1968 Chevy Camaro, so show a little respect."

He ditched me where I stood and walked around to the driver's side and got in. Wheeler leaned over and unlocked the door.

"I'm always surprised when something this old is still running," I said, getting in and smelling the recently polished interior.

"That should be the Breed slogan," he said dryly without a hint of humor.

Which made me smile. I buckled my lap belt and slammed the heavy door. The bucket seats were comfortable, and sitting in the old car brought back memories. I cranked the handle in circles to roll down the window, and Wheeler fired up the engine.

"We'll go to the house you lived at first."

The warm wind felt amazing. Gravel popped on the underbelly of the car as we pulled out of the parking lot and took off down the road at breakneck speed.

Thirty minutes later, we arrived at the house I'd once shared with Hawk. It was an ostentatious dwelling with tall bushes on each side that looked like skyscrapers. Normally they were kept neatly hedged, but now they looked scraggly and in need of a trim. The houses in the neighborhood were spaced apart for extra privacy, and only the orange streetlights illuminated the grounds.

Wheeler swung open the front door, and the cold air made my skin crawl. I cupped my elbows, standing closer to Wheeler than I had been before.

"What if someone's in here?" I whispered.

"Then I'll shift, and my wolf will feast on their bowels," he said indifferently, disappearing down the hall to our left.

I stood frozen in the living room. My eyes floated to the grand piano, the fireplace, the brass-framed paintings on the walls, and all the oversized vases. Before I chickened out, I suffocated the fear and began lifting cushions, turning vases upside down, pulling open drawers, and I even peered inside the piano. I'm not sure where a man like Hawk would have stashed drugs and money, but no stone would be left unturned.

Wheeler, on the other hand, was breaking things. I heard objects shattering and the sound of his shoes crunching on the broken pieces as he went through each room.

After searching the living room, I hurried down the hall and skidded to a halt when I passed a room that Hawk had always kept locked. The door was wide open, the cement floor covered with bloodstains. It's a room Hawk had told me was his private office, and my stomach turned when I noticed the chains on the floor.

"What… what *is* this?" I gasped, shaking my head at the horrifying reality. "Oh my God."

Wheeler hooked his arm around my waist and pulled me into the hall, closing the door. "Stay out of that room." He went into the bedroom, and I followed close behind.

"I slept in here," I said. "There's no way he could have hid anything in this room without me finding it."

Regardless, Wheeler flipped the mattress over and sliced it open with his knife. After ripping the pillows and breaking the lamps, he pulled everything out of the closet.

"What's going to happen to his house?" I wondered aloud. "Did anyone report him missing?"

"I'm handling all that, and you don't need to know the details."

"You know, you're about as warm as a block of ice." I moved around him like a cyclone and headed for the backyard.

The moon lit up the outdoor concrete with a sharp glow. God, I hated that yard. My wolf was a dirt roller and would have loved playing in a yard with grass. I knelt, examining the flat stones near the door to see if any were loose. I could see Hawk doing something stupid, like burying them in the mud. Nothing looked suspicious, so I removed the cover from the hot tub and peered in.

I flipped a few switches until a blue light illuminated the pool of water. Jet nozzles spun around, causing the water to noisily bubble and circulate. It all happened so fast that I didn't have time to gasp for breath. Someone had pushed me in headfirst.

Someone was holding me under.

The motor hummed beneath the water, and the edge of the tub pressed against my stomach. With the lower half of my body still outside the tub, I thrashed and wildly kicked.

Calm. Stay calm, Izzy.

I steadied myself with one arm extended to the bottom and reached around with my right. But I couldn't grab a hold of anything. A hand fisted the back of my shirt and kept me under.

Oh my God, I was going to drown. Panic set in. My heart raced and my lungs began to constrict, aching for oxygen. I writhed, trying to pull my whole body in so I could turn around and get the upper hand, but whoever was holding me down had pinned himself against the back of my legs.

Then my hair tangled in one of the jets and I screamed underwater.

I gripped the ends of my hair when his weight suddenly vanished and I was free.

But I wasn't free.

A set of hands tried pulling me out, but met with resistance. A larger chunk of hair threatened to rip from my scalp if he kept pulling. When he let go, my entire body slipped underwater.

Dark shoes splashed in front of me and Wheeler dunked his head in. I frantically tugged, pleading at him with my eyes.

A butterfly knife appeared and sliced off a chunk of my hair. He hooked his arm around my waist and yanked me up.

"Gahhh!" My lungs wheezed as I gasped for air. I coughed immediately, having sucked in some water.

A loud splash sounded when Wheeler jumped out of the hot tub and paced around the yard, dripping all over the concrete. "Fuck. He got away. Took off just as I came outside."

"Who was it?" My voice strained, and I began coughing up water.

He flipped his knife around until it closed and then tucked it in his back pocket. "One of Delgado's men. I'd bet my fucking right arm on it. Persistent SOB."

"I'm okay. I don't need any help," I said sarcastically as I pulled myself out of the water and swept back my sopping wet hair.

"You should have shifted," he said, peeling off his shirt and wringing out the water.

"It happened too fast and I panicked."

"Your wolf doesn't have long hair, so she would have been able to turn around and bite that asshole. You have to learn to trust your animal enough to protect you."

"I know, Wheeler. I'm just not used to men trying to kill me. Real nice town you have here." I glanced down at my dress, and it clung to my body. I squeezed out the ends and found my shoes scattered next to the hot tub. "Why would he want to kill me? Then he won't get his stuff. Humans aren't very smart."

Wheeler turned off the hot tub and threw the cover back on. "To scare the nightmare out of you. That's a real threat that makes someone comply. Delgado thinks you're full of shit and you know where the money is. I'm sure he's wondering what the hell happened to the man he sent after you at the festival." Wheeler raked his fingers through his wet hair and wiped off his face. "He's fucking with one of *us* now, so he better watch his back. I hope he tries it again."

"What?" I gasped. "You want him to come after me again?"

A dark look crossed his face. "This is the kind of mud that sticks to a boot, and I can get a footprint. Evidence. Reason to take care of this malignancy of a man the legal way, if I can't strangle him with my bare hands. And believe me, if Delgado ever crosses me personally, I will dig a grave and bury him myself."

"I've lived a pretty crazy life, Wheeler, but not until I moved here have I had people trying to kill me. No offense, but don't even think about using me as bait. I have no intention of allowing that human to get the upper hand with me again."

We headed back inside.

"Right. 'Cause you're a badass."

I yanked him back by his shirt and gave him a frosty glare. "My wolf emerged to save April's life. A *human*. I'm not a violent person by nature, but my wolf is aggressive and relentless. I'm not going to talk about what she did to a Shifter in Topeka seven years ago who tried to rape a woman in an alley by knifepoint, but let's just say he'll have scars for the rest of his life, and deservedly so. I have to balance things out with my energy, so forgive me if I'm not putting on spiked boots and twirling a knife in my hands. I don't know how to prepare myself for someone shoving me headfirst into a tub of water."

Wheeler spun all the way around and glared down at me with pale brown eyes. "So tell me why your wolf comes out to save someone else's life, but not yours?"

"It's a long story."

Wheeler had decisive brows, the kind that sloped down in the middle and gave him a sinister expression.

Maybe he wanted to know the answer, or maybe he simply wanted to provoke me, but I wasn't going to tell him my life story. I'd spent my entire youth in a volatile house and had been forced to cage my animal. After a while, my wolf had given up on fighting for me. But after having been penned for so long, she'd become aggressive and wouldn't hesitate to come out when someone else was in danger.

To be honest, that kind of relationship with my animal is exactly why I was so perfect to wait tables in crazy bars. I'd seen waitresses who couldn't control their animal, and all it took was one reckless shift to either get fired or attack someone. Some of those customers could rile you up, but I'd learned over the years to let all the small stuff slide and handle a situation without relying on my wolf.

Plus, she was a pissy little thing. Literally. Years ago, Jericho told me my wolf had pissed on two of his bandmates for taunting her. She didn't understand what they were saying, but she was smart enough to comprehend their tone.

"We're going to start collecting dust if we stand in here much longer. Let's go," Wheeler said.

⸺◦◦◦⸺

"There's nothing here," I said despairingly. I took a seat at the kitchen table in Hawk's second home. "We've exhausted all avenues and haven't found a thing."

After turning the first house upside down, we'd taken a long and arduous drive to the second house, where I'd been held captive. It took a breath of courage for me to walk through that door, but once inside, I remained focused. Wheeler searched the bedroom and basement because I didn't want to revisit that dark period in my life ever again.

I sighed, looking up at Wheeler. "Did you search the floorboards?"

"I've checked every conceivable place, including the toilet tank."

Wheeler was standing on top of the kitchen counter, looking at the space above the overhead cabinets. He finally rested his arm on the top of the fridge, his eyes downcast. "I crawled around in the attic, but I don't think he would have put it up there," he said to himself.

"I don't think it's here," I murmured, circling my finger on the table. "Maybe he sold it all. He could have put the money in the bank."

"Not likely. That's the kind of thing that attracts attention," Wheeler said knowingly. "Men with money like to hide it in overseas accounts, but Hawk seemed like a dumb shit, so I'm not giving him that much credit. A man can leave too many bread crumbs if he starts opening accounts and wiring money around."

My throat became dry, and I shivered. "What if we never find it? I'll have no choice but to leave town."

Wheeler's shoes slammed against the tile when he jumped down. "Maybe some of the others will pussyfoot around the truth, but I'm going to tell you flat out that I don't want you taking Jericho away from our pack. That's a low-down—"

"I'm not—"

"No, let me finish." His eyes darkened with his expression. "The lowest thing a woman can do is break up a pack. If you leave, Jericho is walking. I've known that wolf long enough to know he'll do it. We can't force a man to stay, and in time, we'll gain new pack members. But by then, you've already severed the brotherhood, and the damage is done."

I stood up and had reached out to touch his arm reassuringly when he stepped back.

"Wheeler, that's not my intention. I'd never do anything so selfish as take him away from his pack. I care for him too much to want to rupture old wounds. But if I stick around, Jericho's not going to stand by and watch these guys come after me. That'll leave me with no choice but to skip town. I wish I'd never met Hawk—he was the biggest mistake of my life. Not because of what he did to me, but what he did to those women. To Jericho. And to you…"

"Look, I'll tolerate you because I have no choice. But don't expect me to be nice and warm up to you just because you're sorry—that's not going to happen. I may be in your debt, but I'm not going to let you drag my brother away from the only good thing he's had in this life, and that's his family."

"I told you I'm not asking him to come with me!"

Wheeler shook his head angrily. "Doesn't matter. He'll follow, and you know it. Jericho had a fucked-up past, and whether you want to admit it or not, you were part of it. So don't get the idea that your love is going to weather the storm. He'll resent the hell out of you for making him leave his family, and he'll go back to that same old bullshit we pulled him out of all those years ago. If you split, then do it quietly in the middle of the night and leave him a Dear John. 'Preciate ya."

Wheeler turned away and stalked out of the room.

As much as I hated his abrasive candor, he was right. Jericho would follow me if I tried to leave; I was certain of it. But someday he'd start thinking about his family, and maybe that will be the fissure that finally breaks the dam.

I owed it to him to stick around and clean up this mess. I owed it to him not to bail.

When I searched for Wheeler, a light at the end of the hall caught my attention. It came from the room Hawk had kept me in. I heard the sound of Wheeler ripping apart the mattress and I shuddered.

The living room was small and insignificant. I sat down on the sofa and stared at the television, wondering how Hawk could have watched movies while I was tied up in the bed. It made me furious—it made me want to hurt him. But he was gone now, and I needed to let all that anger go before it ate me up like a cancer. It wasn't good to hold in that much hate; all it does is make your wolf insane.

I stared at an ugly painting on the wall, one with puppies running in a distant field of weeping willows. Hawk liked pastel imagery, and this was a dark oil painting. I got up and stood in front of it, running my fingers down the brassy frame.

"Wheeler?"

"Busy," he barked out.

"Wheeler?" I said more urgently, tugging at the immovable frame.

"Busy," he growled loudly.

"Fine," I yelled back. "Be busy while I'm looking at the drugs and money."

The door slammed against the wall, and he rushed into the room from my left. "Where?"

I pointed at the painting and stepped aside as Wheeler gripped the edges, tugging so hard his biceps looked like painted rocks.

I ran my fingers along the frame while he scraped his nails on the canvas. Wheeler pushed in, and a clicking noise sounded before the painting opened up like a door.

"Slick bastard," he breathed. "Doing it old school. How did you know to look at the painting?"

"Hawk hated dogs."

"And he was dating you?" he said with a snort.

We both stared at the combination lock sunken into the wall. Wheeler was tall, so he leaned in and began turning the dial.

"What was his birthday?"

"Heck if I know. Try the address."

"He wouldn't be that stupid." Wheeler turned the dial and it clicked. "Yeah, he was that stupid. Why the hell did you end up living with a pinhead like Hawk?" Wheeler stretched his arm inside the wall.

"What's in there?"

He pulled out stacks of money and placed them in my arms. I almost squealed with excitement. Then he pulled out bags of drugs—a larger quantity than I'd ever seen before.

"He's got compartments on the left and right," Wheeler said, his voice straining as he reached all the way up to his shoulder and pulled out more money.

"How are we going to get this to Delgado?"

"Maybe we should keep it," he suggested.

"No! Absolutely not."

Wheeler shut the painting and smiled darkly. "That's what I like to hear."

"So you're testing me?"

"Just need to make sure my brother isn't tangled up with a greedy whore."

I snatched the bags from his arms and flounced out of the room. "You need to learn to talk to a woman properly."

"Wait a second," he bellowed, jerking my arm and causing some of the cash to fall on the floor. "We're not walking outside with an armload of drugs and money. Let me get a trash bag or something. We'll put it in the trunk and head back. Lexi took Lynn and Maizy to a hotel tonight in case we found something, and Austin needed to work out a plan. They don't suspect anything because Lynn has a getaway vacation every so often. Austin got the idea so in case we ever needed them out of the house for a night, they wouldn't freak out."

"I just hope Austin knows how to get in touch with Delgado."

A fiendish look of amusement appeared on his face. "Maybe we should leave a note: *Found drugs and money. Call this number. Hugs and kisses—the guy who killed your henchman.*"

CHAPTER 22

J ERICHO REGAINED INNER BALANCE AFTER his wolf had taken over for the entire day. The events of the previous night with Isabelle killing a man had left him rattled. The last thing he remembered was shifting and nuzzling against Isabelle's white wolf as they slept beneath the stars. When he finally shifted back, the sun bronzed the western sky and painted the treetops with gold as it dipped below the horizon in search of night.

He walked inside naked and pulled on a pair of jeans, listening to Denver make a few wisecracks in a cartoonish voice about him hunting rabbits. The mood among the pack was somber, and he found out later that Austin had sent Wheeler to search for the drugs with Isabelle. He hoped going back to the house wasn't too traumatic, but maybe it would help her put those demons to bed.

Jericho's band had made plans weeks ago to write up some new music, and Austin didn't look thrilled when they swung by and trickled upstairs to the game room. It usually went on all night while they sat around, drank beer, scribbled down lyrics, and tested out new sounds. As a collaborative effort, it was important each member participated. This was Trevor's first session, and he was nervous the boys wouldn't like his style of music and ideas. But fresh blood always gave them a new vibe.

Jericho was waiting in the game room when they walked in, and Joker and Ren showed up with a few female companions. Jericho wasn't cool with the distraction, but he didn't want to be rude and throw them out. Joker had his drumsticks tucked in his back pocket, and Ren's guitar was slung over his arm in a case.

"They wanted to tag along and be our muses," Joker said nonchalantly, strutting in the door.

Three girls followed behind, eyes wide as they nibbled on their lips.

Humans.

Joker preferred humans for the obvious reason that he *was* one. Shifter women always had their sights on Jericho, leaving the rest of the guys in the dust. Human women didn't really care who they hooked up with, so Joker always had a fair shot. Ren was young, but the kid had game.

"What's wrong, man?" Jericho asked when Trevor eased up beside him, his hands in his pockets.

"You know," he whispered.

Trevor wasn't shy by any means, but he didn't like intimate situations where he might end up having to explain he was gay.

"Just show 'em how cool you are," Jericho said. "Make them wish they could hook up with you. That drives 'em wild. Do you think I used to hook up with every single hottie who rubbed up against me? They want you even more when you're aloof. Be aloof."

"Aloof," Trevor repeated as a mantra.

Jericho plucked a cigarette from a pack on the bar and tucked it behind his ear. "Where did Reno and April head off to?"

Trevor laughed quietly and shook a few strands of hair out of his eyes. "They had some elaborate date planned. He took her to a concert, and afterward they're staying at the Four Seasons and getting their nasty on. She packed lube; I'm kind of freaked out."

"More than I needed to know," Jericho said as they swaggered across the game room.

"Gina, Tina, and shit… what's your name?" Joker asked as he stumbled through introductions.

The blonde leaned over the pool table, and it made Jericho's body go stiff. He turned his eyes away and headed to the bar to light up his smoke.

"It's Ebony," she said, her tone snippy.

A girl with a low-cut top and a silver pendant tucked between her breasts took a seat beside Jericho. "So you're the famous Jericho. I've seen you play—you're hot onstage."

He lit up his smoke and took a deep drag, deciding he had a fifty-fifty shot at getting her name right. "It's just a job, Tina."

"Gina."

"Right."

Her left hand abruptly squeezed his thigh. "I think you're really sexy." Then she slid off the stool and intruded in his space, inching her hand even higher as her voice became sweet like honey. "If you want to know *how* sexy, show me your room. If you're not up for sex, I'll just give you head."

How juvenile was this conversation? he thought. Not a seductress by any means. And yet Isabelle could make him rock hard from a single glance with her mesmerizing green eyes. They both shared the same eye color, but hers were so vibrant and full of shine whereas his were dull and often compared to a dark jade. Isabelle had always been the better version of him.

"I'm not on the menu tonight, honey. But if you sit back in your seat and have a drink, I can hook you up with Ren. None of you has a shot at Trevor; he's a virgin and saving himself."

Trevor was either going to kill him or thank him for that later.

Gina glared at her friends and then evaluated Joker. She slyly hopped off her stool and poured herself a glass of brandy from the bottle sitting on the bar. Her eyes remained watchful of Jericho, and it made him uncomfortable enough to polish off his drink. While she refilled his glass, he went to help Trevor adjust the level on the amplifier to a volume that wouldn't piss off Austin.

Tina lifted up her shirt in front of Ren and stroked her ample breasts, quickly lowering the hem again and sitting in the beanbag next to him. It was obvious by his hard-on that Ren wasn't going to last long in this session.

All Jericho could think about was Isabelle. The way her wolf had taken care of that human to protect April filled him with pride. He admired her strength and resilience, despite the fact he would have preferred if she took it easy for a few more days.

The diamond ring he'd bought her was sitting inside his dresser drawer on top of her Pink Floyd shirt. Jericho wrote heartfelt lyrics for a living, but he didn't have the right words to give her with that ring. Nor did he know where and when to ask her to be his mate. It had to be right. Didn't all women want hearts and flowers? Shit, his palms were sweating just thinking about it.

When he returned to his seat, Gina had a cunning grin on her face as he took a sip of his drink.

"I think I've changed my mind about your friend," she said. "Why settle for the consolation prize when the trophy is in front of me?"

"Because the trophy isn't up for grabs," he reminded her.

She crossed her legs and licked the edge of her glass, speaking quietly. "We'll see about that."

———⊷∘⊱⊰∘⊶———

I could hardly sit still in Wheeler's Camaro as we headed back to the Weston house. He had stuffed Hawk's money and narcotics in the trunk of the car, although I didn't see the point. If a human cop had pulled us over, Wheeler's scary ass would have initiated an automatic search regardless.

I rolled the window up as the trees thickened, and we took a left turn that led up their private road.

"So, what are your feelings for Jericho?" Wheeler asked unexpectedly.

The headlamps shone eerily across the dirt road, illuminating a set of eyes in the brush that belonged to a wild animal.

"He's my best friend."

"That all?"

"I can't tell you."

He glared over his shoulder with his light eyes. "And why's that?"

I flipped some of my tousled hair back and unbuckled my seat belt. "Because I haven't told him how I feel. Not in all the right words."

"He told you, but you didn't tell him. That's the deal?"

Who is this asshole? He wants to sit here and judge me when he probably hasn't been laid since the early nineteen hundreds?

"I can't talk about this with you, Wheeler. It's personal and…

just know that I care more about Jericho than anyone else in this world. But if I'm going to say the words, I'm not going to say them to you."

"Just don't hurt him," he said under his breath.

Wheeler pressed down on the brake, and I jumped out of the car, excited to tell Jericho the good news about finding Hawk's stash. Once all this craziness was behind me, I planned to find a cute apartment near work. Living with the Weston pack was temporary, and while I would be forever grateful, I couldn't continue taking advantage of their hospitality.

I lightly rapped on the door and heard live music playing, but it was jarring and uncoordinated.

Ben opened the door with an irritated look on his face, which quickly brightened when he set eyes on me. How strange for two men to be so similar and different all at once. Ben's smile threw me off because Wheeler never cracked one.

"Well, if luck don't be a lady," he said admiringly, his eyes roaming down to the damp dress that clung to my thighs.

"Is Jericho here? I need to speak with him."

"Come on in," he said, holding the door with his arm so it left me with a tiny opening to squeeze through.

Before I could walk under his arm, Wheeler forcefully shoved him back and spat curses in low words I couldn't hear.

"Go fuck yourself," Ben said. "Since no one else will," he murmured, stalking toward the kitchen.

Wheeler slammed the door and slouched in a nearby chair. I jogged up the stairs and followed the sound of a guitar string being plucked over and over, then a girl laughing like a hyena.

The thick smell of cigarettes filled the hallway, and it sounded like one of his usual jam sessions. It reminded me of the early years when we'd hang out in hotel rooms with his band. To an outsider, it might have looked like a bunch of guys goofing off, but those were the nights they had written the most inspiring music.

I filled the doorway and scanned the room. Joker was lying upside down in the beanbag chair, tapping his drumsticks on his knees. Ren leaned on the bar with two women attached to him like vultures. Trevor was sitting on the floor making notes on several sheets of paper, strumming a few chords and writing more down. This looked like the tail end of a session and not the beginning, so I turned around and headed toward Jericho's room. A red glow spilled from beneath his door.

I turned the knob, ready to wake him up with the good news. If only I had brought in the money and drugs to show him, although waving narcotics in his face might have been insensitive. I didn't think he'd mind the cash.

"Guess what we found, Jericho?"

In the glow of the cruel light, a blonde sat astride Jericho on the bed. I blinked in horror, lost in a cutting memory from decades ago. Reliving a night I'd spent years trying to forget. As I stood there, the hope of what might have been between us was crushed out like a cigarette in a dirty ashtray.

"Take a picture, it'll last longer," she said over her shoulder.

I stepped back, my feet itching to run. But something caught my eye. She was topless in a pair of panties and had her hands all over his bare chest. Jericho's shirt was pulled up to his neck, but his eyes were closed.

This was so wrong.

"What's going on?" I asked, my voice shaking as much as my hands. "Jericho? Why isn't he moving?"

"Mind your own business," she slurred, leaning down to kiss him. Her mouth ran across his face, and Jericho's head lolled to the side.

Something vicious snapped within me—a fiercely protective emotion that gripped my heart.

"Get off him!"

My heart raced wildly as I rushed forward and fought to pull her off. She scratched my arm, and I tossed her on the floor.

"What the hell?" I heard Austin say. "I leave the house for one goddamn hour…" His voice trailed off, and there was a commotion in the game room of profanities, apologies, and girls vocalizing their complaints.

"Jericho, wake up," I said, slapping his cheek. I pulled his eyelids back and he groaned, struggling to open them.

"Hey, baby," he murmured. Then a string of unintelligible words mumbled out, and I slapped his cheek harder.

"What's wrong with you?"

As soon as the words left my lips, I grabbed his arm, looking for tracks. Then I searched the room for coke, pot… anything.

"Is he awake?" Austin stormed in the room and flipped on the light. "One of the girls spiked his drink with some kind of date-rape drug."

Rage consumed me to the point where I couldn't think straight. I flew out of the room and ran after the trail of voices moving out the front door.

"Is he conscious?" Wheeler asked, running by me up the stairs.

I couldn't answer because all I saw was red. I blew through the front door and onto the porch like a hurricane, cutting a trail through the grass as I approached Jericho's entourage.

I snatched the back of the girl's shirt—the one who had decided it was okay to give drugs to a former addict. She whirled around, swinging her mane of blond hair.

"Hey!"

I punched her in the face and she went out like a light.

Her friends looked at me wide-eyed and began helping her up, dragging her to the car as they hurried to get away from me.

Joker approached me guiltily, hands wide. "I'm sorry, Izzy. I had no idea that was going to happen. Never thought a girl would slip drugs into one of *our* drinks. That's scary as hell," he said, wiping the sweat from his face. "I don't tolerate drugs very well. Ren could give a damn, but *Jesus*, Jericho said he wasn't feeling well, and we got so distracted that I didn't notice Gina had left the room. Tell Jericho I feel like shit about the whole thing."

"Tell him yourself."

I went back in the house and found my keys hanging on the wall behind Jericho's keys, covering the letter *J*. One of the boys had brought my car back to the house, and it was time for me to go.

Not because I wanted to, and not because I despised Jericho for shredding me apart with infidelity.

I was scared.

Scared shitless by how deeply I loved him. My heart had shattered seeing him in that condition, and I realized that maybe I couldn't have it all. Maybe Jericho was just as unattainable as he made himself out to be onstage. Just within reach, but something I could never hold on to.

What scared me the most was how much I wanted to hold him and never let go. The visceral pain of seeing him hurt made me realize how it would crush me if something ever happened to him. I couldn't bear the thought that if I gave him my heart, it wouldn't be enough. He could end up killing himself with this careless lifestyle! I'd never lost anyone before, and as foolish as it seemed, I wanted to let him go now before the choice was no longer mine.

His pack didn't stop me. They were busy helping Jericho, which is where I should have been. Tears stung my eyes as I started up my car and sped down the road, leaving a cloud of midnight dust behind me. I needed time to think—I was so confused and still shaking. I could have shifted and ripped that woman's throat out, that's how close I was to losing control. My heart ached with a torrent of emotions ripping through me: anger, rejection, guilt, and disappointment.

But I was so damn mad that Jericho put himself in that situation. I had been attacked the previous night in the trailer, not that I expected him to be wallowing around about it, but to walk in on him and his band partying with a bunch of groupies?

And in his house! If I moved in with them, who's to say that wouldn't still go on? Women would always be a constant temptation. A constant threat.

And there it was again. So pathetic. Maybe it boiled down to that irrational fear women have that somehow we're not enough. I had all the self-confidence in the world about the kind of woman I was, but was it enough for *Jericho*?

A tingling sensation struck me warmly between the legs—I was going into heat soon, just as the alpha had predicted. Super. Just what I needed. Jake was going to fire me for sure. Technically, he couldn't. There were Shifter laws that protected women from job termination due to hyperactive ovaries, but he was only keeping me on because of Jericho.

When I turned on the radio, the Beatles lamented the death of Eleanor Rigby. I should have changed the channel, but I rolled down the windows and let it go. Human artists seemed to understand the impermanence and sorrows of life. Maybe that's why I'd been so attracted to Jericho's lifestyle when we'd first met, because he shared those views and showed me how to live in the moment.

God, he was unbelievable. Just a shining light in the world, one of those people you meet who you know is going to leave his footprint. How tragic he would never rise to the fame he so richly deserved, all because he was a Shifter. You can fake your death and change your name, but you can't erase your face from people's memories, or your voice.

As the melody ended, I remembered the Beatles song he'd sung in the bar about yesterday. Oh hell's bells, I was turning into a sappy sentimental fool, just like those girls I always rolled my eyes at. But now I understood how confusing and painful love could be.

So many conflicting emotions swept through me that it became impossible to know what the right thing to do was. He'd told me he loved me, and that resonated. Jericho seemed so willing to open up to me, and I was beginning to close like a book that didn't want to be read.

Now *I* was the one with all the insecurities, fears, and trouble. Jericho had cleaned up his act, and here I was dodging drug dealers, playing kidnap victim to my ex, and losing control to my murderous wolf.

That's why packs rarely took in rogues like me. They'd never trust a girl who grew up in a house full of cougars. I felt like fate had steamrolled right over me.

In fact, I began to get mad at myself. I decided to give me the silent treatment.

Of all times to be going into heat. Now I needed to find a motel and ride it out. With luck, it would end quickly.

CHAPTER 23

"E AT," AUSTIN INSISTED, SHOVING A plate of food in front of Jericho.

It must have been around three in the morning, and Jericho had a killer hangover. He wrinkled his nose at the corn and leftover greasy sausage. "I'm not hungry."

Austin angrily rapped his knuckles on the table. "You can pick it up and put it in your mouth, or I can shove it down your throat. You're still unsteady on your feet; I want you to drink more water to flush that shit out of your system."

The last thing Jericho remembered was listening to Trevor hum out a melody, and then everything had gotten fuzzy and tangled. He saw glimpses of images in his head, but he wasn't sure if they were memories from long ago or hallucinations.

He shoved the damn sausage in his mouth to appease Austin even though his stomach roiled. "What happened last night?" he asked around a mouthful of food. It's not a question he'd had a chance to ask because the last two hours had been spent hovering over the toilet. Man, did that bring back some dark memories.

"Your band. Need I say more? It's a good thing Lynn wasn't here."

Jericho rubbed his eyes wearily. Denver was still at the festival, and Reno had gone out with April. Everyone else was asleep. "Can you just tell me what happened? I only had a couple of drinks; it doesn't make sense." He was growing tired of Austin's elusive answers.

Austin rubbed his bristly chin and laced his fingers together. "One of the girls had drugs in her purse, and she slipped one in your drink."

"Ah, Christ."

Jericho had heard of some of the drugs human men used on women, but he'd never experienced it. Shifters were a little more resistant to drugs, and it required more to knock them out. It's why he was awake and not still passed out in the bed. But the gap in his memory made him uneasy. He scooped up a forkful of corn and reluctantly took a bite before washing it down with water. "And?"

"Look, we're all adults," Austin began. "If you want to have sex in the house, that's none of my business. But your buddies were using the game room upstairs like a brothel. That ain't cool."

Jericho snorted. "Joker? I doubt it. He's shy."

"I don't give a damn about shy; that's not the example I want to set for Trevor. He's new to the pack and new to your band. I can't stop him if he wants to be part of your group, but if you mess his head up—"

Jericho's fork hit the plate with a clang, and he scooted his chair back. "Look, Chaz was the only bad influence in our band, and he's out. I'm not going that route again. Trevor's also a grown-ass man who can decide what the hell he wants in life, but yeah, I'm keeping my eye on him. I know what fame can do to your head, and I'll keep him grounded. I'll have a talk with the boys about our sessions and make sure we don't have company in the future. You can bet that idea was all Ren's. He's a young wolf, and you know how horny they get."

"Keep it under control, Jericho. I mean it." Austin rubbed his face wearily. They were both sitting at the long kitchen table that was large enough to accommodate more pack members, should they ever get any. Austin had been taking his time adding to their pack. Some Shifters were all about size—and true, there was strength in numbers. But unless the Packmaster was a dictator, large packs became divided because of strong opinions.

"I'll keep an eye on Trev," Jericho said, knowing Trevor wasn't the kind of guy who was going to fall prey to the rocker lifestyle. "Joker knows he's in the doghouse because of this, so you can bet he'll give Ren an earful before I get a hold of him. You don't have to worry about Trevor. I know his type, and that's not his scene."

"It sure didn't seem to be Izzy's scene," Austin said offhandedly.

He slowly lifted his eyes, struggling to speak. "Say again?"

"I think she decked one of those girls on the lawn. That's what Ben saw from the window."

Jericho lurched forward and seized Austin's arm. "What the hell happened?"

"She walked in on you and that woman."

"Walked in on us doing what? Oh, fuck!" he said, leaning back and tunneling his fingers through his long hair.

"Yeah. Some girl was half-naked on top of you, and Izzy didn't look too happy. Good thing you two aren't mated. If Lexi had seen me in a position like that, her wolf would have torn out that woman's throat. In fact, I'm pretty sure she would have come after me," he said with a low chuckle.

Jericho felt like the lowest scum on the planet. They'd finally reconciled after a tumultuous past, and he'd just made her relive the nightmare all over again.

After a thoughtful sigh, Jericho's voice came out weary and broken. "What else happened?"

"Izzy yanked her off the bed like a heap of dirty laundry. For a minute there, I thought she'd stick around. But when I was hauling you off the bed, she got a crazy look in her eyes and ran out. For what it's worth, I don't think that groupie got far with you." Austin scratched his ear and looked away, as if embarrassed. "She still had her uh… her panties on."

"It doesn't matter," Jericho said under his breath. "She'll never forgive me." He pulled out his phone and dialed Isabelle, but she didn't answer. Sickened by the turn of events, he sent a text.

> **Jericho:** Isabelle, please talk to me.
> **Izzy:** There's nothing to say.
> **Jericho:** It's not what you think. Where are you?
> **Izzy:** Hell.

He threw the phone across the table and reached for his pack of smokes, lighting one up and taking a long drag, his hand shaky.

"Not in here," Austin said.

"Fuck you. Fuck this. Fuck it all."

"That's how it's going to be? You're getting fixated on something you can't have; maybe she ain't good for you."

Jericho kicked back his chair and knocked it over. "You guys have it all wrong!" he shouted. "You keep talking like she was a bad influence in my life, but you didn't know her. She was the best damn thing I ever lost! *Twice* I fucking lost her."

He spun around, squeezing his eyes shut and taking another drag. Such an idiot. He'd blown it. Should have never let those women inside the house. Should have been a better man. Should have proposed to her before he lost her. Should have…

"I think you need to cool it and take a walk," Wheeler said from the entrance to the dining room.

"Go to hell," Jericho spat, pacing the floor, hair falling in his face as he stared at his shoes.

Wheeler gripped his shoulders. "Be chill. Take a long walk and…"

Jericho shoved him in the chest and knocked him back two feet. Wheeler stalked forward and gripped his shirt in a tight fist, and that's when Jericho swung. Austin reached to pull him off while Jericho chanted, "Fuck it all!"

"You can get any damn woman you want!" Wheeler shouted.

Jericho struggled against Austin's vise-like grip. "I don't want another woman! Don't you get it?"

"No, maybe you need to fill me in," Wheeler snarled. "Look at all the trouble she's brought. Look at what the hell she's done to you. You're throwing swings at your own pack brothers. No woman is worth all that."

Jericho shoved Austin off him and staggered back, his voice cracking. Pain lanced through his chest—the worst kind of searing pain that only a broken heart can bring. "She *was* worth all that. She was worth *everything*! I never had a purpose in this world until Isabelle came along. She pushed me into doing the one thing I do well, and that's music. She gave me a reason to live and I *threw it all away*," he growled and shouted all at once. "Every good thing about me I owe to that woman. I fucked up my own life because I couldn't appreciate what I had right in front of me. All those women—do you think they ever meant a damn thing? I've always loved her, I was just too damn scared to think she could love me back. What's to love? I'm just a junkie, a singer who lets women use him—she should have left me long before she did. But Isabelle stuck it out and never gave up on me. She had faith when I didn't." He slid down the wall and covered his face with tight fists. Tears wet his lashes.

"Let's leave him alone," Austin murmured.

Isabelle had put her trust in him, hoping he was a changed man. Maybe Jericho hadn't lain in bed with that woman by choice, but he'd put himself in that situation. He had become a ghost of a man over the years, going through the motions. The women had just become a way to forget how alone he felt.

He picked up his cigarette from the floor and put it between his lips, watching the tip glow orange and crackle as he pulled in a taste. Now he knew with absolute certainty that what he'd felt his entire life wasn't just a figment of his imagination.

Isabelle was his life mate.

She was the woman he was born to love.

Shifters often talked about born life mates—couples who had an unbreakable connection. A man could sense when his woman was in danger, and Jericho had felt pangs of worry on several occasions, like restless insects crawling in his stomach. He'd felt it bad earlier that night when Isabelle was supposed to be with Wheeler. It was so powerful he almost shifted, but no one said anything had gone wrong, so he'd dismissed it. Maybe he was going crazy.

Wheeler swaggered in and took a seat on the floor to his right. He pulled up his knees and draped his arms over them, tipping his head back.

Jericho stayed silent, stoically watching his cigarette wasting away between his fingers.

"You still got the ring?" Wheeler asked. "You should hang on to it. You might find another girl to give it to."

As if that were an option.

"What happened with you two last night?" Jericho asked in a cracked voice.

"We found what Delgado's been looking for. Hawk kept it stashed in a safe in the house where you two were held prisoner. Some asshole was there—one of Delgado's men. Good thing we found the money and drugs. Now we can get that moron off our ass. These damn humans are nothing but trouble."

"Wait, hit rewind. Someone was there with you?"

Wheeler touched his cheek and stared at the drop of blood on his finger, smearing it between his fingers. "Yeah. Some asshole tried shoving Izzy in the Jacuzzi. I would have caught him if her hair hadn't gotten stuck in the jets."

Jericho's muscles tensed. "*What?* Austin didn't tell me this."

Wheeler kept dabbing his finger on the small cut. "No, and he wouldn't have. He was a little preoccupied holding your hair while you puked in the toilet like a little—"

"Get on with your story," Jericho bit out.

"I had to cut off a chunk of her hair with my knife or she would have drowned in that damn thing. It got tangled up in one of those little…" He twirled his finger in a circle. "Anyhow, now I have to go back and drain the tub. If someone gets nosy and finds a chunk of red hair floating around in there, it's going to raise eyebrows."

"And the body won't?"

Wheeler sniffed out a laugh and then groaned. "I have to clean up his house of pain so we can keep our noses clean. Might have to torch it. We should have called cleaners."

"Don't even think about it," Jericho growled.

Reputable cleaners would open an investigation, so usually the shady cleaners were called when someone didn't want the authorities sniffing around. But it wasn't a good idea to involve those guys in too much of your business; some were corrupt and not above a little blackmail. Jericho couldn't risk anyone finding out. Even though Hawk had taken them into captivity, there was an off chance Jericho could receive a jail or death sentence. The mess he'd left in that basement left no question that Jericho's wolf had carried the matter beyond self-defense.

"Has Izzy ever told you she loves you?"

Jericho shook his head.

Wheeler stretched out his legs and crossed them at the ankle. "And you would have proposed to a woman without knowing how she felt about you? Jesus. You've got big balls."

Jericho wearily pushed himself off the floor to go to his room. He still had a throbbing headache from the drugs, but the thought of someone trying to hurt Isabelle when he wasn't there to protect her made him sick to his stomach.

He stopped at the door and spoke without looking down. "Sometimes you just have to take a leap of faith. I don't need to hear what I feel in my heart."

CHAPTER 24

"I'M SO SORRY, ROSIE. I wish I knew how long I'm going to be away from work, but the last time I was in heat it went on for two weeks."

I heard her curse in Spanish.

"Usually it's just a couple of days," I assured her.

Which was a lie. I'd always gone through my heat cycle alone, so it lasted longer than those who were mated.

I switched on the light in my motel room and sat on the bed. I had requested the last room on the second floor. While I wasn't on the Breed side of town, I didn't want to risk a Shifter with a strong nose walking by. There were many rogues on the streets, most of whom didn't abide by the laws.

"Rosie, if Jake's mad and wants to fire me, it's all gravy. I can hardly blame him after everything that's been going on these past few weeks. Just let me know ahead of time so I can start searching for another job. I swear I'm usually one of the most dependable girls you could ever meet. I won't—" I breathed a sigh of relief to hear the understanding in Rosie's voice rather than anger. "Yes, okay. I'll call you later when I know more. Bye, Rosie."

Three days had passed since I'd left Jericho. He'd given up calling me after one attempt. No surprise there. Once again, I'd bailed on him. I wanted to sock myself over the head, but getting over my heat cycle quickly became a bigger priority. It struck me that morning like a tsunami—tingles surging between my legs and my muscles clenching with need.

Biology at its finest.

Shifters didn't have to guess when they were their most fertile; the scent attracted Shifter males within a certain proximity. Other

Breeds were oblivious to the change in our scent, although Chitahs were sensitive enough to detect our amorous emotions. Jericho once told me the scent of a woman in heat was comparable to the most heavenly nectar settling on his tongue, thick and sweet.

I lay down and took a deep breath as I shoved my face into a musty pillow. The last wave had hit two hours ago. It usually began slow and steady, desire flooding my senses until it reached a crescendo. The only way to abate the discomfort and decrease the duration was to have orgasms, and I won't deny that I'd always felt guilty doing that on my own. Not that there was anything wrong with it, but when in heat, it felt mechanical—a means to an end. One year, I ignored my needs to see if it really made a difference. The yearning became relentless, and it was one of the longest cycles I'd ever spent in heat.

I moaned against the pillow in frustration when a knock at the door startled me. My heart raced, and I hopped out of bed and peered through the peephole. Relief swam through me at the sight of a familiar face, and I quickly unlocked the door. "Thank you so much for doing this, Ivy."

She gracefully breezed around me, her braid swishing behind her back. Ivy set down two bags of groceries on the table.

When I closed the door, she tossed her purse in the chair.

"I'll pay you as soon as I get back to work. I'm a little short right now; the guy wanted every dime in my wallet to put down on the room."

"Don't worry about it," she said with a wave of her hand. "It's inconsequential. These are things you need, and I'm more than happy to help."

I'd only asked for a few staples, but much to my delight, she had brought fresh fruit. I didn't have a fridge in the room, so most of my meals were going to be peanut-butter sandwiches and microwave soup.

"Here, we can just put it all on the dresser," I said. "That way I can eat at the table and enjoy my magnificent view."

Ivy laughed softly and shook her head. She had a warm complexion with dark eyes and lush lips, but she didn't doll herself up like most women. Her lashes were elegantly long and black, and her high cheekbones created contours in her face to be admired. Mascara and lipstick would have detracted from her natural beauty.

"Nice mirror," she said, glancing at the sliding closet doors next to the bed.

It felt a little sleazy because it was right beside the bed, and it took no stretch of the imagination to realize what it was put there for. A long dresser filled the right wall with a microwave on the left side. The television wasn't just mounted on the wall; it looked like it had been screwed in there to prevent someone from stealing it.

"I'd make you some coffee, but the machine doesn't work," I said.

Ivy lined up the little plastic cups of soup on the heavy dresser and put the snacks to the right. I guessed she was health conscious, because most of the foods were labeled as whole wheat or organic.

"How do you go through your cycle while living in a pack?" I asked out of curiosity. "Austin's mated. Is he really able to keep all the men away?"

Ivy handed me a green apple, and I sat on the bed while she folded up the paper bag. "As crazy as it seems, they're really respectful. I haven't gone through my heat spell yet, so I don't know what that's like. When I went through the change for the first time, Austin could sense it. He made sure I had privacy, and Lexi was the first one to see my wolf."

"Wow, you're younger than I thought." Ivy seemed like such an old soul that it came as a surprise to find out she was a new wolf.

Ivy tipped her head and smiled. She had a lovely tan that complemented her mahogany hair, which was the richest shade of brown I'd ever seen. A glint of her lavender nail polish caught my eye, and she held her hands out for me to see. "April likes to do my nails. Isn't that a beautiful shade?"

"She has a keen eye with picking the right colors," I said, remembering her suggestions in the store when we'd first met.

"I like April a lot. She's quiet and thoughtful, although young."

"You're young."

"Yes," she replied, a hint of sadness in her voice. "But I had to grow up fast. It's not the numbers that age us in life."

"Where did you come from?"

"The Kizer pack up in Oklahoma. My father traded me off because... Well, he didn't think I was a good influence on his pack. I'm grateful. Sometimes family isn't where we really belong."

"And you belong with the Weston pack?"

She shifted her eyes pensively. "I don't know that *belong* is the right word. I feel protected and cared for, and I guess that's all a woman needs to draw strength." She tapped a can on the dresser with the tip of her finger. "Anyhow, I was getting too old, and it was time for me to change hands. A woman must break from the pack she's raised in; it's not safe. You know how it is."

No, I didn't know. All I knew about packs was what I'd overheard in conversations at work. I turned the apple in my hand, twisting at the stem. "I didn't grow up in a pack."

Ivy looked at me contemplatively, tracing her finger over the dimpled surface of an orange. "Maybe you were lucky. Not all packs are like Austin's."

My brows stitched together. "What was so wrong with the pack you were raised in?"

Her face heated and she folded up the second paper bag, setting them both on the floor. "I came from a different world." When she finally stood upright, a quiet sigh blew past her lips. "My father called me Poison Ivy—that was his name for me. My mother died years ago, and I had no siblings to turn to. I mostly kept to myself in the later years. My father believes in ruling a pack with an iron fist, and that's not always a good thing. Things were different when my mother was alive."

"Do you still talk to your father?"

"I haven't heard from him since the day I left, but Austin mentioned he's called and asked about how I'm fitting in with the pack. It's been just under a year. I was his only child, and you can imagine his disappointment that I wasn't a boy."

"Firstborn a woman?" I asked in surprise.

"Yes. It's not unheard of. Looking back, some of the men

must have seen me as a female who might be able to produce an alpha male child. The Kizer pack treats their women like breeding machines, and most of that was my father's fault for bringing in old blood. It's refreshing to live in a house where I can play horseshoes with Denver or listen to music with Jericho and not have to worry about ulterior motives. Just to be treated as an equal—it's something I've never known."

My eyes lowered to the floor at the mention of Jericho's name.

I lifted a swath of my hair and studied the ends where Wheeler had sliced off a chunk to free me in the hot tub. She stepped forward and touched a few wavy strands. "Do you want me to trim this up for you?"

"I thought about lopping it all off," I said jokingly.

"No, don't do that. You have exquisite hair. It's such a unique shade of light red. I'll get some scissors and come back this afternoon. How does that sound?"

"Better you than me, I suppose. I'd make a mess of it. Thanks, Ivy. I'm so sorry for all this trouble; I swear this isn't who I am. There's no way I can repay your family for what they've done. Did Wheeler tell you what we found?"

She sat on the bed beside me and pulled her braided hair around front, brushing her fingers over the ends. "They had a difficult time getting in touch with Delgado, but Reno arranged a meeting with one of his men and performed the exchange. I don't think that's the last we've heard of him though, and Austin's worried about his pack getting involved with someone as unscrupulous as Delgado. This guy is big-time—even my father avoided drug lords. I'm relieved they handled this the right way."

The elephant in the room was stomping around and swinging his trunk, but neither of us brought up Jericho. As much as I wondered how devastated he might be, I also had visions of him packing up his guitar and heading off to another gig, buying drinks for a girl sitting on his lap, and wondering what crazy Izzy's up to. There's a time in every broken relationship when you face the ugly question of wondering how much you really meant to a person, if you'll be the only one with the broken heart.

"What happens if you find a mate?" I asked. "Who's not in the Weston pack, I mean."

"Then I go with him. This living situation is only temporary, unless I choose not to mate. It would break tradition to have my mate move in with my pack. He would not acclimate to a house full of men who already feel protective of me."

"Are you looking?"

Ivy stood up, and her long braid draped exquisitely down the center of her curved back. "I'm optimistic, but I don't know if there is a man who is capable of giving me the love I require."

My smile withered when I noticed the sullen expression on her face as she looked at her reflection in the mirror. Ivy had a romantic heart, and I felt a kinship to her more than the other girls because of it. Her free spirit inspired me to desire more for myself, and yet something about her was broken.

Then again, maybe we're all a little broken and just trying to find the glue that'll hold us together.

"You could try searching for love online." I grinned at her and suppressed a giggle.

She slapped a hand over her mouth and laughed, her eyes turning into playful crescent moons. "Can you imagine having a human pick me up at the house for a date? I'm afraid I'd end up with six chaperones."

We both laughed at the idea, and I took a bite of my tart apple.

Ivy raised her chin proudly and headed toward the door. "All I want is a good man who can provide for me. I should be so lucky," she finally said, lifting her purse from the small table.

"Well, don't get mated unless he loves you."

"Likewise," she said, waving as she went out the door. "I'll be back in a little while."

———◦◦◦◦———

Jericho was sprawled out on the living room sofa, listening to the Weston pack moving about the house. A few days had gone by since the night he'd been drugged by that groupie. Izzy had taken her car and left for good, and he'd been unable to get his head together. Once the pain in his chest subsided, it was replaced with emptiness.

Maizy darted around the spacious living room, engaged in a game with Denver. Maizy didn't have any children to grow up with or close friends, so Denver provided her with all the entertainment she could hope for. The men enjoyed the vivacious energy she brought into their home. Denver was Maizy's watchdog and would be her protector for as long as she needed. That little girl adored him, probably because he had the same maturity level as she did.

"Denny! Now what animal am I?"

He peeked through his lashes and saw her swinging her arm in front of her face.

Denver pinched his chin and tapped his bare foot on the floor. "A duck."

"I'm not a duck!" she complained. "You're not even trying." Maizy flapped her little arm up and down like an elephant moving its trunk.

"A moose."

She dropped her arms and scowled. "I'm an *elephant.*"

Denver snorted and patted the top of her head. "Not until you eat your dinner. Now skedaddle!"

"Dinner's ready!" Lexi shouted out.

Maizy walked slowly toward the dining room and glared over her shoulder at Denver.

He pointed upward, and his face brightened. "Aha! Now you're a turtle!"

"Well, you're a skunk," she said, poking out her tongue and disappearing.

"Kids," he murmured, raking his fingers through his hair.

"She looks up to you," Jericho said.

Denver sighed. "You gonna sleep on the couch all day, dickhead?"

"No. We have a show later tonight."

Denver stuffed his hand in his pocket and pulled out a bite-size piece of candy. He wadded up the wrapper and tossed it in a blue vase.

"I see," he said with a mouthful of caramel. "Hot babe buffet. I'm not working tonight, so how about I come along?"

"I thought you didn't like leftovers," Jericho grumbled, finally sitting up. All he had on was a pair of black jeans and a leather belt. Jericho rubbed the tattoo on his left arm and watched Denver tuck his hands beneath his armpits, looking irritated, but not enough to blow his chance of scoring a date.

Not that Denver scored much.

"You don't have to ask permission to come to my show." Jericho rubbed his eyes and decided he was going to need eyeliner to camouflage his exhaustion.

"Look," Denver began, pointing back and forth between them. "We both know panties may be flying in your direction, but that doesn't mean the ladies won't want to ride on the Denver carousel of love."

"Seriously?" Jericho laughed and covered his face. "Look, I'll hook you up if all you're looking for is a one-night stand."

"Maybe you could use one too, bro. Might do you some good to move on." Denver quietly walked out of the room.

If the only way for Jericho to get out of this funk was to have sex with another woman, then he was in trouble. Celibacy was looking like a viable option. He couldn't tear his thoughts away from Isabelle. The way she had spread her body out before him, how perfectly her breasts molded against his chest, and the floral fragrance that lingered on her sugary-sweet skin. Isabelle's lips tasted of passion fruit, and just thinking about their tongues twining gave him an erection.

Everything about that girl wrecked him.

Wheeler joked that Isabelle could give him writing material for his next song. They didn't get it. Christ, he couldn't imagine what must have gone through her head when she'd walked in on him. Jericho felt blessed he wouldn't have to go through his life with the expression on her face burned in his memory.

The last time he'd seen Isabelle in human form, she was lying in bed with the afterglow of their passion on her face. For a brief moment, he'd thought he might have a shot at something meaningful in his life.

He got off the couch and went upstairs, unclasping the silver chain that hung around his neck. He closed his bedroom door and knelt in front of his dresser, opening the bottom drawer. On top of the Pink Floyd shirt was the black box. He pulled out the ring and looped it on the chain, putting the necklace around his neck. It settled against his chest, right over his heart.

Where it would stay.

After dinner, Denver gave Jericho a ride to work in his yellow truck. It wasn't one of the newer models, but an old classic that some of the boys called a jalopy. Denver kept it in good condition, even if it looked a little beat up.

"This isn't the way," Jericho said when Denver turned in the wrong direction.

Denver rolled down his window and let the warm wind ruffle his hair. "I promised Ivy I'd do her a solid and drop off something."

"Where?"

Denver's silence answered his question. Ivy had been to see Isabelle earlier that day but had said nothing to Jericho about the visit. He didn't ask.

After grabbing a small plastic bag, Denver slammed the truck door and jogged up a flight of stairs at one of the most run-down motels Jericho had ever seen. It looked a hundred years old—painted yellow with bright blue doors. A couple of the letters had burned out on the sign, and most of the cars in the parking lot looked local based on their bumper stickers, which meant they were either using it for prostitution or a place to live.

Jericho searched the truck for a lighter but could only find a box of matches in the glove compartment. He struck the match and lit the end of his cigarette, tossing the charred stick out the window.

Two big guys were standing by the stairs, watching a woman

rush to her car from one of the rooms. One guy nudged the other with his elbow, and they both laughed in gravelly voices.

"What the fuck are you doing?" Jericho asked himself, getting out of the truck with the smoke between his teeth. He stalked toward the building and chastised himself as he went up the stairs, ascending two steps at a time. It was as if an invisible string were pulling him forward, compelling him to go to Isabelle.

Denver appeared with a startled look on his face. "No way, Jose. You need to turn around and get your ass in the truck." Halfway down the steps, he snatched Jericho's wrist and tried to coax him away.

"Chill out," Jericho said, swiping his arm in a circle.

"It ain't a good time for visits," Denver ground out through his teeth. "Come on, man. Don't make this harder than it needs to be."

Jericho took a drag of his cigarette, the orange tip crackling, and then flicked it over the railing. "I'll just be a minute."

Denver held up both hands. "You're a bag of nuts. If you're not back down in five minutes, I'm leaving without you. Clock starts now."

They headed their separate ways, and Jericho walked in the direction Denver had come from. There were only two motel rooms on the left, and the first one he passed had a couple of toy cars outside the door. He walked to the end unit and knocked on the door.

After a few beats, Isabelle's voice rang out. "Go away."

He put his finger over the peephole. "Isabelle, it's me. I want to talk."

"Please, just go."

He rested his forehead on the door, knowing she must have been doing the same on the other side. She sounded so close.

"I can't leave. Not without seeing you. I'm sorry. I'm so damn sorry."

"I know," she said softly. "It wasn't your fault."

"It wasn't!"

"I *know*. I didn't mean it sarcastically. I believe you."

"Hard to tell from the expression on your door."

He thought he heard her laugh, but maybe it was wishful thinking.

A light flipped on inside and the curtains opened. Jericho stepped to the left and admired Isabelle on the opposite side of the window. Thank God for cheap windows and an old air conditioner that allowed them to hear each other.

"You cut your hair," he said. It was several inches shorter, messy, and had never looked sexier. Just like the rest of her. Her white tank top was wrinkled, too long, and revealed cleavage. Her sweatpants fit snugly and showed off the gentle curve of her hips.

"Ivy did it," she said, touching the ends. "Long story."

Yeah, he knew. "You okay? Wheeler told me what happened."

She nodded, and her eyes slid down his body. "Do you have a show tonight?"

He nodded back.

Isabelle covered her smile. "Who did your eyeliner?"

"Maizy. Why?"

"It's all…" She traced her finger beneath her eye and sloped down her cheek.

Jericho wiped the heel of his hand across his face. He hadn't had the heart to say no when Maizy walked in his room with a smile, holding his smoky eye pencil.

"How long are you staying here?" he asked conversationally, noticing a stack of food on her dresser to the right. Pillows were scattered across the bed and the blanket was pulled back, as if she'd already settled in for the night. The television was off, which made him wonder if Denver had woken her up.

"I'm not sure. It won't be too much longer." She gripped the curtain and lowered her eyes ruefully. "You should go."

Jericho put his palms on the glass and leaned in. "Isabelle, open the door and let's talk. I'm not going to say anything to upset you; I just want to explain what happened so you don't walk away from this hating the hell out of yourself for giving me a second chance. This wasn't your fault. Please, baby, I can't do this through the window."

She theatrically pulled the drapes closed. His heart stammered when the chain slid off the lock and the door cracked open.

He peered into the dimly lit room. "Isabelle, I'll just be a minute. I can't leave without seeing you…"

Then it hit him. She had barely appeared in the doorway when all the blood in his body rushed south and he became hard as granite. All he noticed was how lovely her breasts looked behind that thin fabric, which was sheer enough that he could see the color of her nipples.

Jericho pushed his way in and kicked the door shut. He cupped the back of her neck, running his nose along her damp cheek as she tilted her head up to look at him. "Oh, *fuck*. You're in heat, aren't you?" he breathed.

When she let out a delicate moan, he settled his weight on his right leg and broke out in a sweat. Damn, the sweet scent lingering on her skin filled his senses and clouded all rational thought. Before he knew it, his mouth was on hers and… Jesus—her lips were so pliant and soft, moving with his in sweet rhythm. She tasted like ambrosia, whetting his sexual appetite like he'd never known. They whispered words back and forth, but Jericho couldn't focus.

Her leg wrapped around his, and she moaned against his mouth. Before he knew it, Isabelle was grinding herself against him. "*Please*, make it stop."

Christ, his willpower was about as strong as a thread of hair. Her need for sex consumed him, but he pushed her back, out of breath.

"Wait, Isabelle. Wait. I'm not doing this with you, so stop."

CHAPTER 25

M Y HEART LEAPT IN MY chest when Jericho appeared outside my motel room. What was I going to say to him? I definitely couldn't open the door in my condition.

But he looked so handsome on the other side of the window. Tall and terribly sexy. Wisps of brown hair danced on his shoulders from the southerly breeze. The outdoor light cast shadows on the left side of his body, making his Adam's apple stand out. It also obscured his eyes, but I could feel them on me. Jericho had on my Pink Floyd shirt. Maybe that's what did me in—seeing him in something he knew was mine. Something he wanted close to his body.

He deserved a chance to speak his mind, and I didn't want anything left unsaid. I'd already been down that road. I'd spent years wishing for a time machine so I could have told him my true feelings. I'd often wondered if he would have overdosed had I stayed and confronted him. I realized the importance of not leaving loose ends.

His palms pressed on the glass. Another wave was coming, and I felt my resolve weakening, crumbling to ashes. I opened the door, and his words were abruptly cut off when his nostrils flared and his eyes hooded.

I'd seen that hungry look on a man's face, but never from Jericho while looking at me. He stepped inside and kicked the door shut with his heel. Then he roughly cupped the back of my neck and closed the distance between us.

His bristly cheek pressed against mine. "Oh, *fuck*. You're in heat, aren't you?" he said in a warm breath that skated down my neck.

I moaned as our lips found each other. Carnal need swelled

in me like a hurricane, and I became the storm, crashing against Jericho.

His tongue slid into my mouth and met with mine… God, he tasted heavenly and I couldn't get enough of him. When he moaned into my mouth, it sent a feverish rush of tingles to my core. I wrapped my leg around his body, consuming more of him with my hands, my arms, my legs, my mouth, my breath.

He pulled back. "I need you to stop doing that," he said in a heavy breath.

"What?"

"Moaning against my tongue."

"I'll stop."

His lips touched mine lightly. "And don't answer me in a breathless voice. You don't know what the fuck that does to me."

I couldn't stand it. I needed him inside me.

Now.

No time to undress and refine my seduction skills. No time to even make it to the bed. "*Please*, make it stop," I said in a trembling whisper, nipping on his lower lip and feeling another lick of pleasure shoot through me.

His body responded, pressing against mine, and his strong arms wrapped around my waist.

But then he pushed me away. "Wait, Isabelle. Wait. I'm not doing this with you, so stop."

Did he think I was a compliant female? I bent over and pulled down my sweats and panties, kicking them aside. Jericho backed up a pace, startled by my dominant behavior. He'd never been in the same room with me while I was in heat, and I had never been in the room with another man in this condition. All my body knew was that it wanted him. It felt like a pulse throbbing inside me, and I needed that empty space filled.

Just when I thought he was going to turn and run, Jericho pulled away the end of his belt and unlatched it, curving his arm around my waist as he walked me into the side of the dresser. It bumped against my waist, and he reached out with his left arm and knocked all the contents off the surface.

A clatter of cans and packaged foods spilled on the floor, and as I turned to look, he lifted me up and set me on the end. My legs hooked around his waist and he struggled with his zipper, finally shucking down his pants.

I pulled on his neck, trying to kiss him as he worked diligently to free himself.

"Inside me. Now," I begged. "I need it, Jericho. I need you so bad it hurts."

"It's just the heat talking," he said in a ragged and almost remorseful tone.

Jericho hesitated and leaned into me, his face so close. My knees were bent and I lifted my legs, rubbing them against his flanks and feeling the thick press against my core.

"Isabelle, you could get pregnant," he warned.

I could see his mind was scrambling for a way out of this. Our bodies knew exactly what they wanted to do, and maybe it boiled down to animal instinct, but he was too busy rationalizing. In my mind, it wouldn't be the end of the world if I became pregnant with his baby. Maybe our relationship was all kinds of messed up, but kids weren't a regret in the Shifter world. It was harder for a woman to pair up with a mate other than her child's father—most Shifter men didn't want to take on that burden. But good guys were out there, and I could provide for a baby.

Jericho's baby. Just thinking about having *his* child made me want him even more.

So I kept stroking his sides with my legs, coaxing him to stop thinking and start *feeling*. I lay on my back, knocking an orange on the floor as I pulled off my tank top and tossed it over his shoulder so I was bare to him.

He bent down and stroked his tongue along the crease of my thigh and up to my navel. Then he slowly outlined one of my nipples with his tongue, and I released an anguished moan.

I opened my mouth, gasping for breath as he drove deep inside, stretching me wide and penetrating all the way to the hilt.

"Ah fuck, Isabelle... it's so damn *hot*." It almost sounded like a complaint, but he kept rocking against me, sliding in and out, filling me with an eruption of tingles and waves of pleasure. "Is this what it's like?" he asked in a ragged breath, looking up at me with awareness burning in his eyes.

"I don't know. You're my first in heat."

"*Oh my God*," he breathed more than said. "I've never felt anything this *sweet* before."

His eyelids fluttered as he stood up, holding my thighs and swiveling his hips in a maddening rhythm. Our skin slapped together and the surface of the dresser pulled at my back as I began to slide up.

"Mmmm." I unabashedly moaned and cried out, over and over, gripping the sides of the dresser.

Jericho touched my lower belly, and his thumb stroked my sex masterfully while the other hand squeezed my breast. I felt a pinch here, a swirl there, a squeeze, and then he went faster. Our first time together, we'd made love. But this was animalistic.

Primal.

"Harder!" I screamed.

Jericho lifted my legs straight up in the air and rested them on his shoulders, changing how I felt everything.

"Oh, like that," I breathed, wanting this to last forever.

"I can't stop," he panted. "Tell me to stop."

"Don't stop!"

"Please, Isabelle… Tell me to stop. I'm going to come… Oh fuck, tell me to stop."

I cried out as a wave of heat engulfed me and pleasure squeezed me so tight my entire body locked up. I raised my hips off the surface. "*Don't stop*. Faster, Jericho. *Harder*," I begged, seeking my release. I couldn't even formulate words anymore—I was so consumed by our passion.

He complied, as if his body were going against his will. The dresser made an awful complaint as the drawers shook and more cans fell off.

I bent my knees and lowered my legs, wrapping them tightly around his waist. Beads of sweat touched his brow, and his lips were swollen as he looked at me like a hungry animal. Jericho collapsed on top of me, and as soon as our bodies made contact, I arched my back and the most intense wave of pleasure struck me as I came.

So did he, and our duet of cries sounded better than any damn song he'd ever written.

Jericho tried to pull out, and when I wrapped my arms and legs around him, his eyes hardened like steel. He reached around and gripped a fistful of my hair, kissing me hard and thrusting as deep as he could. I gasped against his mouth. With that one gesture, he claimed me.

My body shuddered one last time before every craving and ache dissipated, as if it never was. So *this* is what it felt like to be sated by a man during heat? *Hell's bells.* Now I understood with perfect clarity why women sought a mate. Usually when I was by myself, the craving still lingered.

Jericho stood up, and the cool air tightened my nipples. I'd never been more uncomfortable in all my life. I also hoped the next people who stayed in this room didn't put their sandwiches on this dresser.

"I can't do this, Isabelle," he said out of breath.

"Do what?"

He raked his fingers through his stringy brown hair. "This… Whatever this is. It's not right. I feel like I'm taking advantage of you. This isn't how I wanted…"

I blinked a few times and covered my chest. My body felt glued to the wood and it was a Herculean effort to push myself up. I blinked in surprise as Jericho turned around, picking up my oversized white tank top and putting it on.

He folded up the Pink Floyd shirt and stood in front of me, tilting my chin up. "Sexybelle," he whispered. His eyes studied the shape of my mouth, and then he handed me the shirt. "Put this on for me."

"Why?"

A sexy grin slid up his face. "So I can take it off again."

"No."

His brows knitted. "Why don't you want to wear this shirt?"

It wasn't mine anymore.

He wasn't mine.

His callused fingers stroked along my cheek and he dipped his head low, searching my eyes. "I love you, baby."

The silence made me feel like the worst kind of villain. Now that all my carnal fire had been extinguished, my brain was starting to kick back into gear, and it always seemed to be in conflict with my heart.

He stroked my cheeks with his thumbs and admired me from the top of my head down to my thighs. "You're the most beautiful song I've ever written."

"You mean ridden?"

An irritated look flashed in his eyes. "You're *not* one of those girls. I want to give you something, but I don't know if you want it."

His cheeks flushed, and he bit down on his lower lip. I'd never seen him look so... nervous.

"I don't know how I feel, Jericho. Not after the other night."

"What you saw at the house—that wasn't what you think. I was—"

"I know. You don't have to explain. She drugged you and it wasn't your fault. I just got confused all over again. I don't know how to explain it."

"Maybe it's time that you and your wolf start making agreements. I know what your animal wants, Isabelle. It's *you* who keeps doubting. You had a good reason to run away from home; no one should treat their sister that way. You ran away from me all those years ago and had good reason; no one should treat a friend that way. But hell, I'm asking you *not* to run this time. I want to show you how you *deserve* to be treated."

I swallowed thickly and looked away.

"My pack won't treat you like that, Isabelle. I know why you're scared."

I brushed my hair away from my face. "Then you can't ask me to do this. You can't expect me to not be terrified of something I've never known before—afraid that I could trust you and..."

He cupped my cheeks and kissed me softly on the mouth. "I'm not pushing you, because I know it'll make you run again. I'm not Hawk—I don't have any dark secrets that I'm keeping from you.

Maybe I have secrets, but they're not the kind that will tear us apart, and I want to share them with you."

"Yeah? What's one of your secrets?" I asked in disbelief. Jericho had a dark past, but he wasn't a dark person.

He leaned in tight. "That I'm going to hunt down the man who tried to drown you and end his life."

"You'll never find him. It was dark. Even Wheeler didn't get a good look."

"Yeah, he did."

My brows popped up. "Say again?"

He tipped his head to the side. "Delgado sent a man to collect the goods from Reno and Wheeler. He made the fatal mistake of making a snide remark to Wheeler about how he should have just cut your throat and slaughtered you like a pig. Wheeler tracked him down, and I have his address burned into my memory."

"You wouldn't."

But yes, he would. Never mess with a Shifter whose wolf thirsts for blood.

"You can't do that, Jericho. They'll put you in Breed jail for killing a human."

He licked his lips, and darkness pulsed in his eyes. "As it turns out, he's not human."

I covered my face and shook my head. "This has just been a crazy month. I'm sitting naked on top of a dresser in a sleazy motel, having a deep conversation with a guy I've spent the last twenty years thinking was in a grave. All these old ghosts are coming back, my ex turned out to be a psychopathic maniac, I had thugs tracking me down, almost died in a hot tub, I'm eating soup out of a plastic container, and I walked in on you passed out with a naked woman. I know it wasn't your fault; I'm just so confused. And it doesn't help that I'm in heat!"

Jericho laughed sexily and smoothed out my hair so that it covered my breasts. "Have you ever told someone that you loved them?"

"The guy at 7-Eleven who bought me a donut when I was fifty cents short."

"I'm serious."

I shrugged. "It was a good donut."

Jericho's lips twitched. He gently touched my shoulders as if we were having an ordinary conversation anywhere. But we weren't. I had my coochie on display while Jericho was swinging in the breeze. He licked his lips, and a smile crossed his expression. "I've got an idea. You with me?"

I nodded.

"All right. Here's the deal. You go through this heat thing…"

"Easy for you to say."

He shushed me with a finger pressed to my lips. "You get through this cycle and then go back to work."

"If Jake hasn't fired me."

"Don't sweat it," he said in a deep voice. "He's cool, just a bottom-line kind of guy. You'll have your job, and I'll go back to playing my shows."

"So that's it? *That's* your plan? Go back to what we were doing?"

"No more women."

My heart skipped a beat. "Say again?"

"I'll give you time, baby, because that's what you need. But guess what? I'm not letting you slip through my fingers again. I'm putting my claim on you, and that means if anyone messes with you, then he'll answer to me. Maybe I can't call you my girl just yet, but I'm going to look after you. I'm going to make you smile and dance at the donut shop with your bad self. We're going to be best friends again, so that means we hang out and watch movies like we used to do. What we have ain't just about the sex, and damn, the sex is off the charts. It's about the spark, like you're the melody and I'm the words." His voice fell to a soft whisper. "You don't have to tell me you love me—just put on this shirt." He handed me the Pink Floyd shirt, and I put it on my lap. "When you decide to wear it, then I'll know."

"Know what?"

He leaned forward and his luscious lips met with mine, easing into a deep kiss. His tongue filled my mouth, and his kiss was so hot that I expired right then and there.

Jericho's kiss abruptly ended, and he pulled me in with a magnetic gaze to answer my question. "I'll know when I see you in that shirt again that you love me."

CHAPTER 26

L EAVING ISABELLE ALONE IN THAT motel room was a testament to his strength, but Jericho reluctantly did the right thing. A woman going through heat wasn't in her right frame of mind, and expecting her to work out relationship stuff was unrealistic.

Especially after having hot, delicious sex on a dresser. Man, it was even better than the first time. Not just because of how blissfully good her sweet apple pie was—it had everything to do with the way she watched him with hooded eyes. The way she lay down for him, how creamy her skin looked against his tanned hands, her red hair splayed across the wood, and the sensual feel of her thighs wrapped around his waist. It was abso-fucking-amazing. Enough to make his wolf howl.

Turns out, he'd spent an hour in her motel room. Didn't seem like it, but Denver had taken off by the time Jericho made it to the parking lot. So he began walking and gave Joker a call to let him know he wasn't going to make the show.

"We can't cancel, man. Where the fuck are you?"

"Send Trev into the lion's pit," Jericho suggested.

"You want him to take your place?"

"Make it or break it time. Unless you wanna sing."

"Hell no."

Jericho hung up the phone, and his mind drifted back to Isabelle. As tempting as it was to go back, he wasn't about to start up a relationship based on sex with the one woman who mattered to him. Then again, it was too late for that.

He kicked a beer can and realized he was strolling down the

street wearing a woman's tank top and a thin sheen of sex sweat on his face.

"I didn't know you were turning tricks," a voice said from a car on his left. Jericho glanced at the vintage Camaro as Wheeler leaned over to the passenger side. "Get in, sweetheart," he said with a dark chuckle.

Jericho opened the door and sank into the seat. "How the hell did you find me?"

"Denver. He's pissed off. Guess he thought he was getting some tail going out with the rock star."

That made Jericho feel like shit, but Denver would get over it. He was insufferably picky, and chances are he wouldn't have hooked up with a girl anyhow.

Wheeler rubbed his nose. "You smell like sex."

"You smell like peanuts."

A bag appeared in front of Jericho's face, pinched between Wheeler's fingers. "Take some. I bought the unsalted ones by accident."

"I can sweat on them if you like," he suggested, pushing the bag away. "I called Joker about tonight's show—Trevor's going in my place."

"That what you're upset about?"

Jericho fumbled through the glove compartment and swept his hand beneath the seat. "You got any smokes in here?"

"No smoking in my car. 'Preciate ya."

Wheeler reached into a bag between the seats and grabbed a flat stick of beef jerky, which he immediately began gnawing on.

"Way to perpetuate the stereotype," Jericho said. "Want a dog biscuit when you're done to freshen your breath?"

"Shut the fuck up," he muttered, still chewing.

Jericho noticed Wheeler had grown some stubble along his jaw. He reached out and poked Wheeler's cheek, only to get a retaliatory punch in his chest. "You should let it all grow in instead of that scruff around your chin. Or shave it all off. Women like men who are decisive. Your facial hair looks like it's having an identity crisis."

Wheeler slanted his eyes at Jericho's ensemble. "You buy that shirt on clearance in the misses department, sweetheart?"

"Don't be an asshat. Where are we going?"

"Had a thought running in my head. You know that prick who played bobbing for apples with your girl? It just so happens he's at home. Reno's been scoping out his place the last couple of days, and he sticks to a routine. He's a Shifter—that much we verified—but I don't know what his animal is. All I know is he owns a damn cat."

All humor evaporated from their banter. A wave of fury rolled through Jericho as his wolf snarled and snapped from within, demanding to be uncaged.

"Feel like paying him an unexpected visit?" Wheeler suggested. The motor thrummed an answer as the car increased in speed.

Wheeler shut off the headlights and the hot engine made tapping sounds.

"You sure he's home?" Jericho asked. "It looks dark in there."

"Maybe he went beddy-bye," Wheeler said, rubbing the scruff on his chin. "Little pig, little pig, let us in."

The houses were spread apart with a few acres of property surrounding each one. The dirtbag lived in a one-story brick that looked a few decades old. He didn't have a garage, only a carport cover with a white car sheltered beneath. A few poisonous vines crawled up one of the live oaks to their right, and the driveway was cracked and narrow.

Jericho twisted off his rings. "Does he have a family?"

"What the hell kind of woman would mate with a guy like that? No, Reno did a check. He lives alone with a cat. I hate those damn things."

The front door violently swung open, and a middle-aged man emerged with a shotgun in one hand, stalking toward their car. "You two had better get the fuck off my property!"

"And boom goes the dynamite," Wheeler said, exiting the vehicle.

Jericho hopped out of the car and kept a steady pace ahead of Wheeler so this asshole knew who was gunning for him. The man had a shaved head and looked pretty seasoned for a Shifter. The small tattoo on his hand was nothing compared to the grotesque skull with black wings inked across his chest.

"You better step back and tell me your business before I blast a hole in your chest," the man said.

"I'm Jericho, and you tried to snuff out my woman."

He pursed his lips as if recalling a memory. "The redhead, huh?" He sized Jericho up with his beady eyes. "Are you what I think you are?"

"You mean badass?" Jericho took off his necklace with the ring on it and handed it to Wheeler. "Keep this." Then he peeled off his tank top and approached the man. "Tell me your name."

The man raised the shotgun and shifted his stance. "Shane. You plan on taking me out on a date now?" Shane belted out a villainous laugh.

"Put the gun down, and let's settle this like men."

"Why should I?"

"Because a Shifter with a gun is nothing but a pussy with a weak animal. Nobody messes with my girl and walks away alive."

Shane's thumb stroked the barrel of the gun, his gaze traveling between them. "How do I know your friend there isn't going to join in?"

"I'm not into threesomes," Wheeler said. "What's the matter, can't hold your own?"

Jericho turned around. "Get in the car. Stay there, no matter what happens."

"I'm not leaving you out here, baby bro."

"Yeah, you are. Get in the damn car. This is my battle to fight, so the pack stays out."

Wheeler stroked the hair on his chin, contemplating the request. "Fine. But you realize if something goes wrong, then brother or not, Austin will toss me out of the pack for watching it go down?"

"You two need a moment for good-bye kisses?" Shane asked.

Jericho inched in close and lowered his voice. "Look, Wheeler, we both know you love a good fight, but this one's mine."

"You don't have official claim on Izzy."

"I've had claim on that girl for decades. Just get in the car."

Wheeler stalked toward the Camaro and got in, slamming the door and staring through the windshield as he moved his mouth, talking to himself.

Jericho turned to face his enemy. "Put down the gun and let's do this."

A crooked smile curved up Shane's cheek as he put the safety back on the gun and set it on the ground. "Only one animal walks out alive, so feel free to put your tail between your legs and go back home. I don't fight for honor or fun—I fight to kill." He kicked off his motorcycle boots and unlatched his belt. "And by the way, I'm not a wolf."

————◦◦《◎》◦◦————

Wheeler gripped the steering wheel, his knuckles turning white. Maybe it *was* Jericho's fight, but a pack fought together. Then again, what dignity would Jericho have if someone else won his battles? Wheeler didn't understand the whole "fighting for love" bit, except it must have been some irrational instinct in their wolves that couldn't be controlled. No woman was worth dying for, except his mother.

He leaned forward and narrowed his eyes. Jericho approached Shane and must have been at least a foot taller than the man. Through the open window, a smoky scent hung in the air, as if someone had been burning trash. Threats turned into curses and the men circled each other, eyes alight and lips peeled back. Without warning, Jericho shifted. His wolf stood on top of a pile of clothes, teeth bared and body stiff, ready to attack.

At first, Wheeler thought Shane might go for the gun. Maybe his animal was a deer and he just talked a good game. Wheeler tensed, ready to jump out of the car if that dumb shit decided to do something stupid. Instead, he shifted, and Wheeler spat out a curse.

Shane was a black bear.

Had he been a grizzly, this would have quickly escalated into a pack fight. Luckily, the bear wasn't as big as some that Wheeler had seen in his time. That didn't make his sharp claws and teeth any less capable of tearing through flesh and cutting bone, though.

They circled each other beneath a canopy of moonlight, the fierce bear swiping his massive paw as Jericho's wolf bowed his head, seeking an angle of attack. He pounced a few times, snarling and growling, testing the bear's reflexes.

Once a Shifter lost control to his animal, his mind would sleep. Only some of the alphas had retained the ability to remember the shift and maintain some level of control. The rest were at the mercy of their animal.

Wheeler anxiously watched Jericho's wolf snapping at the bear's legs. He must have gotten a good bite because the bear suddenly roared, stretching out his neck and silencing every living creature within earshot.

Bingo. The wolf lunged, shaking and thrashing his head in violent motions after locking on to the animal's neck. The bear swiped his paw and the wolf yelped, leaping back with a limp.

"Jesus, Jericho. Come on. You got this," Wheeler whispered to himself.

The circling and quick attacks continued for several exhausting minutes. Wheeler almost pulled a cigarette out, except he didn't smoke. His phone suddenly went off, playing "Thunderstruck" by AC/DC.

"Dammit, Reno, not now," he murmured, turning off his phone.

When the wolf charged from the opposite side, the bear whipped his head around and took a nasty bite out of the canine's shoulder. The wolf scurried around him, and Wheeler could see blood matted in his fur. Probably a combination of both of theirs, but he couldn't tell since the bear's fur looked like black satin in the moonlight.

Each animal moved with merciless grace, seeking a bite on an artery that would draw blood and weaken his opponent. It splattered on the concrete driveway like black rain. Wheeler didn't know if Jericho's wolf had ever faced a bear, but he sure as hell gained some mad respect for his brother. He'd never seen Jericho so calculated, so bloodthirsty, so vicious.

When Jericho's wolf went for the jugular, the bear suddenly

twisted around and grabbed him with both paws. Wheeler could no longer see his brother—only a mass of fur and muscle.

His heart raced, damn near cracking a rib as hard as it was pounding against his chest. Wheeler flung the door open and stood immobile, holding on to the frame of the window, trying to decide what action to take. Instinct dictated he should fight with his pack, but Jericho would never forgive him for stripping away his honor. Sometimes that's all a man had. That idiot was about to die for a woman who wasn't even his mate.

Within seconds, the struggle ended. All Wheeler could see was a tangle of the wolf's legs protruding from beneath the bear.

Wheeler stalked toward the shotgun and picked it up off the ground. Honor or not, that bear was about to get a bullet in the head.

He approached the limp mass of bodies and paused, hearing a low grunt. The bear's jaw hung lax, and blood poured from an open wound on his neck. Jericho's wolf had torn out his throat.

And now he was suffocating underneath three hundred pounds of bear.

"Jesus!" Wheeler shoved the bear as hard as he could until it flopped over on its back.

"Jericho, *shift*," Wheeler said harshly. He tossed the gun aside and lifted the wolf's muzzle. "Shift, goddammit."

In a fluid movement, the wolf changed over to a man. Jericho lay naked on his side, still suffering nasty wounds to his body. Bite marks were on the front and back of his left shoulder, and a long gash separated the skin on his thigh. It was hard to tell how many wounds he'd sustained because he was bathed in blood.

Wheeler lifted his eyelid to see how responsive he was. "Shift!" The healing magic was effective only when you were able to shift soon after an injury, and multiple times if necessary.

Jericho groaned, shifting back into his wolf. It looked better. Good enough that Wheeler picked him up and carried him back to the car.

The carcass of the bear would remain in animal form. Wheeler's ass was going to be toast when Austin found out what went down, but for now, he needed to focus on getting Jericho back to health.

CHAPTER 27

I T TOOK FIVE DAYS BEFORE my heat cycle finally subsided, but not without a strange set of occurrences having taken place. Two days after Jericho had left, police sirens woke me up in the middle of the night. I drew back the heavy curtains and peered out the window, observing a group of curious men surrounding a dead bear in the parking lot. I didn't know if bears lived in Texas, but being so far in the city, it led me to believe it must have been a Shifter.

But the peculiar part was that the animal was lying on the hood of *my* blue car. I wanted to throw on my robe and dash outside to make sure my vehicle wasn't damaged, but it would have been too risky in my condition. Animal control finally showed up and dragged its heavy carcass away.

I returned to work and had a candid discussion with Jake. If all he wanted me for was to keep Jericho's band around, then I would be turning in my resignation. He sat back in his chair, patting his stomach, and laughed heartily. He confessed that in the beginning, that was his intention. But after hearing good things about me and seeing an increase in profits, there was no way in hell he was going to let me go, regardless if Jericho stuck around or not.

"Your red hair draws them in, and your personality keeps them coming back," he said. "Maybe I should fire you for the stunt you pulled in announcing to the whole bar you're a wolf, but you know what? No one's complaining. In fact, we got a few new customers when rumors began circulating about our sassy waitress."

God bless men like Jake. I wasn't sure how long I'd be doing the waitress gig, but Howlers felt like home. Jake even gave me an advance so I could put a deposit down on an apartment.

I hadn't spoken to Jericho since the night we polished the dresser, so perhaps he wasn't as serious about us as he had led me to believe. I couldn't blame him. The poor guy had been under the powerful influence of all those pheromones flying out of my pores. I'm sure it made men say things they didn't mean. I'd returned to work a week ago; the man could have at least called.

I kept the Pink Floyd T-shirt neatly folded on my coffee table. The table Rosie had given me because she's awesome like that. She took off work over the weekend to help me furnish my apartment with some things she didn't want or need anymore.

The marks on my wrists were mostly gone. Mostly. I'd have a permanent scar on my left wrist. I saw Denver each night when his shift began, and we'd mended the weirdness between us. In fact, he turned out to be one of the funniest people I'd ever met. I didn't bring up Jericho's absence, and neither did he. I needed to stop holding on to something I could never have and just accept the man Jericho was and will always be—a man with a good heart, but not someone willing to give it to just one girl. I couldn't hate him; I just wish he hadn't made all those promises to me.

I was wiping down a table when I heard a little girl scream. I stood up, eyes alert, and saw little Maizy bounding through the room with a smile on her face. Denver came around and lifted her up, setting her on the bar. He pinched her nose and she giggled, fishing her hand in a bowl of pretzels.

Lexi strutted through the front door with Austin two steps behind her. He grabbed her hips and pulled her back, whispering sexily against her neck. I couldn't help but notice the guys sitting nearby looking her over, and maybe that's why Austin tucked her a little tighter against him. You could feel her strong personality, and combined with her lovely legs showcased in her jean shorts, every tongue was wagging. She wasn't showy; her shirt was an oversized cotton tee, and she preferred sneakers over pumps. But some girls just had that thing about them and never realized it.

They relaxed on a couple of barstools, and I approached with a smile. "It's good to see you two. Can I get you something to eat?"

Lexi smiled wide. "I'm starving, but I'm kind of getting tired of hamburgers."

"How about I bring out a steak? Maybe some fresh green beans on the side."

Austin's brow arched. "Make that two."

My eyes were downcast, and I took a breath. "I hope you don't hate me for everything. I feel like I'm constantly apologizing, but I don't know how to make it right. Just know that I'm grateful for all the help you've given me. I did what I could to protect April; I just didn't know it would come to that, and he left me with no option."

Lexi patted Austin's arm and cleared her throat.

He ran his fingers through his hair, his pensive glance swinging around the room. "I appreciate that. I think you know my position as a Packmaster. You're an old friend of Jericho's and I can't sever that history between you two, but I also don't want it severing my pack, if you get my meaning. Now that I know who was behind all your troubles, I don't think we could have avoided the mess. Let's just put it behind us and move on."

I quirked a smile. "A second chance sounds like a great idea. I've never had siblings who had love for me the way you do for Jericho. He's a lucky guy."

Before I turned, he caught my arm and leaned in privately. "Just so you know, we're the lucky ones. Look, I don't know what exists between you two, but don't confuse him. Just figure out what you two are to each other and make it loud and clear. That's all I'm asking is that you be straight with him."

Austin was right. Since reuniting with Jericho, our relationship had been nothing but a whirlwind of emotions. We'd pushed, we'd pulled, and Jericho had made promises I didn't know if he was ready to keep. His absence had made me doubt what he said in that motel room, and we needed to sit down and have an honest discussion that didn't happen right after sex.

I nodded. "Don't worry. I'll settle it the next time we see each other. He has a show tomorrow night."

He smiled handsomely. "Good girl. And I like my steak rare."

I went in the kitchen and passed along the order, taking out a tray to one of my tables. They were setting up the stage for the next act. It hadn't been announced on any flyers, so I wasn't sure who was up. Maybe Jake had a surprise in store, or maybe he'd just decided to have an open mic and let anyone up there to karaoke. Oh God, please no.

"Miss Izzy!" Maizy waved, and I walked up beside her.

"Hi, sweetie. Is this too loud for you?"

I worriedly looked to Lexi and she shook her head, confirming Maizy had no issues with all the excitement going on.

"Look what Denny gave me," she said, opening her hand.

I laughed and watched her eat a piece of chocolate. Denver must have had a box of candy stashed behind the bar.

Denver pulled Frank to the side, and they had a private conversation. Frank wasn't supposed to be in that night, so I guessed Denver had called him up to swap out his shift.

Maizy swung her legs excitedly, making silly shoulder movements to the music on the jukebox as she watched Austin twirl Lexi around in a dance.

One of the waitresses, Nell, walked out with a tray full of sodas. I curled my finger for her to come over. "Which is the virgin?" I asked.

"The one with the cherries, of course."

"Do you like cherries?" I asked Maizy.

"Uh-huh!"

I lifted the tall glass of soda and took a sip to make sure there wasn't alcohol in it. "Sorry, Nell. Can I swipe this one?"

"No problem," she said, winking at Maizy. "Anything for the cutie-pie."

Maizy carefully held the glass and slurped on her soda.

Reno and April were making their way inside, weaving through the crowded room. April's blond hair looked so attractive on her with the edgy cut that made her hazel eyes shimmer. I smirked when I noticed some of her lipstick on Reno's neck.

"Hi, Izzy!" She gave me a quick hug and then got lost in Reno's thick arms.

"Are you two hungry?" I asked. "We've got steaks on the fire."

"No, we had Sonic on the way over."

Lexi snorted. "Reno couldn't wait, huh?"

He leaned forward. "When a man's hungry, he eats." His hands slipped around April's waist, and she blushed wildly.

"Oh, Lord. You two are going to set this place on fire," I said with a grin.

Denver returned and sat on the stool in front of Maizy. She grasped his head with her hands, forcing him to turn his head in different directions. It was good to see a wolf take over as a watchdog for a young girl, even if she *was* human. I'd heard it was a strong bond and that the male would fight to the death for the life he vowed to protect.

Austin kissed Lexi on the cheek as their spontaneous dance ended. He turned his back to me to face Lexi, sipping his cold beer. Some of his tattoos peered out from the sleeve of his shirt, and her fingers smoothed over them. The way she looked at him told me she had eyes for no other man.

"I like your hair shorter," Lexi yelled out over the noise. "Looks good on you."

I pinched the ends of my hair, which fell below my shoulders— still long, but not as long as it once had been.

"Ivy's pretty handy with the scissors," I replied.

People moved toward the stage when a finger tapped on the microphone a few times.

"I wonder who's playing," I mumbled. Jericho's band wasn't scheduled to go on until tomorrow night, and the other two bands that played in the bar didn't have a show scheduled this week.

When Jake walked onstage, the jukebox cut off. "Ladies and gents, we have an unexpected surprise for you this evening."

"Free beer!" someone shouted, and laughter followed.

"Hop on, Peanut." Denver patted his shoulders and Maizy threw her legs over them, holding on to his head and sitting up tall. He walked toward the back edge of the crowd, and the main lights lowered a little.

"No, not free beer, you jackass," Jake said with a tight grin. "We have a familiar face with a new sound, and tonight you have the pleasure of hearing their debut album that will only be available to Breed. You can buy the songs online exclusively at our website, but this is Breed only. If this goes viral, I'm going to hunt your asses down."

I was impressed that one of our own was making an album, which was unheard of.

"Put your hands together for *Heat*."

Denver whistled with his fingers, and the crowd gave them solid applause.

"Oh my God," I murmured.

The men shuffled onto the stage and hooked in their equipment. Jericho stood with his back to the crowd, wearing the sexiest pair of jeans I'd ever seen on a man. They were cut up, revealing a peek of black underwear. A long chain hooked from the back pocket to his belt loop, and the lights overhead cast shadows on the ropes of muscle on his toned arms. Women screamed and threw up their hands, forcing me to lean to the left so I could get a better view.

My heart raced as I watched the girls gyrate to the beat of Joker's drums. Jericho kept his back to the crowd, strumming his guitar sexily, and it was then that I noticed April screaming for Trevor.

"He looks so good up there!" she said excitedly.

Trevor had on a pair of sunglasses, his hair gelled in different directions, and he was wearing a button-up shirt with a pair of oxford shoes. He looked like a rocker in disguise behind clean-cut clothes, and that had several women gravitating toward him.

Jericho turned his head, peering over his shoulder and delivering his signature panty-dropping smile.

He seduced with his wanton voice, singing into a microphone with his back to the crowd and a blue light enveloping him like a cloak. No one rushed the stage, but a few were beginning to recognize him. Jericho tilted his body to keep his tattooed arm out of sight. He continued engaging with the microphone stand, making love to it with words that rolled out in a sound I could only describe as sexrock. A steady beat, slow and rhythmic, increased in tempo as it would during lovemaking. His lyrics melted like honey into the mic and sweetened the crowd.

As fast as I could, I ran out of Howlers and sped away in my car.

———◦◦◦———

"Nervous?" Jericho asked, watching Trevor retie his shoes for the twentieth time. "It's not like you haven't done this before."

"Yeah, but that was a larger crowd," Trevor said, leaning forward in the chair where they waited backstage at Howlers. They were going up in a few minutes to introduce their new sound as part of a "sneak peek" promo Jake had arranged.

Jericho laughed. "Usually it's the other way around."

"A smaller crowd is more intimate—I can see their faces up close, and I feel like they can tell I'm an imposter."

Jericho lightly tapped his palm on Trevor's forehead and then collapsed on the crappy sofa next to him. "You're not an imposter. It always feels like that at first, when fame is new. We're regular guys, but they look at us as gods or something. Been there, done that, you get over it. Here," he said, tossing Trevor a pair of black sunglasses. "Put these on. You'll be surprised how easily you can become someone else hiding behind a pair of shades. Just pretend when you get up there that everyone wants to have sex with you. Funnel that energy into your instrument and make love to it."

"I'm not humping my bass."

Joker laughed from the other side of the room, tapping his drumsticks rhythmically on a footstool. "Dude, *that* might actually sell more tickets. Hump away."

Ren ignored everyone, strumming a melody on his guitar from an armless green chair.

Jericho eyed Joker suspiciously. He had an impish smile on his face that meant he either just got laid, he was going to get laid, or he had a practical joke planned. Earlier, Jericho had searched the room and inspected the instruments for anything suspicious. It came up clean, but he knew Joker had something up his sleeve.

They heard Jake making the intro.

"Come on, boys. We're up. Let's sell the shit out of this music, and then we won't have to perform as much. It'll sell itself online." Jericho rose to his feet nervously.

Yeah, nervously.

He'd been in front of an audience a thousand times, but this night was different. This night was special. Minutes before, Jericho had been watching Isabelle from the back of the room. She looked abso-mazing, even with her hair a little shorter. It drew attention to the lovely features of her face. When his heart began to race with desire, he'd disappeared backstage and hung out there for the rest of the evening.

No one knew Heat was about to make their debut. A new sound, new bassist, and their songs would be made available online. It was a great way for them to earn extra money without having to book as many shows. Jericho knew some of the audience might recognize his voice, but the way he was going to perform the first song would throw them off. He planned on singing with his back to the crowd, hair covering his face, with a sultry voice like he'd never used.

But that's not why his palms were sweating and his mouth was dry.

Isabelle's diamond ring rested at the end of a long silver chain tucked beneath his cutoff shirt. He had only removed the ring once since putting it on the necklace, and that was when he killed the Shifter who'd tried to drown Isabelle. Tonight, every note, every syllable, and every beat of his heart would be hers. Maybe he should have called her after that night in the motel, but he'd been so inspired by her that the band had been working day and night to write new music. He was going to let his music do all the talking, and it was something he'd been planning since the night he bought the ring.

The band made their way onstage as the lights cut off in the back. The stage lights behind them shone toward the crowd, creating a silhouette effect until an overhead blue light switched on above Jericho's microphone. He turned his back to the crowd, and Joker tapped his sticks and kicked off the beat.

Jericho took the pick out of his mouth and sang the opening lines as Joker followed with a slow and steady rhythm. The bass rolled in next, and then Ren hit the chords. He peered over his shoulder and smiled when he caught a glimpse of Isabelle at the bar.

He'd die for that woman. Jericho proudly wore scars on his shoulder and leg. A bear claw hung on the outside of his shirt as a token of his kill. He'd taken it right after he and Wheeler dumped the Shifter on Isabelle's car as an offering. They'd tried to get the carcass up the stairs but failed miserably.

It was a Shifter thing.

Trevor was killing it onstage. The audience ate up their performance like sweet cake, devouring Trevor's sexy moves with his bass, and Ren worked the crowd on Jericho's right. Even Joker was in rare form, playing at a level of magnificence they'd rarely seen. Human or not, that guy attacked his drums, and some of the girls were biting their knuckles as they watched him play.

Mid-song, Trevor fell to his knees and thrust his hips upward, creating a ripple of screams in the crowd. When he rose up and provided backup vocals, Jericho knew that Heat finally had a new audience. He had co-written a couple of songs with Trevor and planned to pass him the mic for a song or two. Trevor probably wouldn't stick with them for long; the kid was awesome, but he wasn't cut out for this lifestyle. So why not give him a few songs and let him in on their first recorded album? What an awesome memento. Their job required traveling, odd hours, no routine, lots of warm-ups, and the monotony of repeating the same act again and again, which wore out a lot of musicians. Still, he'd let Trevor enjoy it for as long as he wanted.

With impeccable timing, they went silent on the last note of the song. The crowd roared, and a thong flew over his shoulder and landed on Joker's drums. There was always at least one in every crowd, especially the Shifter bars. Man, the buzz of energy swelled in the room, and Jericho had never felt more alive. Just knowing Isabelle was in the sea of faces—watching and listening—made this so damn worth it.

A woman suddenly rushed the stage, hobbling clumsily in heels, and planted a kiss on Trevor. Joker burst out laughing when the woman ripped off her wig, revealing she was a man.

Dammit, Joker. He'd taken his practical joke too far, not knowing Trevor was gay.

The crowd whistled and a few people laughed. *So much for Trevor's life in the spotlight.*

But the joke was on them.

Trevor suddenly stepped forward and kissed the man hard, biting the guy's lower lip in the most erotic way. To Jericho's surprise, the women in the crowd were cheering—all for it.

In a *Shifter* bar, of all places. Shifters were one of the few Breeds who could have offspring, so they didn't take it lightly when one of their own turned their nose up at it. Maybe they accepted it more readily because the band was putting on a performance, but in any case, Trevor got all the acceptance he needed. He pushed the guy away and started up a bass line, walking the stage like he owned it. And he did.

Joker turned beet red.

Jericho revealed himself to the crowd, slowly turning to prepare for the next song. A wave of surprise spread across their faces when some of them recognized they were staring at Jericho Sexton Cole.

But he didn't see them. All he saw was the empty space where Isabelle had once been standing at the back of the bar.

CHAPTER 28

"COME ON, COME ON, COME on. Hurry up," I chanted at the red light illuminating my windshield.

The moment Jericho hit the stage, I'd known right then and there that I loved him something fierce. I'd always known it, but that moment solidified everything I'd ever felt for him and everything I wanted to feel for the rest of my life.

There was only one thing left to do, and that was run.

Run home to get that damn Pink Floyd shirt and put it on!

Hell's bells, I hoped Jericho hadn't seen me running out, although I doubted with all the luscious women in the front row that he'd noticed me in the shadows.

Blink. The light turned green and I hit the gas, sailing down the street like a racecar driver. I'd left in such a hurry that I'd forgotten my purse.

I couldn't stop grinning as I approached the bar. My vintage T-shirt was a little big and came to the ends of my shorts, but it still smelled like Jericho, even though it had been in my apartment for over a week. It's like every breath of him was in that fabric—every breath of us. A story of our past, present, and future—woven into the fibers of a threadbare T-shirt.

My heart pounded against my chest and I cursed, unable to find a parking space anywhere near the bar.

"Dammit!" I shrieked.

Word must have spread about their performance because people were parking across the street and jogging toward the door. I couldn't take it. After circling twice, I double-parked and hopped out of the car.

"Hey, you can't do that!" someone shouted from behind. I

turned to look while running toward the bar and stumbled, twisting my ankle.

Pain lanced through my foot and I hissed, pulling up my leg and debating on whether or not to shift in the street to heal myself or suck it up like a big girl.

I sucked it up.

Hobbling on one leg toward your true love isn't the most graceful way to find your happily-ever-after, but that's exactly what I did. I provided a few laughs for some onlookers, hopping like a lame kangaroo as I made my way to the front door.

Thankfully, I still heard Jericho's voice, calling to me like a siren.

"What the hell is wrong with you?" Denver shouted over the music.

"Honey, is your foot bothering you?" Rosie said, coming up on my left.

"Get out of my way!" I shouted, hopping through the crowd. I got pushed left and right as people wanted to get as close to the stage as possible.

I screamed his name like a silly fangirl, so naturally he didn't look in my direction. I squeezed my head between two large men, hoping maybe Jericho would see my bright hair and look my way.

"Over here!" I shouted.

My heart stopped when he looked right at me. But then I saw it. That look. The one that told me he was pissed off. The one that said maybe he didn't care about me like I had hoped. The one that said there were a million other girls out there, and I was nothing special.

His eyes dragged back to the front row of girls as he sang to them.

Them. Those big-breasted blondes with tattoos. The ones he always fell for.

My lips tightened in anger, and I spun around, running into Wheeler.

I snatched his shirt and balled it up in my fist. "You owe me one."

He lowered his head to the left. "Yeah. And?"

"Put me on your shoulders."

His eyes widened with disbelief. "You want what?"

"I want you to put your head between my legs and lift me up."

Someone patted him on the shoulder and laughed. "If you don't take her up on that offer, I will. I'd love to put my head between her—"

Wheeler knocked the guy in the jaw and then spun around. I nervously gripped his hair as he lifted me off the ground. Damn, Wheeler was strong, and his shoulders and arms felt like granite. He handled me as if I weighed nothing.

There I was—the one and only thing that Jericho couldn't possibly ignore. My red hair was illuminated beneath a low spotlight directly overhead.

Jericho abruptly stopped singing, but the music kept going. His eyes slid from my red hair down to the Pink Floyd shirt.

The one that said "I love you" by simply being on my body. The one he'd asked me to wear when I was ready to tell him what he meant to me.

I held my breath and vaguely heard Wheeler complaining about how tightly I was fisting his hair.

Hell's bells, Jericho looked lickable. Smoldering eyes pulled me in like magnets. Strands of his long hair had lighter shades of brown, just enough to make you notice him a little bit more. He had on his smoky eyeliner, not that I went for guys who wore makeup, but it had always been part of his act. He said onstage it worked to a man's advantage to draw attention to his eyes when they were light in color. My brows knitted when he turned away and dragged the microphone stand to Trevor, patting him on the shoulder. The tempo changed to a different song, and Trevor took over, singing a slower ballad in a hungry voice that made a few women gasp.

Jericho leapt off the stage and sliced through the crowd as he moved in my direction. I got the shivers just watching his swagger and the animalistic way in which his eyes devoured me. I remembered his heated kiss, the way he made me laugh, and the way he loved me. I remembered a guy who sat next to me on a rainy day at a bus stop and held a magazine over my head in a failed attempt to keep me dry, who invited me for donuts and coffee until the rain stopped.

It had gone on for three days, and it seemed like that's how long we stayed in that shop together, talking and realizing the friendship between us was effortless. Jericho made me a stronger woman, and I wanted to make him a stronger man. I wanted to see him succeed in life and have everything he'd ever wanted.

But right now, it looked like he only wanted one thing.

"Isabelle, is there something you want to tell me?"

I looked down at him with a foolish grin, his brother between my legs, flanked by his pack who'd begun to close in on us. In front of everyone who mattered and others who didn't, I told him what I'd been holding back for decades.

"Jericho Sexton Cole, I love you to pieces. I love the man you were, the man you've become, and most of all I love the way you love me."

His shoulders sagged as if he'd been holding his breath. "Come down here."

Wheeler set me down, and my stomach knotted when I saw that Jericho wasn't smiling. He didn't kiss me, twirl me, lift me into his arms, or do any of the silly romantic things that I thought might happen after giving him my declaration of love.

"Are you mad?" I asked.

His mouth formed a grim line, and he shook his head. "You bailed on me tonight during the first song."

"Are you serious?" I said, my voice raising an octave. "I had to drive all the way home in hellacious traffic. I hit almost every red light, I almost hit a cat, and all so I could put on this shirt!" I said, tugging at the fabric. "Are you seriously upset that I didn't hear you sing?"

"Yeah, I kind of am." He stepped forward and tilted his head to the side. "I had plans."

"Did I miss the striptease act?"

"Baby, there's only one thing I want to take off for you."

He reached beneath his shirt and lifted a long silver chain from his neck. My knees weakened when a smile tugged at his mouth and he fell to one knee, holding my left hand.

"Isabelle Marie Monroe, will you be my life mate?"

A ring slid on my left ring finger, and it sparkled like nothing I'd ever seen before—like a supernova. The chain still hung from it, and my hands trembled. Jericho's cheeks flushed, beads of sweat appearing on his brow as he looked at me expectantly.

Nervously.

Uncertain.

"But we don't do rings," I protested.

"If your wolf loses it, I'll buy you another, but that ring is going to sparkle on your pretty hand. So don't be a stubborn wolf; give me your answer."

I leaned down and cupped his cheeks, placing a soft kiss on his mouth. "Yes, sweetheart. I'll be your mate, your friend, and maybe a pain in the ass, but I'm here for good. No more running unless it's into your arms."

Then his tongue entered my mouth. Heat slid down to my core, and our bodies married as he rose up and we fell into a lover's kiss. A few claps erupted around us, and Austin patted his shoulder, walking off with Lexi. I loved that despite it all, his brother supported his decisions.

"I'm sorry I missed your show," I whispered.

"That's okay, baby. You get the encore." Jericho smiled wide and snared my arm. "Let's go. Time to do some consummating."

I hopped on one foot with eagerness.

"What's wrong with your leg?" He glanced down at my swollen, shoeless foot. I had left it somewhere in the parking lot between the street and fire hydrant.

Ignoring him, I touched the bear claw hanging from his neck. "What's this?" Then my eyes roamed to the puncture marks on his left arm, and I pulled his shirt back, noticing more on his chest. "And what are *these?*" I exclaimed, horror sweeping over me.

"A souvenir. No one messes with my girl," he said, stroking my soft hair with his dexterous fingers.

Then I knew. The man who tried to drown me must have been a Shifter. A bear. The one that was left on my car as an offering. Jericho had challenged him for my honor and had chosen not to heal all the way, as is custom. A Shifter who fought for his mate's life wore his battle scars proudly.

I stroked my finger over the puncture wound closest to his tattoo and kissed it. "Jericho, you didn't need to get me a ring. *You're* my diamond. Strong, resilient, and one of a kind." I traced my finger around the scar.

In a swift movement, he bent down and swept me off my feet. "Are you trying to win my heart?"

"So what if I am?"

"Baby, you already had me with the shirt. Hell, you had me the day we met in the rain when you told me to get lost."

I laughed against his neck. "Well, you *were* a persistent pain in the ass. Not to mention you used a porn magazine to cover my head."

He chuckled. "The centerfold made for extra coverage."

"Are you really going to carry me out of here *An Officer and a Gentleman* style?"

He kissed my cheek and belted out a few words to the song at the top of his lungs. I slapped my hand over his mouth and laughed. "Don't you *dare* embarrass me while sweeping me off my feet. You have an image to protect. You know—the *badass* image. Singing a sappy song from last century? No, sir."

"I'm not going to lie to you, baby. I'm staying with the band. Austin's offer to work in the shop isn't what I'm about. This is who I am. Late nights, rehearsals, zoning out at dinner and scribbling lyrics on a napkin—that comes with the package. I'm sorry if I can't wrap it up in a neat bow."

I placed the palm of my hand on his chest and nestled my head against his shoulder. "I'm all right with it. The stage is where your heart is, and you should always follow your heart."

I squeaked when Jericho set me on top of the bar and eased between my legs. Someone's drink tipped over and rolled on the floor, but he ignored the complaints and kissed my forehead.

"Baby, *you're* my heart. You're the only girl I've written music for. The only girl I want to wake up next to and make blueberry pancakes and bacon for. The only girl I want to kiss on the neck, love with my mouth, eat donuts with at two in the morning, and go on road trips with. Music is how I express myself, but I could never love anything more than what I've got right here," he said, softly kissing my mouth.

I leaned back a little. "There are a million other girls out there. You sure about this?"

His hands splayed across my thighs. "You're stuck with me. I'll love you no matter what we go through together, because that's what a good mate does. And we're gonna have unbelievable sex together," he said, waggling his brows. "I think we both know that's a *fact* and not an assumption. Speaking of, I'm going to make good on that promise starting in the next twenty minutes."

I gripped the bear claw in a tight fist and looked at him tenderly, still in disbelief. "What makes you so sure you want to be my life mate?"

Hell's bells, the grin that appeared on his face made me realize why I'd gotten butterflies the first time I laid eyes on him.

"Because, Isabelle, you're more than just the girl who stole my heart—you're my sexy little redhead."

CPSIA information can be obtained
at www.ICGtesting.com
Printed in the USA
LVHW011542210319
611421LV00003B/628/P